Praise for Jennifer Snow

"*An Alaskan Christmas* is heartwarming, romantic, and utterly enjoyable."
—*New York Times* bestselling author Melissa Foster

"Prepare to have your heartstrings tugged! Pure Christmas delight."
—*New York Times* bestselling author Lori Wilde

"Jennifer Snow is one clever writer."
—*RT Book Reviews*

"Never too late to join the growing ranks of Jennifer Snow fans."
—*Fresh Fiction*

"Ms. Snow brings the drama, heat, and heart along with a great cast of characters."
—*Harlequin Junkie* on *Pushing the Limits*

"Grab some hot cocoa with this one and enjoy Snow's latest."
—*RT Book Reviews* on *The Mistletoe Melody*

JENNIFER SNOW

An Alaskan Christmas

ISBN-13: 978-1-335-04150-0

Recycling programs
for this product may
not exist in your area.

An Alaskan Christmas

www.HQNBooks.com

Printed in U.S.A.

For all of the members of search-and-rescue organizations worldwide, who selflessly put their own lives at risk to save others in times of need—thank you!

An Alaskan Christmas

CHAPTER ONE

HER ARMS FULL of patient files, Dr. Erika Sheraton tipped her head back as Darren, her premed intern, poured a double shot of espresso down her throat. The hot liquid delivered the instant adrenaline boost she needed to get through the rest of her fourteen-hour shift.

Dinner? A quick glance at the clock on the wall above the nurses' triage station revealed it was almost nine. A late dinner.

"How are you not vibrating? That's your third in two hours." Darren crumpled the paper cup and tossed it into a recycle bin as they walked.

"Caffeine stopped affecting me a long time ago. Now it's about the taste," she said, only half kidding. Double course loads and all-nighters in college and then med school had prepared her for the long hours she put in now as a general surgeon, and caffeine had been her best friend.

The twentysomething looked like he could use a cup himself, as he stifled a yawn. His sandy-blond hair poked up in the back as though he'd crawled out of bed at the last possible minute and his hazel eyes were bloodshot. If he was tired now after only eight hours on shift, he'd be reconsidering this particular profession by midnight. The staff at Alaska General Hospital never rested. The revolving doors at emergency constantly rotated with broken bones, heart attacks and bleeding patients filing in. No day was ever the same. Unpredictability kept Erika alert and on her toes.

"After these rounds, I'm going to need you to check in on Mr. Franklin—he's in recovery. His family is wondering when they can see him." The man's entire extended family was camped out in the surgical ward waiting room—fifteen or sixteen of them at least. They couldn't see the man, but they all refused to leave. Each one took turns driving the nurses on duty crazy. "Make sure they know only immediate family can go in. He needs his rest."

Darren nodded, but a look of hesitation appeared behind his dark-rimmed glasses.

"What?" She checked her watch.

"I just… Well, shouldn't you talk to them? I know his wife wanted to thank you…"

Erika shook her head. "Keeping him on the low-cholesterol, low-sodium diet I've prescribed—and off my operating table—will be thanks enough," she said, scanning the top folder on her stack.

"Okay, but…"

She shot him a look.

"No problem. I'll check in on him."

"Thank you." She continued down the hall toward the next high-priority patient.

"Don't forget, your dad still wants to see you," Darren said, struggling to keep up to her half sprint.

"I know." And she could do without the hourly reminders. Her father rarely requested her presence during her rounds, so whatever it was wouldn't be good. If she put him off long enough, maybe he'd forget.

"Top chart—Mr. Grayson. He's scheduled for an appendectomy in a few hours," she said, approaching the man's hospital room.

Darren nodded as he smiled. "This old guy is hilarious. Did you know he was a stunt motorcycle driver in the circus in the '80s?"

"No." She knew he had an inflamed appendix and had waited far too long to come in. She knew his vitals and that in an hour, they'd be prepping him for surgery. Knowing personal details of a patient's life didn't make her job any easier or guarantee a better outcome. She juggled the files on one arm as she reached into her pocket for a new set of sterile gloves.

"Hey, before we go in there, can I talk to you?" Darren asked, stopping her outside the room. He stared at the checked patterned floor tiles.

Damn. "You're requesting a transfer to a different physician." He wasn't the first medical student who'd gotten reassigned. She'd made it a month with Darren—a new record.

Another intern bites the dust.

He nodded, obviously relieved that he hadn't had to vocalize it himself. "You're amazing, Dr. Sheraton, and I feel so fortunate for the opportunity to work with you, but you're also very busy and unavailable…"

The sharp sting of the words was familiar. She'd heard the same speech from interns and boyfriends alike. She'd successfully eliminated the problem in one group right after her first year of residency…interns were hospital-assigned and therefore out of her control.

"I mean I just need all the training I can get and between patients and your research work…"

She didn't need an explanation. She was busy. Too

busy to have someone following her around in fact. This was totally fine with her. "I understand."

"You're not upset?"

"Only about having to get my own coffee from now on," she said.

The joke missed its mark and the intern's eyes widened. "I can still do that…"

Wow, was she really that scary? She was demanding and expected the students to put in the hours she did. She may not be the friendliest doctor on staff, socializing after work and remembering birthdays and such, but she gave these interns a real picture of their future in medicine. Wasn't that what they were there for? "I was kidding, Darren."

"Oh…right."

"Dr. Sheraton, please report to emergency. Stat."

The call over the hospital intercom had her handing Darren the stack of folders. "Please take his heart rate and blood pressure," she said, practically running to the elevators. "And don't forget Mr. Franklin."

"Got it," he called after her.

The quiet twenty-six-second elevator ride to the first floor was the closest thing she got to a spa day. It was the only time she was forced to slow to a pace other than her own usual breakneck speed. But even that half a minute was too long. It gave her time to think. Think about her previous surgeries and replay the details— what went right, what went wrong, what she could do better next time. Constantly reevaluating herself made her a better surgeon, but too often it left her feeling like she was coming up slightly short of her potential. Her type A personality left little room for failure or complacency.

Checking her phone in her lab coat pocket, she scanned her schedule for the rest of the evening, evaluating what she could push back if this emergency demanded her immediate attention. The number of things marked *urgent* made her will the elevator to move quicker. She'd be lucky to get out of there by 2:00 a.m.

A text popped up from Darren.

If you change your mind about Mrs. Franklin…

She wouldn't. She ignored the text from her intern—former intern—and put the phone away.

As the elevator stopped, she took a deep breath, expecting to see a flurry of organized chaos as the doors opened. Stretchers, ambulance lights flashing and sirens wailing outside, paramedics and nurses… Instead, she ran square into her father.

No emergency, just his six-foot-three frame and his usual neutral expression. It was impossible to read her father, as his face gave nothing away. His emotions were never too high or too low, just infuriatingly balanced no matter the circumstance. His calm presence and rational thinking made him fantastic at his profession, but sometimes he was irritating as shit as a father.

"Hi. I was just coming to see you." Eventually.

"Walk with me," he said, turning on his heel and nodding.

Her jaw clenched so tight her teeth might snap. This was so like him—assuming she could drop everything at his command. He may run the hospital, but he often had no idea how hectic her schedule was. "Can we talk as I do my rounds? Darren is…"

"More than capable," he said, leading the way to his first-floor corner office. "And requesting to be transferred, I see."

His tone made her palms sweat. He should be happy that she was pushing these interns to their limits. What awaited them once they graduated wasn't for the faint of heart. Better to get used to grueling days and nights now, performing on little to no sleep, living on caffeine and leftover Halloween chocolate bars, than to realize they couldn't cut it when lives were in their hands.

Unfortunately, he didn't always agree with her beliefs. He wanted the interns to feel at home at Alaska General so they'd apply here once they graduated. The hospital was short-staffed and more doctors would benefit everyone, but Erika preferred to work alongside the best.

Her father had an open-door policy—literally—so when he closed the office door behind her, she knew the head of General Surgery hadn't called her in to discuss Thanksgiving dinner plans.

She glanced at his wall calendar as she sat. Especially since Thanksgiving was a week ago.

"Dad, this intern thing is just ridiculous…"

He held up a hand. "This isn't about your inability to effectively manage others."

Kick to the gut delivered and received. She clamped her lips together.

He opened his desk drawer and handed her a letter as he sat in the plush, leather chair behind his oversize mahogany desk.

Her eyes widened, seeing the Hospital Foundation logo on the top of the page. "Is this the final approval from the board for the clinical trials?" They'd submitted the application six months ago to start trials on a new antirejection drug, after years of research, and they were waiting on the formal go-ahead to start with a test group.

Would Darren reconsider staying with her if he knew he could be part of a medical breakthrough? He'd been a lot of help in the past month.

"Just read it," her father said.

She scanned the letter from the board of directors, feeling her excitement fade and anxiety rise with each word. "Recommended vacation? What is this?"

"I don't like it either, but the board is reviewing policies and making sure we are following them," he said, the edge indicating he'd been outvoted in this decision. He certainly didn't believe in time off and had never encouraged her to take any. Her life was her career, just like him.

"But any day now we will be starting clinical trials on the new drug." It had taken her father and his team almost three years to get the experimental antirejection product approved for testing on organ transplant patients, and they'd finally gotten it. They'd worked around the clock for a year to make sure they did. Subjects were undergoing assessment right now to be ready for the trials.

Now was not the time to take a break.

Her father looked as though he'd made the same argument to the hospital board. "The team will have to handle it."

So *recommended* actually meant *forced*. "Why now? I'm fine. I don't need a break." At twenty-nine, she was eager to prove herself as one of the top general surgeons in the state. Between her surgical success record and the research time she'd invested in this new drug, she was close. Helping her father get one step closer to winning the Lister Medal was high on her priority list. "Come on, Dad, you know I'm good. My last two operations were impossible surgeries…"

"*Improbable* surgeries."

Erika clamped her lips together again, forcing her argument to stay put. It wouldn't do any good. Three years working alongside her father and she'd yet to prove herself. Despite two back-to-back *improbable* surgeries that she'd performed successfully, he still doubted her abilities. His micromanagement over her research team had driven her insane, but he'd reluctantly agreed to let her run her own set of clinical trials on the antirejection drug, and she'd foolishly believed she was making progress with him.

Now she was being forced into taking a break.

What the hell *was* a break? She hadn't had one since starting university. She'd graduated with her bachelor's in three years instead of four by doubling up on courses and then had applied directly to med school. She'd interned at Alaska General and secured a position there shortly after graduation. She couldn't remember the last day she had off, let alone…she glanced at the letter. *Two weeks?*

What the hell would she do with all that free time?

Her chest constricted and air struggled to make it to her lungs. "Okay, maybe I could take a few days, but two weeks is crazy."

"Darren told me about the one-way street," her father said.

Last time she was driving *him* home. "It was a mistake. It was nothing." Accidentally turning down a busy one-way street—in the wrong direction…in rush hour…after an eighteen-hour shift—had frightened the bejesus out of her and Darren, but she wasn't about to admit that to her father.

Had that near-death experience had anything to do with Darren's transfer request? Did he actually think she was starting to burn out?

She wasn't. The truth was, her mind had been elsewhere on the drive home that day. November 20. The anniversary of her mother's death. Each year that day weighed heavy on her. But bringing that up to her father would do more damage than good.

"It's a sign you're working too hard," he said.

Again, an edge of irritation in his voice. Her father didn't acknowledge weakness. He believed in pushing through, working hard to overcome exhaustion and stress. She'd failed to do that in his eyes, and she couldn't be truthful with him. They never talked about her mother.

"So I can't fight this?" she asked, her jaw tight as she struggled to keep her voice steady. This wasn't fair. It was unnecessary, but throwing a temper tantrum wouldn't help.

"The decision is final." He ran a hand through his salt-and-peppered hair and reached for his glasses, picking up a file on his desk.

She was dismissed. "Effective?"

"Immediately. Dr. Hipstein has been called in to complete your rounds."

Dr. Hipstein. A veteran doctor who was semiretired. Staff and patients loved his fun, uplifting demeanor. Standing, she said, "Okay, well, I'll see you in two weeks."

He nodded, not glancing up as she left the office and headed down the hall. She took the elevator to the fourth floor, leaning against the cool metal wall as she watched the numbers light up. Going into her own office, she closed the door, kicked off her heels and lay down on the uncomfortable cot she'd wheeled in to try to catch some sleep between patients. She stared at the dark stain on the ceiling tile above her and forced several deep breaths.

Two weeks.

It may as well be two years. What the hell was she going to do with herself?

She had no hobbies. She had no boyfriend. She had no friends besides colleagues, who were more acquaintances. She didn't have a pet. Heck, even her houseplants were plastic.

Feeling her chest constrict, an anxiety attack looming, she forced another breath, but it barely made it past her throat. A vacation. She'd never been on one before. Ever. Not even as a child. Raised by her workaholic father, the farthest she'd ever gone was camping with Cassie and her family every summer…

Cassie.

She hadn't seen her childhood best friend in years. They'd been inseparable growing up, but their lives and careers had gotten in the way of the friendship over time. Her free-spirited friend was an adventure tour guide, still living in their hometown of Wild River, while Erika worked herself into forced vacations at the hospital in the city. Fun and leisure activities had never found their way onto her priority list. A drive to succeed pushed away any desire to relax. Eventually, when she'd reached her career goals, she'd slow down a little…enjoy life, but for now, she was focused solely on her career.

Right now, she wouldn't even know how to find fun if she had a direct map to it.

Sitting up, she glanced at her calendar on the wall. It was November 30 and the weather that fall would ensure great skiing conditions on the slopes. Not so great for mountain driving, though. She'd never admit it, but the close call on the one-way had her feeling a little nervous on the roads these days.

She bit her lip. She could take the train.

Going to her computer, she confirmed times to Wild River for the next day. Less than a two-hour ride. The mountains weren't that far from the city.

Finding accommodations for that length of time proved to be challenging, though. Ski season was always booked well in advance, and with the village holiday activities starting that week, no hotel or B and B could accommodate the two-week stay.

Should have checked that first.

Opening Facebook, she went straight to Cassie's page.

When was the last time they spoke? Actually spoke, not quick Facebook messages or a "Merry Christmas" or "Happy Birthday" text, but an actual conversation?

Flipping through her friend's recent photos of winter camping and hiking through the trails, group shots of happy-looking adrenaline junkies on a heli-skiing trip…her already fragile confidence in the idea waned. Did they have anything in common anymore? As teenagers, it had been their differences that had connected them. She was studious and focused—exactly what Cassie had needed to help her survive the course load in high school. Someone to make sure she went to class and did the assigned work. Erika had tutored her friend in math and physics to make sure her grades were high enough to graduate on time. And in return, Erika had learned to relax and have fun once in a while from her high-on-life friend. Cassie forced her to take breaks, even if it meant stealing her textbooks for a few hours, and without her, Erika would have had no social life at all.

Her gaze fell to her exposed wrist at the edge of her white blouse. The faint lines of a tattoo were starting to show through her tattoo concealer. The word *Friend* only legible because she knew what it said.

The *Best* and *Friend* tattoos had been their gift to one another when Erika moved to Anchorage for university. They'd promised not to let life get in the way of their friendship. Erika almost always kept hers covered these days. She really should have it removed—it was hardly professional—but each time she made the appointment, she canceled it.

She opened Messenger and hesitated. Could she really spend two weeks in Wild River? Would her friend be happy to hear from her?

She released a deep breath and started to type. Only one way to find out.

CHAPTER TWO

THIRTY-SEVEN HOURS into the search and the twisting in Reed's gut grew worse by the minute. The call from the state troopers' office reporting a missing ten-year-old girl on the side of Wild Canyon Peak—where she'd been snowshoeing and camping with her parents—had sent over fifty search and rescue volunteers out on the mission immediately. November in the mountains was cold, unpredictable and they'd already experienced one small avalanche earlier that month.

Reed pulled up his scarf and readjusted his head-lamp. At six thirty, it was already pitch-black outside, making the search harder and his confidence fade. The bitter wind that had picked up since nightfall cut through his thermal jacket and the crew members near him—walking the trails where the young girl had last been seen—looked as tired and anxious as he felt. They were reaching a critical point and his only consolation was knowing that the girl had been dressed for the weather. Her parents claimed she was wearing a full snowsuit, gloves, hat and scarf.

Snow crunched beneath his boots as he neared the edge of a cliff, peering over in the hopes of seeing the little girl. Snowdrifts made visibility in this area tough. His mouth felt like sandpaper, but he didn't stop to take a drink. Not yet. Only on scheduled five-minute rests.

He checked his watch. Nine more minutes until they took a mandatory break. He scanned the area as he took slow steps forward…his ten years of experience on the Wild River Search and Rescue making his senses sharp and focused, despite lack of sleep and the intensity of the unpredictable weather in the high altitude.

As he approached the drop-off, he saw an orange scarf caught on a tree branch to his right. He almost released a sigh of relief—it was the first physical sign they were in the right area where the girl might be. But the proximity of the scarf to the edge of the cliff had his pulse racing. The high angle, steep incline was treacherous…the slippery rocks a major hazard.

"Orange scarf located," he said over the radio. "Proceeding with caution to edge of Wild Canyon Peak, hoping to obtain a visual." Hooking a carabiner to his belt and fastening the harness support to the tree, he moved toward the edge.

It was dark and the light reflecting off the snow hindered his ability to see into the depths, so he shut off the light as he scanned the rocky edge. "Rebecca!" he called, his voice reverberating off the mountain.

To his right, several other rescuers approached. He motioned for them to stay back, as a block of snow gave way beneath his right foot, shaking him slightly off balance. The child may not have realized how close she was to the edge, because of the unsteady footing and false ground.

"Rebecca!" he called again, moving closer. Rocks covered in shimmering frost were like glass beneath his boots. He peered over the edge, a shiver running through him as he took in the thousand-foot drop. No one could survive that fall.

"Hello."

The sound was barely audible above the howling wind, but a rush of heat flowed through him as he turned toward it, about twenty feet below him to the right. Turning on the light again, he scanned the area. There she was. Sitting on a six-inch-wide ledge, her head rested against the side of the mountain, her eyes shut tight. Wind beat against her with so much force, Reed feared she could be blown off the ledge any second.

The clock was ticking. They needed to move fast.

"Hi, Rebecca. I'm coming to help you. Just stay right where you are. You're doing great." He had no way of knowing if that was true or not, he couldn't assess her well-being from this distance, but he needed to reassure her. Providing relief and a sense of safety was an essential part of the rescue. If the endangered believed they were now safe, they were more proactive in their rescue.

"I've located Rebecca. Side of Wild Canyon Peak. She is responsive," he said over the radio, as two crew members approached after securing their own harnesses.

"How are we proceeding?" Wade Baxter, one of the rescue leaders, asked.

It was Reed's month as head rescue leader, therefore he was calling the shots. "I'll rappel to her, assess injuries and check approach angles. Get a litter ready in case we need it."

The man nodded, motioning forward two support crew members who dragged the carrier on the snow behind them.

"Frank, can you belay me?"

"Yes." The older man, who'd been a team member for over twenty-five years, was the best person Reed could have at his side in that moment. Since retiring, he rarely came out on rescues anymore, but when there was a child involved, alone and lost, it was all hands on deck.

Reed began his descent. "Rebecca, I'm going to come to you. Stay where you are. Just relax and don't move."

Her nod was small.

He could see she was clutching several branches protruding from the mountain. She'd lost her right glove, as well as her scarf, but other than that, her skin was covered, protected from the elements. Thank God. Frostbite set in within minutes in this cold.

His own cheeks—his only flesh exposed to the elements—stung in the wind. They could expect her right hand to need medical attention. His boots slipped against the rocks and several gave way, falling to the base of the mountain.

He moved lower and lower until he reached the ledge. Not trusting it to hold both their weight, he hung next to it. "Hi. I'm Reed. Can you open your eyes for me?" He wanted her to know she was safe, that she could trust him…but he would need her cooperation to get them out of there as quickly as possible.

"No."

He saw the shape of her lips more than he heard the word.

"Afraid of heights?"

She nodded.

"Okay. Well, I'm straight ahead of you. So just open

your eyes and look straight ahead. You'll see my goofy grin," he said.

Slowly, her eyes opened and the terror in them made his chest tighten. He ignored the what-if scenarios running through his mind and cleared his thoughts.

Save the kid, get everyone back safe. Simple. Yet, not an easy task. Expect the unexpected.

"You're doing great," he told her. "Are you hurt?"

"My hand was hurting but not anymore…"

Frostbite. Hopefully, they weren't too late.

"And my leg."

He glanced toward her legs, where her snowshoes still dangled from her feet. The right leg was twisted in a grotesque angle. Numb and in shock right now, she couldn't feel the severity of the injury, which was good. He hated to think that she'd been out there that long alone, scared and in pain. Keeping his voice calm, he radioed. "We will need the litter. Start lowering it to the left."

"Is my leg broken?" she asked, daring a glance at it.

"Yes." He wouldn't lie. She would need to be prepared for what came next. "But we are going to get it fixed up in no time. We have an ambulance waiting on the trailhead. Just a few more minutes…and your parents are there…"

"No!" She moved away, clinging to the branches. New fear on her face.

"Whoa, hold up. Stay still." He'd seen this before. Lost children were surprisingly terrified that their parents would be angry. He knew after interviewing hers that nothing could be farther from the truth. The young couple was going crazy—worried about their little girl. Relief would be their only emotion when she was brought back safely. "Your mom and dad are not mad. They are worried and they love you. They can't wait to hug you." Reunions after rescues were the only consistent element to this job.

Tears slid down the little girl's cheeks. "I was supposed to stay with the group," she whispered.

"Getting lost happens. This isn't your fault." He glanced overhead and saw the litter approaching. To the left of it, Wade rappelled down the mountain. About two minutes away. Adrenaline soared through his veins as he mentally prepared for what came next—getting her off the ledge and onto the carrier and getting her to the ambulance on standby, waiting for them.

"I'm really scared," she said, glancing up toward the litter.

"Can I tell you a story?" he asked her.

She nodded.

"When I was about your age…" It was closer to fifteen, but he wanted her to identify with him. "My mom took my sister and me and our best friends camping just a mile from here. I decided to take a hike in the woods close to nightfall…and I got lost." He actually hadn't been alone, but the story worked better this way.

Rebecca's eyes widened.

He glanced up. The litter was about five feet away. "I thought I knew the way back to camp, but as I started walking, I only got more and more lost." The truth was, he had known the way. If he hadn't been lost with his sister's annoying, smart-ass best friend, who'd insisted the way back to camp was in the opposite direction, and if he hadn't been gentleman enough to not let her wander off alone and get lost, he wouldn't have been stranded with her overnight as they'd waited for the search crew to find them.

Erika Sheridan. He'd told countless variations of this story over the years but the deep irritation he felt for her was always the same.

"Night fell and I was still lost, so I thought really hard about what I'd learned from a Hug-A-Tree program I'd taken…" May as well turn this into an educational experience. "I remembered that the best thing I could do was to find a tree in an open clearing and stay next to it. Hug it if I felt nervous…" A memory of Erika, terrified and trembling in his arms that night fifteen years ago, flashed in his mind and he lost track of what he was saying. She'd been irritating right up until that moment when darkness had fallen, they were tired and hungry and he'd learned she was afraid of the dark. At that moment, he'd caught a glimpse of a different girl…

Of course, her vulnerable side disappeared again as soon as they were rescued.

"How long were you there?" Rebecca asked, her voice trembling as she shivered. Her body was going into shock.

"Only one night, but it was scary and I was relieved when rescuers found us…me," he said. "And now I help other kids who need it."

"I'm glad you found me," she said, as the litter reached them. "What's that?" Fear was back in her voice.

"It's kind of like a stretcher. It will help me get you back up the mountain safely, without hurting your leg." Too much.

"How do you want to do this?" Wade asked, dangling next to him.

"I'm going to move closer and harness her in case that ledge decides not to hold," he said as quietly and calmly as possible. "Then I need you to bring the litter closer. The right leg is broken and I can't assess any other injuries right now."

Wade nodded. "Copy that."

Reed turned to Rebecca. "Okay. My friend Wade and I are going to get you to safety and I need you to be as brave as you have been out here alone, okay?"

She nodded. "And you're sure my parents aren't mad?"

He smiled. "Darling, believe me...if there's anything crazy on your Christmas wish list this year, about an hour from now will be the best time to ask for it." He winked at her and her frostbitten lips curled into a tiny smile.

Time to get her home.

CHAPTER THREE

SIX MINUTES IN Wild River and already Erika was regretting this impulsive move. Which was why she never did anything impulsive. Waiting on the train station platform, she felt more than a little out of place. Her thin-heeled, three-inch leather boots and dressy cashmere winter coat looked ridiculous among the ski suits and winter boots the other travelers wore. She didn't own anything like that anymore. She rarely went outside in Anchorage.

Her large suitcase contained more of the same non-casual clothes, but she thought she'd packed at least one pair of jeans. She hoped.

She forced a breath, taking in her surroundings. She hadn't been back to Wild River since she left for university. The town nestled between the Chugach and Talkeetna Mountains was small with only two thousand residents. It was breathtakingly beautiful with its snow-covered peaks and untouched wilderness, but it was also her past and already she felt slightly claustrophobic.

When Erika spotted her friend behind the wheel of a large SUV with the Snow Trek Tours logo on the door, Cassie gave an apprehensive wave, which didn't fill Erika with confidence in her decision to come. As the vehicle stopped in front of her, Erika opened the back, put her suitcase inside, then climbed into the passenger seat. "Hi…"

"Hey!" Cassie went in for a hug just as she extended a hand. Her fingers poked her friend in the chest and Cassie moved away. "Oh…okay…we're shaking hands."

Erika pulled her hand back at the same time Cassie reached for it. "We don't have to…sorry, that was dumb."

Cassie nodded, turning her attention back to the road. "Shall we just go, then?"

"Yes," she mumbled.

As Cassie pulled her vehicle away from the train station, Erika stared longingly at the departures drop-off zone in the side mirror.

She'd talked herself out of canceling a dozen times since booking the trip, and reaching out to Cassie the night before had required several glasses of wine. Her friend had seemed more than a little surprised when she'd responded to Erika's Facebook message, but she'd invited her to stay for as long as she wanted. Erika hadn't mentioned that this spur-of-the-moment vacation wasn't her idea. In all honesty, she'd be back on a train headed home if the next train wasn't scheduled to leave for Anchorage days from now.

Especially if this awkward silence continued. Obviously, the ten years between them might be about ten years too long.

Erika started to sweat beneath her coat, suddenly feeling like she'd accepted a ride from a stranger.

Which was ridiculous. They'd been best friends. They'd shared their deepest secrets. Time couldn't have changed them that much, could it?

She cleared her throat, unwrapping her scarf from around her neck as a blast of warm air reached her. "So...you like living here?"

"I do." Cassie glanced at her. "And you—you're happy living in the city?"

"My apartment's a few blocks from the hospital, so it's convenient."

Cassie nodded.

Silence.

"You're an adventure tour guide?"

"I own a mountain adventure company."

"Own it? Wow."

Cassie shot her a questioning look.

Erika's face grew hot. "Not like wow as in I didn't think you could own your own company...but wow as in, I'm impressed... Owning a business is really hard and a lot of work..." God, she was making it worse. "Just that I'm happy for you." *Just shut up, Erika.*

"I knew what you meant... I think," Cassie said, looking over her shoulder as she changed lanes.

Other than the fact that her friend's blond hair was now shoulder-length and not hanging down her back, she looked exactly the same as she had when they'd graduated high school. At five-two, Cassie had always had a petite, athletic figure... Erika had always envied her friend's perky B cup boobs and muscular body. Erika had skipped training bras and gone straight to double Ds the moment she hit puberty, and without the stress of her job and her too-busy-to-eat schedule, she'd be two hundred pounds. All she had to do was think about eating a stale donut in the hospital staff room and she'd gain weight.

And unlike the dark circles Erika tried desperately

to cover with concealer, Cassie's skin was still smooth and wrinkle free. If running her own company was stressful, you couldn't tell by her friend's relaxed, easy-going demeanor.

"Is the company busy this time of year?" she asked. With the holidays approaching, the mountains would soon be bustling with families enjoying the Christmas festivities. Wild River boasted the best year-round ski resort in Alaska. Unfortunately, their five-star lodge was completely booked until New Year's.

Cassie nodded. "Summer and fall are our busiest. Winter months tend to be slower because families are here mostly to hit the slopes, but we still keep busy with snowmobile and snowshoeing tours." Her expression clouded slightly.

"You okay?" Years might lie between them, but she could still read Cassie's face.

"Yeah, I'm fine…now. There was just a rescue last night for a little girl who'd gone missing on a snow-shoe tour a few days ago."

Instantly Erika was yanked back in time to her own misadventure in the mountains, being lost overnight… with Cassie's brother, Reed. She shivered even now just recalling the incident she usually refused to think about. That day had been one of the worst days of her life.

"She's okay. They found her," Cassie said a little harshly when Erika was silent.

"Right…that's great. A relief," her voice trailed off. This reunion wasn't going well. How she'd expected them to just pick up where they'd left off, she didn't know. Why had she come here by train? She should have driven so she wouldn't be stuck here, at the mercy of the train schedule.

Though that was precisely why she'd done it.

Noticing Cassie's wrist tattoo—the word *Best* visible beneath the sleeve of her coat—she decided to try again. Their tattoos had been more than just words at one time and their shared history had to mean something. "So…your company—how many employees work for you?"

"I have a team of six tour guides during the busier seasons and four during the winter."

"Do you have an office?"

"Yes, on Main Street."

"What's the name of the business?"

"Snow Trek Tours."

"Right. The logo on the door…" Opening the search engine on her phone, Erika typed in the name.

"Don't believe me?" Cassie asked, glancing at the phone as the company's professional-looking website appeared.

Erika closed it down and shook her head. "Sorry. Research is a habit of mine, that's all." Though maybe she should have researched her friend's Facebook page a little more. Or reached out to her before now. But she was genuinely interested. "Other than snowshoeing and snowmobiling, what else does the company offer?" Snow Trek Tours couldn't possibly survive on those activities alone and Cassie said summer was a busy time.

"Winter camping is popular this time of year, before the temperature drops in the negative… Also corporate events—we host a lot of executive team-building trips."

Erika nodded. "I can imagine there's a lot of liability insurance needed…" Her body jerked forward as Cassie stopped the truck abruptly at a stoplight.

"This is starting to feel a little like an interview," she said.

"Sorry." Socially awkward was a term that readily came to mind when she described herself. She'd always struggled to fit in with other kids, and based on her lack of friends now, that trend had continued into her adult life. Despite her professional success, or maybe *because* of it, Erika had a hard time relating to people and having a conversation that wasn't work related.

Much of her identity was wrapped up in her career, and outside the comfort of the operating room, she wasn't quite sure who she was.

But this was Cassie—her best friend…or at least she had been. She could relax. She could be herself… or at least the closest version of a normal person she could muster.

But Erika couldn't think of anything else to say and a moment later, Cassie reached forward and turned up the volume on the holiday music station playing "Rockin' Around the Christmas Tree."

Right.

Erika glanced out the window as they drove along Main Street, the late afternoon sky casting a beautiful glow over the town, already decorated for the upcoming season. Lights and garlands were wrapped around the streetlight poles and the storefront window displays competed to be the most elaborate. They held a contest every year and visitors could vote on their favorites. When Erika was a kid, her mother would bring her to Main Street for a shopping trip the week before Christmas and they always agreed that the secondhand bookstore—Wrinkled Pages—had the best display. They'd drink hot chocolate and shop for a new train set for her father at the Hobby Shop—he'd collected miniature sets back then—and she'd looked forward to his fake surprise when he'd opened the gift every year. Christmas when her mom was alive had been something to celebrate, and the traditional shopping trip was etched in her memory.

The season in Wild River was magical and the sights outside the window reminded her that this was the season of miracles. If she survived medical school, she could survive a vacation.

But her friend was quiet.

Was Cassie contemplating ditching her on the side of the road?

She released a slow, steady breath before asking, "Is there a bar nearby?" It was before five but it was already getting dark, daylight growing shorter this time of year, so drinking was acceptable, right? It might help her relax a little. Anything to help her vacate her life.

Cassie nodded emphatically, as though she, too, had come to the conclusion that alcohol might be their only savior that week. "I know just the place."

"DON'T EVEN THINK about turning down those drink offers."

Reed laughed. "If you're cool with a drunk-ass bartender this evening, I'll toss them all back." The outpouring of congratulations was the same after every successful rescue, but yesterday's rescue had everyone breathing a deeper sigh of relief. Rebecca had suffered a broken tibia and femur and frostbite to her fingers on her right hand, as he'd predicted, but she'd been released from the Wild River Community Hospital that afternoon.

The bar's owner, Tank—affectionately nicknamed for his six-foot-five height and two hundred and seventy pounds of solid muscle—hesitated, then shrugged before heading toward his office in the back of The Drunk Tank. "I don't care. Just don't forget to lock the place up."

"You're leaving?" Reed asked, twisting off several beer caps and setting the bottles on the bar in front of Wade and Tyler—two other rescue team members who'd been on the search the night before.

Tank turned and held out a shaky hand.

Reed nodded. "Got it." Tank was a support member on the search and rescue crew, had been for far too long. He should have applied to be a full member by now, but he couldn't get past the lingering anxiety after the rescues. Admittedly, the ones that hadn't gone successfully left their scars and took some time to bounce back from, but the successful ones left Reed pumped.

Tank—the biggest softy on the planet—had a tougher time. Especially when kids were involved. A single dad, last night's emotional reunion between Rebecca and her parents had Tank ditching the scene immediately.

Reed worried about Tank being on the team when he had so many other responsibilities, namely Kaia, to take care of, but they each had their reasons for being on the crew. And they certainly needed the members.

"Okay, grab your backpack, let's go home," Tank said, reappearing with his coat.

Kaia climbed down from the barstool and slid into her coat, tucking her dark hair into her hat and grabbing the Wonder Woman backpack that was a million years old but she refused to part with. "Bye, Reed. Thanks for the chocolate milk."

"Anytime." He waved as they left, turning his attention to Wade and Tyler. "You guys good?"

"Yeah. I mean, last night was brutal, but it ended well. That's what matters," Wade said.

"Do I get promoted to lead now?" Tyler asked, leaning an elbow on the bar.

Only the third time he'd asked that day. "You've been on the team a year. Stick it out, keep proving yourself and you'll be bossing the rest of us around soon enough," Reed said. Tyler was one of the best S & R members he had, definitely one of the hardest working. But he was also young and impulsive, and Reed couldn't fully trust his decision-making. However, he knew the guy also had different aspirations. He'd applied to become a volunteer firefighter in Wild River. If Reed didn't help promote him to lead soon, he might move on. Reed would hate to lose him. Good, qualified team members were hard to find and even tougher to keep. The team was lucky—they were all as close as family. They looked out for one another on and off rescues.

"How's Cassie?" Wade asked.

"She's okay. Rebecca's family reassured her that they don't hold Snow Trek Tours responsible. They had gone against Mike's advice." The family's assigned tour guide had suggested a different trail because of the unpredictable terrain, but they'd insisted on the more experienced trek. They took full responsibility for what happened. Still, he knew his sister had been just as stressed and worried as everyone else during

the rescue hours. Her company had an amazing reputation in Wild River and he knew it was because she
always put the safety of her clients and employees first.

Seeing her enter the bar now, he nodded and smiled.

But his smile faded when he saw she wasn't alone.
He squinted in the dim lighting of the bar.

No shit.

The girl who'd crossed his mind just the night before was walking toward him with his sister. Unfortunately, she was hardly a girl anymore. Dressed in a
red-and-black-checked cashmere coat, cinched at her
tiny waist with a leather belt, a red hat covering her
mocha-colored hair and three-inch, impractical yet
sexy leather boots, she was definitely not a little girl
anymore.

What the hell was she doing here?

Tyler and Wade gave up their barstools to the
women, waving as they headed toward a booth.

"See ya, guys," he said. Then, turning to his sister,
"Hey, Cass, who's your friend?" He wiped the bar in
front of them and set down two new coasters.

His sister shot him a look that resembled a plea for
help…or for something strong. Obviously this visit was
as much of a surprise to her. He reached for the top-
shelf premium vodka and held up the bottle.

She nodded, removing her scarf and coat. "Make it a
double. This is Erika… You remember her, don't you?"
She placed her coat over the stool before climbing up.

Erika was still scanning the bar as though she hadn't
decided yet if she was going to stay.

"Um… Erika." He pretended to think. "Right, yes,
I remember—how've you been?"

She finally looked at him, her eyebrows furrowed. "We've met?"

Unbelievable. He'd only held her in the woods overnight so she didn't have a panic attack.

"You have to remember my brother, Reed," Cassie said, motioning for him to be quicker with her drink.

Erika's mouth gaped slightly.

There you go. He knew he'd changed over the years. In high school, he'd been tall and lanky...skinny was a better term. Food wasn't always plentiful at home and being active in every sport that he could play for free had him burning energy faster than his body could keep up. Luckily, he'd discovered weight training. "Hard to believe this hunk is the same guy, huh?" he asked when she continued to stare.

Her look of disbelief was quickly replaced with a disapproving, incredulous one. "Do you own this place?"

"Nope. I'm just here to encourage copious amounts of alcohol and misbehaving," he said, his jaw tight. Within seconds, she had him feeling like the teenage kid who wasn't sure he'd ever amount to anything. Over the years, his confidence had grown along with the size of his biceps. Very little shook him, so how this woman he hadn't seen in years had him agitated, he didn't know. No doubt, their history was part of it.

"He makes the best cranberry martinis in Wild River. Have a seat," Cassie said, gesturing to the barstool next to her.

"Or don't." Reed shrugged when Erika hesitated.

She ignored him as she examined the barstool. Picking up a napkin, she wiped the seat before removing her coat and sitting, folding the coat over her legs. Ready for a quick exit if needed.

"Wow," he muttered, pouring alcohol into the shaker. At Cassie's desperate expression, he poured a little longer. Reaching into the fridge, he ignored the opened carton of cranberry juice and grabbed a new one, irritated by his desire to please Ms. Better Than Everyone with fresh juice. "So, Erika, how've you been?" Second and last attempt at polite conversation.

She unwrapped her red scarf but left it dangling around her shoulders. The contrast of the red scarf against the white cashmere V-neck sweater pulled his gaze downward to her chest. The swell of her soft-looking, full breasts spilled slightly over the top and he remembered summer days when his gaze, hidden behind sunglasses, had been on nothing else. She'd always been a pain in the ass, but her body had been rockin' even back then. Apparently, she still had an effect on him. The front of his jeans was uncomfortably tight.

"I'm a surgeon now," was her reply to his question.

And modest. He grinned, feeling his semi disappear. "Impressive. That's like a doctor, right?"

"Are you making fun of me?"

He shook his head as he tossed ice in the mixer and shook. "Not at all." He grabbed two martini glasses from the back wall and inspected them just to freak her out a little. "Clean enough," he said, pouring the red liquid into the glasses. Grabbing several lime wedges, he attached one to Cassie's glass.

Erika held out a hand. "None for me, thanks. People sneeze and touch the garnishes left on bars," she said. "So many germs." She shuddered.

"Nah… These have only been sitting out for a week, tops," Reed said, attaching the lime slice to her glass and handing it to her.

Her mouth opened then snapped shut again, as though she were biting back a smart retort of her own.

Too bad. He'd like to see what she was made of. She had to possess more than this frosty exterior… though he'd only ever gotten evidence of that once, and only briefly.

Next to her, Cassie removed the lime wedge and took a long sip of her drink.

"What brings you to Wild River?"

"A vacation," she said tightly. Her eyes scanned the bar and he'd never been so proud of the tacky holiday decorations. The look of disgust on her face when her gaze landed on the Santa figurine peeing in the snow that was attached to a beer tap was worth every penny the thing cost.

"Most people find those fun," he said, sliding a bowl of bar nuts toward his sister.

"Really? I can't imagine why," Erika said, sipping her own drink.

He waited to see if she liked it, annoyed that it mattered, but she left him hanging, turning her attention back to her surroundings. She glanced from side to side over her shoulders toward the back.

"Bathroom's in the far corner, past the pool tables on the left."

"I'm fine." She crossed her legs to sit awkwardly on the stool.

Right. Germs. "How long are you staying?"

"Two weeks."

Cassie's drink flew out of her mouth, showering him

with sticky cranberry juice. He reached for a napkin and wiped his forearm, handing her one for her face.

"Two weeks? Wow," Cassie said, grabbing a handful of bar nuts and stuffing them into her mouth.

Erika nodded. "Or not... I don't know yet."

Holy awkwardness. Obviously his sister and her former best friend were learning quickly that sometimes friendships didn't last into adulthood.

"Was that a little girl I saw leaving before we came in?" Erika asked.

"That was the owner's daughter," he said, glancing at his sister. As suspected, the mere mention of Tank and Cassie's thoughts were written all over her face. His sister and his friend had been doing this protracted dance around one another for years now. He wasn't sure what was going on, except that Cassie got flustered and flushed whenever Tank was around. She often babysat Kaia for Tank and the two had been friends for years. He suspected the man's single dad status might be the main reason the two hadn't hooked up yet.

"He brings his daughter in here?" Erika sipped her drink again.

"Until the bar starts to get busy, yeah."

She shook her head.

"You got an opinion on that, Ms. PhD?" He leaned against the bar. She was there five minutes and had succeeded in insulting the bar, the bar's owner *and* him. She had a knack for putting people off. Always had, but for some reason, it irritated him more now.

Before, she'd had a reason to judge them. They were poor, living in a shitty part of town, wearing hand-me-down clothes from kids they went to school with. Wild River was small enough that everyone knew everyone else's business, so trying to hide how much they struggled as kids was impossible. But he and Cassie had both come a long way.

"It's actually an MD."

He blew out a long, slow breath.

"And I just don't think a bar is an appropriate place for a kid."

He glanced at Cassie, but she just sent him a look that said, *can't win, don't try.* Seeing several regulars enter, he stood straighter and waved in greeting. A trip down memory lane with Erika was obviously not possible if the woman didn't even remember that he and Cassie had spent far too many evenings in a corner booth in a bar while their mom worked. Their mother's small dive bar in Willow Lake, the next, even smaller town over, had been a second home to them. They'd helped her clean up after closing almost every night and he'd worked there before he was legal. It wasn't an ideal upbringing, but it was about survival and working together as a family.

Their way of life hadn't been Erika's reality. Why *would* she remember that not everyone had been as blessed as she was?

Obviously, she'd been successful in forgetting a lot of things.

CHAPTER FOUR

COMING TO WILD RIVER was feeling less and less like a mistake the more cranberry martinis Erika consumed, so she raised her empty glass for another.

The crazy-hot bartender she barely recognized as the scrawny, tall kid that had never particularly liked her hesitated as he dried a shot glass with a towel and she wrinkled her nose.

"Allowing dishes to air-dry is a lot more sanitary," she said.

"Another drink it is. Maybe it will make you less annoying... So far, that hasn't been the case, but here's hoping the third one's the charm," he muttered as he reached for the shaker.

"I heard that."

"You were meant to." He shook the shaker and the insult was quickly forgotten as her eyes fell to his arms. Thick, sexy biceps beneath the black T-shirt held her stare far too long. Damn, they were hot. She wondered where they came from. They certainly hadn't been there before. The Reed she remembered could barely open a pickle jar. This Reed could probably smash the jar with his bare hand. He was all mountain strong... was that a thing? Mesmerized by the way the muscles looked flexed all the time, she jumped when he snapped a finger in front of her face.

Busted. Her cheeks flamed as bright as the tacky red garland draped along the bar. "What?"

"I said, another double?" He grinned, having caught her checking him out.

She shrugged. "Why not?"

"You want another one?" he asked Cassie.

"I don't know… I'm feeling the first two…"

Reed grinned. "Only the first one had vodka in it. You two aren't drunk. You're high on sugar."

Cassie laughed. "In that case, definitely. The more sugar I drink, the more bearable she becomes." Her friend gave her a gentle shove to soothe the sting of the comment and indicate she was kidding. Mostly.

After one double martini and a lot of refined sugar, Erika was starting to see herself as the annoying, stuck-up twat they thought she was. She released a deep breath. Just relax. Vacations were an excuse to vacate one's life. She desperately needed to escape her own mind. Checking her cell phone for calls and messages from the hospital was useless as it seemed the bar killed any kind of cell reception. And she wasn't exactly in the best frame of mind to deal with hospital stuff right now anyway. Tomorrow, she'd be more responsible. Tonight, these cranberry martinis were a lifeline.

Cassie turned on the barstool. "These martinis remind me of that party we went to in tenth grade—Kylie Fresco's Sweet Sixteen?"

Cassie hadn't needed to clarify. It was the one and only party Erika had attended in high school. After her father had caught her sneaking back into the house, vomiting on the hall rug at 2:00 a.m., new, stricter rules had been put in place.

But that had been good. Going to the party had been stupid. Getting drunk and acting irresponsible got no one anywhere in life.

Where the hell was her drink? She gestured for Reed to speed it up as she nodded. "I remember the aching head the next day while I studied for my biology finals."

"I think that was the first and last time we drank together," she said.

"Really? Are you sure?" She thought hard but another night didn't immediately come to mind. She'd known better than to disobey her father's no-partying rule, not that she'd gotten many invites anyway. She wasn't fun and cool like Cassie. Other kids didn't get her and eventually she'd stopped trying so hard to fit in. After high school, she'd gone straight into university, while Cassie had worked a bunch of part-time jobs to save money to travel to Europe. Her adventurous spirit had taken her on a three-month trip and they hadn't seen much of one another after that...

Cassie leaned over the bar and grabbed a bottle of tequila from Reed, who had just finished pouring several shots for a group sitting at the end of the bar. "Shot glasses, please."

He placed two on the bar with a disapproving shake of his head. "You sure about this?"

Reed hesitated, looking at Erika. Deep blueberry-colored eyes made Erika shift on the barstool. She'd always felt uncomfortable around Cassie's older brother. He hardly hid his true feelings about her and she'd heard him call her a snob once... Not that she maybe didn't deserve the label based on outside appearances, but she really wasn't the person he thought she was.

Or the woman her coworkers thought she was. Or the daughter her father expected her to be.

Although if everyone thought she was a certain way, could there be some validity to it?

Drinks. More drinking, less thinking.

She turned to Cassie and scoffed, "Whatever. We don't need his approval to drink. We are two strong, independent women." She took the bottle of tequila and filled the shot glasses. Then, stretching along the bar, she grabbed two lemon wedges and handed one to Cassie.

"Not worried about where that lemon has been?" Reed asked.

Ignoring his amused stare, Erika clinked her glass against Cassie's. "To a fun night with no regrets," she said, tossing the liquid back, letting it burn the common sense right out of her.

OH, SHE WAS going to regret this night all right.

Two hours later, outside the bar, Reed shot his sister an annoyed look as he escorted them the two blocks from The Drunk Tank to Cassie's condo above Snow Trek Tours. Thankfully it was still early and the servers could handle things for five minutes.

"Don't look at me like that. It's not like you've never been tipsy before," Cassie slurred.

Tipsy? They were shit-faced at eight thirty-six.

Real party animals.

"Okay, let's keep walking," he said, as Erika stopped to admire the Christmas display in the Chocolate Shoppe's window. The life-size sculpted Santa made out of chocolate made his teeth hurt just looking at it.

"I'd kill for chocolate right now," she said, practically licking the window.

Gone was the uptight, stick-up-her-ass professional and it had only taken two shots of tequila.

"I have to get back to work." Taking her arm, he led the way around the corner to the back staircase that led to his sister's condo.

Erika took one look at the stairs and shook her head. "That's not going to work." She lifted one boot-clad foot so he could see the high heel and he caught her as she toppled off balance.

He gritted his teeth. Of course—her nonsensical, yet sexy as all fuck heels. Heels on boots that hugged her shapely calves nicely and forced a distracting sway in her hips when she finally did go to the restroom at the bar, but not exactly grate-friendly.

He sighed as he scooped her up.

"What are you doing?"

"Getting you upstairs," he said, jogging up the stairs with her in his arms. She wasn't heavy and he held his breath, the scent of her soft perfume overshadowing the smell of tequila on her breath.

He was glad they were calling it a night before the bar got really busy. She was far too distracting, especially once she'd let her guard down. Her unexpected smile had mesmerized him and her easy-sounding laugh had surprised him. Her body was smoking hot, but it was her dark eyes and full, pouty lips that had him fighting an odd attraction to his sister's best friend all evening.

When she stopped spouting bullshit, she was even kind of funny in a dry humor, self-deprecating way.

Too bad she couldn't have a sense of humor like this when she was sober.

"Shit. I forgot my gloves," Cassie said behind them. "Here's my keys, I'll be right back." She tossed the keys at him and turned to head back toward the bar.

He caught the keys. "What? No...what am I supposed to do with her?"

"Just set her down on the couch. I'll get blankets and a pillow when I get back," Cassie called as she disappeared down the street.

"Great," he muttered.

"Oh come on. Don't act like you're not enjoying this macho act of heroism." Erika struggled with the pronunciation. "You were always the protector type." She touched his chest and her eyes raked him in. She was looking at him the same way she'd gazed longingly at the chocolate Santa moments before.

He wasn't sure which unsettled him most, the look in her eyes, the fact that she remembered something personal about him or the hardening in his pants at her touch.

He unlocked the door and nudged it open with her body. Then he promptly discarded her on the couch as instructed.

Done. She was there safely. Just leave.

Hearing them enter, Diva, his sister's Siberian husky pup, came running to greet them. She saw him, but noticing their new guest, went straight for Erika instead with a welcoming yelp.

Erika sobered in record time, bringing her legs up to her chin on the couch and making herself as small as possible. "What is that?"

"Cassie's dog. Erika, meet Diva." Obviously, his

sister had forgotten to mention her pet to her house-guest. Though how Erika could miss the daily dozen pictures of the dog his sister posted on social media, he didn't know. Diva in her Halloween costume dressed as a banana, Diva in her new snowsuit, Diva in the bathtub... If his sister ever had kids, he was blocking her on Facebook.

"That thing is huge."

He laughed. "She's still a puppy." And she was super cute.

The dog jumped onto the couch and continued to yelp, pawing Erika's shoulder.

"Can you get it away?" she asked, her eyes closed, hands clutched in front of her.

"You allergic?" he asked, approaching and lifting the dog into his arms.

"No. Terrified."

"Don't worry. Diva doesn't eat city folk." He brought the dog to the kitchen and set her down by her food dish.

Erika glared as she removed her coat and scarf. "It's not like we have a certain smell or anything." She kicked off her boots and leaned back against the cushions.

He shrugged as he reached for a blanket from the back of the couch. "I don't know about that," he said. He bent toward her and paused near her ear to sniff. The action was meant as a jerk move to annoy her, but damn, it backfired. The tantalizing sweet scent of honey on her neck was subtle and provocative. He hadn't been close enough to be tempted by it when she'd been in his arms, but now it clouded his senses.

Luckily, she shoved him away before he could do something moronic like lick her.

He tossed the blanket over her quickly and stood. "Okay, so you're all good?"

She nodded, but her gaze was on his midsection. And her unblinking stare was full of unconcealed attraction. The same way she'd checked out his biceps in the bar.

He glanced down to see that his T-shirt had risen slightly on the right side, exposing his stomach.

Obviously his abs were to her liking.

"Erika."

"Huh?" Still staring.

"It's been a while, huh?"

She frowned, finally pulling her gaze back to his. "For what?"

"Since you've had sex."

Her mouth gaped.

"I mean, that's why you're staring at my stomach like I'm a piece of chocolate."

"I was not," she said, but her cheeks flushed. "And I'll have you know, I have plenty of sex…all the time. Men beating down my door for it…" she mumbled.

That he wouldn't doubt, except he knew from Cassie that she was a reclusive workaholic and he was willing to bet the only penises she saw were on her naked patients.

"And anyway, even if that was the case, you'd be the last guy I'd want to break my dry spell."

Okay, now he was intrigued. Especially since he'd made no motion to fix his shirt and her eyes were glued on his abs again, betraying her words. He crossed his arms, making sure to flex his biceps for her viewing pleasure, as well. She wasn't going to get him, but all of a sudden, he wanted her to want him. "Oh yeah, why's that?"

"Because I don't think you'd be any good."

What?

"Hot guys are rarely good in bed. They don't think they need to be. They are selfish and rarely leave a woman satisfied."

She'd obviously been with the wrong dudes. "In your expert opinion?"

She nodded. "As a doctor and woman. Yes."

Damn, he'd like to kiss that smug expression right off her face, but the voice in his head told him to leave her drunk ass alone. "Okay, then. Good night."

"What? Not even going to try to prove me wrong?"

In two strides, he'd reached her. Pulling back the blanket, he lifted her and, seating himself on the couch, he set her down on his lap. A leg on either side, she straddled him. "You sure you want to eat your words?"

Instead of answering, she gripped his face and kissed him. Hard. His surprise faded fast as his mouth suddenly craved hers. The taste of tequila mingled with her cherry lip gloss and he forgot he was the one teaching her a lesson. Her legs gripped his and she pressed her chest against him, the feel of her breasts beneath the soft cashmere making his heart pound against them.

His hands moved down her neck, over her shoulders, down her back and rested on her ribs, squeezing tight as his breathing became increasingly difficult. Her body was tight and hard under the thin, soft fabric.

Her arms circled his neck and she pushed her pelvis forward against his dick, which was suddenly straining against the front of his jeans as she slipped her tongue between his lips and deepened the hot and heavy kiss. Her fingers crept up the back of his neck and tangled in his hair as their tongues danced and fought for position…locked in a power struggle…

His sister's best friend was an incredible kisser and completely boner inducing. He couldn't help but wonder if it was the alcohol running through her blood making her uninhibited or if she'd be this torturously sexy even sober?

His hands left her rib cage to grip her waist as she began a slow rocking motion with her hips, pushing her pelvis against his increasing hardness. No way could he handle that and be able to go back to work. Besides, she was drunk and Cassie would be there any second.

Probably the only thing powerful enough to make him pull his mouth from hers and hold her body away from him was the fact that he didn't take advantage of women—drunk or sober.

Her eyes flew open and she looked slightly dazed.

He knew the feeling. "Care to reevaluate your opinion?" he asked hoarsely, his dick throbbing and his mind reeling from the effect of her kiss. Her unexpected response to his.

He watched her swallow hard, but immediately the look of lust was gone, replaced once more by the infuriatingly annoying stuck-up, dismissive look. "I've had better," she said with a shrug, climbing off him ever so casually, as though she hadn't just been prepared to ride him rock-hard.

He stood, readjusting himself in his pants, then covered her with the blanket as she stretched out on the couch once more. "Fair enough. For the sake of all hot guys, I tried."

"And failed," she said, closing her eyes as she rolled into the couch.

Unbelievable. "I guess so," he mumbled. A temptation to kiss her cheek overwhelmed him. She was definitely a complicated woman…and unfortunately, for him, the more complicated the better. Only the sound of his sister's footsteps on the stairs outside snapped him back to reality.

"She asleep already?" Cassie asked as she came indoors.

"Um…yeah. Out like a light. See ya later, sis," he said, escaping the apartment quickly, hoping the cold winter wind would help to extinguish the spark that had been ignited in his core.

CHAPTER FIVE

I<small>F SHE COULD CLEARLY</small> remember every detail from the night before, Erika was pretty sure she'd be feeling remorse...or at the very least, embarrassment.

Lucky for her she didn't.

She was, however, feeling like her head was being squeezed in a vise. Groaning, she opened one eye and surveyed the condo. Located above Cassie's adventure tour company on Main Street, the loft-style condo was exactly what she'd pictured her friend living in. Light blue walls made the place feel bigger and the open-concept living room, dining room and kitchen was exactly Cassie's style. The winding wooden maple staircase leading upstairs to Cassie's bedroom and bathroom added a touch of sophistication to the place.

Which was of course downplayed by Cassie's choice of artwork. Dogs Playing Poker was placed over her marble wood-burning fireplace and an altered *Mona Lisa*, featuring the iconic lady sticking out her tongue and crossing her eyes, took up most of the dining room wall. Her friend hadn't changed at all over the years.

After the initial awkwardness, she'd let her guard down and was reminded how much she'd missed Cassie over the years. Her friend's jokes were as lame as ever but her stories about her travels had awoken a wanderlust spirit in Erika. Europe and Australia sounded amazing and Cassie had somehow managed to find a balance between working hard and playing hard.

Maybe she needed to try harder to find that balance. Or more realistically, she'd forget all about her alcohol-influenced promises and resolutions the moment she arrived back in Anchorage.

Tossing back the comforter, she swung her legs over the side of the couch. "Cassie!" she called up the stairs to her friend's bedroom.

Silence.

Going into the kitchen, she saw a bottle of Gatorade and two aspirin.

Thank you, friend!

Next to it was a note.

Had to leave for work, make yourself at home. See you tonight. Maybe we'll stick to wine this time.

Good idea. She popped the pills and gulped the Gatorade, then stood in the kitchen. What did she do now? She might be on vacation, but her friend still had a job to do. Which left her to her own devices…

A vague memory of some sort of beast jumping her the night before flashed in her mind and she turned in a quick 360, checking for a dog, but the condo was empty.

Had she dreamed it? She wasn't sure. One dream stood out vividly though… Reed. Naked. And the most mind-blowing sex dream that had nearly given her a real orgasm in her sleep. She still couldn't believe he was the same guy she'd known years before. He'd certainly filled out—the muscles straining against the fabric of his T-shirt the night before had practically made her drool. Muscles she'd touched every last inch of in her dream…

Coffee. She needed coffee. Stat.

She surveyed the uncluttered counter. No Keurig? No coffee maker? Was her friend kidding?

She opened every cupboard, standing on tiptoes and bending low to search every corner for the lifesaving appliance, but nope.

Holy shit. Her friend didn't drink coffee yet she was up and off to work at…she searched for a clock… 7:00 a.m.? Was she a robot?

A thorough search through the pantry revealed Cassie still had a kid's cereal addiction, but not even instant coffee could be found.

There's no way Erika would survive two weeks without coffee in the morning, which gave her a new daily purpose.

She'd gift her friend the miracle of caffeine. An early Christmas present.

Hearing a key turn in the front door, her heart raced slightly until she saw Reed enter, then it echoed off the open-concept walls.

Damn, he looked far too hot for 7:00 a.m. She quickly ran a hand through her hair and wiped her raccoon eyes.

"Morning," he said, juggling a tray of coffee and a bag that smelled like it had a piece of heaven trapped inside. Erika's stomach growled and she quickly did an underarm sniff test as Reed closed the door…behind a beast on a pink leash attached to a bejeweled collar.

Great, so she hadn't imagined the dog.

And right now the thing was staring at her like he wanted to eat her face.

She moved to put the kitchen island between her and the animal as Reed unhooked the leash. "Hi…"

He smirked as he watched her back around the island, away from the dog. The thing was relentless in his attempt to get to know her, rubbing the damp fur on his back against her and rotating in circles by her feet.

"Will he bite?" she asked, not taking her eyes from the creature as he sniffed her leg.

"Not unless you bite her first," Reed said.

"Very funny," she mumbled, though she was grateful when the dog lost interest and went to its oversize pink food dish.

And then immediately fell into it. Out cold, completely limp, legs sprawled out behind him.

"Oh my God… Is he okay?"

"Diva—*she*…" Reed said.

Right. She always assumed all dogs were male.

"And yes, *she*'s fine, just asleep," Reed said, going to the dish and scooping her up into his arms, cradling her to his chest as he carried her to her dog bed near the window.

A fuzzy memory of being the one Reed put to bed flashed in Erika's mind and her cheeks flamed. He'd carried her inside…had she cuddled into him? Yep.

Just focus on the dog. "What happened?"

"She's narcoleptic. She could be out for a minute or an hour."

Was he kidding? "A narcoleptic dog?"

"Yep."

Okay then…

"I brought you coffee and breakfast," he said, opening the paper bag.

"Why?" Glancing down, she saw her nipples pointing through the fabric of her thin tank top. She folded her arms across her body. Her bra was draped over the back of the couch. She hadn't expected visitors.

Reed picked up a coffee and closed the gap between them in two easy strides. "Because, I told you last night that I'm not the kind of guy who has sex with a woman and then doesn't call."

Her mouth gaped. No freaking way. It had just been a dream. "We…no…there's no way…" She shook her head, but a flashback of him laying her down on Cassie's couch the night before had her panicking slightly.

Nope. There was no way. She was sticking with that. "We didn't."

But her confidence wavered as he grabbed her hips and pulled her closer. "Final answer?" The intensity in his blue eyes made her shiver. His soft, manly smelling cologne made her mouth water slightly as her body stiffened. Shit, if they had, she just might not regret it…

Reed grinned. "You're right, we didn't."

She pushed him away and reached for the coffee. "I knew that." She took a desperate sip, the hot liquid scorching her tongue and the back of her throat as she forced it down.

"You kissed me, that's all," he said with a shrug, opening the bag and taking out a plastic-covered container.

She scoffed. "You're so full of sh…" Oh crap, she had kissed him. Reality had somehow blended with her dream, but she was starting to distinguish between the two. She had kissed him. And it was a fantastic kiss… "Oh, that was nothing… And so completely out of character for me." Damn, she'd really let her guard down the night before.

"Why? Because I'm just a bartender and you're a brilliant, beautiful surgeon?"

Her cheeks flamed, her mind still caught on beautiful. Ignoring the question, she reached for the plate of food piled high with scrambled eggs, bacon, sausages and toast, but he pulled it back out of reach.

"This is mine." He took out a small container of what looked like oatmeal and handed it to her. "You said last night you only ate 'clean.'"

She'd said that? Man, she must have sounded like a complete holier-than-thou asshole. His breakfast looked so good and the greasy food was exactly what she was craving that morning, but she squared her shoulders and accepted her fate. She could always head out for a second breakfast once he left. "The oatmeal's perfect." She opened it and, grabbing the plastic spoon, she forced herself not to gag on it. She normally skipped breakfast and sometimes lunch with her busy schedule. But she was on vacation and she planned to eat. A lot. And the faster she could get rid of him, the faster she could get to the breakfast diner on Main Street.

Reed grinned, watching her put another spoonful of the thick, tasteless gunk in her mouth. "Good?"

"Delicious."

He folded a piece of crunchy bacon and popped it into his mouth. "Mmm. I love bacon."

Setting the oatmeal down, she stole a piece off his plate and closed her eyes as the grease hit her tongue.

Reed laughed, sliding the plate toward her. "I was kidding. This is yours. I actually do eat 'clean' most of the time," he said with a wink as a chime sounded from his pocket and he reached for...

"A pager? What are you, a drug dealer?"

"Don't *you* carry a pager at the hospital?"

She sighed. "Yes, but there are very few professions

where they're needed these days… I can't imagine the bar has an emergency at this time in the morning."

"The bar—no. Snowcrest Mountain—yes," he said, grabbing his coat.

She narrowed her eyes at the search and rescue logo in the corner of the red-and-yellow jacket. Okay, so that was unexpected and more than a little hot. "You're mountain search and rescue?"

He nodded, checking his watch. He hesitated when his gaze locked on hers once more. A brief second of conflict registered in his baby blues before he said, "If you can tear yourself away from that coffee, why don't you get dressed and I'll show you *my* emergency room?"

CHAPTER SIX

INVITING ERIKA ALONG had been an impulsive move. One Reed was immediately wishing he could undo. Since the kiss the night before, he hadn't been able to shake his annoying attraction to her. Her taste lingered on his lips and her taunting words replayed in his mind. She could say what she wanted, but she'd definitely been as turned on by the kiss as he was. His freezing walk back to the bar had little effect on the heat coursing through him. He hadn't expected such passion from her, but she'd rocked him. So much so, that he'd turned down a very enticing proposal to spend the evening with a bombshell blonde tourist that promised no strings attached.

Of course, it was all physical with Erika. She was the sexiest woman he'd had the pleasure of putting to bed in a long time, but she was irritating and stuck-up and so far from his type…it was merely physical.

Her braless state when he'd entered Cassie's an hour before had given him a semi-hard-on that only the emergency call had been able to deflate. Soft-looking, round breasts visible under the tank top she'd been wearing had practically begged to be touched and the long, shapely legs that had straddled him on the couch had stolen his attention more than once. Messing with her had been a mistake…putting his hands on her body after a sleepless night of thinking of nothing else had only made the torture worse.

He couldn't act on the temptation. She was his sister's best friend, a woman he'd grown up with, and her attitude drove him insane. Hot sex with her wasn't worth the headache.

And now, watching her climb the side of Snowcrest Mountain with three support members and the head of the ski patrol unit, he definitely regretted inviting her along. Tyler, Wade and Marcus seemed more focused on getting to know Cassie's houseguest than they were on the task ahead of them.

Tyler especially. He was going to have a chat with the young team member. Reed wasn't going to act on his impulses toward Erika, but he didn't want anyone else to either. She should get to enjoy her vacation without being pawed at by his team.

He hadn't even expected her to agree to come along. But after only the slightest look of consideration, she'd hurried to Cassie's closet to find an extra ski suit—one that fit his sister's body like a glove and therefore hugged every last inch of Erika's taller, curvier frame like it was clinging for dear life.

If he was jealous of anything, it was the fabric.

Of course, her excitement and eagerness to join him had nothing to do with him, but a doctor's instinct combined with the prospect of boredom, holed up in Cassie's condo all day. From the moment he'd entered, he'd felt a restless energy from her. He would be surprised if she lasted five days on this vacation.

"So, this is a first," Tyler said, falling back from the others to walk alongside him.

"What's a first?" Tearing his gaze away from Erika's ass, he turned to the guy.

"You bringing a morning-after out on a rescue."

His jaw tightened at Tyler's casual dismissal of the surgeon as just another lay. "Not a morning-after. She's just a friend of my sister and she's a doctor. Thought we could use the help." That hadn't been his motive at all. He'd wanted to show her that there was more to him than she saw.

Why did he still want some sort of validation from her? What Erika Sheraton thought of him shouldn't matter at all, but it did.

"A doctor? Shit. Beauty and brains. She single?"

Reed shrugged. "She's on vacation alone."

"So, you think she's available then?"

Tyler's interest wasn't surprising. Erika was beautiful and Tyler made it a habit of dating the beautiful tourists. Reed didn't judge. He hooked up with his fair share, too. The search and rescue jacket was like a beacon for some women and he wasn't one to turn down a good time. Difference was, the women he had fun with knew it was just a one-night stand. Tyler had a way of leading them on, making them believe there could be more to it. Then ghosting them the minute they left the mountain.

Reed didn't like the idea of Erika falling prey to Tyler's charms, but there was little he could do about it.

"You know, I didn't check her Facebook relationship status," he grumbled as Erika joined them. "Why don't you take a turn with the litter?" he told Tyler.

"Yes, boss." Tyler gave a mock salute as he took over from Wade. He grinned at Erika. "I'll buy you a drink at Tank's later."

"Oh...okay, sure," she said, looking slightly confused.

Was it possible that she didn't realize how hot she was?

"Any update from ski patrol on suspected injuries?" she asked, and he shook thoughts of her body from his mind.

Ski patrol was already on-site, waiting for his injuries to be assessed so they could determine the safest way to get him back down the mountain to the ambulance waiting to take him to Wild River Community Hospital. Reed's initial reaction was to tell her she couldn't be privy to the info as she wasn't officially supposed to be there, but he'd been the one to invite her. "Nothing more than the broken leg reported so far," he said. "But he is complaining of pain in his right arm and upper chest and they aren't moving him until we arrive on scene."

She nodded, unzipping her jacket slightly as the mild temperature and the trek uphill brought a flush of heat to her cheeks and neck.

Catching a glimpse of the tank top beneath the jacket, he shook his head. "Are you just wearing the tank top and shorts beneath that?"

"You said to hurry."

Damn. She was still braless. Despite the thickness of the borrowed winter coat preventing any visibility to her tempting body, he felt himself harden again.

They were just breasts. He saw breasts all the time. Okay, maybe not all the time. But a lot. And this particular set—while amazing—was attached to a woman that drove him crazy. And not in a good way.

The entire drive to the base of the mountain, she'd been glued to her cell phone, typing furiously—texting or answering emails, he wasn't sure. But he was willing to bet it was work related. And when he'd cranked the soft rock station, she'd flicked the stereo off.

Annoying. As. Fuck.

And he'd do well to remember that, he thought as his eyes drifted back toward her exposed chest and his mouth went slightly dry.

Luckily, the ski patrol snowmobile came into view a second later and immediately his focus returned to the rescue...and only the rescue.

Mostly.

Picking up their pace, they heard the skier before they saw him.

"What's taking so long? I'm freezing to death on this snowbank," the guy on the ground said.

Hardly. It was forty degrees outside. And the guy should be thankful for the cold ground beneath him, it was no doubt dulling some of the pain from his injuries. His left leg was twisted and his skis had been removed. Ski patrol was trying to calm his ranting, but the guy continued to beak off.

"We're here," Reed said, approaching the two ski patrol guys kneeling on the ground next to the injured man.

"Thank God," Jimmy, a young ski patrol crew member, muttered. "He's been talking smack about suing for forty minutes now."

Doubtful. Reed had read and signed enough ski resort release forms to know the man wouldn't have a legal leg to stand on. All injuries are the fault of participants. Ski hill conditions and unpredictable weather made this sport a "do at your own risk" thing. "We got it," he said, doing a visual assessment of the skier. "What's his name?"

"Kent," Jimmy said.

Kent was in his midthirties, Reed would guess. Five-ten, two hundred pounds. The litter should work. A quick glance at his left leg confirmed it was broken. The odd angle of the knee joint was slightly sickening and he shot a quick sideways glance at Erika to see if she turned even the slightest bit green.

Nope. Her own critical gaze was assessing the scene same as his. Unfazed. Calm. Thorough.

It was a little hot.

"Is someone going to help me? This fucking hurts," Kent said.

Erika dropped to the snow next to the guy. "It hurts more when you expel too much hot air unnecessarily," she said.

Reed's eyes widened. Her bedside manner could use a little work, but the guy did zip it.

"Broken leg…where else are you experiencing pain?" she asked.

"Right shoulder. I think it's dislocated…" Kent said, calmer now. "Why aren't you dressed like these guys?" he asked as she moved closer to his arm.

"I'm not search and rescue."

Reed bent next to her and stopped her as she reached for the zipper on Kent's coat. "That's right. You're not. You are just here to observe." There were two thick gloves between their flesh, yet the contact resulted in an electric current shooting up his arm.

She yanked her hand away from his. "Bullshit. I'm a qualified surgeon. Under my oath as a doctor, I have to help in an emergency situation."

He forced a breath. Arguing in front of the injured man would be unprofessional, but he wasn't letting her take lead on this. It was his job, his team, his responsibility…his ego. "We are fully trained to deal with these types of injuries…"

She ignored him, unzipping the coat and shaking her head. "Not a shoulder dislocation. Looks like a clavicle fracture. It's swollen pretty badly. Do you hear any grinding when you move your arm?"

The guy looked like he was about to pass out from pain as he attempted to move his arm. He nodded as he swore under his breath. "Definitely grinding."

Erika leaned closer.

Kent's gaze dipped to the opening in her jacket and Reed snapped a finger. "Eyes up here."

Erika was oblivious. "The bone is off center. I can see it protruding here. It needs to be readjusted as soon as possible."

Readjusted? On the mountain? No way. "Erika, you need to step down. We will get him on the litter and to the emergency room at Wild River Community, where the doctors there will set any broken bones."

She shot him a look. "The leg—there's nothing we can do here. It's too far gone…"

Jesus. Kent looked horrified. "Your leg will be fine," Reed said.

"But the clavicle, I can help. An hour from now, this bone will be that much harder to put back in place. This guy will be wishing for death," Erika said.

The guy's eyes widened and he looked ill.

What was Erika like with her own patients? He was glad he wasn't one of them. "We are not authorized…"

"*You* are not authorized. I am," she argued, her

steely gaze igniting a fire in him. Infuriatingly impossible to deal with. Yet, there was the smallest part of him that found her challenge attractive.

"As fun as this is to watch, can you two maybe argue later?" Tyler said, moving closer to act as referee between them. "This guy is in pain. Whatever we're going to do, we need to do it now."

Backing down was not in Reed's wheelhouse. Tearing his gaze from Erika's, he looked at the injured skier. "I recommend we get you to the hospital, where they can properly assess the situation and set the bone in a more comfortable environment."

Erika's jaw clenched, but she remained silent.

Kent looked back and forth between them.

"It's your life," Erika said.

Kent nodded. "If it's all the same, I think I'll go with the surgeon."

Erika beamed victoriously. "Well there you have it. Excuse me," she said, kneeling closer to Kent, forcing Reed out of the way. She pulled off her gloves. "Okay. This is going to hurt, but in three seconds the bone will be set and the pain will ease a little…"

The guy nodded, his hands clenched at his sides. "Just do it before I change my mind."

Chicken out, more like it.

Erika placed a hand on the center of his chest and gripped his arm. "Take a deep breath. I'm going to count to three and then…"

Snap.

"Ow! Jesus!"

"There. Done. Feels better already, right?" Erika asked the guy, as she stood, putting her gloves back on.

The guy's look of anger dissipated quickly as he

nodded. "Actually, yeah. A million times better. Thank you," he said as Tyler and Wade lifted him carefully onto the litter hooked to the snowmobile. They buckled the safety straps and the vehicle headed slowly down the hill.

"That wasn't nice," Reed said as he stood next to Erika, watching the crew disappear over the side of the mountain.

She shrugged, looking far too pleased—whether with her performance or having won the battle of wills with him, Reed wasn't sure. "Hurts less when they don't expect it."

TWENTY MINUTES LATER, unexpected nostalgia overwhelmed Erika as she entered the hospital's emergency room. Sure, she worked in a similar environment every day, but this place was special, embedded deep in her psyche. Even the smell of the iodoform awakened memories of visits to see her father when he'd worked here years before.

Her love of medicine had started the first time she'd walked into Wild River Community Hospital. At six years old, she'd felt the energy and excitement of the fast-paced emergency room, enjoyed the quiet, comfortable silence of the nursery and sensed the passion and dedication of the doctors and nurses. Every day after school, she'd beg her mother to drop her off at the hospital to do her homework in the doctor's lounge, and she'd take every opportunity to annoy the doctors with her thousands of questions whenever they'd come in for a break. They marveled over her interest and her ability to retain what they taught her.

Most children hated hospitals, but she loved her

afternoons there. The best part was when her father would let her go on his rounds with him. How he was with his patients and the way they looked at him with admiration and respect had made her feel such pride, even at a young age. Back then he was a real-life superhero.

She'd wanted to be just like him.

Maybe she should have waited in the search and rescue van.

"Are you the doctor who set the shoulder?" a young physician asked her as they approached the triage desk.

She nodded. "The fractured clavicle—yes."

The doctor, whose name tag read Ford, checked the chart he held. "Right. I just have some paperwork for you to sign."

"Paperwork?"

"Releasing the hospital from any complications that could arise based on you setting the shoulder on the mountain instead of waiting for the patient to come here."

There wouldn't be any. She could have set that clavicle anywhere, but she understood. She reached for the clipboard.

Reed frowned next to her. "Wait. The patient authorized her to do it and he was a lot better off for it."

The young doctor shook his head. "Doesn't matter. I'm sure it's fine, but it's procedure. I'm sure you can appreciate that, Dr. Sheraton."

He recognized her?

Wasn't a complete surprise. She had given several presentations to the Anchorage Hospital Association regarding the new antirejection drug the year before.

And her father's reputation as a top surgeon in Alaska had a way of shining light on her and her career, as well.

"It's no problem. I'll sign it." Truth was, she hadn't really been thinking about procedure on the mountain… or the search and rescue's policies and standard operating. While she'd done what she thought was best for the skier in the moment, she'd overstepped.

She probably owed Reed an apology—*that* would be tougher.

"Here you go…it's front and back. You can just leave it with triage when you're done. We'll add it to Mr. Jansen's file," Dr. Ford said.

Taking the clipboard, she sat in the emergency waiting room, read through the release and signed quickly, letting her actions sink in. She wasn't one to question her decisions, but she also wasn't one to act hastily in these kinds of situations. Luckily, her assessment about the fracture had been correct, otherwise she could have done more damage than good.

How much of her uncharacteristic impulsiveness on the mountain had to do with Reed and the fact that she'd been determined to be right and maybe impress him with her skills?

She glanced at him now, checking his cell phone as he paced the emergency room, waiting for her. His invite to tag along had surprised her—they'd never been friends and she knew his breakfast delivery had probably been under pressure from Cassie.

A memory of his hands gripping her waist in the kitchen made her flush. She'd kissed him. Drunk Erika had courage sober Erika would never have. She'd rarely dated in high school and college, instead focusing on her studies and the volunteering experience she needed for her medical school applications. But when she did go out with a guy, it was usually someone as studious as she was…often her dates had turned into study sessions. She never dated guys like Reed—outgoing, laid-back and hot as hell. Guys like Reed had never been interested in her and now, she was too busy to notice if they were or not.

"Oh my! Look at you." A deep, familiar voice made her smile. "When the nurse said Dr. Sheraton was here, I knew it couldn't be your father, but wow," Dr. Smyth said, approaching with arms outstretched.

Erika stood and accepted the older man's hug. "Hi, Dr. Smyth. How are you?" She hadn't seen her father's former colleague and mentor since moving to Anchorage. He looked exactly the same. He'd always had white hair and deep-set wrinkles even in his forties and now in his late sixties, he'd seemed to stop aging. He'd always insisted she call him Grandpa and he'd been as much a part of her family as her real grandparents… until her mother died and her father had stopped entertaining in their home, withdrawing from everyone. Even her.

"Trying to get in as many days here as I can before they kick me out," he said, but his smile revealed he was looking forward to his upcoming retirement. She'd read about it in the hospital association newsletter the month before and had been meaning to reach out with her congratulations. A month ago? Wow. Her days at the hospital were a blur.

"I'm sure they'd keep you. Let me go tell them you want to stay on a few more years," she teased.

He grabbed her hand as she made a move toward the triage desk. "Don't even think about it. My golf times are already booked in Palm Springs. Jillian's there now." She knew he'd finally gotten married five years ago after being alone his entire life. His work had been his focus—giving back to his patients and community through countless charity organizations he was part of. But apparently, later in life, he'd developed a need for companionship. She'd meant to reach out to congratulate him on that news, as well. Had she even RSVP'd to the wedding invite? Guilt was easier to repress when she was holed up in her tiny office...now it drowned her. She should have attended the wedding.

"Congratulations on everything—the retirement, the wedding..." she said, and from the corner of her eye, she saw Reed watching them. She turned slightly so he was out of view.

"How's your father? I invited him to the wedding, but he RSVP'd that he was out of town that weekend."

Her father was never out of town...he was barely ever out of the office, but at least he'd responded. Or his assistant had. She forced her voice to sound light as she answered. "He's good... As busy as ever."

"Yeah, I reached out to him a few days ago, on the anniversary of your mom's death, but he didn't respond."

The mention of her mom made her chest tighten, then she felt slightly embarrassed. Her father had once thought the world of Dr. Smyth. The man had mentored him into the fantastic surgeon he was now. Yet, her father felt no ties or obligations to the hospital where he'd developed his skills. "He's been really preoccupied working on the new antirejection drug. Pending final approval, we start clinical trials right before Christmas."

"Yes. I'm on the committee that approved the trial start date yesterday," he said, nodding. "Wonderful new product."

She fought hard to hide her surprise at the news. The committee had approved the trials and her father hadn't told her yet? She'd checked her emails on the way to Snowcrest Mountain and there had been nothing from him or any of the other members of the team. "Yes, it is. It's been a long time coming, but we feel we may have a breakthrough product." One that might save lives without doing more damage than good. If only this drug had been around when her mother was fighting her battle with polycystic disease, she might still be there.

"I believe you do," he said sincerely.

Erika beamed, his support meaning so much to her. "Thank you. I should have known you would be part of the approval committee." Dr. Smyth had been nominated for several awards in clinical research himself.

"You're doing great work. Both of you. Your mom would be so proud."

The unexpected lump that rose in her throat at the second mention of her mother was tough to force down. She rarely talked about her mom, as her father refused to discuss her, but she was on her mind a lot. "I hope so," she said. Her mother had died from complications of a kidney transplant before she could see Erika grow up and achieve her dream of becoming a doctor. The empty chair in the auditorium when she'd crossed the stage to accept her high school diploma, her college diploma and then her medical school honors achievement had made each accomplishment shine just a little less.

Her father's pride was a given, but then he always expected success. Anything else wouldn't do.

Dr. Smyth placed a hand on her shoulder. "We could use a surgeon of your qualifications around here. Not that I'm poaching you," he said quickly. "Just letting you know that if you're ever looking for a change… a month from now there's a position opening up." He smiled.

She'd never give up her position at Alaska General Hospital, but Dr. Smyth's belief in her felt good. "Thank you, but Alaska General is my home. That's where my true passion is—with the opportunities to do so much good in medical research." She cast a glance at Reed and he looked away quickly as though he hadn't been listening to every word.

Dr. Smyth nodded, his gaze drifting in the direction hers had gone. He gave her a look she didn't fully understand. "The opportunities here are different for sure."

"Excuse the interruption, but Mr. Jansen wants to see you," Dr. Ford said, coming to a stop next to them.

"Me?" Dr. Smyth asked.

"No. Dr. Sheraton."

Erika shook her head. "Oh no, I only stepped in to help on the mountain. He's in good hands here." Wild River Community was not her hospital. She'd already crossed boundaries.

"I think he just wants to thank you. His girlfriend is in there, as well."

Her pulse raced and her hands sweat a little. Beyond the doctor's shoulder, Reed was still watching, listening…

"Can you tell him I had to go, but I wish him a

speedy recovery?" she asked, handing him the signed release form and heading toward the door. "It was great seeing you, Dr. Smyth," she said, desperately fighting to not read too much into the older man's expression.

"You, too. Say hello to your father for me," he said.

She nodded and escaped outside. She doubted very much that she'd be telling her father anything about this experience.

CHAPTER SEVEN

"To your first successful mountain rescue," Cassie said, raising her wineglass. After that morning's hangover they were sticking to their wine-only plan.

"To her *only* mountain rescue," Reed muttered from behind the bar of The Drunk Tank as Erika raised her own glass to accept the toast. No hard alcohol that evening. She couldn't trust her lips to behave.

"We'll see," she said, enjoying the fact that he was so bothered. He was right. She had no intentions of venturing out on any more rescues with him—the liability only one reason, the odd, adrenaline-induced rush she'd gotten from the experience another—but she wasn't about to tell him.

"Besides, an injured skier wasn't a real rescue," he said, yanking on the Santa head so that beer "peed" out into a pint glass.

"What's up your ass tonight? Erika helped that guy today," Cassie said, shooting her brother an annoyed look.

He shrugged, pouring three more pints and placing them on a tray for the waitress.

Erika would like an answer to that herself. After all, it had been his idea for her to tag along and he had to know that as a trained medical professional, she couldn't not step in to help the poor guy, and she had apologized for being slightly pushy. Sort of. Her "I'm sorry, I had to pull rank" in the van on the way back to the station had been met with a grunt and eye roll, but it was as good as it got from her.

The other search and rescue crew members had been complimentary when they'd arrived back at the station...particularly Tyler.

He was cute. A little younger than her, but funny and sweet and less...intimidating than Reed. She wouldn't mind seeing more of him while she was there. And before she'd left the station to head back to the village, he had offered to take her heli-skiing... something she'd been wanting to try. Skiing was the only sport her father had approved of. That and golf. And only because the board organized semiannual retreats and he believed it would somehow reflect badly on their operating skills if they weren't good at both. Therefore, she'd taken private lessons every winter since she was twelve. Regular slopes held little challenge for her anymore, so she planned to take Tyler up on his offer...

"And feel free to keep that ski suit, it looks way better on you," Cassie said.

"It's too tight on her," Reed said.

Both women's jaws dropped.

His face turned the same shade as the nose on the Rudolph ornament hanging from the garland above his head. "I just meant, it was...tight."

"Yeah, you said that. Now's the part where you apologize for the assholic comment," Cassie said.

Erika waited, her emotions wavering between pissed off and embarrassed. Her friend was a lot smaller than she was, the suit had been tight, but come on—who said something like that?

"Sorry, that came out wrong..." Reed said through clenched teeth. "I meant that it may get you some unwanted attention while you're on vacation," he added as his gaze wandered past them to Tyler entering the bar.

His jaw set in a tight line as the younger guy waved at them.

Erika didn't get it. The two men worked together on the team. They seemed to get along just fine...until the ride back to the village. The more Erika and Tyler had chatted, the grumpier Reed had gotten. His annoyance had been evident, but was it more than that? Jealousy perhaps? She'd caught him staring at her ass in the too-tight ski suit, and there was a sexually charged tension between them, but they couldn't stop bickering for five minutes. What did he care if she took Tyler up on his date offer?

Ignoring his scowl, or maybe because of it, she enthusiastically returned Tyler's wave. "Maybe I'm okay with some attention," she told Reed.

A hard stare met hers before he moved away to serve several customers at the other end of the bar.

"Man, he's in a mood," Cassie said, standing. "I'll be back, I have to pee."

"He sure is," Erika mumbled as her friend walked away. She watched as Reed snapped the lid off several beer bottles, placed them in front of the patrons at the bar, then crossed the room toward Tyler, ignoring a couple of women in a booth who were trying to flag him down.

Tyler stopped in his tracks and his grin faded to

a look of annoyance as Reed said something to him. Then a second later, he left the bar.

What the…?

"What did you just do?" she asked when he returned.

"What do you mean?"

"Just now. What did you say to Tyler to make him leave?"

"Nothing. He just remembered he has the night shift at the station." He shrugged as he grabbed a dish towel from the bar.

Her eyes narrowed. "Are you cockblocking me?"

Dropping the towel, he leaned against the bar, his nose just inches from hers. His musky cologne filled her senses and she held her breath as she felt submerged in the deep blue sea of his eyes. The five o'clock stubble along his jawline was decidedly sexier than his clean-shaven look, and she resisted the urge to touch it to see if it felt soft or rough. "Was cock what you were hoping for on this vacation?" he asked.

Her mouth felt like sandpaper and her knees shook a little beneath the bar, but instead of retreating, she only closed the gap between them even more. "Not yours."

"So you said last night."

Had she? They'd actually talked about his penis? What else had they talked about? "Well…good. So we are clear on that." His eyes penetrated her gaze and the words had come out sounding weaker than she'd intended, but she refused to give a fraction of an inch. Unfortunately, this close to him, her thoughts were fuzzy.

"Crystal clear," he said, moving away as Cassie returned.

Thank God. Her mind and her body had been locked in a battle of wills. Why was Reed so hot when he was aggravating as fuck? She wasn't attracted to those kinds of men—the ones that would just as easily drive her insane as they would drive her to lust. She dated safe, nice guys…when she did date. Ones she wouldn't get attached to, lose her heart to. Guys like Tyler.

Never guys like Reed.

Never *Reed*.

"What was that about?" Cassie asked, looking back and forth between them.

"Nothing." They spoke in unison.

"Okay…" Her cell chimed on the bar and, picking it up, she read quickly before saying, "I'm sorry, but I have to go." She grabbed her coat from the stool.

"Where?" Panic filled Erika's tone. After her stare-down with Reed, the last thing she wanted was to be left alone with him.

Right?

"It's Tank's night at the station, so I usually spend the night at his place with Kaia." Cassie wrapped a hand-knitted multicolored scarf around her neck and grabbed her gloves from her coat pocket.

Erika raised an eyebrow at Reed. "*Tank's* night at the station?"

He lifted a shoulder. "Guess I must have read the schedule wrong."

Sure. She turned her attention back to Cassie. She'd deal with Reed later. "You stay at Tank's? Overnight?" Was there more going on than her friend had let on? The night before, they'd caught up on most things, but

Cassie's relationship status hadn't come up. She'd assumed her friend was enjoying being single the same way she enjoyed all other aspects of her life—with a carefree abandon.

"I stay over when he's *not* there," she said, her annoyance evident.

Was it possible her friend had a thing for the single dad? Erika had momentarily suspected it the night before, but now the feelings were written all over Cassie's face. Sexual frustration across the board that evening.

"You can come with if you want…"

To babysit. Probably not. Children weren't her thing—she couldn't relate to them. "Nah, that's okay. I'll finish my wine, then head back to your place." To do what, she had no idea. Downtime was going to be the death of her.

"Here's the key to the condo. Sorry, I know I haven't had a whole lot of time to spend with you, but I have a few evenings off coming up."

"It's cool. I crashed in on your life. I'll keep myself busy," she said, a sideways glance at Reed.

"Okay, see you tomorrow," Cassie said, rushing out.

Erika glanced around the bar, but other than Tyler, who'd been conveniently chased away, there was no one else she recognized. It was possible there were others she might know from high school, but unfortunately, she hadn't kept in touch with many people from her small town. Would they even want to reconnect with her?

She took a sip of her wine as she watched Reed work, his back to her as he restocked the clean beer glasses behind the bar. His black T-shirt stretched across his broad back and shoulders and tapered at his waist. Tucked in haphazardly to one side of his jeans, it gave her a nice view of his ass. It was a nice ass. Too bad *he* was a bit of an ass.

He continued to work, ignoring her, and she tapped her nails against the bar, checking her watch. It was barely eight o'clock. How was she going to get through the night? Cassie no doubt had Netflix—she could binge-watch the entire first season of one of the popular shows the nurses talked about.

But what she really wanted to do was call her father and ask why he hadn't told her about the trial approval yet. All afternoon, she'd waited for a call or email from him. Nothing. Confronting him would get her nowhere though, and she wasn't allowed back at the hospital anyway. She'd never wanted special privileges for being his daughter, but it almost felt like the reverse was true. He treated everyone else on staff with a lot more respect.

Reed shot a look over his shoulder. "That's kinda annoying."

She stopped tapping her nails and sighed.

God, she was bored. She looked around the bar, almost wishing someone would choke on a bar nut or something.

She cleared her throat. "So, that's why you work here… It makes sense now."

A guarded look appeared in his eyes as he turned all the way around. "What makes sense about it?"

She had no idea what she'd said to offend him, but the set jaw as he waited for her reply meant she clearly had. Man, could they just have an uncharged conversation—sexually or otherwise? He seemed to want to make everything an issue. "Just that it gives you the flexibility to be a part of the search and rescue team."

"You think that's the only reason I bartend?"

She shifted uncomfortably on the stool. "There's nothing wrong with bartending. I just think there are other careers you'd be suited for." He'd always been an honors student in school and she remembered hearing him talk about university after graduation. This career choice of his had surprised her, but it had started to make sense after realizing that he wasn't only a member of the search and rescue crew but one of the team leaders. She knew—after Googling it that afternoon—that the position required a huge time commitment and the ability to drop just about anything when a call came in.

"*Better* careers you mean?"

Geez, why was he taking this so wrong? She was trying to say that he was smart enough to have a… Shit. She sighed. "Okay, fine, that was a shitty thing to say."

His shoulders visibly relaxed. "Now we're even for my equally shitty comment about the ski suit."

Had they somehow just declared a sort of truce?

"And you're not entirely wrong," he said slowly.

Finally, a brief respite from the tension they seemed to keep creating whenever they were alone.

"I do like the flexibility this job provides, and Tank understands where my priorities lie. But it's more than that. I love the people here in Wild River. The business owners in the community are a team. We take care of the tourists and treat the locals like family. It's nice.

And I make enough to survive and really who needs more than that?"

She did. Or at least she'd been raised to think she did. Cassie's life was simple, exciting and carefree... and despite her friend's example of success, Erika didn't think she could live this way. Surviving paycheck to paycheck and hoping for a good season would stress her out. Erika liked security and that came with a big salary and health benefits.

"I take it you disagree?" he asked in her silence.

"No. I'm just not sure I would feel comfortable..."

"Without a six-figure payday?"

"Now, *you're* being offensive again."

"Don't mean to be. To each their own, I guess." He leaned his elbows on the bar and studied her. "But, you know, if you ever consider a career change, we are always looking for new members."

"On the search and rescue crew?" A volunteer position? Even if she allowed herself to believe for an instant that she could be fulfilled simply by doing something altruistic, to walk away from her career and move to the mountains? She shook her head. "As you said, today's adventure was a one-time thing." She meant it. She was there to try her best to relax, to unwind until her two weeks were up, then she was headed back home. Where her clinical trials had been approved. The thought reminded her that she needed to check her email again when she got back to Cassie's. By now, surely someone—most likely not her father— had notified her.

"What about that kiss?" Reed's voice interrupted her thoughts. "Was that a one-time thing, too?"

Her breath caught in her chest when his blue eyes

blazed into hers. What was the right answer? The *yes* her brain was cautioning her or the *no* her body was screaming. Her gaze broke away from his to stare at the full mouth...so tempting... "Yes. *Both* just a one-time thing," she said, hoping she sounded more confident to him than she did to her own ears.

He straightened as several customers claimed the free stools next to her. "That's too bad. I'm not sure which one disappoints me more," he said with a wink, moving on to serve them.

And damn, if that simplest gesture didn't make her wish she could change her answer.

CHAPTER EIGHT

It FELT AS though he'd just closed the bar and now he was back. Tank was sleeping off his night shift at the station, therefore it fell on Reed to do inventory that month. He unlocked the back door and secured it again before heading into Tank's office for the supply sheets. He could ask the waitstaff to help, but he preferred to take stock alone. It was faster and it would be done right.

This time of year, their inventory doubled—the shelves were fully stocked with all their regular alcohol and mixes and then the addition of the holiday-themed junk. He wished Tank would just change the names of their drinks to festive sounding labels instead of making him come up with actual Christmas-inspired cocktails, like Candy-Cane Explosion and Frosty Twist, but it was his buddy's bar and there was a reason it was the local hot spot.

Grabbing the sheets, he worked his way through the bottles of wine in the cellar, double-checking the counts before moving on. When his gaze landed on the California merlot Erika had been drinking the night before, an image of her licking a drop of wine from the rim of her glass flashed out of nowhere.

A dozen women had ordered this particular wine and yet none of *their* pretty faces and delicious-looking lips sprang to mind. Nope. Just hers. Man, having her around for two weeks might be the death of him. One minute they were on the edge of flirting and he was tempted to kiss her and the next they were arguing, and it only made him want to kiss her more. She was his sister's friend and most siblings had a rule about these things, but it had never really applied to them. Growing up, Cassie had crushed on or dated almost all of his buddies and in recent years she'd set him up with a few of her friends.

But none had gotten a rise out of him or stolen his focus quite like Erika.

Her words about his chosen career had lingered with him longer than he liked. He'd taken offense to them because she'd struck a nerve. He'd been honest when he said he loved bartending…that didn't mean he wouldn't prefer doing something else. His high school grades had been good enough to get him into college and he'd worked since he was fourteen, putting money aside for his future. He'd just decided not to enroll that September, instead joining the search and rescue crew. Then it had been impossible to leave.

But for a split second last night, he'd wished he was someone she'd see as successful. Important.

Jesus.

Losing count of the bottles, he started over and forced himself to concentrate. He had to quit allowing this woman from his past to mess with his head.

"Cassie, where are your wineglasses?" Erika called from her friend's kitchen as she continued to search through the cupboards. The only thing she could find to hold liquid were cereal bowls and an eclectic collection of beer mugs that ranged from hilarious to NSFW.

Her friend hadn't changed a bit. She'd always had an uninhibited, unapologetic sense of humor. Her set of shot glasses featuring the entire tantric library of impossible poses was a testament to that. Where did she even find this stuff? Most likely on her travels around the globe.

Cassie appeared in the kitchen behind her, her poop-emoji slippers scuffling on the tiled kitchen floor.

"Those are the worst slippers ever."

"Funny though, right?" Opening a drawer, Cassie took out a package of multicolored extra-long straws. "No glasses. Just straws." She selected a pink one and put it into her bottle of pinot grigio. "What color do you want?"

Erika laughed. Her friend was crazy. "I'll take a blue one." She wasn't planning on consuming an entire bottle of merlot herself, but she wasn't about to critique her friend's hospitality. Especially after the rough start to their reunion.

This girls' night was long overdue and Erika was curious to get to the bottom of the Tank situation. As well as other questions burning in her mind that she wasn't sure how to bring up.

Cassie slid the blue straw into the bottle and carried them both into the living room, as Erika grabbed the popcorn and the peppermint-flavored fudge she'd bought earlier that day at the Chocolate Shoppe. With Cassie working all day, she'd had plenty of time to explore the village. So much had changed in ten years, with a lot of chain stores moving onto Main Street, including name-brand snow gear and clothing companies. She'd been tempted to buy herself a new ski suit, but remembering the look in Reed's eyes when she'd worn Cassie's, she'd saved her money and splurged on the expensive, handmade, hip-widening fudge instead.

And it was definitely the better choice. Popping a piece into her mouth, she closed her eyes and savored the perfect balance of cocoa, mint and sugar on her tongue. The taste immediately brought back a memory of her childhood Christmases before her mom's death. They'd always buy peppermint fudge weeks before and would have to buy more closer to Christmas Day. There was no such thing as willpower where peppermint fudge was concerned. Even her father had once been weak against the temptation.

Maybe she should bring him back some. Maybe a reminder of happier holidays might have an effect on him. Though what Erika expected, she wasn't sure. She'd yet to find a way to get close to him since her mother's death, and it would take more than peppermint fudge to piece her father's shattered heart back together.

"Oh my God, these are so good," Cassie said, her mouth full of her own piece.

"You have a chocolate factory minutes away—how are you not a thousand pounds?" Erika asked, sipping her wine.

The combination of wine and chocolate in her mouth was sinful.

"Staying active helps—all the skiing and hiking definitely counteract the calories...and I've placed myself on their do not allow list."

"Like for addicts?"

She nodded. "For chocolate addicts. You'd be sur-

prised how many of us locals have had to add our-
selves to it. I swear they lace this stuff with cocaine.
It's crazy addictive."

Erika didn't doubt it for a second. She may be adding herself to that list before the week was up. But until
then... She reached for another piece. "I'd forgotten
how different small-town life is," she said, curling her
legs under her on her friend's couch.

Immediately, Diva jumped onto the cushion beside
her and sat staring at her mouth, a thin line of drool
escaping her muzzle. "Forget it. Even if dogs could eat
chocolate, we're not good enough friends yet for me to
share," she said, but softened the words by tentatively
petting the dog's head.

Diva shot her an arguably adorable look that said
"Give me time, I'll wear you down with my cuteness"
and lay beside her, resting her chin on her front paws,
butt stuck up in the air, tail wagging back and forth,
contented.

"Don't be fooled. She's not giving up that easy,"
Cassie said.

Just to be safe, Erika moved the plate farther out of
the dog's reach. "So, when did you open Snow Trek
Tours?" The opening day pictures Cassie had posted
on Facebook could have been a week ago or six years.
Life seemed to blur past.

"Four years ago...after Mom sold the pub. She paid
off the house, took a job from the new owner and then
split the rest of the money between Reed and me."

Erika hoped her friend didn't notice her cheeks
flush at the mention of her brother. He hadn't been far
from her thoughts all day as she'd wandered through
the shops on Main Street. His words about kissing

her again had played over and over in her mind. It's not that the idea wasn't tempting, but he was Cassie's brother. The odd connection and irresistible pull she felt to him were an issue. She hadn't experienced real feelings for a man in a long time. She'd be reluctant to claim she'd ever truly been in love, so she had no idea how to label these emotions that were popping up out of nowhere whenever she was around Reed, but they weren't harmless—that much she knew for certain. Therefore, when she'd seen him leaving The Drunk Tank around noon, she'd hightailed it in the other direction.

"So, you just decided to open your own business?" That took courage.

Cassie nodded. "I was working for an adventure tour company in Girdwood and I decided why not start my own?" she continued.

Erika could have talked herself out of taking such a big leap of faith with a dozen different "why nots." But her friend's ambition and belief in herself was something she'd always admired and slightly envied. Cassie didn't need the same reassurance from others that Erika did. "This is none of my business, but the money from your mom was enough to open up shop in Wild River?" She didn't know much about Wild River real estate, but a storefront on Main Street couldn't be cheap. Rent alone on these buildings could cause a new venture to struggle.

"It was when Reed gave me his half," Cassie said, grabbing a handful of popcorn.

Erika's eyes widened. "That was nice of him." Really nice. Admirable. Respectable. Had her questioning what she thought she knew about him and regretting every bad thought she might have ever had. The siblings had always been close, but this went above and beyond. She ignored the tug at her heartstrings.

"That's my brother. He's always had a protective nature. It's what makes him so great with the search and rescue team. Always putting others first."

Erika had always envied Cassie and Reed's relationship. An only child, she'd longed for a sibling. Cassie's family had been the next best thing, and despite not particularly liking her, Reed had kinda assumed a protective role over her whenever she spent time with the family.

"I think he felt it was his job to be the man of the house after Dad disappeared," Cassie said, her expression changing slightly as she mentioned her dad.

One day, Cassie's father had gone to work with a logging company in the forest and hadn't returned. It was just months before Erika's own mom died. Losing a parent had only bonded her and Cassie even more. It was a tough time in both of their lives, but they'd helped one another through it. Their friendship was the only thing Erika had to depend on back then. With her father withdrawing, she'd felt alone. Cassie had been there.

"Anyway, I still feel bad about taking the money from Reed. He'd been saving to go to university, but as soon as I mentioned the business idea, he handed me a check. I've tried repaying him, but he won't hear of it. Man, he's so pigheaded sometimes," Cassie said, but affection for her brother was the only thing Erika heard in her voice.

"What was he planning to study?" Not that it mattered, if he was putting that goal permanently on hold, but she was so curious about him. In two days, she'd gotten to see various sides to him and it only left her wanting to learn more.

"He wanted to be an EMT...possibly a nurse. He's smart enough for med school, but he doesn't believe that."

Or maybe he just knew the cost of that degree was something he'd struggle to afford. Growing up, Erika had never had the financial worries that her friend did. And it sucked that it might have been what prevented Reed from following a passion. Obviously, with his original plans sidelined, he was doing the next best thing here in Wild River.

"Anyway, once he started volunteering on the S & R team, there was no dragging him away. He's one of their best. I, for one, feel better knowing he's out there."

Erika, too. There was no doubt in her mind that if she was in trouble, he'd find a way to help her. She swallowed hard—the damsel in distress, needing to be rescued feeling was one she rarely entertained. She was strong, independent and didn't rely on men for anything, yet the idea of Reed being equally as strong and independent was sexy. "Are there many rescues during the year?"

Cassie nodded. "The team responds to an average of three hundred a year. Ski patrol requiring assistance, like yesterday, happens a few times a week. Missing hikers, who've gotten turned around or followed the wrong trail, are common but longer searches are rare."

"Hardly a dull moment around here, huh?"

"We keep busy and the adrenaline fuels us, binds us all together. Living here, you come to see everyone as family. We look out for one another. You must re-member that," Cassie said, reaching for more fudge.

Reed had expressed something similar the night before and Erika felt an odd sense of longing for that kind of community. After her mother died, Cassie's family had been the closest thing to a support system she'd had—her father burying himself in work to dull the pain. After graduation, Erika had followed her father's footsteps, throwing herself into her studies, then work. She'd traded friendships and connections for long hours and getting ahead in her career.

And she'd been okay with that. Until she was suddenly faced with an up-close look at the other things in life she'd never thought she'd needed.

Cassie's cell buzzed with a new message and she read it quickly. The dreamlike expression in her eyes made Erika suspect it was from Tank.

She was right.

"Tank. Thanking me again for hanging out with Kaia last night." She replied to the text quickly, then tucked the phone under her leg on the couch.

"So, what's the deal with you two?" Obviously Cassie had feelings, but did Tank see her as just a baby-sitter and someone he could count on? Or was there more to the relationship?

"Wouldn't I love to know?" Cassie said, popping a handful of popcorn into her mouth and chewing furiously. "There's attraction there and we are best friends, and I love Kaia…" She shrugged. "It's complicated."

"The situation or Tank?" Erika had only seen the guy briefly, twice. He seemed nice enough in a quiet, mysterious sort of way and she wondered if Cassie had yet to solve his mystery.

"Both. Kaia's mom left them when she was a baby. Kaia doesn't remember her and Tank straight-out refuses to talk about her. No one has a clue who she is or where she is or what the circumstances are. And we all respect Tank's privacy enough not to ask." She sighed. "He's very…cautious about bringing someone else into their lives."

Fair enough, but it sounded like Cassie was already ingrained in the family's life. Babysitting his daughter overnight meant Tank obviously trusted Cassie, and that was a huge thing in relationships. They already had a solid foundation of friendship, so giving in to the romance developing between them would only be a good thing. "But if the mom's not in the picture, how could moving on with a new relationship be bad? Tank deserves to be happy, so does Kaia…and so do you."

Cassie nodded with a sigh. "We're making progress, I think," she said, scooping up a passed-out Diva and carrying her to her doggy bed.

The puppy flopped onto her back, all four paws straight up in the air, snoring loudly for such a little thing. "It's really unsettling how she just passes out like that," Erika said, watching her friend cover the dog with her pink blanket.

"Yeah, it was trippy at first. But the vet says she's fine and she might grow out of it." She sat on the couch next to her. "Anyway, enough about my sad, nonexistent love life. What about you? Anyone you're pining away for back in Anchorage?"

An image of Reed flashed in her mind and her cheeks flushed, giving her friend the wrong idea.

"There is, isn't there? Who is he? Dish." She turned on the couch, moving closer to hear the scoop.

But there wasn't one. Erika shook her head. "Unfortunately, mine is even sadder and even more nonexistent." Unfortunately? Where had that come from? She wasn't missing a relationship, was she? She liked her life alone—her own space, her own independence, sole control of the television remote...

"Oh come on. You're gorgeous, successful and smart. There's no way men aren't interested."

"Truthfully, I wouldn't have time to notice if they were. Work is all I do." And the other doctors at the hospital were too much like her, too much like her *father*, to evoke any feelings of attraction. She'd dated several after med school, but there wasn't a connection worth pursuing. Her time was better spent in the lab. Science made sense. Love didn't.

Cassie frowned. "But you date...sometimes, right?"

She wished she could remember the last time she'd been on a date, just to give her friend the impression that she wasn't a complete loner. "Not lately. I mean I'm not still a virgin if that's what you're thinking." She laughed. "I've dated in the past. I even had one semi-serious relationship while I was still in premed, but once I graduated and started working at the hospital with my dad, I was too busy. Brian...the guy I was seeing...said he didn't want a part-time girlfriend." She shrugged. She hadn't been able to argue with him or promise to change. Her career was her passion and she'd yet to meet a man to challenge that. He'd been a nice guy—solid and kind, pursuing a law career—but there hadn't been a spark. No butterflies. No passion.

Damn, why did Reed keep popping into her mind!

"How's that relationship?" Cassie asked.

"With my dad?"

Cassie nodded, sipping her wine.

Erika's chest tightened. Such a loaded question. One she had no idea the answer to. They got along fine, they worked well together. But it hadn't been the same father-daughter relationship they'd once had in a long time. "Complicated in a different way."

"Still struggling for his approval?"

Her friend's "getting it" without her having to say anything proved that despite time and distance, Cassie was still the one person who truly did "get" her. She should have made this visit sooner. She wouldn't allow ten more years to pass without another one. "Yes. But you know, I'm not sure it's even attainable," she said.

"Why does it matter so much? I get it when you were a kid, but now you're a success. And you're happy, aren't you?"

She paused. "There's different definitions of happy, right? I mean, I'm not unhappy...or at least I stay busy enough that I wouldn't notice if I were." Staying busy seemed to keep a lot of hidden wolves at bay. She didn't like that they all seemed to be closing in now that she wasn't keeping up her usual frantic pace. And her honest vulnerability in that moment made her slightly uncomfortable. Few people got to see this side of her.

"Your mom would be proud," Cassie said. "And she'd be thrilled that you're working with your dad on that new clinical drug."

Erika frowned. She hadn't mentioned anything about that to her friend. "How did you know about that?"

Cassie grinned. "We may not have kept in touch much, but I've been silently stalking you on social media."

Erika shook her head. "I haven't posted anything to social media since 2005."

Cassie laughed, raising her hands in defeat. "Fine. Reed told me when I stopped by the station to have lunch with him today."

Okay, *that* was unexpected. He'd obviously been paying attention to her conversation with Dr. Smyth. But then he'd also talked to Cassie about her? "What did he say?"

"Not much, just that Dr. Smyth at the community hospital was very complimentary to you and said this new antirejection drug might be a medical breakthrough."

"Dr. Smyth has always been supportive of my career and my dad's." It was too bad her father didn't think it was important enough to stay in touch.

"Anyway, Reed was impressed."

She scoffed, but her heart missed a beat. His approval obviously meant something to her.

"No, really—he was. And even though he acted like a jerk after the other day on the mountain, he said you were really great at helping that injured skier."

"Well, snapping bones back into place is my thing," she said with a light laugh. Reed had told his sister she'd done a great job? He was talking about her? Did that mean he was thinking about her as well? The idea that he might not have been kidding the night before in the bar made her stomach queasy. Or was it just too much peppermint fudge? She prayed it was the latter. No entertaining thoughts of her and her best friend's brother.

"Let's not lose contact this time when you return

to your life, okay?" Cassie said, extending her wine bottle in toast.

Erika clinked hers against it with a nod, unable to verbalize the promise. Despite all her best intentions, she knew herself, and the vow had a good chance of getting broken.

REED LOCKED UP the bar after midnight. Main Street was nearly empty as he walked to his truck. Except for a few tourists taking pictures near the ten-foot Christmas tree at town hall, all was silent. It was one of his favorite times of day. Late at night, Main Street was a ghost town, the snow falling in the illumination of the streetlights the only movement. Usually it was alive with holiday shoppers, festive music playing on the storefronts' outdoor speakers, so the stillness normally calmed him. But tonight, he was restless.

And he knew the cause. Erika.

He'd hoped she would come into the bar that evening so they could have a normal, nonsexually charged exchange—just one that might help to ease the dull throbbing in his pants that she stirred with her offensive obliviousness. If they could move into a friendlier, platonic territory, then maybe the sparks flying between them would sizzle out. His goal was to be polite, nonargumentative and as distant as possible the next time he saw her. No more interfering with whatever she and Tyler could possibly have going…and just mind his own business.

But she hadn't come in.

Driving past his sister's place, he saw the lights in her condo still on. They were still awake. He could stop by…

For what?

He kept driving and arrived at his own apartment a few minutes later. Going inside, he tossed his keys onto the entrance table and his coat over the back of his old, worn recliner in the living room—it had once belonged to his father and despite the man disappearing years before, Reed had been unable to blame the chair. It was comfortable. He'd needed furniture when he'd first moved out on his own, so he'd kept it.

Sitting at his desk, he opened his laptop and navigated to the Alaska Search and Rescue Board website, scrolling through the list of outback S & R organizations. That week's rescues and mission reports were slightly longer than usual—typical of this time of year when tourists and less experienced skiers and hikers flocked to the mountains. He quickly scanned the ones near Wild River, Willow Lake and surrounding areas, but as usual didn't find what he was looking for.

Shutting down the website, he sat back in the chair and sighed. It was fifteen years ago. He had to let it go. Let *him* go.

If only he could understand what had happened to his father. So many times he'd replayed that day in his mind, but he couldn't find that clue, that missing piece, that indication that something was off.

His father had been leaving for work before dawn, heading to Whitestone Logging Camp where he'd spend two weeks on duty before heading home again for a week. He'd come into Reed's bedroom to say goodbye. He'd seemed to be in a good mood. Nothing was out of the ordinary. Reed had been half-awake and had mumbled a few words before going back to sleep.

Now, he wished he'd woken up. Spent those last few minutes with his dad...

They hadn't known something was wrong until their father's boss called the house looking for him two days later. He hadn't shown up for work the morning he'd left.

And he'd never come home.

Where he'd gone and why—all remained a mystery.

Still, Reed searched for a ghost, reviewing the Search and Rescue Board site every day, hoping that one day his father's name would pop up on the list. Found. Safe was too much to hope for by now, but something to give them all closure was what he was really searching for.

He stretched his legs out under the desk and laced his fingers behind his head, staring at the computer screen. Then, leaning forward, he typed Erika's name into the search engine and waited for the information to load.

Pictures of her in her lab coat appeared among articles about the new clinical trials she'd mentioned were starting in a few weeks. He read quickly, growing more and more impressed with each word. A new antirejection drug they were testing that would be as effective as the ones currently on the market, yet wouldn't do as much damage to the patient's immune system.

Her mother had died from a failed kidney transplant, so it didn't take a genius to figure out the motivation behind this particular research.

He leaned closer to the screen and studied the picture of her, obviously taken just after graduating med school. She was smiling, but the upturned lips couldn't hide the absence of happiness he saw reflecting in her mesmerizing dark eyes.

She looked beautiful, but cold. Not at all like the woman he'd caught tiny glimpses of in the last few days. Relaxed, confident, open and happy. The doctor in this picture looked nothing like the one in the too-tight ski suit, commanding the situation and not afraid to get her hands dirty.

"So, who are you really, Erika Sheraton?"

Just the fact that he wanted to find out should be enough to make him stay away.

CHAPTER NINE

"CASSIE, WHAT IS THIS?" Erika asked, picking up a green plastic tube that had fallen out of her friend's over-stuffed backpack as they descended the back stairs the next morning.

Cassie turned. "Oh, that's a Shewee. Thanks," she said. Taking it and opening a side pocket, she tucked it inside.

"A She-what?" Erika shivered as a blast of morning mountain air blew her hair into her face. Struggling under the weight of Cassie's thick sleeping bag and tent, she stopped near the Snow Trek van.

"It's a portable toilet. That tube will help me pee into the bowl without having to go outside of the tent at night or remove all my warm clothing on hikes."

Erika wrinkled her nose. "Gross."

"You wouldn't say that if you were out in the middle of nowhere, cold at night and your bladder was about to explode."

"That's the thing—*I* would never be in that situation. I can't believe all this outdoors stuff is your idea of fun," she mumbled as she readjusted the weight of the heavy camping gear in her arms. How her tiny friend was going to carry all of this into the mountains, trudging through deep snow up her knees, Erika had no idea. The last-minute corporate booking for the excursion had been disappointing. She'd been hoping to have more girls' nights, but now Cassie would be away for several days.

Cassie had invited her to tag along as a tour guide in training, but this adventure, Erika had declined. Camping in the summertime was not exactly her thing—winter camping had zero appeal.

"So, I'll be gone for five days. Make yourself comfortable...and if you need anything, just call Reed."

Not even if she was on fire.

Putting distance between them was her plan. If she could stay away from him, she couldn't be tempted by whatever insanity was taking hold. "I'll be fine." She handed her friend the tent and sleeping bag, then wrapped her arms around her body, shivering as she stepped from one booted foot to the other. The temperature had dropped several degrees in the last few days and the thick, heavy clouds threatened snow. Without the mountain sun warming the ground, everything was covered in a thin veil of frost.

Pretty. But cold.

Cassie hugged her quickly. "Thanks for your help. I'll see you in a few days."

"Bye. Be careful and have...fun?" She couldn't imagine why anyone would want to do *one* overnight in the woods in this mind-numbing cold, let alone four.

"You really should try this sometime. You'll see, it's not that bad."

"I'll take your word for it."

Cassie laughed and waved as she climbed into the van and drove away. Erika hurried back up the stairs and inside the condo.

Now what?

She'd eaten breakfast already and cleaned up the kitchen. Another day shopping didn't appeal to her. She could go to the spa a block away and indulge in some well-overdue pampering, but getting a last-minute appointment might be tough and she wasn't sure she could relax anyway.

Sitting on the couch, she reached for her laptop and logged in to her remote desktop. The hospital board might be able to force her out of the office, but they couldn't stop her from responding to emails. She scanned the newest ones first. Several patient results from the lab that she noticed Dr. Penders was cc'd on as well, so no need for her to review... Delete. The announcement for the annual staff Christmas luncheon—delete. She never attended. She never had time. She'd hear the nurses and interns and other doctors laughing and having a good time in the staff lounge, but she'd always breezed past on her way to another emergency. This year, she wouldn't even be there to ignore the festivity.

An email from Darren caught her eye and she opened it.

Hi Dr. Sheraton,
Sorry, I opened my big mouth and got you in shit with your dad. Hope the vacation is going well. I wasn't sure if anyone had reached out to you yet regarding the clinical trials, but we've received the approval.

Oh, and I decided not to go through with the transfer request.
Hurry back,
Darren

Closing the email, she scrolled through the rest, but there was nothing from her father.

Unbelievable.

She shut down the connection and closed the laptop, resting her head against the couch cushion.

Feeling Diva's weight next to her a second later, she opened one eye and peered at the dog. Her pink sequined leash was in her mouth and she danced in a circle, wiggling her fluffy tail.

A walk it was.

"I can't believe you let her make you wear this," she said, attaching the blinged-out leash to the matching collar. "Don't you have any self-respect?"

Diva licked her face.

"Gross. We've talked about the licking," Erika said, standing. In the last few days, she and Diva had silently come to some sort of understanding. The dog was adorable—especially when she fell asleep at the oddest times—but they still weren't at the licking phase yet.

Excited paws danced around Erika's feet as she slid into her coat, hat, scarf and mittens. She nosed her pink booties hanging on the bootrack to dry and Erika shook her head. "No. You're a dog. Let's go." She opened the door and followed her down the stairs. "Lead the way."

The dog headed right…in the opposite direction of The Drunk Tank.

Good. Not like she could go into the pub with Diva anyway, even if she did want to see Reed. Which she absolutely didn't. Nearly two days without a sight of him wasn't bothering her at all. Reed and his kiss had been the farthest thing from her mind. She and

Cassie had been bonding, and she looked forward to her friend's return so they could continue rebuilding their friendship. She hoped for more shopping on Main Street, night skiing on the slopes, dinner at the Meat & More Grillhouse—Erika's treat—and more peppermint fudge and chick flick marathons.

But while Cassie was away, how could she stay busy enough to avoid the temptation to visit the bar?

Reed was impressed by her. It was the only thought on repeat since the night before. Weird. He had an odd way of showing it. She wondered if he'd noticed they weren't at the bar last night. Or cared.

She shook her head and sucked in a big, fresh, cleansing breath, hoping the icy chill entering her lungs would cool her body from the heat flowing through her thinking about her friend's brother.

Turning her attention to the mountains in the distance, which surrounded the village, she stopped to appreciate how beautiful they actually were. She could see them from Anchorage, but rarely in her day-to-day life did she get an opportunity to stop long enough to take in the beauty around her. Her body and brain were constantly shifting from one thing to another. Here, things were different. Still early in the morning, the stores were just opening and the village was starting to come to life.

Watching as Diva gracefully dodged every puddle as she strolled along Main Street made Erika laugh. The husky had a serious complex—she really did believe she was a six-pound poodle, not a forty-pound beast.

Only her friend would adopt a pet as unique as this one.

As they rounded the corner near the coffee shop,

she saw the search and rescue cabin across the street. The small structure attached to the fire department was painted red and yellow, and the Wild River Search and Rescue logo was painted above the door. The fire station's garage door was open and inside were fire trucks, the S & R van, several snowmobiles and rescue equipment. About twenty kids lined up outside the cabin door.

Diva yanked her in their direction.

She hesitated. The dog wouldn't harm a flea, but that wasn't her only concern. Reed could be inside and she was hell-bent on sticking to her avoidance plan. But at Diva's persistent insistence, she jogged across the street as the crosswalk lit up.

"Diva!" A little girl wearing a camo-colored ski suit rushed over to them as they approached. "Hi, girl," she said, bending on one knee to shower the puppy with attention. Her dark brown hair fell into her face and she pushed it back behind an ear with a gloved hand.

The dog practically purred. She pranced and her tail wagged like crazy as she did circles around the little girl, tangling her legs in the pink leash and pulling Erika closer. She jumped off the ground, desperate to be picked up.

"You two know one another?" Erika asked.

"Yeah… Diva's uncle works with my dad," the little girl said, laughing as she stepped free of the leash.

Erika smirked. She wondered how Reed would like being referred to as uncle to a canine. Though they all seemed crazy over this dog, so he probably wouldn't mind. "What are you guys lined up for?" She looked toward the entrance, where more kids gathered inside.

"The Hug-A-Tree program. I've taken it already, but now I volunteer to help out," she said proudly.

Erika had seen posters around town for the safety-training program for kids. When she'd attended Wild River Elementary, her class had participated in a similar wilderness preparedness field trip, but she'd been sick that day and missed it.

"Have you taken it?" the kid asked.

"No… I haven't."

"Then you should," she said, taking Diva's leash and heading toward the door as the last kid in line disappeared inside.

Erika reached for it back. "Oh no. Diva can't go inside." Her gaze fell on the building and she strained to see inside. Was Reed in there?

"Sure she can. Cassie brings her by all the time. We're training her for the Alaska dog search and rescue team."

Ha! The only thing this dog could track down was the day spa.

"Come on," the little girl said.

"Well, I'm not a kid…"

She shrugged, and Erika realized she was the same little girl she'd seen in the pub the first night she arrived. Tank's little girl who Cassie babysat. She seemed a lot older than her nine years. "The program is for everyone. Backwoods safety is everyone's responsibility," she said. "If you're going to be spending time here, you really should learn some basic survival skills."

"I'm a doctor."

"But you wouldn't want to have to use your skills on yourself, right?" she said as they reached the door.

Smart-ass had a point, but Erika wasn't really in a

hurry to go trekking through the mountains anyway. Skiing was about as adventurous as she planned to get. But noticing Tyler checking off names on his clipboard inside, she started to rethink it. With Cassie gone for five days, she was going to go crazy. That heli-ski trip he promised might keep her busy for a while and distract her from thoughts of Reed. She hadn't run into him since the day of the rescue, so now might be her only chance to see him again, without purposely seeking him out. She removed her mittens and tucked them into her coat pockets. Taking off her hat, she smoothed her flyaway strands. "Okay. I'll take the course."

"Great. I get five bucks for everyone I recruit, so tell them you're with me—I'm Kaia."

"And here I thought you were concerned for my safety," Erika said with a laugh. The smile died on her lips as she entered the classroom and saw Reed among the group of search and rescue crew members leading the program. She turned to glance at Tyler, but he'd yet to notice her. Talking to him with Reed there would be weird, though it shouldn't be. It wasn't like they were going to act on the odd tension between them. Sure, they may have a physical chemistry, but they couldn't be around one another five minutes without arguing.

Though the angry sex in *Mr. & Mrs. Smith* didn't look all that bad… And those two were trying to kill each other.

"Actually, you know what…" She turned back toward the exit and checked her watch for effect. "I can't stay." She reached for Diva's leash but the puppy tugged it in the opposite direction.

"You should."

Reed's voice behind her made her heart race. She

forced a polite smile as she turned, and Tank's daughter took off across the room with Diva. Fantastic. "Why's that?" Was it possible that he got better-looking every time she saw him? Faded jeans that hugged his thighs and the black T-shirt with the search and rescue logo stretching across his chest had her mouth actually watering. Given the choice between the peppermint fudge and his pectorals, she'd be hard-pressed to make a decision.

Neither one was healthy for her.

He shook his head slowly. "No reason. Everyone should know the basics about backwoods safety, that's all." His blue eyes seemed to penetrate straight to her soul, and the fact that he cared about her safety had her feeling slightly faint.

"I'm not planning to venture too far from the village."

"Are you planning to visit The Drunk Tank again?"

So he had noticed that they hadn't come in the night before. "Cassie's away for a few nights. I don't usually drink alone."

"Sit at the bar. With me," he said.

Her pulse raced. "Oh…um…" Jesus, where was her tongue?

"Reed, all of the registered kids are here," Tyler said, coming up to them.

Thank God for the interruption, she'd forgotten how to breathe.

"Good…okay," Reed said, looking annoyed by the guy's sudden presence.

"Hey, Erika, how's your vacation going?" Tyler asked her.

"Great!" she said, cringing at the overly enthusiastic

response. He was wearing the same outfit as Reed—jeans and search and rescue T-shirt—yet the sight of him didn't have the same effect on her.

Damn.

But actually that was a good thing. That meant Tyler was safe. Someone she could spend time with while Cassie was away and then leave in two weeks without anything getting complicated. Purposely avoiding Reed's gaze, she added, "I was serious about the heli-skiing... If you have time..." Her flirty smile was one she didn't use often, so she prayed it didn't make her look psychotic.

Tyler smiled. "Definitely, I'll make reservations..." Then, after a quick glance at Reed, he shook his head. "Sorry... I, uh, forgot I'm pulling double shifts at the station for the next...week?"

Reed cleared his throat.

"Two weeks. Sorry, Erika... You really should check it out, though—it's an amazing adrenaline rush," he said, before walking away.

Erika glared at Reed. "What's your problem?"

"No problem. You're my sister's best friend and I told her I'd keep an eye on you while she was away."

What was she? Six? She raised an eyebrow.

"Not keep an eye on you like you're a child...just if you need anything."

There were definitely far too many implications in that solitary word. *Anything.* She could think of a few things she needed, but she'd been hoping to get them from no-strings-attached Tyler, not complicated-as-all-fuck Reed.

"Tyler's just not...the right person to take you heli-skiing," he continued.

Silence followed, and if he expected her to ask him to take her, he'd be waiting a long time. Tyler might not be the right person to keep her company while she was on vacation, but she already knew spending time alone with Reed was just dangerous. Like, stupid dangerous.

"Reed, we're ready to get started," an older man said from the front of the room as another volunteer, dressed head to toe in a tree costume, came into view.

Kids cheered and Reed hesitated for a brief second, causing her heart to rise in her throat. "Anyway, you should stick around for this," he said and walked away.

With Diva napping, lying on her back with all four paws in the air next to Kaia, it didn't look as though Erika had much choice. She took a seat at the back of the room on a wooden bench along the wall.

"Hey, everyone, have you all met Woodsy?" Reed asked the group as he wrapped an arm around the tree.

"Yes!" the chorus of kids called out.

"Great, well, with Woodsy's help, we are going to go over the most important rules for backwoods safety…"

He was really great with the kids.

How many other roles and responsibilities did he have as a lead member of the search crew? When did he ever have time off? Between the bar and his volunteer position, she figured he must clock in as many hours in a day as she did. Maybe that was why he was single. Too busy to date? It didn't seem likely that the women around here would let him use that excuse, though.

From the corner of her eye, she saw several moms paying real close attention to the demonstration, as well.

No doubt, Reed had his pick of women, so why was he flirting with her? Was he flirting? Or was it simply his promise to Cassie that had inspired his invite for her to hang out at the bar?

This was exactly why Erika didn't do relationships. Who had time for all these games and second-guessing? Not her.

"What's the first thing you should do if you realize you are lost in the woods?" Reed asked the group.

Several tiny hands shot up in the crowd.

"Yeah, you. What's your name?" Reed asked a little boy in the front row.

"Tim."

"Okay, Tim. Whatcha got?"

"Try to find your parents," Tim said.

"Nice guess, and I'm glad you said that. Who else thinks that is the right answer?" He surveyed the crowd, but his sweeping gaze didn't include her.

Almost all hands went up, including her own before she could stop herself.

Luckily no one seemed to notice.

"Come on up here, and I need a few other volunteers…" Reed selected several other kids from the crowd and with their help, he set the stage. Parents at a campground. Kid lost, out of sight…and how he might head in the wrong direction if he started wandering.

"So, we see that's probably not the safest thing we could try," he said. "But it was a great suggestion, Tim. Anyone else have an idea?"

Tank's daughter raised her hand when no one else did. "Hug a tree?"

"Exactly!" Reed said. "So, everyone let's practice. On three…hug a tree!"

Thirty kids rushed toward Woodsy on Reed's count, and Erika hid a grin as the guy inside the suit went wide-eyed as the wind was knocked from his lungs on impact.

"Stay with your tree. Make yourself as big as possible by lying down on the ground. Helicopters circling overhead have a better chance of seeing you if you lie down."

And fan out your limbs... Wave them around when you see the helicopter... Erika's heart pounded, a long-repressed memory spiraling back.

Reed had said those exact words to her.

Years ago. The day she'd found out that her mother's kidney transplant had failed and she was living on borrowed time. The antirejection drugs had failed to help her body accept the new organ, but they'd been successful in weakening her immune system. Within weeks after her surgery, her mother had pneumonia and her body was refusing the transplant. The family's worst fears were coming true. They were losing her mom.

She hadn't wanted to go on the overnight camping trip with Cassie and her family, but her mother had insisted, saying it would help take her mind off things.

Terrified and sad, not wanting to leave her mother's side, she'd continued to refuse, until her father had asked her to give them that night alone. She'd felt even worse at the idea that she was being shut out. She'd felt the most alone she'd ever been. Her parents had one another to cope with the devastating news that day, but neither of them were there for her.

Cassie was.

She wouldn't have known how to get through that day or the others to come without her friend...or her friend's family.

Of course the trip hadn't taken her mind off her

mother and when she'd needed some time to herself and had wandered down an unfamiliar trail, she hadn't even noticed Reed following a few feet behind. Adrift in her sadness and fears over losing her mom, she hadn't realized she was lost until the sun had started its descent over the mountains and she hadn't recognized her surroundings.

Reed's sudden presence in the woods had scared her, but she'd felt immediate relief not to be alone, even if it was Reed—a guy who didn't even try to hide how annoying he thought she was. Though that day, he'd been nicer to her than usual…

But that didn't last when they disagreed on the right direction back to the campgrounds and they'd gotten even more lost, moving farther into the woods, away from the campsite.

She still couldn't say for sure whose fault it was, and she'd probably deny it was hers until the day she died… But watching him now, she had a sinking suspicion that she was to blame.

He knew exactly the right things to do in a situation like this.

Just as he had that night.

She remembered how he'd removed his jacket to place over her shoulders as night fell and the temperature dropped, and how he'd held her, not asking any questions as tears fell down her cheeks and how when she'd finally fallen asleep, exhausted and worn-out, he'd stayed awake all night…protecting her.

A tightening in her gut increased when his gaze met hers as he wrapped up the session.

He'd been a source of comfort for her on the worst day of her young life.

And she'd forgotten how much that had truly meant until that very moment.

Damn, things with Reed could get so out of hand if she let them.

Kaia approached with a wide-awake Diva, and Erika stood, helping to clean up by adding several plastic chairs to the pile a volunteer was forming. "So, did you learn a lot?" the little girl asked.

More than she'd thought possible. Mostly about Reed. Mostly about just how wrong she'd been—had always been—about him. "Very informative."

"Great!" Kaia beamed, then she glanced at her boots. "Do you know when Cassie will be back?"

"In five days."

She looked relieved. "Oh good. She's supposed to take me shopping for a Christmas concert dress… I'm in the school junior choir and I'm singing a solo this year, so I'm supposed to wear something nice. I don't have a dress, and Dad doesn't know the first thing about fashion, so Cass said she'd help," she said.

Wow, Cassie had really taken on the role of female confidant to the little girl. "I'm sure she will as soon as she gets back. Maybe I can tag along—I've got pretty good taste in clothing."

Kaia sized her up. "Okay, sure. Will you be here for Christmas Eve? We always have a big party."

All of a sudden, she wished she would be. By Christmas Eve she would be back to her busy life in Anchorage and starting the clinical trials. Which was far more important than celebrating the holidays. "Afraid not."

"Kaia, come on!" another kid yelled from the doorway.

"Gotta go. Bye, Diva," she said before rushing to follow some kids her age as they left the station.

Erika hung back, waiting until the last of the kids and their parents had gone before slowly approaching Reed. "That was great." She had no doubt that the kids had learned information that could save their lives in an emergency.

"Think you could handle the backwoods now?" he asked, a look on his face that told her he'd never forgotten their night in the woods.

She nodded. "I think more than anything, I just need to learn not to be so stubborn and listen once in a while." It was the closest thing to an apology/admission of guilt he would get from her.

He seemed to accept it. His warm smile was unlike the grins or smirks he'd cast her way since she'd arrived. This one held sincerity and genuine friendliness and it nearly knocked her on her ass.

Arrogant, annoying Reed was hot enough, she didn't need him getting all nice on her. If that happened, she'd be dead in the water…or snow, as the case might be.

"I should get going," she said as Diva tangled her legs in the leash, eager to get back outside where the kids were playing on the snowbanks. After her "nap," she was once again all energy.

Reed nodded. "Yeah, I have to get some work done here before heading to the bar tonight."

Whether that was another invite, she couldn't decipher, but she wasn't about to read too much into anything. In fact, putting distance between them was what she'd decided was for the best, right? "See you." She turned to leave, but his voice stopped her.

"Hey, Erika…"

"Yeah?" Turning back, she held her breath.

"If you want to go heli-skiing, I'll take you. I mean, if you want... I'd be happy to."

Her heart raced as her thoughts spiraled. She hoped her excitement and turmoil at his offer wasn't too obvious. "Because you think I need a babysitter?"

"Because I want to."

Oh God. Her knees felt slightly unsteady beneath her. An hour ago, spending time with him seemed like a mistake...now, as the memory of their night in the woods together returned, it seemed like an even bigger one. Unfortunately, knowing something was a mistake didn't always prevent people from making it anyway. "When?"

He didn't hesitate. "Tomorrow morning. I'll pick you up at 6:00 a.m."

CHAPTER TEN

REED DIDN'T NEED his alarm. He'd barely slept. Anticipation of the helicopter ride over the adrenaline-junkie ski trails was nothing. It was spending the day with Erika that had him worked up.

He should have let her enjoy her vacation, then wave adios as her curvy ass left town. Putting distance between them was the smart thing to do, especially when the memory of their kiss was driving him crazy. He'd dated a lot of women over the years, but no solitary kiss had played on his mind so much. And it was stupid—they had nothing in common, they argued all the time and she was leaving in ten days, probably not to be seen again for another ten years. Still, he was unable to ignore this magnetic pull to her.

She was different. Beautiful, smart, successful... but also determined and strong-willed. She challenged him and drove him insane, and it only had him wanting more. In all of his previous relationships, things had been easy, comfortable. They lacked a certain intensity. One he felt all the time around Erika.

Getting through the Hug-A-Tree session with her sitting in the back of the room had been tough. He'd fought to keep his gaze from straying her way, wondering if any of it was ringing a bell, triggering a memory of their night together in the woods.

The semi-admittance of guilt and the expression in her eyes had told him it had.

He showered and dressed quickly. Contemplated shaving, then decided against it. He'd seen the way she'd eyed the scruff along his jawline a few nights ago. He gelled his hair and sprayed cologne on his sweater. Then he stared at his reflection.

"Hope you know what you're doing, man."

Pulling up in front of Snow Trek Tours ten minutes later, she was waiting on the sidewalk. In that too-tight ski suit.

Damn. He'd been secretly hoping she'd buy her own suit. One that was big and bulky and hid the body beneath. His only chance of survival on the treacherous snow hills that day had depended on it.

Looked like he was screwed.

She waved, and her smile was tentative as she opened the passenger-side door. She was feeling as weird about this as he was. The only time they'd ever hung out together was with Cassie and usually a group of other friends. They'd never had a reason to be alone—except that one night.

Now, they were *completely* alone.

Alone in the silence of the cab of his truck with a thick sexual tension nearly fogging up the windshield. He could feel warmth radiating from her even though she sat as far away from him and as close to the door as possible, her gaze surveying Main Street and her hands toying with the tag on her gloves.

Hopefully, by the time they reached the Chugach Mountain Range, things would feel less awkward.

After all, this wasn't a date. It was just him playing tour guide to a friend of his sister.

A hot, tempting friend who smelled like vanilla frosting. He couldn't figure where the smell was coming from exactly—her hair? Her skin? Her lip balm? His eyes fell to her glossy pale pink lips, and the urge to taste them to see if his suspicions were right made him clutch the wheel tighter and turn his attention to the road.

He cleared his throat. "Good morning," he said as she clicked her seat belt.

"Hi."

"Did Tank pick up Diva already?" he asked. His buddy had offered to take care of the dog while they were gone that day so they wouldn't have to rush back. The day trip would have them on the slopes for most of the daylight hours.

"About ten minutes ago," she said. "He seemed a little worried about this trip Cassie's on… Is it dangerous?"

Reed shook his head. "Winter camping is always unpredictable, but Cassie knows what she's doing." He worried about her, too, but no one had ever been successful in telling his baby sister what to do. And she was a more experienced adventure guide than anyone else in Wild River.

Erika nodded. "So, where are we headed?" She frowned when he took the village exit onto the main highway.

Obviously she wasn't one for surprises. "The best slopes are west of Chugach Mountain Range. I've arranged a day pass with Snowpeaks Powder Guides." He'd spent the afternoon before arranging the details, wanting everything to be great. He'd never wanted to impress someone as much before, but Erika was used to the best. If she'd been planning this, she would have spared no expense, so that's what he'd done. This time of year, he'd had to call in a few favors to secure the full-day ski and lunch on the mountain package, but he was looking forward to showing her the best heli-skiing experience of her life. Better than if she'd gone with Tyler. "It's a full day on the slopes, so I hope you got a good night's sleep."

"Not really," she said, biting her lip. Her hands were clenched tight on her lap.

Oh no. "You do know how to ski, right?" He took the highway exit and stopped at a light, glancing at her. If she'd allowed him to book an adventure designed for advanced skiers and had never been on skis, he was calling off the day. Cassie would kill him if anything happened to her friend.

"Of course I ski." She was nodding but staring at him as though there was something she wasn't saying...

But there was definitely something on her mind. "Don't worry, these guides are the best and there are varying degrees of ski trails from beginner to extremist. Snow Trek partners with them all the time..."

"I'm not worried about the skiing."

"Okay." *He* was. Worried he'd smack right into a tree, staring at her ass. They should probably stick to safer trails. From the corner of his eye, he took in her sexy thighs hugged by the dark blue fabric and his mouth watered slightly.

And she was still looking at him funny.

"What?"

"Nothing," she said too quickly.

"Spill it. Are you regretting agreeing to this?"

"No. I'm looking forward to it."

"Wishing Tyler was the one taking you instead?" His stomach tightened as though preparing for the blow. Maybe he shouldn't have stood in Tyler's way. If she preferred him...

"No," she said. "I'm glad it's you taking me."

Didn't sound convincing enough to save his ego, but he'd take it as truth. "Well, what's up? And don't say nothing. If you're having second thoughts about this, it's not too late to cancel." It was totally too late to get his money back, but if she was nervous, he'd happily take the financial hit.

"Reed, the skiing will be fun. It's just... Well, I just feel like I should apologize..."

He glanced at her. "You already apologized for taking over my rescue the other day."

"Not for that. I mean, for judging you without knowing you."

He shifted in his seat and cleared his throat. "I think maybe we're both guilty of that." He slid a look at her and she smiled. The pretty, upturned lips and the genuine, expressive eyes nearly making him go off the slippery highway.

"And I think it was really great of you to help Cassie start her business." She blurted the words out quickly, true-to-Erika fashion.

Ah, so his sister had told her. He wished she hadn't. Giving Cassie his share from the sale of their mom's old pub in Mat-Su Valley had been a no-brainer for him and she had to get over feeling like she owed him something. He shook his head. "I didn't do anything.

She had everything she needed—the business plan, the great idea... I just helped with the funds. And really, it wasn't even my money, so..." He shrugged.

"But I know how much she appreciated it."

"Me, too." His sister was not someone to take advantage and if she said she could make her business idea work, he believed and supported her the entire way. There was nothing he could have done with the money that would have made him feel better than seeing his sister's business thriving. He was proud of her.

"Well, I think you're great. I mean, what you did... *It* was great," she said quickly, but not before he could take advantage of her slipup, his ego refueled.

"You think I'm great?"

She rolled her eyes. "Oh God. I shouldn't have said anything."

"Admit it, you've always had a crush on me."

She snorted. *Actually snorted.* And it was the sexiest snort he'd ever heard. He couldn't hide a smile as he pulled his truck into the parking lot of Snowpeaks Powder Guides and cut the engine. He turned in the seat to face her as he unbuckled his seat belt. "Come on, be honest. You're *still* hot for me."

Her jaw dropped slightly, but she quickly recovered. "You wish."

"Maybe." It was suddenly hotter in the cab of his truck, as the truth of the simple word hit him. He did want her to want him.

"Well, I'm sorry to disappoint you, but that night in the woods, a long time ago, was the one and only time I'll be falling asleep in your arms," she said, opening the door and climbing out of the truck.

It was more of an escape.

Remembering the way she'd kissed him a few nights ago, Reed couldn't help but hope that she might change her mind.

THE SEVEN-MINUTE scenic helicopter ride over the Chugach Mountain Range would have been breathtaking, if Erika could have focused on the mountain peaks and valleys, covered in the freshest dusting of powder on earth. But seated next to Reed in the back of the helicopter, her pulse was racing and her heart echoed loudly in her ears.

Thank God for the hum of the helicopter and the large, noise-reducing headphones they wore. She didn't want him to know how much he affected her. How right he was in assuming she was hot for him. Playing it cool and unfazed was her game plan for the day—one she'd spent all night figuring out.

Too bad it had gone straight to shit the minute his truck had pulled up in front of Cassie's. For a day that wasn't a date, it was the closest thing to one that she'd had in a long time, especially with a man as gorgeous as Reed.

He was dressed in a dark blue ski suit that hugged his muscular body in all the right places, and Erika suddenly wasn't as interested in skiing. His thigh was casually resting against hers in the small space of the Eurocopter AS350 but the contact, even through layers of clothing, felt anything but casual. Heat continued to rush through her as he moved closer to point at the trails coming into view beyond the trees.

He smelled amazing—like a combination of fresh mountain air and sexy alpha hunk—and she found herself leaning closer to breathe him in.

Such a big mistake. She clenched her legs together as her body sprang to life like awakening from a long, deep slumber.

It had been months since she'd had sex...scratch that...years. And most days she was too exhausted after her eighteen-hour shifts to even think about using the vibrator that was still in the packaging on top of her closet.

Since reuniting with Reed, she'd been more turned on and more in tune with her body's desires than ever before. She wanted him.

Bad.

The way his gaze swept over her, especially when he thought she wasn't looking, had her pulse going crazy. She couldn't remember the last time anyone had looked at her that way—with unconcealed desire and appreciation. But it had to be superficial. After all, they'd reached a truce in the truck, but they didn't really like each other, right? He'd only offered to take her today to keep Tyler away.

Best to remember that before tearing all his clothes off the next chance she got.

They neared a clearing and her excitement rose. She'd always been a strong skier and she was looking forward to the first exhilarating pass down the mountain. She could also use the distraction and distance from Reed.

She looked through the small window at the mountains moving closer. Another helicopter had touched down already and several skiers were preparing for their run, strapping into snowboards.

When was the last time she'd felt this excited about something?

"We're going to set down about two miles from here," the helicopter pilot announced through their headsets as he began their descent.

Reed gave a thumbs-up and turned to look at her. "Ready for the thrill of your life?"

Erika read his lips more than she heard the words and she gripped the bench seat tightly.

She suspected ready or not, she was going to get it.

REED MAY HAVE exaggerated when he said he had heli-skied before. He'd gone on countless search and rescues for heli-skiing days gone wrong, but he'd never actually skied the untracked powdered slopes himself.

Mainly because of the higher price tag on the day adventure. But the look of pure adrenaline on Erika's face as they disembarked the copter moments later made him glad he'd dipped into his savings. Her dark hair whipping around her rosy cheeks as she took in the breathtaking scenery at the top of the mountain was stealing his breath…and his focus.

He barely heard a word their guide said and he hoped his team wouldn't be out rescuing *him* later that day.

"Um…are you sure these fat skis are a good idea?"

The guide nodded. "Absolutely. They feel a little weird, but they will help make the transitioning to powder easier and make for a much smoother run. They're the same as regular skis. The only difference is you need to keep your weight even on both, instead of pushing against that downhill ski. Got it?"

Reed nodded. So did Erika.

"So, we will start here on *Bunny Hop*, what we call our beginner run…it's clear sailing straight to the bottom. Not many trees or ramps or sudden drops," Garrett, their guide, said, snapping into his snowboard. "I know you both have skied before, but a few tips—keep your upper body facing down the fall line, hands forward and poles planted. Make sure to coil and uncoil through the few turns on this run and stand tall over your feet."

They both nodded.

"And remember, there's no need to lean into the back seat to keep those ski tips from diving—the fat skis got this. We cool?" He gave two thumbs-up.

"Got it." Erika snapped into her skis and lowered her ski goggles, looking ready to go.

Only Reed hesitated as he stared down the wilderness slope. They were pretty freaking high, and that incline was steep for a beginner run. Luckily the weather conditions were great and he knew the company had emergency responders at the base of the hill... But these fat skis were odd.

"Your husband looks a little nervous," Garrett said to Erika, nodding toward him.

The twentysomething professional snowboarder had come highly recommended for first-timers, but already Reed wasn't a fan. Tall and muscular with a laid-back, casual charm, the guy reminded him of Tyler.

Erika shook her head. "Not my husband...just a friend." Her voice carried over the wind and echoed on the mountains around them.

Why did those words bother him? They *were* just friends. Barely friends, in fact.

That didn't mean he liked the way the guy's attention went from ski instructor friendly to full-on interested in a matter of seconds.

"And he's just afraid I'm going to race him to the bottom," she said.

Actually, right now the only thing he was nervous about was the overwhelming feelings of jealousy causing his jaw to tighten as the guy continued to flirt with her. His gaze drifted over her body, and Reed gripped his ski poles. "If he's smart, he won't let you get too far away," Garrett said with a wink.

Erika's flirty smile in return was too much. First Tyler, now Garrett. Erika was too beautiful for her own good. If she wasn't careful, she'd get her heart broken by one of these mountain players. Moving between them, he blocked the other guy. "Are we going to ski or chat all day?"

She shot him an amused look. "See you at the bottom," she said, pushing off and heading fearlessly down the mountainside.

He stood watching her sexy hips swish back and forth expertly as she left a cloud of powder behind her. She looked like a natural on the slopes. Her hair trailing behind her was a sharp contrast to the glistening white snow, and he almost forgot she'd challenged him to a race.

Garrett was also checking her out.

Reed held a gloved hand to the guy's chest, as he went to push off. "When she said friend, she meant... *good* friend."

"But not boyfriend?" Garrett said. "Snooze you lose, man," he said, taking off after her.

Unbelievable. Reed knew one thing, he hadn't paid a small fortune to have his girl swiped out from under him. Pushing off on his right ski, he took off down the mountain, flying past the guide, surprising himself by his speed. He didn't plan on snoozing or losing.

He also didn't want to wipe out and roll down the hill. Looking like an amateur next to the snowboard god wasn't the way to win Erika's attention. He slowed his pace slightly and tried to enjoy the ride, but seeing Garrett quickly approaching on his right, he regained his lightning speed.

Garrett laughed behind him, and Reed was fairly certain the guy was letting him win. Didn't matter. He'd take the nondeserved victory.

Out of breath and amazed he hadn't died, Reed stopped several feet from the chalet, then made his way toward Erika.

"Wow! That was crazy," she said, her windblown hair messy around her flushed cheeks as she raised her ski goggles up over her hat.

"Yeah, crazy…" At the moment he didn't care about the run. In fact, on a mission, he'd barely paid attention to it. "Listen, if our guide is acting like a jerk or making you uncomfortable, I can see if there's someone else who can guide the rest of the day," he said, fighting to catch his breath. Someone older and married, perhaps.

Garrett had reached the bottom and stood chatting with another instructor near the chalet. Both of the men were looking at Erika. Suddenly, Reed didn't like the idea of any guide helping them out that day. He wanted to spend the day on the slopes with her. Just her.

She shook her head. "No, it's cool. He's cute."

Cute? "You know, Erika, these mountain ski resort guys are real players. You should be careful around them."

She raised an eyebrow, but her lips curled into an amused grin. "You're acting like a babysitter again."

Screw that. He took several strides closer and reached for her waist, awkwardly gliding her skis into the space between his. "That wasn't my intention," he said, brushing the hair away from her face. He saw her swallow hard as her eyes flitted between his.

"What was your intention?" she whispered, staring at his lips.

The chill of the air disappeared as heat rushed through him. Damn, he wanted this woman. Right or wrong. Smart or stupid. Didn't matter. She was stirring up cravings he hadn't experienced in a long time. And that delicious scent of vanilla was definitely coming from her lips, he decided.

He pulled her closer and bent at the knees slightly to lower his head toward hers. He studied her for any sign that he should stop, but she tilted her head slightly to the right as he went left. She wanted this.

"You two *friends* ready for another run?" Garrett's voice interrupted the moment and Erika backed away slowly.

At the end of the day, Reed was filling out a customer complaint card. He forced a deep breath as he nodded. "Yep."

"We sure are," Erika said, but her look told him to try that kiss again.

She didn't have to worry. He had every intention of trying as often as it took to get a taste of those vanilla-flavored lips…and any other flavors she might taste like anywhere else.

By lunchtime, Erika had had enough of Reed and Garrett's dick-measuring contest. Flattering at first that the twenty-two-year-old guide found her attractive, it was quickly turning unprofessional.

And Reed should really know better than to put his safety at risk, with his breakneck pace down the slopes, to try to impress her or win her attention.

He didn't need to try. The more she got to know him, the more time she spent with him, the more impressed she was. She was attracted and interested and having a hard time focusing on skiing. Their almost kiss after the first run had her longing for another opportunity. His hands on her waist and the way he'd looked into her eyes had weakened her knees and filled her with anticipation.

"Here you go... One hot dog with just relish," he said a moment later, handing her the barbecued hot dog and joining her at the picnic table on the outside patio of the small ski hut at the base of the mountain.

The outdoor lunch setup was beautiful, and the midday sun shining against the snow-covered mountains cast a glistening effect over the terrain. It was an experience she wouldn't soon forget and it seemed Reed had gone all out to make sure of it. No one had made such an effort for her before.

"Thank you," she said, unwrapping the foil. She took a bite, savoring the taste. She was starving, having worked up an appetite on the slopes. And she'd forgotten how much better food tasted in the outdoors. She swallowed the bite, then hesitated before saying. "You know you don't have to compete with him, right?"

He turned to face her. "I'm not having to work that hard to match him on the slopes," he said.

"I meant for my attention," she said softly, touching his bare hand on the picnic table. His skin was warm below her cool flesh and he looked surprised by the gesture, but immediately took her hand in his.

"But you said we were just friends."

"We are…but…" Her eyes couldn't decide where to look. His crystal blues held a question she didn't know the answer to and his full, pink, wind-chapped lips beckoned. He'd looked so sexy racing down each new, slightly more challenging slope. The unexpected intimacy that came with taking on these challenging trails had her struggling to resist the urge to touch him, kiss him all morning. The short helicopter runs back to the top of the mountain had never felt long enough, yet with each one, new undeniable sparks had gone off between their bodies.

Now she was touching him, and if she just leaned a little closer…

He made the decision easy for her. Wrapping his other arm around her waist, he pulled her closer on the bench, until one of her legs was draped over his. Cupping her chin with his free hand, he brought her mouth closer to his. "I've wanted to kiss you all day," he murmured, his lips barely grazing hers.

She was on fire. Heat rushed through her core and anticipation was making it hard to steady her thundering pulse. "Well, what are you waiting for?" She was desperate for his mouth to meet hers. Dying to give in to the desire that had only made the morning that much more exciting and uncertain. The fact that she was craving this excitement and uncertainty, was starting to get addicted to the high, surprised her.

Where had her sensible, calculating, careful side gone?

And where the hell was her kiss?

Reed released her hand and cupped her face with his hands as he closed the tiny gap between their lips.

Finally.

She sucked in a breath. She didn't plan on coming up for air anytime soon. She closed her eyes and sank closer.

Still no kiss.

She opened one eye. He was so close, staring at her.

"You are definitely not what I thought you were," he said, pulling away slightly.

Both eyes open. More talking, really? "You really thought I was horrible?" She knew she came across all wrong in most situations. Her cold exterior was a shield she'd worn for so long and she wondered how many fantastic kisses she'd missed out on because of that. That, and the fact that she didn't stop moving long enough for any guy to keep up. She gave no one the chance to get to know the real her.

What if they didn't like what they found?

"Not horrible…just not this freaking amazing. You're surprising the hell out of me and that doesn't happen often," Reed said. "I'm usually a good judge of character, but I've gotten you all wrong all these years."

She swallowed hard, the world around them disappearing as she lost herself in his gaze, his arms, the gentle way his fingers stroked her cheek. Amazing. No man had even come close to complimenting her that way. She'd have settled for not horrible.

He was Cassie's brother and that should be reason enough not to let things go any farther. Hell, she could list a dozen reasons—most of them having to do with her lack of experience with relationships, even casual, physical ones, but she suspected it was already too late to cool things between them. She didn't want to.

He moved closer, but this time she pulled back. Suddenly, she had to know. "Why did you follow me that day?"

He didn't ask for clarification. "Because I understood how you were feeling…and I didn't want you to be alone."

Of course his situation had been different—with his dad just disappearing one day without explanation—but of course he had understood how she was feeling. And at the time, she'd instinctively known it. "I'm glad you were there."

He pulled her closer again. "I'm glad you're here."

Her heartbeat echoed on the mountains as his lips inched closer.

She was so ready for this kiss. He looked and smelled so great and he was saying all the right things, touching her and looking at her the way she longed to be touched, admired. She closed her eyes, feeling his breath against her mouth.

"You two better eat, we have more skiing to do," Garrett said, leaning over the picnic table, his face suddenly just inches from theirs.

Seriously?

Luckily, he moved away, laughing again before Reed could deck him. "Son of a…" he muttered.

Erika silenced him by placing a small peck to his lips. Not the passionate, desire-filled one raging inside of her, but a soft, tender hint of what she hoped was to come.

"That was hardly enough," he said, his voice husky.

"Well, maybe you can convince me to try again

later," she said, a flirty adrenaline soaring through her as she moved away and continued to eat her hot dog. Not that she was hungry anymore. She could survive solely on this incredible feeling forever.

"You better count on it."

CHAPTER ELEVEN

"THANK YOU AGAIN for today," Erika said as Reed pulled to the side of the road outside Cassie's place. The sky was dark and the light snowfall that had started on their way back now blanketed the village with a pretty, glistening effect. Holiday lights on the lampposts and in the closed store windows created the perfect Christmas card scene.

Exhausted but rejuvenated from the day on the slopes, Erika was disappointed that it was coming to an end. Reed had held her hand in the helicopter several times during the afternoon runs, but as they'd moved to more challenging terrain, their focus had turned to the mountains, and while kissing was still in the back of her mind all afternoon, they'd both resisted.

Now that her safety was no longer at risk, the temptation of Reed's lips was forefront in her mind.

"You're welcome. You killed it out there," Reed said, turning in his seat to face her.

He'd removed his jacket, and the way his black crewneck sweater hugged his biceps as he rested his arm against the steering wheel almost made her mouth water. Watching him expertly move his body down the rugged terrain had her on fire.

"When did you learn to ski like that?" he asked, obviously as reluctant to end the day as she was.

"I took lessons for years. It was the only sport my dad thought was a good use of my time." She hoped her strained relationship with her father wasn't evident in her voice. She really didn't want to end the day on anything other than a high.

"Your dad must be a great role model," he said, and she heard a longing in his voice. No doubt getting through the troublesome, confusing teen years without his was tough. Reed had been close to his dad and his disappearance had hit him the hardest. She remembered the brief stint of rebellion he'd gone through—skipping school, getting in with the wrong crowd... Luckily his mother had been strong enough to set him straight again.

Funny how he envied her relationship with her father and she'd give anything to have a mother in her life.

"My father is a fantastic example. I've learned a lot from him."

He squeezed her hand. "He may have been tough on you, but look how successful you are."

Again, longing in his voice. Therefore, she didn't argue. Her privileged upbringing wasn't something to complain about. So, her father had never been there for her emotionally, but he'd provided everything else she'd needed. "You're right."

He glanced at the time on the dash. "Well, you have the place to yourself... Tank texted to say Diva can stay overnight with them. Kaia's not allowed to get a dog, so any chance she has to keep Diva longer, she's all over it."

Cassie would be okay with that. Tank and his daughter were probably better at caring for Diva than

Erika was anyway. And the dog's reaction to seeing Kaia the day before assured Erika that Diva wouldn't have any complaints.

"Take a hot bath to ease those aching muscles, have a glass of wine…" Reed continued, his voice going slightly hoarse as his gaze burned into hers.

A hot bath, a glass of wine…all sounded a million times better if he'd join her.

"Damn, I wish I could, but I can't. It's my night at the station. Marcus is sick, so I'm filling in for him," he said.

She blinked. Had she accidentally voiced the thought? "Can't what?"

"You just asked me to join you."

Her eyes widened. "Oh, I…uh…"

He cupped her face with both hands and every coherent thought vanished. "Believe me, I want to."

She couldn't breathe. Air. Where was air when you needed it?

His burning gaze had her body aching for him as his hands tucked her hair behind her ears. Such a simple, smooth gesture, yet it made her feel safe. Vulnerable yet completely in control of her desires. "Hey, how about dinner instead? Nothing fancy, just takeout at the station. You could keep me company."

She should let the day end. Let him get to work. She'd had fun for the first time in forever and she'd felt things for a man she'd forgotten she could feel, but that was why she needed to put the brakes on. Despite liking him, despite wanting him, despite the temptation of spending more time with him, she couldn't. She was only there for a break, then she was returning to reality and she didn't want to make that harder. She'd barely thought about work all day and she would have expected to be feeling guilty or anxious.

She felt neither. Still, "I should probably call it a night..."

"I like you, Erika."

Again. No air.

"I mean, when you first got here, man, were you annoying."

She glared at him but couldn't argue the point.

He grinned. "But I was still attracted to you...and the last few days, that attraction is growing. I know you're only here for another week, but I'd really like to spend more time getting to know you again... Or, I guess for the first time."

She looked down at her hands clenched on her lap.

To what end? She couldn't make things work with a man who lived in the same condo complex...miles away would be next to impossible.

But admittedly, she was getting ahead of herself. Reed hadn't said anything about what happened when the week was up. Just that he liked her and wanted to get to know her and damn, if those feelings weren't mutual.

"Dinner. Just dinner."

Oh, he made that sound so promisingly simple, but she knew in her gut it wouldn't be. It was already so much more than just dinner. His touch was more than just a touch. His long stare held so many questions and revelations. And she knew the deeper she got, the closer she got, nothing at all about Reed would be simple.

"Okay," she said finally, no other answer possible when he was this close, touching her, smelling so great, after their invigorating day in the mountains. If she left him now, she'd always wonder what might have happened if she'd said yes. For the second time that week, she was going with impulsive.

He smiled, reluctantly returning his hands to the steering wheel. "Okay," he said, pulling the truck back onto Main Street, heading toward the station.

Meanwhile, her heart was headed straight for trouble.

WELL, IT WASN'T wine and a bath, but he had pizza and Erika's company, so he'd call it a win. Reed had sensed her reluctance in the truck and he'd silently hoped she'd agree to spend the evening with him. The day had been the best nondate he'd ever been on. The more he spent time with her, the stronger his feelings for her grew. And not just the semi-hard-on feelings he'd struggled with all day. The thought of letting her go had made his gut hurt. He didn't want to think about how it might hit him when she actually left Wild River.

"I didn't know the team leads had to take these overnight station shifts," she said, removing her ski jacket and tossing it next to his on the tiny, uncomfortable cot in the corner. The twelve by twelve space was busting at the seams with a desk and extra gear stashed everywhere. When the county provided funding, they bought as much equipment as possible, whether they had space for it or not. That equipment could mean the difference between life and death for someone needing help, so they turned nothing away.

"Normally that's true, but we try to keep it fair with responsibilities around here. We have a great team, so we all pull our weight," he said. "Music?"

"Sure."

He turned on the old stereo on the desk and tuned to

the local holiday music station. "This okay?" he asked as a slow, romantic song played.

"It's great. I can't remember the last time I listened to Christmas music. I'm usually so busy at the hospital that Christmas is just another day."

A wistful longing in her voice made him glad she was there for the season. Even if she could only appreciate it for a little while. He opened the pizza box lid. The smell of meat and cheese escaped on the steam and his stomach growled. He was famished.

He'd been relieved when Erika had claimed to like the same meat-filled, double cheese pie that he normally ordered. If she'd preferred some chicken or veggie crap, he may have had to order them separate meals. He reached into a cupboard above the cot. "Paper plates okay? Or I could run into the fire station to see if they have real ones…"

"Paper plates are perfect," she said, and it actually sounded like it was. Man, could he have been so wrong about her when she'd first arrived? It certainly seemed like he'd been too quick to judge. What had come across as arrogance was actually something a little more endearing—a socially awkward bluntness he was starting to understand.

All trace of the stuck-up doctor had vanished that day on the mountains. Or maybe he was just seeing beyond the self-preservation facade.

He dished up the pizza and scanned the space. They had few options for eating. "Desk or lap?"

"Lap is fine," she said, sitting on the cot. She shook her head and laughed as she tapped the hard mattress. "Wow, this is about as comfortable as the one in my office."

He nodded as he sat next to her and handed her a plate. "If it was too comfortable, we'd sleep through calls." He laughed. "No worries about that on this thing." The cot was an old one they'd been gifted from the fire station, and the IKEA mattress was maybe three inches thick.

"I get it."

"You work all kinds of shifts at the hospital?"

"I work every shift," she said, taking a bite of the pizza. A small drop of tomato sauce appeared on the corner of her mouth and she licked it away.

His eyes were glued to the lips he'd kissed ever so briefly hours before, and the grumbling in his stomach was momentarily forgotten. He couldn't wait for another taste of her. He wasn't even going to try to pretend that it wouldn't happen again. His "just dinner" line was a lie. And they both knew it.

"I don't have to, of course, but things are extra busy right now," she continued, and something in her tone helped to check his hormones for the moment.

"I'm guessing this time off wasn't your idea?"

She swallowed her bite of pizza and shook her head. "Forced vacation... Or as the letter stated, *recommended* vacation."

He wondered if his sister knew that Erika's out-of-the-blue appearance hadn't just been a desire to reconnect... He pushed it aside. They'd gotten off to a rocky start, but it hadn't taken long for Cassie and Erika to pick up where they'd left off, so he wouldn't mention this new info to his sister. "Are you enjoying your time off at least?"

"Thanks to Cassie...and you," she said, her gaze meeting his and holding.

Forget food. There was only one hunger he needed satisfied.

Taking her plate and his and setting them aside, he pulled her to her feet and into his arms. "I need to kiss you again," he said, his voice hoarse as his arms tightened around her waist.

"I'm okay with that," she said, her gaze flitting frantically between his eyes and his lips. "Now?" she asked when he hesitated.

"You bet," he said before crushing her mouth with his. Vanilla lip gloss mingled with the taste of pizza sauce, making him crave her more than ever. His hands traveled up her back, firmly massaging the tense muscles along her spine and shoulders before cupping the back of her head beneath her tangled, windblown hair. His tongue separated her lips and continued to explore her mouth as he deepened the kiss.

Her hands were against his chest and the muscles beneath the thin fabric of his faded search and rescue T-shirt twitched. The soft moan that escaped her lips had him hardening fast and when she pressed her body closer, his erection was impossible to hide.

Her eyes snapped open as she broke the kiss. The look of surprise in her dark eyes was killing him. She had to know the effect she could have on a man. "I did that?" she asked.

He laughed gently, pulling her even closer against it. "That was all you."

She grinned as her hands crept around his neck, her fingers tangling in his hair as she guided his mouth back to hers. "Let's see how hard we can make it."

He nearly growled as he devoured her mouth again, his grip on her waist moving lower to cup her ass in the ski pants. Smooth, thick fabric beneath his hands wasn't cutting it and he quickly slipped his hands down the waistband. The tightness cut off circulation in his wrists, but he didn't care. She wore thin yoga pants underneath. He could tell by the soft, thin, stretchy fabric hugging her like a second skin.

Damn, her ass was hot.

She pulled away slightly to run her tongue along his bottom lip, then captured it between her teeth, biting gently, driving him crazy.

The spectrum of emotions she'd evoked since arriving were all cumulating into one strong, overwhelming desire to have her—all of her. Every little inch of her sexy body, every brilliant thought and every piece of her unreachable heart.

But he needed to slow things a little or he'd never last. And he wanted this to last a long time. He broke the contact between their lips as another slow Christmas song started to play. "Dance with me," he said, taking one hand in his and wrapping his arm around her waist. She wasn't getting that far away.

"I don't know how," she said, breathless.

"Just sway," he said, leading her in a slow circle.

She rested her head against his chest and he kissed the top of her head. His grip tightened on her hand as the carol wrapped around them. The pulsing in his veins subsided just a little to let him appreciate holding her, feeling her...

She sighed and he could feel her heart beating against his.

As the song came to an end, he tilted her face up toward his. "You're beautiful," he said.

She stood on tiptoes and captured his mouth again,

and all waiting was over. He wanted her now, and the frantic, demanding way she was devouring his lips revealed she wanted him just as much.

Lifting her, he wrapped her legs around his waist and backed her toward the cot. He placed her on top of the uncomfortable mattress and fell on top of her. She immediately reached for him again, clenching his shirt in her hands as she held him glued to her body.

His penis strained against the fabric of his underwear and ski pants. It had been months since he'd been with a woman and that in itself could be blamed for the intensity of his hard-on, but he knew not just anyone would have this effect on him. Erika was by far the most tempting, beautiful woman he'd ever met. The fact that they had a shared history had this new connection sparking more intense, uncontrollable flames of desire. Despite never being close friends, she knew him and he knew her. They'd spent one night together, united by a common fear and hurt, connecting in a way that he'd effectively pushed aside all these years.

He separated her legs with his and placed his hardness against her. Their thick ski pants making it impossible to get any relief from the aching throbbing.

Less clothes. Right away.

She moaned, raising her hips higher to grind against him.

Fuck. He wanted her so bad.

She wasn't hesitating or second-guessing or making him hesitate or second-guess. They both wanted this.

He pushed harder against her, seeking some form of relief, but the ache just grew stronger. Her frantic kisses, her tongue circling his and her hands all over his body had the intensity and urgency dialed all the way up.

Struggling for a breath, he broke away from her mouth and kissed her neck. The soft smell of her jasmine-scented perfume made it hard to think as his tongue licked along her flesh. Goose bumps surfaced on her exposed skin and she swallowed hard. "How bad do you want me?" she asked, the words coming out a strangled sound. Her hands had dipped lower to his waist and she was tickling his exposed abs by trailing her fingers delicately across his skin.

"Bad," he whispered against her ear, feeling her body tremble. "Can I have you?"

The reply was torturously slow in coming, but as she slid her hands higher beneath his shirt and started pulling it off over his head, his cock spasmed with the knowledge that soon it would be buried deep inside her. Her eagerness for him was such a turn-on.

He sat up and helped her remove his shirt, and the appreciative look in her eyes made him grateful for the time he put in at the gym. Being physically fit for his job was important, but seeing the effect it had on Erika in that moment was even more fulfilling. He reached for the base of her sweater and slid it slowly up her body. Her lower stomach, her belly button, her ribs all came into view in a devilishly slow reveal and he was buzzing with anticipation as he raised the fabric higher…revealing bare, perfect breasts.

His jaw dropped. *No bra. Fuck me.*

She shrugged. "You were right about the ski suit being too small. A bra wouldn't fit."

"You've been braless all day?" he asked, peeling the fabric up over her head and tossing it aside. Immediately he cupped the soft mounds with perky erect nipples begging to be fondled. It's a good thing he hadn't known or they may never have gotten out of his truck.

"Yes." Her eyes closed at his touch and her head fell backward onto the thin-as-paper pillow, a soft sigh escaping her. "That feels amazing."

His eyes raked over her flat stomach and thin waist as his hands continued to knead and massage, his fingers pinching the hardened buds until her breathing became labored. A turned-on woman had to be the sexiest thing on the planet. The way her body reacted to his touch, his kiss had him feeling dizzy. He needed to be closer to her. Feel every inch of her pressed against him. "What do you like, Erika? Tell me what you want."

"More of this. Much more of this," she said as he kissed along her collarbone and down to her breasts. Capturing one nipple in his mouth, he sucked gently, twirling his tongue around it until she was almost panting.

"You like that?" he asked.

"Yes," she whispered, guiding his head to the other breast.

He happily obliged. He could lick and suck on these amazing breasts all night long.

"I want you so bad," she said.

Climbing off her quickly, he undid his ski pants and pulled them off, along with his underwear.

From the cot, she watched, her eyes falling to his exposed, erect cock. "Excited?" she asked, the teasing glint in her eyes torturing him.

"Little bit," he said. He reached for her pants and removed them, dragging the fabric of the yoga pants along with them and tossing the clothing to the floor. He was desperate to remove the underwear as well, but he needed confirmation that things weren't moving too quickly. That she was still okay with this.

And for the first time, a look of hesitation flashed in her eyes.

Shit. Please don't let her put the brakes on now. Blue balls would be uncomfortable, but not getting the opportunity to touch her, lick her body everywhere and feel what it was like to be inside her would be torture. But if she said stop. He would.

"Is the door locked?" she asked instead.

Relief flowed through him as he hurried to lock it and pull the blinds closed further. "It is now."

Then returning to her, he climbed back between her legs, kissing her again. He could kiss her all night. Her mouth was soft and welcoming. Her lips were juicy and delicious and the way her tongue danced with his—it was like they'd been kissing one another for years. An unsettling familiarity, a startling connection that vibrated between their mouths continued throughout his entire body as he rocked his pelvis against hers.

Wetness escaped the tip of his cock as he pressed against her underwear. She was wet, too, and the thought that she was so willing, so ready for him nearly put him over the edge.

"These need to go," he said, reaching for the waistband and yanking them down to her knees.

She wiggled her legs, moving the fabric lower then kicking them off one foot. They fell to the floor next to his.

Erika Sheraton was naked beneath him and he'd never have expected it in a million years.

He took a moment to appreciate every inch of her, every curve, every hollow. He let his hands slowly trail the length of her sides, appreciating the smooth hourglass shape, then across her flat stomach, circling the gorgeous belly button, then up her rib cage to squeeze her beautiful breasts once more. His cock throbbed with need as his hands moved lower again, retracing the path back to her hips and then down her sexy, muscular thighs and back toward the opening between her legs.

Her body trembled on the cot beneath him, and the desire reflecting in her dark eyes had them looking almost black as she took in every inch of him. "You really have filled out," she said, her eyes on his cock.

"And you keep getting more and more beautiful by the second." He allowed one finger to dip inside her wet folds. "And so revealingly wet."

Shit, she was just as ready for him as he was for her.

"I want you inside me," she said, arching her back to raise her pelvis against his hand, seeking release of her own.

"Now?" he asked.

She nodded frantically, reaching for his arms and pulling him back down against her. She kissed him hard as his cock settled between her folds, rubbing up and down against her clit.

Damn, she was sexy. Erika Sheraton was sexy. Words he'd never thought would be racing through his mind just seconds before he was inside of her.

Her hands were seemingly everywhere at once, as though she couldn't get close enough to him as she rocked her pelvis up and down along his length.

Hating to move away from her, he quickly reached

for his ski pants and retrieved his wallet. He removed a condom and, tearing it open, he slid it on fast. The motion made his ache even worse. His entire body was on fire, a desperate desire erasing all other thoughts.

Erika's chest and stomach rose and fell with her heavy breathing. "I want you so bad, Reed," she said.

The feeling was mutual…and he couldn't help but wonder if they shared other feelings. He knew this went beyond the physical for him. It wasn't just a one-night stand with his sister's best friend. This was a connection years in the making. He'd always thought his feelings for her were disdain and dislike, but even those had been strong. Maybe they'd been something else.

They certainly were now.

Lowering himself on top of her, he slid between her legs and brushed her hair away from her face, staring into those big, chocolate-colored eyes as he slipped inside of her.

Her breath caught. She closed her eyes as her muscles squeezed tight around him.

Fuck. He wouldn't be lasting long. The moment didn't even feel completely real. Erika…it was Erika. Erika's body he was inside of. Erika's hands touching him. Erika's mouth just inches from his. Her breath warm and coming hard against his cheek. He went deeper.

She moaned beneath him and tightened her grip on his shoulders. Her nails dug into his flesh, but it didn't wake him from this dream.

"Look at me," he said, taking her hands and holding them above her head as he plunged deeper again.

Her eyes opened and she held his stare as their bodies rocked together in perfect rhythm, faster, harder, growing more desperate as he neared the brink of orgasm.

"This okay?" he somehow managed to ask.

"More than okay," she whispered.

His arms shook on either side of her and his hips dug into her thighs as he moved faster, harder... He was so close. The intense sensations building made it impossible to hold off any longer.

"I'm coming, Reed," she said suddenly, and thank God because he couldn't hold his own orgasm back much longer. Plunging deeper and faster still, he felt her tighten and spasm around him as she let out a loud moan of satisfaction.

The feel of her wet body wrapped around him, her soft skin pressed against his, the smell of her sex tantalizing the senses, he erupted in waves of pleasure, squeezing her hands tighter. His gaze never left hers. She was beautiful. She was real. In that moment—for that moment at least—she was his.

And why that thought didn't terrify him, he didn't know.

His body collapsed a second later and he rested his forehead against hers. "Damn, that was good," he said, kissing her gently.

"Definitely unexpected," she said with a satisfied smile. She hugged him closer and he felt her continue to vibrate and clench around him, driving him crazy again already. "I have a new answer to your question now."

"What question?"

"About whether I'm enjoying this vacation," she said, kissing him again. "I'd say it's the best one yet."

He laughed. "Because it's your first and only one?"

"Because of you."

ERIKA HAD NEVER felt so comfortable on a three-inch, hard-as-rock mattress. Of course, most of her body was draped across Reed and not actually on the bed. Sleeping on the cot in her office would be so much better if he was there. Obviously, she'd be less productive.

"So, do you bring all the girls back here?" Suddenly, she wondered about his dating history. He was obviously single. She knew he wasn't the type to sleep around or cheat on a girlfriend. He'd always been nice and considerate and thoughtful to the girls he'd dated when they were teens. So why he was single now was a complete mystery. He'd filled out over the years and she'd admired his muscles through his clothing, but the straining fabric of his T-shirts hid an even more amazing physique than she could have imagined.

And for one night, he'd been hers.

"I haven't dated *all* the girls," he said with a smirk.

She hit his arm playfully. "The ones you *have* dated, smart-ass."

He shook his head, pulling the thin blanket up over them a little more. "Believe it or not, this is not part of my game."

She eyed him. "Your game? So you're saying you're playing me?" Why did her heart beat so loudly? It wasn't like it mattered if he was. She wasn't looking for anything serious from him. This was fun. Casual. No strings attached. Probably the first and last time.

Damn, she hoped not.

He smoothed her messy hair away from her face and the look in his eyes told her far more than his words. "Not at all," he said, his voice serious.

Too serious. She was relieved this wasn't meaningless to him. She just wasn't sure she was ready for it to mean something. Relationships were a mystery to her. Human anatomy, fixing people she was good at. Building friendships, connections and long-lasting commitments were as foreign to her as another language. And she couldn't help but wonder if she was too old to learn.

"Has there ever been anyone special?" she asked.

He stared at the ceiling, twirling a strand of her hair around his finger. "I don't think so. I mean, after high school there was one girl I dated for over a year. She was great and we were great together. Things were comfortable, predictable…"

"That's not good?"

"It would have been if I wasn't looking for something more," he said.

"Like what?"

"Sparks. Fire. Intensity. I mean, I know they say those things fade in a relationship, but they should be there at the start and they just weren't with her…or anyone else."

She stiffened. She'd felt sparks between the two of them. Had he not?

"Until now…"

Her shoulders relaxed. She traced a fine white line on his chest above his heart. "Where did you get this scar?" Changing the subject seemed necessary.

He glanced down at her finger. "That one was from my very first rescue mission as a recruit. Three hikers went missing on the side of Snowcrest Mountain. It was spring and the snow had started to melt. The ground was muddy and avalanches had been happening in the area. I was inexperienced, had no idea what to expect.

As we trekked along the mountain, I fell against a jagged rock."

"Ouch."

"Yes, it was. Eight stitches," he said with a laugh. Taking her hand, he kissed it, entwining his fingers with hers.

The intimate gesture had her heart racing more than the frantic, explosive sex.

"But luckily, I've gotten a little better at the job since then."

"Accidents still happen." She saw them all the time. People's lives and health suddenly in jeopardy just doing things they did a thousand times before. Skiers, hikers, campers, wilderness enthusiasts—she saw them all in the emergency room. She'd once removed a tree branch that was three inches thick from a man's shoulder. Out here, nothing was predictable.

"You're right—they do," Reed said. "We are as careful as we can be." His fingers trailed up and down her arm, making her shiver. He misread the goose bumps for cold and pulled her closer. "Out there, our main priority is the safety of the search team, then it's the safety of the person we are trying to find. That's why we go only as far as we do. We could potentially search forever in some cases." His voice sounded strained at the reality of the situation.

"How often do things...not work out?"

"They *do* more often than not. We have a good success rate...not as good as we'd like," he said. His fingers stopped trailing. She'd obviously touched a nerve.

"Sorry, that's probably not something you want to

think about or talk about." She bit her lip as she stared at his chest.

"Not with Cassie out there right now, no," he said tightly.

She forced a breath. She had to get better at this. Communication and sensitivity. She knew she struggled with both. "Again, I'm sorry. I'm not good at... I lack a certain sensitivity. I really don't mean to offend."

His body relaxed a little and he hugged her closer. "I know. It's okay." He cleared his throat. "Is that why you wouldn't go see that injured skier when he asked for you at the hospital?"

"Yes." And she'd thought about that decision and how it must have looked to the other doctors, to Reed, a few times since, before pushing it away. It was in the past. She couldn't change it. But she wished she could stop feeling a slight pang of regret about it. Unlike the emergency room, where she had plenty of other patients and a hectic schedule to use as excuses for not following up or being available, here she'd had no excuse. Except her own awkwardness and reluctance to see patients as people once they didn't need her help anymore.

"I take it you prefer to distance yourself from patients?" No judgment in his voice, just a genuine curiosity.

She nodded. Inadvertently, she distanced herself from everyone. Her mother was the compassion and source of comfort in her home...after she died, Erika's father retreated and she was left to either toughen up or be lost in sadness. "I need to in order to do my job effectively. If I'm emotionally invested in a patient, the surgery has an added element of pressure. If I don't know anything about them, I can operate the same on everyone, without placing values on life."

He nodded. "I understand. I think. But then every patient is just another medical file?"

Her spine stiffened. "It sounds cold when you put it that way…but I can't say it isn't true." Cold as it was, she couldn't deny that each patient became a series of numbers and tests. Their probability of survival was the only way she knew to determine the outcome of the procedure. It didn't matter if one person had three kids and a mortgage to pay or if they were a single, middle-aged billionaire. Everyone got her best—in the operating room, at least. And that's really what they needed from her. Friends and family could provide comfort and support. They couldn't save them. That was her job.

When Reed was silent, she leaned on an elbow to look at him, expecting to see him look at her differently now. It would be hard for him to understand. He was full of compassion and empathy and she doubted he could as effectively remove emotions from his chosen career.

The respect and admiration in his eyes was a source of relief. "Things are just different—stressful and fast-paced in a different way in the hospital setting."

"I get it. I do. You don't have to explain yourself to me," he said, touching her cheek.

Yet, she wanted to. Worse, she wanted to be different. She wanted to be that doctor who could get to know their patients and their families and not risk jeopardizing their skill in the operating room. She rested her head against his shoulder. "My dad used to be so amazing with his patients—when he worked here at Wild River Community Hospital…before Mom died. He was caring and sympathetic and everyone truly felt as though they were his only priority." She'd felt like a priority back then, too.

"Like Dr. Smyth?"

She nodded, once again feeling a pang of regret for the relationship her father had let lapse. Though who was she to judge? She forced a breath. She was fixing that. She was here mending her broken friendship with Cassie.

Though not exactly at the moment. For the first time she wondered what her friend would think about this situation. She would probably be happy for them. Her friend didn't possess a single jealous or mean-spirited gene. Cassie was the best.

"How did your mom die?" Reed asked, breaking into her thoughts. "I know it was kidney failure, but I've never known what the actual cause was."

"She had polycystic kidney disease and her transplant failed. While the antirejection drugs didn't help the body accept the new organ, they were powerful enough to destroy her immune system," she said, the sting of it still as raw as the day she'd found out.

"That's why you're working on the new antirejection drug." He twirled a strand of her hair around his finger, letting it fall in a ringlet beside her face.

The gentleness in his touch, the sympathy in his voice made it so much easier to open up to him.

"Yes. We hope to create another drug that's less

damaging on the body with its side effects but just as effective in ensuring the success of the transplant organ." It was too late to save her mom, but she hoped to help millions of others.

"Do you think it will work?"

His genuine interest warmed her, and her excitement about her research surfaced. For years they'd been examining the effects of different drugs, and she thought they might actually have one that would react with the body the way they wanted. She nodded. "Clinical trials start just before Christmas."

His expression clouded slightly. "I'd forgotten for a second that you're leaving again," he said, pulling her back down toward him and kissing her.

So had she. Lying there in his arms was the only thing that mattered in that moment. Crazy as it sounded, nothing else seemed to exist when he was holding her. Both an amazing feeling and a terrifying one. The idea that she could let everything else fade away so completely was something she'd never expected.

The silence held too much meaning. Too many unsaid thoughts. So she shifted her body so that she was on top of him. "Well, I'm here now," she said. Taking his hands, she pinned them over his head and leaned down to kiss him again. Hard. Then, pulling away slightly, she slid her tongue along his bottom lip. "What are you going to do with me?"

He grinned, freeing his hands with ease and gripping her waist. Flipping them over, he lay on top of her, forcing her legs apart as he wedged himself between them. "I've got a few ideas," he mumbled against her mouth.

And for now, those ideas of his were the only things she couldn't wait to explore.

CHAPTER TWELVE

"HELLO? I THINK the door's locked."

Erika's heart pounded in her chest as she untangled her body from Reed's. Sprinting from the cot, she collected her discarded clothing. She hadn't meant to spend the night, and they'd just fallen asleep less than two hours ago.

Reed was only seconds behind her. "Shit. Morning crew."

"Do they have a key?" she asked, frantically trying to free her yoga pants from the inside-out ski pants. Her underwear and backward sweater, which she'd put on in the middle of the night when they'd finally taken a break from sex to eat the cold pizza, wasn't the outfit she wanted to get busted in by other members of the search and rescue team.

Reed glanced at the schedule on the wall. "It's Harrison. He's new, so no." He yanked his T-shirt on and pulled on his jeans, and Erika was sad to see his sexy body disappear. The body she'd had the pleasure of exploring three times the night before. She still couldn't believe her physical reaction to Reed. She couldn't get enough of him. She gazed longingly at his crotch as he zipped his zipper but another loud knock had her shoving her legs into the ski pants, tangled yoga pants bulging up around her thighs.

Screw it. She'd fix it later. She found her coat, but Reed grabbed her before she could put it on. One hand cupped her breast through her sweater as he drew her into his body. "I had a great night," he said.

So close to him, she nodded, trying not to breathe. Morning breath was not sexy and in the light of day, this was all slightly awkward…though not regrettable in the least.

He kissed her and she kept her lips shut tight. She hadn't brushed her teeth since the morning before.

Pulling back, he grinned. "You're beautiful—messy hair and morning breath and all."

She smiled, knowing exactly how he felt. His messy hair and sleepy-looking expression was actually the sexiest look of all. She wanted to rip his clothes off and push him back onto the cot. Go another three rounds by lunch.

But then a knock on the door had her retreating from his arms and pulling on the ski coat. "How do we explain this?" she whispered as she ran a hand through her tangled hair. Windblown from skiing, then tangled even more against the bedsheets all night, she may never get a brush through it again.

She didn't care. It was all so worth it.

Reed shrugged as he went to open the door. "Pretty sure no one will believe any story we can come up with anyway…"

She held her breath as the door opened and a young guy walked in. "Did I wake you?" he asked Reed, then noticing her, he grinned. "Ah… Hello. Erika, right?"

How the hell did he know?

"Tyler mentioned you," the guy said, tucking his

long, wavy hair behind an ear and extending a hand to her. "I'm Harrison."

She shook his hand quickly, ignoring Reed's annoyed expression at the mention of Tyler. She hoped she wasn't interfering with the two men's working friendship. It should be clear to him now, after the night before, that he was the one she wanted. "Hi…nice to meet you."

She grabbed her boots and slid them on the wrong feet for an uncomfortable walk of shame back to Cassie's. "Well, see you…" she said to Reed.

"I'll walk you out," he said, and she was relieved that the other guy had gone straight to the leftover pizza and didn't give them a second glance as they headed outside.

She turned to face Reed, the bright light of day highlighting everything the night before had concealed. They'd actually had sex. Three times. Together. Her and Reed. Undeterminable emotions ran through her. Lust mixed with a slight embarrassed feeling. How was he feeling that morning? Was this it? Or did he want to spend more time with her? Have more mind-blowing sex? She'd be okay with that. "Thank you again for yesterday. It was…"

"Unexpected," he finished.

"In a good way," she said. She danced from one foot to the other, waiting. Would he ask to see her that evening? Did she want that? Physically, things had heated up between them fast…but she couldn't deny that emotions had played a role in the night before. She liked him. A lot. He was a part of her past that she'd temporarily forgotten, but after only a few days together, an odd, comforting sense of familiarity was mixing with exciting newness to create undeniable chemistry between them.

But she was going home in a little over a week.

And that was just one of the reasons they should be thankful for the amazing night they'd had and go their separate ways.

"So, seeing as how I promised you dinner last night and you didn't get a chance to eat…at least not while the food was hot, how about a do-over tonight? A real restaurant with real plates and no convenient uncomfortable cot to distract us?" He stepped closer and touched her cool cheek. Heat radiated through her.

She'd readily go for paper plates and uneaten pizza again, but they really should cool it a little. Still, the idea of seeing him that evening had her heart leaping with excitement, so she didn't even consider saying no. "Okay. Seven?"

He checked his watch. "That's eleven hours from now. Pretty girl, I'll never make it that long without seeing you. I was thinking more like five."

She laughed, loving the feelings of warmth that were flowing through her at his words. Loving them and also terrified by them. "That's a little early for dinner…"

"If the restaurants opened earlier, I'd suggest three."

Happiness like she hadn't felt in a long time had her practically floating. "Okay. Five it is."

REED WATCHED ERIKA walk away, fighting the urge to jog after her for one more kiss. This was crazy. She was literally still within sight and he missed her already.

He ran a hand through his disheveled hair. He had to get a grip.

Seeing Wade's truck pull into the parking lot, he waved as the older guy got out. "Hey...was that Erika I saw walking away from here?"

"Yes it was," Reed said, unable to hide a grin as he followed the other guy back inside.

"So, you two?"

"Are having dinner tonight," he said, forcing the new recruit out of his chair and sitting behind the desk. "You're getting pizza sauce on your shirt. Use a plate, man." He liked giving the new recruits a hard time and that morning, nothing could deflate his mood.

Wade shook his head. "You boys and your casual flings with these tourists. Be careful. Someday, you'll get attached to one of them, like I did." He removed his coat and hung it on a hook. "Kim was here for less than a week on a girls' trip. I still don't know how it happened. One minute I'm casually flinging my brains out and then bam! Couldn't live without her." He pointed a finger at Reed. "Don't tell her I said that."

Reed just laughed, but he suspected Wade was more right than he knew. The night before had been amazing—Erika was hot as hell and her passion had been a complete surprise. But Reed already knew it was more than just sex.

"Hey, did you guys see this printout?" Harrison asked, placing a fax from the state troopers' office on the desk.

Reed scanned it.

Alaska Search and Rescue had found the remains of a male body during a training session with the Coast Guard on Chichagof Island the day before.

His heart pounded in his chest as he continued to read the details.

The body was currently undergoing an autopsy and investigators at the station were going through missing person files. His hand shook slightly as he looked for the time of the printout.

3:00 a.m.

Around the same time he'd been making love to Erika for the third time. He hadn't even noticed the fax come in. He didn't regret their night together, but a slight unease in the pit of his stomach told him having her there at the station overnight hadn't been the right thing to do.

"Wow...looks like this body was out there a while," Wade said, reading over his shoulder. "Probably wouldn't have found him if loggers weren't cutting back that section of the forest aggressively this past year."

Loggers. The body was found near the Whitestone Logging site.

He thought he might be sick. His stomach churned and saliva coated the inside of his mouth. He checked the time. Almost nine. "Um...can you guys do a routine check on the vehicles? Tyler mentioned one of the tracks on snowmobile two was a little off the other day."

Wade nodded. "Sure, man. Harrison, shove that pizza in your face and let's go."

Once the men were gone, Reed picked up the landline and called the state troopers' office.

"Wild River Station."

He cleared his throat. "Hey, Sergeant Keller, it's Reed Reynolds from Wild River Search and Rescue."

"Hey, Reed, what's up?"

"I'm calling about that body found near Whitestone… Any updates on that yet?" He held his breath. He didn't know what answer he was hoping for. Closure on his dad's case would bring relief, but then what? His father would really be gone. He'd lived with the uncertainty for so long, how would he feel knowing for sure?

"Oh yeah. You know, that find was a crazy fluke. One of the crew slipped and rolled down the bank toward the creek. Rolled right into the body… Just give me a sec and I'll see if anything has come in yet."

He heard papers riffling in the background and he rested his forehead against his hand. For years he'd searched, waited, expected news like this to arrive someday… He wasn't nearly as prepared for it as he should be. If this was his father, how did he tell his mother? Cassie? He took several deep, slow breaths.

"Reed, you still there?"

"Yeah, I'm here. Anything?"

"A report came in about five minutes ago from the coroner's office. Male. About midforties. Caucasian…"

His heart raced.

"Dental records match a missing person by the name of Everett Parsons."

Not his father.

Disappointment fought with relief in his chest. Still no answers. No closure. But no concrete proof that his father was dead. Meaning, he could still be out there… "Okay. Thank you," he said, disconnecting the call.

He sat back in the chair, hearing Wade reenter. The older man placed a hand on his shoulder. "Not him?"

Reed shook his head. "Not him."

ERIKA HUMMED "JINGLE BELLS" as she carried her peppermint mocha up the stairs to Cassie's condo. The stares and whispers as she'd entered the café—her boots on the wrong feet and her hair a disheveled mess—hadn't bothered her one little bit. Nothing could spoil her mood that morning. She unlocked the door and went inside. Removing her winter gear, her cell chimed in her pocket.

New email messages.

Grabbing her laptop, she sat on the couch and curled her legs under her. She sipped the holiday-flavored coffee as she waited for the remote connection. Only nine more hours until dinner with Reed. She could keep herself busy until then.

Opening her inbox, she saw the first message was from Snowpeaks Powder Guides. She clicked on it and saw photo attachments.

Pictures of their heli-skiing experience. She opened up the file and smiled as she flipped through the pictures of her and Reed in the helicopter, skiing down the slopes... The photographer had even captured their near-kiss on the picnic bench during lunch. She sighed looking at the photo. She barely recognized herself. Her flushed cheeks and excited expression had so much more to do with Reed than the exhilarating day they'd been having.

It was the moment he'd told her she was amazing.

She hugged her coffee to her chest, butterflies in the pit of her stomach as she looked at his handsome face.

Five o'clock couldn't come fast enough. She didn't even care if they made it to a restaurant. Food could wait until she got back to Anchorage.

Her cell rang and she jumped.

Caller ID said Unknown.

"Hello?"

"Hey, it's Darren. Did you get my email?"

"I'm just checking them now…" She closed down the email from Snowpeaks and scanned her inbox. "I don't see one."

"I sent it thirty seconds ago, hit Refresh," he said.

No doubt he believed she was sitting around in a hotel room somewhere, clicking Refresh a thousand times. He'd be shocked to know what she'd really been doing on this vacation.

"Is it there yet?"

Man, he was impatient. And slightly frantic. "What's wrong with you?" She was usually the high-strung one. Then the email popped up.

A forwarded email from her father. The subject line made her mouth gape.

"He's selected the clinical trial study patients without me?"

"I couldn't believe it either."

While it was surprising, it wasn't completely out of character. This wasn't the first time her father's executive decision-making had left her out in the cold. Working with him on the new drug had tested her, but she believed in what they were doing.

"When do you get back?" Darren asked.

"Not for another nine days." She stared at the list of participants. If only her father had made a mistake, she could call him and let him know that not waiting for her was wrong. However, each candidate was exactly what she would have chosen. How could she be upset? And the main thing was that the trials were approved and would be starting soon.

She'd be back before they did.

"You're not upset?"

"He did a great job choosing the candidates."

"I'd be pissed," Darren said. "You sound...different."

She felt different. "I'll see you soon, Darren. Thank you for letting me know."

She disconnected the call and forced a breath. "Damn it, Dad." She really should call him, but what could she say? There was always too much to say, but neither of them did.

Her mother's funeral had marked not only the end of their time with her, but also of the closeness Erika and her dad had once shared.

After everyone else had left that day, she'd found him alone in his office. Head in his hands, sitting behind his desk. Throughout the ceremony, he'd stood stoic, unemotional, and as they'd lowered her mother's casket, he'd stared expressionless.

But finally, he was showing his devastation. Alone. "Dad?"

He'd glanced up and his red-rimmed eyes looked pained for a moment before he'd sat straighter, clearing his throat. "Did you need something?"

Yes—comfort, reassurance...a hug.

They'd barely spoken since her mother died a few days before and she was struggling with sadness and a feeling of helplessness. They hadn't had time to process their grief yet and she was depending on him to help her through it.

Entering the room, she wrapped her arms around his shoulders, but he didn't hug her back. "She's gone," he said and she sensed he wasn't talking to her. "She's really gone."

Fresh tears had burned her eyes as she'd squeezed

his neck. She'd never seen him so destroyed, so heart-broken, so lost...

But a moment later, he untangled her arms from around his neck, cleared his throat and stood. "I need to go into the hospital for a while."

"Today? But I thought you had some time off..."

He shook his head as he reached for his coat. "Time off won't bring her back."

He'd left the office and Erika knew she was alone to deal with her grief. Her father had decided the only way he'd survive his was to bury it with her mother.

Reopening the email from Snowpeaks, she stared at the image of her smiling at Reed. Her father was right. Time off couldn't bring her mother back, give her back what she'd lost, but she had nine days before she returned to reality and she planned to make the best of them.

CHAPTER THIRTEEN

HIS PAGER SOUNDED just as Reed hit Send on the text to Erika letting her know he was leaving his place and would be there to pick her up in five minutes. It was four thirty, a little earlier than they agreed, but damn, if he didn't see her soon, he'd go crazy. Since she'd left him that morning, he'd thought of nothing else.

Shaking off the news of the body that had been found had taken a bit of effort and seeing her would help erase it from his thoughts. Erika Sheraton had turned out to be one hell of a surprise. And he wasn't quite sure what to do with that just yet.

Glancing at the pager, the distress call on the display told him he wouldn't get the chance to find out anytime soon.

A quick call to the station while he dressed in his search and rescue gear and he had all the details. A group of teenagers was hiking in avalanche territory and they hadn't been heard from since the morning before. They'd been scheduled to return yesterday evening and no one had been able to reach the group by cell phone. The state troopers' office had requested help in launching a search immediately.

He dialed Erika as he climbed into the truck, his chest filling with emotion at hearing her voice.

"You can't be here that fast," she said.

"Unfortunately, I need to cancel. I just got an emergency call." He felt horrible. It was the first time he was annoyed by the demands of his job, and having to cancel their date at the last minute. He reached for his seat belt and secured it as he pulled out of his driveway.

But Erika didn't seem fazed. "That's fine. Change of plans. I'll come with you."

He hesitated. As much as he'd take any opportunity to see her, this was an actual call. Not an injury on the slopes. She wasn't a team member and this search could be dangerous.

"I'm a trained medical professional. I don't need to be an official crew member to offer assistance," she said, obviously reading his silence. "I read it in the S & R manual online today."

His jaw dropped as he headed down Main Street. "You read the manual?"

"Yep. Wanted to be prepared to argue with you if this opportunity arose," she said, sounding pleased with herself. She'd switched to speakerphone and he could hear her getting changed—the sound of a zipper, the rattling of hangers…

Damn, she was hot. He sighed. And she was right—as a trained physician, she was allowed to assist. With several crew members not available that evening, they could use all the help they could get. "Okay. I'll be there in thirty seconds. But just so we are clear, you're there to assist, not take over."

"No promises."

He couldn't keep the grin from spreading across his face. "Fine. But for the sake of the rescue, please wear a bra."

"Again, no promises."

THE WORRIED EXPRESSIONS on the faces of the teens' parents gave Erika an unsettling feeling as she sat quietly in the station while Reed and Wade questioned them about everything from last point of contact to the size and brand of winter boots they were wearing.

Every last detail could be important to the search and they weren't leaving any question unasked.

Erika had been more than willing to go on the rescue, but she hadn't been prepared for this part. Seeing the distraught families made her feel slightly nauseous. The teens ranged in age from sixteen to nineteen and it was their first trip in the mountains alone. The fathers looked a mix of worried and pissed, while the moms' expressions were pure terror. Erika couldn't even begin to understand what they were going through.

Her only source of comfort came unexpectedly from Diva. The puppy could obviously sense the tension in the air and remained glued to her feet, as though waiting for her own rescue orders. Maybe someday, she would make a great search and rescue dog. Today, she'd be staying at the station with Tank. Not knowing how long she'd be out on the mission, Erika hadn't wanted to leave her alone at Cassie's, so she'd brought the dog along.

Reed had thought it was a good idea to have the dog there, as well. She could provide a sense of comfort to the parents while the team was out searching.

"The colors of the jackets and ski pants?" Reed asked, jotting down the answers. He gave a reassuring nod. "Red and yellow—great. Those will be easier to spot."

Since picking her up, he'd been on alert. He'd been

friendly and obviously happy to see her, but his mind had already been on the rescue.

Hers had taken a little longer to shift from the excitement of being near him to razor focus on the task they were about to embark on. Watching him, she marveled over his dedication and commitment to this volunteer role. Saving lives, putting his own at risk... His selflessness made her six-figure salary for doing the same thing seem frivolous.

"Okay, I think we have everything to get started," he said, zipping his jacket. "Tank will continue to ask further questions and if you think of anything...even something small, be sure to tell him. He'll communicate with us over the radio." He slid his hands into thick gloves and pulled a yellow hat on his head.

"If we can't reach the kids by cell phone, how will you be able to communicate by radio?" one of the fathers asked. A big, burly guy in a camouflage ski jacket. His Wild River Hunter's Club badge on his shoulder suggested this was the guy who'd taught the teens to love the wilderness.

Erika just hoped he'd taught them enough about survival in these winter conditions.

"It's possible we could lose contact with the station, so if you don't hear from us in a while, don't panic. And no one else rush out into the trails for their own search. Having to find you as well will only make this more difficult," Reed said, obviously reading the man's on-edge, eager demeanor properly.

"You expect us to sit around here and wait while our kids are missing?" he said, moving closer to Reed.

Reed's six-foot frame towered over the other man, but the guy had at least twenty pounds on him.

Erika shot a worried look at Tank, but he was briefing the crew members as several others arrived.

"Yes," Reed told the father. "I do. You're more help
to us here, answering questions and not giving us all
more to worry about. Keep trying their cell phones.
Call other friends and family to see if anyone has heard
from them. You're more help to us and your kids by
staying put. For now, at least."

Erika swallowed hard. For now. She knew if the
search went on too long and entered a critical time
it would be all hands on deck and everyone would
quickly become a volunteer, searching the safer re-
gions led by an experienced rescuer.

"But…" the man started.

"Honey, Reed is right," a small woman said, touching her husband's arm. "We'll wait here," she told Reed.

Reed nodded. "Thank you." He started to turn toward the group of rescuers but the woman grabbed his
hand. "Please, please find our son."

Erika looked away. It was too hard to watch. She'd
had families plead with her in the past, early in her
career, to save a loved one and it put a lot of pressure
on. She never knew what to say. She couldn't promise anything and therefore she could rarely offer the
comfort they sought. Not having the answers for them
had eventually caused her to retreat from dealing with
the families. Now, she left that communication to the
assisting surgeon or head nurse. Someone better at it
than she was.

But Reed hugged the woman quickly and whispered,
"I'll bring him back to you, I promise."

She swallowed hard. Fear made her chest tighten.
She had no idea what to expect once their search began.

Was she really ready for this? Reed was right—the injured skier was nothing like a real rescue.

"You have the best of the best heading out there. Try to relax as much as you can and think of anything else that could help the search," Tank said, taking the woman by the shoulders and leading her back to her husband.

A moment later the search officially began, and eight hours after that, the only thing keeping Erika awake was pure adrenaline. Freezing cold wind whipped through her jacket and pierced her skin like needles. Dampness in the air chilled her to the bone. Despite her thick gloves, her fingers hurt and her toes were numb even in the extra pair of minus forty winter boots Tank had given her at the station. Every minute felt like hours. A shiver ran through her and her blood ran cold. How could anyone survive out here in this weather?

Luckily the teens had been camping. According to their parents, they had packed all the right supplies to keep them warm and safe in unpredictable weather and they had enough food and water to survive days.

Still, the concern on Reed's face as each hour ticked by with no sign of the kids or their campground made her feel that she was right to be worried. At first, he'd been confident and calm as they'd headed out toward the camping grounds the kids had reserved, but now she could tell he was starting to question the reassurance he'd given the mother.

They'd slowly trekked through the area for hours. They'd walked the trails surrounding the campsites. Talked to other campers in nearby areas. No one had seen the kids that day...or at all that week.

That wasn't a good sign. The teenagers hadn't been completely honest with their parents about this trip. Suddenly any predictability they'd had based on the teens' plans disappeared. They could be anywhere.

Man, she'd never really thought about having kids of her own and she certainly hadn't been able to identify with the parents back at the station, but obviously her maternal instinct wasn't completely buried—she wanted to strangle these kids herself…after she hugged them…if they found them.

When. When they found them. She had to stay positive.

Wind howled through the trees, blowing her hair into her face, but she could barely feel the strands brush against her frozen cheeks. Her respect for the search and rescue crew grew exponentially with each passing second. She was a visitor to this way of life. They did it all the time, whenever they were needed.

Reed expertly led the team on the search. He seemed to know every inch of these woods and he was making decisions on the most probable actions of the teens. He was alert and focused and seemed to anticipate the needs of his crew members before they even knew what they needed. He wasn't letting the stress affect him and yet he was sympathetic and understanding to the crew members whose anxiety was on display. He was nothing short of amazing, and she was just trying to keep it together.

"How are you doing?" he asked. Moments ago, he'd stopped their combing the backwoods trail at a snail's pace. He poured her a mug of coffee and handed it to her.

"I'm fine," she lied, taking a sip before handing it

to him. The weak, lukewarm, hours-old coffee would do nothing to keep her awake and alert. Where was her intern with her double shot of espresso when she needed him?

She wondered what Darren would think of her in that moment. If he knew she was out there... What would her father think? Unfortunately, she knew the answer to that one.

Reed tossed back the liquid in one gulp and then, opening his backpack, he cracked two new hand-warmer packs against his thigh and handed them to her. "Stuff these inside your boots."

"Reed, seriously I'm fine." By now, she wasn't sure she still had toes anyway. And she didn't want to hold up the search. As it was, her lack of expertise and skill on these missions might be hindering the team, and that was the last thing she wanted.

"My toes are freezing and my boots are thicker than yours. If you insist on staying out, you need to take care of yourself or you won't be much use to us."

He had a point. "Thank you," she said, taking them.

"You're welcome," he said, touching her shoulder briefly before going to check on the others.

Stuffing the packs deep into her boots, instant heat filled the space and circulation returned to her toes, the warmth expanding into her legs, as well. She prayed the missing teens had enough foresight to have these on hand.

Then she thought of Cassie. Her friend led groups out here in the wilderness all the time. She obviously knew how to be prepared and how to handle these elements, but still Erika worried about her. She'd be glad when Cass was home.

In silence, listening for any sound near or in the distance, they continued to comb through the dark, eerie trails. As night had fallen, the temperature had plummeted and the only saving grace was that it was too cold for the forecasted snow to start and hinder the search further.

As she scanned the woodsy areas on the left, she forced herself not to think about the what-ifs in this situation or how worried the parents must be with every new hour that passed.

Instead, she allowed herself to think about the man next to her. The brave, intelligent, sexy man who only appealed to her more and more as she spent time with him, got to know him. She was glad he'd allowed her to come along on the rescue, otherwise she'd be worried to death about him by now.

Was his chosen profession another reason he was still single? She could understand if it was. Being in a relationship with someone as selfless as Reed could make for a lot of sleepless nights. But she understood that drive to sacrifice oneself. While her career wasn't as dangerous as Reed's, she understood sacrifice for the greater good.

Their personalities couldn't be more different, but they were a lot more alike than either of them would have predicted. Alike in ways that mattered…ways that just might be enough for a relationship to survive.

Relationship? She glanced at him quickly. If she'd ever contemplated having one, it was now. With him. But would she still feel the same when she returned to her life in Anchorage?

A moment later, Reed's radio sounded with the

words everyone had been hoping to hear. "Teenagers located on south side of High Ridge."

She breathed a sigh of relief along with several other support team members. Reed continued to communicate with Wade, getting the exact coordinates before turning to them. "About a mile south of here. All four are safe. Minor injuries."

The look of relief on his face tempted her to reach out and touch him, but they had an audience and teens who still needed help.

THE OUTCOME OF every rescue was always uncertain. Weather conditions, how long the search went on, the preparedness of the people who were lost—all played a role in whether or not it was a success. This time it was, and Reed's energy shifted from anxious adrenaline to a steady determination to get the teens out of the cold and back to safety as quickly as possible.

His promise to their families had weighed heavy on his shoulders throughout the search. He knew he shouldn't have, but he'd been unable to leave the station, to leave those parents, without some sort of hope. He knew what it was like to lose someone. To search for someone. To feel that dread and uncertainty, and he'd wanted to offer some reassurance to help ease their minds and hearts.

Now it was the teens who should be nervous. High Ridge was known as the stoner campground and it wasn't where they'd told their parents they'd be camping. But that was up to them to deal with once they were back. His job was to bring them back safely, not save them from being grounded.

Arriving at the rescue site, he visually assessed the

four teens and their surroundings. A tent was up but the fire next to it had burned out a while ago. The dampness in the air making it hard to sustain even a small blaze. A pot still sat on a small portable stove, so at least they'd eaten recently.

Wade and Tyler had them wrapped in thermal blankets and each held a steaming mug of hot water. "Injuries?" he asked.

"A few cuts and bruises but mostly just exhaustion and dehydration. They only had three liters of water and one filter that malfunctioned. No way to melt snow as they dropped some of their gear farther back to lighten their load when the high altitude and added miles started to take their toll," Wade said.

Discarding essential gear was never the right course of action, but now wasn't the time for a lecture. Radioing their location in to the station, he requested assistance from three ski patrol units. He wanted them all out together and quickly. "And let the parents know all four are safe," he said.

"Where are they?" He heard a male voice in the background of Tank's radio. No doubt the aggressive father.

"The parents want to know where they are," Tank repeated.

Reed hesitated. "They will be safe soon enough. Tell them to sit tight." He'd let the kids disclose their location to their parents themselves. Give them a chance to come clean and sort things out. After all, he had no proof the kids were up to no good and he'd give them the benefit of the doubt.

"What can I do?" Erika asked, approaching.

Having her out there with him had been a source of

comfort and yet had elevated his anxiety. Taking care of his search crew was number one priority for him... taking care of her soared straight to the top, surpassing everything.

Keeping a level head with her so close had been challenging. He hated that he was putting her safety at risk. It was dark, freezing and she wasn't dressed properly or trained for long periods in the wild. His protective nature had to be kept in check several times.

He'd been out there to find the teens and he'd needed to focus on that, but now that they were found safe, he was happy she was there. "There are no injuries to treat," he said, unable to resist the temptation to rub her arms gently. He couldn't wait to get her back to warmth and the safety of his arms.

"Just put me to work. Whatever you need," she said, seeming to have caught a second wind as relief flowed over the group. "Should I help Tyler and Wade pack up?"

"Um..." The idea of her working closely with Tyler didn't appeal to him. He glanced around. One of the teens was off by himself, away from the group. Sitting by a tree, he swayed back and forth, his gaze straight ahead, locked on nothing. Reed could see his body trembling, despite the blanket.

"That kid seems to be going into shock." It wasn't uncommon in these situations that fear could take over, even once the lost were found. "Can you sit with him? Maybe just talk to him until the ski patrol units arrive?"

She looked like she'd rather set a bone, but she nodded. "Sure."

As he continued his contact with the station and

directed his crew, he watched her from the corner of his eye...

He'd given her a tough task. She'd admitted that comfort was not in her medical bag and as she sat next to the kid, he saw her hesitate before touching the boy's shoulder.

Surprisingly, the kid leaned into her...and she wrapped an arm around him. He couldn't hear what she was saying to him, but within minutes, the boy was responding and the faraway look in his gaze disappeared.

When the boy reached for Erika's hand, she held his trembling one, Reed's mouth went slightly dry. She continued to amaze him. He barely recognized her as the woman who'd walked into The Drunk Tank almost a week ago. "You guys okay?" he called out when she glanced his way.

She gave a tired smile and nod in response.

Man, he couldn't wait to get her home. "The ski patrol are almost here and the van is waiting on Mountainview Road, where the trails meet," he told the group.

Erika said something to the boy, then stood and approached him. "Are the parents coming?"

"They'll meet us at the hospital. He okay?" He nodded toward the boy.

"He's worried he's going to be kicked off the football team and mess up his chances of a university scholarship. Apparently his dad is coach," she said, looking to him for answers to save this kid's butt.

He touched her shoulder. "He's going to have to face the music, Erika."

"His biggest concern is disappointing his father," she said, her expression distraught.

Ah, that's where the sudden connection had come from. Erika had dealt with a similar fear for years. She hadn't said it the night before, but he'd sensed a shift in her when he'd mentioned her dad. "Look, kids make mistakes. They don't always get it right. Let's hope his dad sees that."

She nodded, but she bit her lip. No doubt her own experience with a strict father caused her worry for the kid. "I'm going to wait with him."

Hearing the Ski-Doos in the distance, he nodded, watching her go back to sitting on the ground. She said something to the boy and he smiled. Then she smiled and the stress of the search melted from Reed's shoulders.

Replaced by the stress of a new challenge, one that was going to be impossible. Not falling in love with Erika Sheraton.

THE APARTMENT DOOR had barely closed behind them before Reed's lips were on hers. His hands worked to unzip her coat, sliding it off her shoulders and letting it fall to the floor. Her own hands were unzipping his ski pants, yanking them down his legs. They stumbled forward into the apartment, tripping on discarded clothes as they removed everything in a frantic abandon.

After reuniting the teens with their parents and debriefing at the station, they'd driven like crazy to his apartment. They'd barely spoken. They didn't need to. Not tonight.

She struggled for a breath as she kicked off her boots, her mouth never leaving his. The rescue was over but the adrenaline still pumping through her was providing a new source of energy. She should be exhausted, but right now, sleep could wait. Her body throbbed with desire for him. A need so bad, it scared her.

He broke the connection with her mouth, lifted her in his big arms and carried her into his bedroom. She barely noticed the apartment around her or his bedroom as he placed her on the bed and continued removing clothing. "Too many layers," he said, lifting her sweater and T-shirt simultaneously. He unclasped her bra and she undid her jeans, wiggling free of them. She couldn't get naked fast enough.

Standing, he tore off his own T-shirt and jeans and underwear, then climbed back onto the bed, settling between her legs. The only thing between their bodies was the thin fabric of her lacy underwear. Feeling his already erect penis pressed against her pelvis, she moaned. "Jesus, Reed... I've been wanting you all day."

"Believe me, the feeling is mutual. If we hadn't found those kids so fast, I would have been calling a ten-minute break to take you behind a tree." He nuzzled against her neck.

He was kidding, but she'd felt the same way. Something about the danger of the situation had only fueled the intensity of her attraction to him and now that the danger was gone, a lingering sense of adrenaline had her vibrating.

His mouth on her neck was driving her insane. His warm breath against her still cool skin was making her tingle. Reaching between their bodies, she wrapped her hand along his thick shaft. She loved how quickly she could turn him on. How fast he was ready for her. She'd never had this effect on anyone before. It gave her a confidence she hadn't realized she'd been missing.

"Mmm, you're so soft and warm," he said, leaving love bites along her collarbone as he massaged her breasts. The feeling of his hands on her body was unlike anything she'd ever felt before. Sex had always been just sex. She'd never felt cherished, appreciated, worshipped before, the way she did with Reed. He ran his thumbs over her nipples and an ache ran through her. She tightened her grip around his cock, stroking faster.

"I want to feel your mouth around me," he whispered.

She could happily oblige. Shifting him off her, she reversed their position, straddling him on the bed.

"This is a fantastic view," he said, his gaze drifting over her exposed body. She loved the way he looked at her. She didn't feel self-conscious with him. No desire to hide herself. *Any* part of herself.

Which terrified her a little.

She moved lower and lower on the bed until she was bent over him. Cupping his balls with one hand, she stroked the length of him with the other. Up and down, excruciatingly slow. His jaw tightened and his hands clenched at his sides. "Your touch is driving me wild."

"Just relax." After that night, he deserved to lie back and relax, let the stress and pressure of the rescue fade away. She would do everything she could to help with that.

He laced his fingers together behind his head, and lust filled his gaze as he watched her stroke him. "That feels incredible, Erika," he said, his voice husky and deep. "Having you here with me is incredible."

There was no place else she'd rather be.

Keeping her gaze locked with his, she lowered her mouth to him. Starting at the base of his cock, she ran her tongue all the way to the tip. The moan that escaped him gave her even more confidence. She'd never felt competent in bed. Sex wasn't something she had tons of experience with. But right now, she felt empowered, in control...

She flicked her tongue around the tip of him, tasting the precum that escaped. She felt her own body get wet. Pleasing him, turning him on was making her own body awaken. In the past, orgasms hadn't been easy for her. Shutting off her overactive brain long enough to give in to physical sensations was a challenge. But with Reed, she was in the moment. Her body, mind and heart were present, and she was shocked at how easy it was with him.

That had to mean something.

"Erika, you're killing me. I want to be inside your wet, warm mouth."

She took all of him into her mouth, sucking gently, twirling her tongue along the length of him as she moved her head up and down. Her hand followed the motion of her mouth—up and down, slowly at first, growing more frantic and desperate as his moans of desire increased.

Knowing he was enjoying this made her want to do it even more. She hadn't been sure what Reed liked, but a desire to please him made her uninhibited.

He tasted so good and he was so big, so thick...

Just the thought of him inside of her was enough to have her dripping wet. She was so close to her own orgasm already and he wasn't even touching her.

"Erika, I'm close," he said, his voice hoarse, his hands now fisting the sheets at his side.

She slowed her pace but didn't stop. Couldn't stop. Never wanted to stop.

She sucked and licked, bringing him close, then easing off until he was breathing hard, demanding release. She squeezed the base of his cock and sucked harder, faster, bringing him to orgasm. He cried out as he toppled over the edge and she slowly, reluctantly removed her mouth and hands from his body.

Instantly, he reached for her, rolled her onto her back and slid his hand down her stomach, dipping beneath the waistband of her underwear. She shivered at the ticklish sensation along her sensitive skin. His fingers didn't even pause before two plunged into her wet, ready body. "Oh my God, Reed."

She closed her eyes and arched her back, lifting her hips off the bed, pressing her body closer to his hand, wanting his fingers even deeper. She clenched the walls of her vagina tighter, craving the intensity. His thumb flicked against her clit, back and forth, circling the swollen flesh, as the fingers pumped in and out. "You are amazing," he said as he pleasured her with his fingers.

He was amazing. Everything about him, but specifically, right now, the way he made her body respond in ways no one else ever had. "That's it, Reed. Faster... harder," she said, reaching for his face. His mouth covered hers and she didn't care about breathing, all she wanted was him. His tongue separated her lips and explored her mouth as his hand brought her over the edge.

Her orgasm rippled through her seconds later and her body trembled beneath Reed. Her breath caught as he broke the connection with her mouth, giving her the air she needed. He gently removed his fingers and softly kissed her lips.

She smiled up at him, exhaustion finally arriving. "Thank you," she said, touching his sleepy-looking face. The scruffy beard was so freaking sexy, she wanted to stay awake and stare at him all night. But her eyes felt heavy and the day had finally caught up to them.

"Thank *you*," he said, kissing her again before rolling to his side and pulling her into him. He spooned her and pulled the bedsheets up over their connected bodies.

She snuggled closer to him, feeling so safe in his arms, feeling so happy, so content. So many foreign feelings for her. Ones she hadn't known she was missing. Ones she wasn't sure she could live without once this vacation was over and she returned to her life.

He brushed her hair away from her face and kissed her cheek. "Think you can sleep now?" he whispered into her ear.

She barely heard him, her eyes already drifting closed.

CHAPTER FOURTEEN

ERIKA ACCEPTED A glass of wine from Reed and leaned back on her barstool. The Drunk Tank hadn't yet opened for the evening—Tank had left the bar closed all day to give everyone time to rest up after the rescue. Arriving back at Cassie's that morning, just as light had started to creep over the mountain, Erika had slept until two, showered, ate a salad then headed to The Drunk Tank to see Reed.

He was dressed in a black shirt with a search and rescue logo and jeans that hugged his ass and thighs—what she'd come to learn was his usual uniform. Sitting across from him, she found herself wishing he was on station duty tonight instead of working at the bar. She didn't know how he kept the pace of his lifestyle. Saving lives in the wilderness one moment, then bartending hours later.

He was gorgeous and sexy as hell, the only man in a long time to set her heart beating out of her chest. But he was also smart and driven and dedicated to his role on the team. His first priority the night before had been making sure his team members stayed safe throughout the search and that everyone made it back uninjured.

He was calm and clearheaded in an emergency, which wasn't a skill a lot of people possessed. She'd seen doctors and nurses lose their cool many times.

Hell, on her worst day, even she had trouble keeping it all together.

And he'd paved the way for the boys to come clean to their parents at the hospital, if that's what they needed to do. The kids had insisted that they'd only been meeting friends at High Ridge, so Reed had casually mentioned to the parents that while they'd found the kids in the questionable location, it didn't necessarily mean they were up to no good. Once the kids were released, they'd gotten quite a lecture from coach dad, but Erika had been relieved to see the older man hug his son as they'd left the hospital.

Relieved and slightly envious.

Staring at Reed now, she knew he was exactly the kind of man she could fall in love with…if her life gave her time to fall in love.

What would Cassie think of her adventures the night before…or the newfound light she was seeing Cassie's brother in? She sipped more wine, turning away from his gaze, suddenly extremely aware that they were alone. The Christmas music echoing off the wooden walls and the dishwasher running behind the bar were the only noises competing with the pounding of her heart.

"So, you're handing in your resignation at the hospital and applying to become a member of the team, right?" he asked, drinking his coffee, his eyes holding a teasing gleam above the rim of the mug. He was joking, but there was a hint of sincerity in the words.

She laughed. "Probably not."

He leaned his arms on the bar and studied her. "But you gotta admit you felt a rush, right? An adrenaline like nothing else…and then total fulfillment at the end knowing we'd done something great."

Yes. One hundred percent yes. At the hospital, surrounded by machines and other doctors and nurses, the chaos of an emergency was different. It was about routine and protocols. Everything they needed was on hand. She knew what she had to do and it was different yet similar in every situation. Here, each rescue was nothing like the one before. Each one held unique challenges, depending on so many varying factors. Being adaptable and quick thinking meant the difference between a success or failure. "I don't have to admit shit," she said finally.

"I'll take that as confirmation," he said with a grin that had her pulse racing. Damn, had her friend's brother always been so sexy? As kids, he'd ignored her. Even as they got older and started hanging with the same crowd, he had never paid any attention to her.

He was now. And his intent stare told her she wasn't fooling him.

"Okay…" she said reluctantly. "It was thrilling." Being on the side of the mountain, moving quickly, working alongside the search and rescue crew and the ski patrol members had definitely set her blood pumping. "Very different than being at the hospital."

"Better?"

She hesitated. "Different."

He nodded. "Okay." He paused. "I was kidding before, but if you do ever get tired of the six-figure salary and want to try slumming it up here, we'd be happy to have you." He reached across and touched her hand, sending an electric current straight to her heart. "*I'd* be happy to have you."

She swallowed hard. While it was reassuring to know she wasn't in this alone, that he was feeling this connection between them as strongly, she thought maybe it would be easier in the end if it was one-sided. If it was only her heartache she had to deal with when she left, she could handle that. "I'll keep that in mind," she said, before an unexpected yawn escaped her.

Despite the sleep she'd caught up on that day, she was completely wiped out. Her eyes struggled to stay open and the wine wasn't helping.

Reed smiled, reaching into his pocket for his truck keys. "Here. Why don't you go to my place and take a nap?"

She frowned, taking the keys. "I could just go to Cassie's."

"You could, but then I'd have to come wake you up at midnight to take you back to my place."

Her mouth went completely dry. A direct contrast to what was happening between her legs. Just like that, she wasn't so exhausted anymore.

"This way, you'll already be in my bed." He took her hand and brought her palm to his lips, where he placed several soft kisses that had goose bumps surfacing on her skin everywhere. "Go. I'll be there as soon as I can."

Midnight couldn't come fast enough.

HE WAS BAGGED. The rescue followed by the evening shift in the crowded bar had him struggling to keep his eyes open, but the moment he saw Erika sleeping in one of his T-shirts in his bed, he caught a third wind. He hoped she'd gotten enough rest, because they probably weren't going to do much more sleeping that night.

She was there for one more week. And he planned on making every minute count.

Diva slept curled up on the foot of the bed, and he carried the heavy, out-like-a-light pup to the extra doggy bed Cassie had given him for "sleepovers" such as this. Well, maybe this wasn't exactly the kind of sleepover his sister had in mind.

He'd worry about Cassie and how she was going to react to all of this later. For the first time, he was experiencing a real connection to a woman and he wouldn't think about the consequences right now.

Returning to his bedroom, he removed his clothes and, lifting the edge of the dark blue blankets, he slid in next to Erika. The warmth of her body near his cold one made him immediately hard. Before Erika, it had been months since he'd gotten laid. And now, after their previous nights together, he knew finding another woman who could make him feel so good wouldn't be easy.

Letting her leave the following week wouldn't be easy either.

He wrapped an arm around her, pulling her into him, and placed a kiss on her shoulder. She smelled like vanilla and faintly like his cologne from being in his bed. He hoped to leave a more permanent mark on her heart, not just a scent on her body. Reed wasn't sure what to expect from her and he was desperate not to let his emotions run away with him, but having her in his arms, so close, so perfect...

He moved her hair away from her neck and kissed her there gently, his hand slowly, softly, moving the length of her body, down her waist, over her hip and slipping below the fabric of the T-shirt. Pressing his palm to her soft skin at her waist, he slid it upward until he cupped one breast.

She moaned, stirring in her sleep, and his body sprang to life. His erection pressed against her ass as he pinched the nipple, which hardened instantly under his touch. "You're home," she whispered, a smile in her voice.

The words made his breath catch in his chest. Home. This was *his* home. But what if coming home meant coming home to her?

So much for not getting too far ahead of himself.

"Are you still tired?" he whispered in her ear, biting her lobe gently.

She wiggled closer to him, pushing her ass back against his erect cock. "Nope."

"Good, because I've been wanting you since the last time I had you and I'm not interested in sleeping at all tonight," he said, squeezing her breast.

She shivered slightly and he let his hand trail down her body once more to caress her thigh, moving inward and upward until he reached the silky fabric of her underwear. She shifted her legs to give him access and he felt the moistness there already.

He loved that a simple touch, a gentle kiss was all it took to get her excited. He loved turning her on. He hardened even more when she reached down to slide the fabric to the right, granting his fingers access to the wet, soft folds of her vagina.

He swallowed hard as he stroked along the opening, flicking his thumb against her clit.

She moaned again and her legs trembled slightly. "That feels incredible," she said, her breath slightly labored in anticipation.

He reached for the waistband of the underwear and she rolled onto her back and lifted her hips to allow him to remove them. He slid them slowly down her legs, pausing to kiss the inside of her thighs, her calves and her feet before dropping the underwear to the floor. "You look amazing in my shirt." She looked amazing all the time, but this look was quickly becoming his favorite. Her lying in his bed, naked except for his shirt, messy, tangled hair and sleepy, lust-filled eyes illuminated only by the light from the streetlamp outside streaming through the gap in the curtains.

By far his favorite. A sight he could easily get used to.

She smiled, her eyes scanning his nakedness in the dark. "You look amazing out of it. You should be naked all the time." She raked her fingers along his abs.

He laughed. "Might get a little cold on rescues."

"Might make more tips at the bar," she teased. She went to lift the shirt over her head, but he stopped her.

"Leave it on and turn over," he said. He needed to see that beautiful, sexy ass up close. The last few times they'd been together, he'd been so desperate for her, he hadn't taken the time to explore her body as fully as he'd wanted to. The situation or their surroundings hadn't lent themselves to a lot of exploration. Tonight was different. He wanted to see her...all of her. Explore parts of her he hadn't yet. See how far she'd let him go.

She did as he instructed, climbing onto all fours on the bed in front of him. "Like this."

"Just like that." His mouth went dry as she arched her back, resting her body on her elbows and pushing her ass into the air, giving him full access to her. Fully exposed and vulnerable to him.

"You are so hot…" He placed both hands on her ass and gripped hard. "I could stare at this ass all night," he said, moving one hand lower to cup her, feeling her wetness drip onto his palm. "Fuck, you're so wet."

"I can't remember the last time I've been this turned on," she said, her voice sounding slightly hoarse. Her body trembled and her fingers gripped the fabric of the bedsheets at her side.

She'd need to hold on tight for what was coming. Kneeling on the bed behind her, he gripped her hips and pulled her ass toward him. He slid his cock between her legs, pushing the tip against her folds. Her wetness covered him and he closed his eyes, as the pleasurable sensation rushed through him. Her body was so ready, so willing to accept him it was impossible to focus. He felt dizzy, dazed—lack of sleep mixing with an intense desire to be inside of her making him feel slightly intoxicated. He was drunk on her, on this attraction he had for her that was so strong, so unexpected, so real… He slid back and forth, pressing himself against her opening but holding back, never entering, until she was panting and clutching the pillow above her head.

"Reed…oh Reed…"

Damn, he could listen to her say his name all night. "Do you want me to fuck you, Erika?" he asked, reaching down to stroke his cock.

"Yes… Like this, Reed. Take me from behind."

Reaching for a condom in the bedside table, he tore the package open with his teeth and slid it on, tormenting himself with the stroking motion. His cock was thick and fully erect and dying to be inside her. This wouldn't last long. The moment he was buried deep inside her wet, warm body, he was going to explode.

His craving of her, his desperate need of her was confusing and terrifying. He'd never ached for a woman as badly as he longed for her. He was mentally and physically exhausted, yet his body only wanted one thing—her.

He held her steady against him, with one arm wrapped around her waist and his palm pressed against her lower back, forcing her body down toward the bed and her ass even higher. "I want to get in deep," he said, just the words alone making him harder.

She nearly whimpered in response. The trembling of her body was driving him crazy. Her legs shook slightly and he could see her wetness dripping down her inner thighs. The knowledge that he was having this effect on her was sexy as hell. Seeing her so vulnerable yet holding all the cards had him so close to the edge already. She had no idea the power she had over him.

He slid his cock along the folds slowly, torturously careful…moving back and forth while his hips thrust forward against her ass. Her perfect, shapely, sexy ass…

"Please, Reed… I need you inside me… I'm so close and I need to feel your hard, thick cock inside of me," she begged.

She only had to ask once. He plunged in deep, hard, and the unexpectedness made her cry out, but then the sound turned to a deep moan of pleasure that had his own breath coming heavy as he pumped inside of her.

"Fast or slow?" he asked, pulling all the way out to the very edge, then sliding all the way back in.

"Fast. Really fast… I can't last long," she said.

He made several deliberate, slow movements in and out—the pleasure so intense it was almost painful. He could feel his own orgasm rising. The intensity increasing with each stroke. Faster, harder he thrust into her…over and over, gripping her ass, his fingers digging deep into her soft flesh, rocking desperately into her body.

Her fingers tangled with the bedsheets and her legs trembled furiously, supporting both of their weight as he rested against her, going deeper with each thrust.

"Oh my God, Reed…"

"Look back at me," he said, reaching for her hair. He gripped it in one hand as she turned her beautiful face to look over her shoulder toward him.

Her gaze locking with his was more of a turn-on than any other sensation.

The timing of their climax was perfectly in sync. A final thrust later, she let out a cry, just as his own orgasm knocked all other thoughts out of his mind. He closed his eyes as he held on tight to her, riding out the waves of pleasure wrapping around them both.

He thought he was going to pass out.

He took a deep breath as he slowly slid out of her, removed the condom and fell onto the bed next to her. Drawing her into him, he kissed her finally, desperate for a taste of her mouth. Lips he wasn't sure he could ever get enough of. His tongue fought with hers, searching for more, craving more…never ever getting enough. He held her tight and she clung to him just as desperately.

One more week… Would he be strong enough to let her go?

HOURS LATER, ERIKA rolled to her side in Reed's bed and reached out for him, but she didn't feel Reed next to her. Opening her eyes, she sat up and scanned the room. He wasn't there.

She listened, but the apartment was silent. Had he gotten a call from the station and gone out without her? She wouldn't have heard him get up or leave. Sleeping in his bed had given her the best sleep she'd gotten… maybe her entire life.

Swinging her legs over the side of the bed, she stood and left the room. Following a faint stream of light, she made her way down the hallway to the living room.

He was sitting at his desk, laptop open, his back to her. Still partly naked, he took her breath away. He was gorgeous inside and out and he made her feel so many different emotions all at once. For someone whose life didn't normally include emotion, the effect was dizzying, but it was quickly becoming a high she craved.

He didn't turn—obviously he hadn't heard her come down the hall—so she took a second to stare at him. The shape of the muscles in his back and shoulders, the messy dark hair… How was she going to leave him?

This forced vacation had quickly become exactly what she'd needed. She'd successfully vacated her life. She barely recognized this relaxed, sexual woman she'd become in a few days.

"Hey…did I wake you?" he asked, turning, perhaps sensing her presence.

"No. I just woke up and missed you."

He quickly minimized the browser on his laptop as she walked toward him.

She shook her head, glancing at his desktop background—a picture of the S & R team in front of the rescue chopper. "Looking at porn?" she teased. Though she was curious about what could have him up out of bed when he'd practically passed out next to her only an hour before.

He grinned, pulling her toward him. "Don't need that with you here," he said, pulling her down onto his lap and burying his face in her neck. "You smell amazing."

She shivered at the feel of his warm lips pressed against her collarbone. "What were you doing?"

"Nothing. Couldn't sleep, that's all." His hands slid the length of her thighs, disappearing beneath the edge of the T-shirt.

God, his touch drove her crazy. She clenched her legs together, already feeling a pulsating in her vagina. Would she ever get enough of him? Could she wear out this urge, these feelings and walk away with just some incredible memories to help her get through her long days and frantic schedule back at the hospital?

His fingers inched higher, up over her stomach and ribs, and his hand cupped her breast. He massaged gently, then pinched one nipple. "I love these breasts," he said, biting her earlobe.

She closed her eyes, savoring the pleasurable sensations of his mouth, his touch.

"So, I'm fairly confident I know the answer to this... but I have to ask—there's no one special in your life back in the city, is there?" he whispered.

She wasn't at all offended by the question or his assumption. "No one."

He smoothed her hair away from her neck as he continued to place kisses along it. "My last relationship ended about three years ago." She could barely label it a relationship, but for lack of better term.

"Was it serious?" His hands continued to massage her breasts as he kissed the hollow at the base of her throat.

"It could have been, but it just didn't work out. My chosen profession makes it challenging to fully commit to someone. Late nights at the hospital, being committed to the job more than anything else." She shrugged. It was a trade-off she had always been okay with.

Reed nodded. He understood that. His career was similar.

"I'm not an easy one to love," she murmured, resting her head against him.

"That's where you're wrong," he whispered.

She shivered. She hadn't exactly worked through her feelings for him yet, but love didn't seem like an impossibility. Was he already there?

"Any bitter heartbreaks along the way?" he asked, running his hands along her sides. Grabbing her waist, he lifted her and repositioned her on his lap. Her body straddled him and she felt his cock hard against her leg.

She shook her head, pressing her pelvis against him. "I don't think I've ever been in love. For real." Right now, she wouldn't have been able to recall anyone else even if there had been someone special in her past. All she could think about was him. And he was making it difficult to think.

Reed slipped a hand between her legs and immediately slid two fingers inside her. She sucked in a breath as his thumb circled her clit. Damn, it took nothing for her to get excited. A simple touch, a few kisses and she was ready to go.

He stood, lifting her body onto the edge of the desk. "I've been wanting to do something…" he said, lowering himself onto his knees in front of her and placing her legs over his shoulders.

She gripped the edge of the desk, her heart racing. "What's that?" she asked, knowing the answer.

"I want to taste you. Lick you. Put my tongue inside this delicious body," he murmured, his lips moving closer to her folds.

She'd never had anyone go down on her before and her mind raced. "Are you sure?" Sex had never been adventurous for her. She was opening her mind and body to a lot of new experiences with Reed.

Opening her heart, as well?

"I'm definitely sure," Reed said. He grinned at her before lowering his head. A second later she felt his tongue lick her wet folds.

Holy shit. She couldn't breathe as he continued to lap up her wetness eagerly, his hands pressing against her inner thighs, holding her apart, giving him better access to every inch of her. "Oh my God…do you want to stop?" she asked, though it was the last thing she wanted.

"Not on your life. I'm just getting started," Reed said, immediately returning his lips to her. He sucked on her clit as he slid a finger inside slowly, then another one. She clenched tight around them as he continued licking and sucking her folds. His tongue flicked her clit as his fingers moved in and out.

She struggled to hold on to the desk as her orgasm rose. So fast. What the hell was wrong with her? She'd never been this sex-crazed before. Now she couldn't get enough. She'd definitely been missing out.

Would he let her return the favor? The thought had her pulse racing. She had enjoyed it the night before. The idea of taking Reed in her mouth again brought her dangerously close to the edge. "I'm going to come, Reed."

"Good. Come for me. Let me taste you…" he said against her. The words caused a rippling vibration to rush through her.

When his tongue returned to her folds, she pushed her pelvis forward, craving more. He gripped her thighs tight, holding them farther apart as his fingers worked their magic inside, bringing her to orgasm. The intensity of the pleasure was unlike anything she'd ever experienced, and her arms nearly gave out as she struggled to support herself on the desk.

Reed moved away slowly and stood. "How was that?"

She reached for him and pulled his mouth toward hers, kissing him hard, aroused once more by the taste of her on his lips. Her tongue slid inside his mouth and she clung to the rippling tremors of her orgasm aftershock. He pulled back slowly and lifted her in his arms. "Let's go back to bed," he said, carrying her down the hall.

"Tired now?" she asked, kissing his neck and snuggling into his solid, warm chest.

"Not even a little bit," he said.

CHAPTER FIFTEEN

DOGGY BREATH WAS her morning wake-up call. Opening her eyes, Erika saw Diva inches away, staring at her. Her tongue dangled from the side of her mouth and she panted as though she'd run a marathon. She pawed the bedsheets but kept her distance.

"You're really trying hard not to lick me, aren't you?" she said, petting the dog's ears. She was cute with her white-and-gray fur and crystal-blue eyes.

"*I* am," Reed said, appearing in the doorway of the bedroom with a mug of coffee.

Erika smiled as she sat up. "Coffee delivered to me in bed. I could get used to that," she said.

"Who said this is yours?"

She extended her hands. "Give me my coffee."

Reed laughed, propping up several pillows behind her and handing her a cup before sliding back in beneath the sheets. "If delivering morning coffee is all it takes to keep you here, it can certainly be arranged," he said with a wink.

Her chest constricted slightly. They still hadn't talked about what was going on between them or if there was anything to hold on to when she went back to Anchorage. She wasn't great at initiating conversations about feelings, so she sipped her coffee.

"So, I have to ask…"

Shit. Here it was. The conversation she wasn't ready for yet.

"Why the forced vacation?" he asked.

Oh. That was easier. Though not by much. She sighed. Most hospitals were forcing their doctors to work overtime every day, not encouraging them to take time off. Understaffed and overworked was the reality of most hospitals, including Alaska General Hospital. "The board of directors is coming down hard on policies these days. They saw the hours I was working and thought I was getting a little burned-out."

"Were you?"

She hadn't thought so, until she'd started to relax that week and the stress began to melt away. "I don't know. Maybe. I certainly didn't agree a week ago, but this break has definitely made me realize that I'd been going too fast for too long." She paused. "I'm definitely feeling more focused, more relaxed…ready to go back."

She felt him stiffen slightly and realized what going back meant. She sat a little higher and turned to face him. "I'm not necessarily ready to leave you…" She avoided his gaze, staring at his smooth chest and upper abs that were partially hidden by the bedsheet. Definitely not ready to leave this body and the things he could do to hers.

"That's good to hear," he said, taking her hand in his. "I'd like to spend as much time with you as possible this week."

She did, too, but, "What about Cass?" Her friend was due back that evening and she wanted to spend time with her, as well. How would Cassie feel about her and Reed? Could they all hang out together? Would that be awkward?

In truth, she never wanted to leave this bed for the rest of her vacation.

"I think she'll be okay…" he said, but even he seemed to think things might be awkward. Especially seeing as how they could hardly be around one another without kissing or touching or ripping each other's clothes off. How would Cassie feel if she wanted to spend the nights in Reed's bed instead of crashing on her couch?

She bit her lip.

"Look, don't worry…we'll figure something out."

Would they figure something out for after this week was over as well? Or was this just a nice perk to her vacation—an unexpected, wonderful enhancement to her break from reality.

"Hey, I said, don't worry…" Reed said, squeezing her hand. "Cassie will be fine. She'll be happy to see that you're enjoying your vacation." He leaned closer and kissed her.

His lips brushed hers gently, barely grazing, teasing, erasing her worry and doubt. All she felt was peace and comfort and an insatiable desire for this hot, sexy hero who knew all the right places to touch, to kiss, to tease… Maybe she wasn't as ready to go back as she thought. Given the choice in that moment, it would be a torturous decision to make.

Diva moved into the space between them and started to circle, wagging her tail.

"Someone has to pee," Reed said, releasing her hand and tossing the bedsheet back. "I'll take her for a quick walk, pick up breakfast and be right back." He set his coffee mug on the bedside table and reached for his discarded jeans from the floor.

Erika watched as he zipped and buckled them, her

mouth salivating at the sight of him in just a pair of low-hanging denim. Damn, it was the sexiest thing she'd ever seen. He reached for his shirt, but she stopped him. "Wait!" Reaching for her cell on the table, she opened the camera app.

"Are you taking a picture of me?" His amusement was evident, but he dropped the shirt and struck a Superman pose.

She laughed as she snapped several pics.

He flexed his biceps, then turned to give her an amazing shot of his ass as he leaned against the door-frame, one arm extended overhead, accentuating those delicious-looking back and shoulder muscles. "Did you get enough or should I keep posing?" he asked over his shoulder.

"This should be good," she said, scrolling through the pics. "Something to remember you by."

Crawling back across the bed, he kissed her again. "I hope I've already given you a few things to remember," he said against her lips.

If Diva wasn't about to pee on his bed, she'd pull him back beneath the covers right now and ask for more memories. But the dog's high-pitched whine suggested they better get a move on.

"You better go." She tossed the sheet aside and stood when her phone chimed with new emails. "Wow—I haven't had good cell reception at your place and suddenly all my emails come in..." She groaned as eighty-six new ones appeared.

Nope. Definitely not ready to go back to work just yet.

"Can I use your laptop to answer a few of these?" she asked, noticing several questions from board members regarding the clinical trials. No one else on the team had been cc'd on them. They'd be expecting her usual immediate response. Maybe she should make them wait until she returned from the vacation they insisted she take. Forward them a copy of her *forced vacation* letter.

"Of course. There's no password and it connects to Wi-Fi automatically." He pulled on his shirt and a new pair of socks. "I'll be back soon. Make yourself comfortable," he said as they walked to the living room.

"I'm naked under your T-shirt—can't really get much more comfortable than that," she said with a laugh, leaning on tiptoes to kiss him again at the door.

"True enough." He tugged on his boots, grabbed Diva's leash and his coat and left the condo. "See you in a bit."

She carried her coffee to the desk and set it down right where he'd gone down on her the night before. Her cheeks flushed at the memory. It was definitely one she wouldn't forget. Nothing about him was anything she could forget.

Seeing more emails appear on her phone, she opened an internet browser and logged in to her hospital email account. She scanned them quickly, looking for urgent ones first. The first few were simple answers she could do without pulling up her notes from her own computer—questions about the selection of the trial candidates. The main criteria was a weak immune system. They were looking to help patients whose success rate was in jeopardy.

Other emails contained questions that she'd need some time to figure out. And unfortunately, they were ones that needed addressing soon.

She fought the urge to point out that this was why she didn't take time off—they had to see their mistake by now. She sighed as several more emails arrived.

She wasn't sure what Reed's plans were for the day, but suddenly, she was going to be working through these at Cassie's. The idea of not getting to spend the entire day with him disappointed her, but she'd see him later at The Drunk Tank.

Shutting down her email, a search engine icon on the bottom of the screen caught her eye. The statewide search and rescue system.

Was that what Reed was looking at the night before?

She bit her lip. It was none of her business. She wasn't a snoop. She wasn't that woman—the one who creeped her boyfriend's computer... Boyfriend? Friend? Sex addiction partner?

Sipping her coffee, she stared at the icon. What had he been looking for on the site? Information about their own mission the other night or a different one? She hit the icon and the screen lit up with a list of rescues and calls from all over Alaska.

Nothing unusual, and this was his job, after all, so why had he minimized the screen and acted secretive?

Then she noticed the search box at the top of the screen. His father's name was typed into it. George Reynolds.

He was still looking for his father? He still believed the man had gone missing? Was still missing?

Her stomach turned, the coffee in her mouth tasting bitter. She knew the truth. George wasn't missing. Three years ago, a man had come into emergency with a severed finger that needed to be reattached—a chainsaw accident in the forest where he'd been working with a nearby logging company. He'd registered under a different name, claiming to have lost his health insurance card, but she'd have recognized Cassie and Reed's dad anywhere. The man had Reed's blue eyes and the same dark hair. He had a dimple in his chin and a birthmark on his forehead. It had been him.

And the moment he saw her had confirmed it. He'd recognized her despite the years and he'd immediately requested a new surgeon to perform the reattachment. That had been fine with her. She'd been slightly shaken anyway. The way the man had abandoned his family had angered her and he was lucky the hospital had a policy of not turning anyone away.

She'd remembered the day years before, when her friend's dad hadn't shown up for his scheduled shift. For three days, they'd had search and rescue out looking for George, but there hadn't been any sign of him.

Cassie and Reed had been devastated. The lack of closure had been worst of all, but then Cassie had discovered a journal her father had kept secretly for years, talking about his depression and his unhappiness…and she'd started to believe that her father's disappearance hadn't been an accident. She had made her peace, believing her father had committed suicide, and even after her encounter with the man, Erika hadn't reached out to her to tell her any different. She'd tried a few times but hadn't been confident it was the right thing. Cassie had found her closure, and reopening old wounds seemed hurtful and unnecessary. Obviously, George had no intentions of going back to his family.

Reed had never believed his father had committed suicide. Apparently he still didn't.

He was still looking for his dad. Was that why he

was so dedicated to his position on the search and rescue team? Was he hoping one day the call would lead him to his father…or at least to an answer?

An answer *she* had.

She felt slightly nauseous. She knew the truth. But did she have the nerve to tell Reed? Would he even want to hear it? Would he believe her?

LEAVING DIVA OUTSIDE, tied to a pole and being adored by a dozen ski school kids, Reed waited at the front of Wild Blossoms for the florist. Setting their breakfast takeout on the counter, he scanned the bouquets in the freezer behind him.

All flowers looked alike to him and they seemed like a waste of money, but he wanted to surprise Erika with something and none of the other shops were open yet.

Lilies? Roses? What color said *I'm into you, don't hurt me*?

Did she even like flowers?

"Hey, Reed, how are you?" Mrs. Cartwright came from the back, carrying several poinsettias.

He rushed to help her with them. "I'm great, Mrs. C. I'm just looking for something for a…friend."

She set her poinsettia down and glanced at the bag of breakfast on the counter. "One-night stand, you mean?" She wiped her hands on her apron.

"Um…" They had had sex, but this was definitely not a one-night stand. "No. We've known each other for years actually." He glanced at the poinsettia in his arms. "Think she'd like this?"

"Is she seventy?"

"No."

"Then probably not. Besides, you can't have these around Diva."

Right. "Well, I'm open to suggestions."

Picking up her glasses, she slid them on, approaching the freezer. "Well, what kind of flowers does she like?"

Reed shrugged. "She doesn't strike me as someone who'd like roses... Would daisies seem too cheap?"

"Do you want to have sex with her again?"

He blushed. Discussing his sex life with the eighty-two-year-old woman who'd known him since he was ten was a little weird. "I'd like that very much, yes," he mumbled.

"Okay. What's her favorite color?"

"Not sure." She wore a lot of red. The more vibrant the shade the better. It contrasted beautifully with her dark hair and eyes...

"Her birthday?"

Shit. He should know this one. But he couldn't remember her ever having a birthday party. Too bad he couldn't text Cass—she'd know all of this. He bit his lip. "Sometime in summer, I think?"

Mrs. Cartwright rolled her eyes. "What are her hobbies? What is she into?"

"She's a workaholic, so I don't think she has any." He was confident in that answer at least.

The older lady sighed. "I have just the thing."

"I knew you would."

Going behind the counter, she picked up a small hardcover book and handed it to him. "This is for you. Not her."

Things You Should Know About a Woman Before

Sleeping With Her. Romance Advice from Fifty Years of Marriage. Written by Mrs. C.

Reed cleared his throat. "Right. Thank you," he said, tucking the book into his coat pocket.

"That will be sixteen dollars," she said.

"What? I thought it was a gift?" He reached for his wallet.

"There's solid gold relationship advice in that book—that shit's not free."

He laughed. "I'm sure it's worth every penny." And she did have a point. For knowing Erika almost his entire life, he didn't know much about her.

Though that wasn't entirely true. He knew how to please her in bed, knew how to get under her skin, knew how dedicated she was to her career, how driven and passionate she was. He may need to find out some of these other superficial things, too, but he did know her, despite what Mrs. C might think.

He placed the cash on the counter and reached for the takeout bag.

"One more piece of advice that's not in the book?" she asked, stopping him.

"Will it cost me?"

"This one's free."

"In that case, hit me."

"A one-night stand gets takeout. A friend you're falling in love with gets a home-cooked meal," she said with a wink.

Damn, she was right. "Enjoy," he said, leaving the food on the counter and heading outside. "Change of plans, Diva. We're headed to the grocery store."

Twenty minutes later, he juggled the tray of coffee and the bags in his arms as he entered his apartment.

"I hope you can wait a little longer for breakfast," he said, seeing Erika sitting at the island in his kitchen. She was dressed already, which was a mild disappointment. He'd been hoping to eat, then climb back into bed with her.

"Um...actually, Reed, I'm going to have to pass on breakfast," she said, standing and walking toward him.

He set the bags on the counter and handed her a coffee. "Why? Don't trust my cooking?"

She smiled but something felt off. His gut twisted.

"Hey, everything okay?" he asked, wrapping his arms around her waist and pulling her closer.

She held back slightly, keeping her coffee cup between them. "Yes, everything's fine. Just work, that's all."

She was definitely preoccupied. "Well, you're more than welcome to use my laptop, and I'll cook as quietly as I can. Let me feed you, at least." This awkward tension hadn't been there an hour ago.

Maybe he should have gotten the flowers anyway.

She shook her head. "I should get back to Cassie's. I need to make some phone calls and this could take a while."

Be cool. She said everything's fine.

"Okay, no problem."

She touched his cheek and some of the tension evaporated. "A rain check on breakfast?"

"My kitchen's always open." And his bedroom and unfortunately his heart.

She kissed him softly and he tightened his hold on her for just a second before releasing her. "I'll see you later?"

"Yes."

She grabbed her coat and slid her feet into her boots. "Come on, Diva," she said, taking the dog's leash and heading toward the door.

"Hey, Erika. What kind of flowers do you like?"

She frowned as she opened the door. "Flowers remind me of funerals."

Dodged a bullet there.

CHAPTER SIXTEEN

ERIKA'S HASTY EXIT had him stressing all day as he worked at the station, organizing the new gear that had arrived. Reed accepted the fact that she was busy, but there was something different in her demeanor when he'd returned from walking Diva. He wasn't sure what he'd done, and he was trying his best not to be paranoid, but something was definitely different in her gaze, her kiss and her goodbye.

"Hey, man, I thought you were taking the day off," Tyler said, entering the station.

"I was going to, but there's a lot to do around here..." He glanced past him to see a flatbed pull up into the garage. He frowned. "What's that?"

"For the float."

He'd forgotten the station was entering a float into the town's Christmas parade the following weekend. They usually joined forces with the fire department, but this year they had a friendly rivalry going on for most creative display. The parade was one of the highlights of the season in Wild River. As kids, Reed and Cassie's dad used to take them every year. Reed had stopped going after his dad disappeared, the tradition just not the same without him. He'd probably opt out of the float construction. Hopefully, Erika would help keep his extra time occupied...

"You okay?"

He nodded. "Yeah, I'm fine." He suppressed a yawn.

"Late night?" Tyler asked with a knowing grin.

"What do you know about it?" He could blame his mood on lack of sleep the night before, but he knew that wasn't it. Though, he probably should call it a day and get some rest. He'd be useless if he was needed on a call or at the bar that evening. He was hoping to avoid both. The snow had picked up throughout the morning and the howling wind made it a great opportunity to stay inside under the covers all evening with Erika. He'd had her three times the night before and just the thought of her made him instantly hard again.

He hadn't known his body capable of coming so many times in one night, but his need for Erika had surprised him.

Cassie's reaction to them together was still a concern, but he knew despite her annoyance, she'd be happy that they were happy. And he hoped his sister didn't mind PDAs because keeping his hands and lips off Erika, no matter who was around, just wasn't happening.

Same went for his crew at the station. Tyler in particular.

The guy shrugged. "Nothing, man...just fucking with you. Someone's in a shitty mood," he said to Tiffany, the crew member in charge of the Christmas float.

She frowned and tossed an armful of tangled lights onto the desk. "I thought you were finally getting some."

Shit, did everyone know? Well, if they thought he was in a bad mood now, they'd really have to put up with his crappy attitude once Erika left. "I think I'm going to head out." As annoying as they were, they were right. But it wasn't the marathon sex and lack of sleep making him so grumpy, it was Erika's exit that morning and the fact that he'd yet to hear from her.

The blaring of the station phone made his stomach drop. The number for the state troopers' office lit up the display. So much for sleeping off his shitty mood.

"Wild River Search and Rescue. This is Reed." He cradled the phone between his ear and shoulder as he grabbed the printout that came over the fax machine.

"Sorry to have to tell you this, Reed, but it's your sister's camping group. We just received a 911 call for assistance on the east side of Chugach Mountain."

His heart all but stopped.

"Her group is trapped in avalanche territory. We had contact for about three minutes, but we lost cell reception. I couldn't make out their exact coordinates or determine if anyone was injured. This weather is messing with the phone lines. Can your crew find out all the info they can and begin the search?"

His throat was as dry as sandpaper. "Yes, of course. We're on it," he said, hanging up the phone and immediately dialing Snow Trek Tours.

"What's going on?" Tyler asked.

He handed him the printout with the info as he waited for one of Cassie's employees to answer the damn phone. Cassie always left detailed plans of each tour in her office in case of emergency—where the group was headed, their planned trails in and out of camp, and the stats on everyone participating. All the information they'd need would be in her trip folder.

Answer the damn phone!

Was no one working that day? Six rings then voice mail.

He hung up and immediately redialed, trying to remember which of the tour guides were going on the winter camping trip with Cass and how many people in total they'd be searching for. Unfortunately, the details were fuzzy. He'd been preoccupied by staring at her friend when she'd talked about the trip the other night in the bar.

No answer.

He ran a hand through his hair and, grabbing his cell, he dialed Erika next. They didn't have time to waste.

She answered on the second ring. "Hi... I was just about to call you."

The relief he'd have felt at her words three minutes ago didn't come. "Hi. Listen, I'm wondering if you could do something for me..." He didn't wait for an answer. "Cassie leaves a spare office key for Snow Trek Tours on the hook near the door. The keyring is a picture of Diva in a...in a tutu." His sister was insane...but right now she was in trouble and his mind and pulse were frantic.

"I found them," Erika said. "What's wrong?"

"We just got a call that her camping crew needs assistance. They're caught in this weather. We have no details, so I need your help. Can you go to the office and look through her files for info about this trip? Anything you can find about number of campers and their hiking plans...anything." His usually clear head was fuzzy and his hand shook slightly. He forced a breath. If he ever needed to remain calm and in control, it was now. "There should be a file labeled with the name of the company and this week's date."

"Yes, of course," she said and he could already hear the wind howling through the phone. "I'll find it."

"I'll be there to meet you right away. Start searching for whatever you can find."

"Okay…and you know I'm coming with you."

He didn't have time to argue and it would be futile anyway. His own worry echoed in Erika's voice. "I'll be there soon."

CASSIE'S ORGANIZATIONAL SKILLS hadn't improved much over the years. As Erika sorted through the files on her messy desk, she mentally lectured her friend. Employee time sheets…new survival skills training brochures…a file labeled Frankie's Construction Weeklong. All she could find on the desk were folders from trips several weeks before.

File shit away when you're done with it, Cass!

Pile after pile of paper, there was nothing.

She grabbed the inbox and started riffling through the papers there. Expansion details to acquire the space next door, several résumés…a bunch of invoices and statements…

She paused at one. A payment sent to the Anchorage Addictions Treatment Center? She scanned it quickly, suppressing a feeling of guilt. She shouldn't be snooping but she couldn't help herself. Cass wasn't struggling with addictions…her mother?

Intake and Thirty-Day Treatment for George Reynolds.

Her father? Cassie knew the man was alive and she was paying for his addiction treatment? Erika hadn't thought it possible for her heart rate to increase even more. She was wrong.

Did Reed know about this? He couldn't, if he was still searching for his dad. Cassie was keeping knowledge about her father's whereabouts—the truth—from her brother. Erika's gut twisted and her palms sweat. This was not good, and it was knowledge she wished she didn't have.

Damn it, why had she read the invoice?

She had to shake it off. They had more important things to focus on right now.

Stuffing the papers back into the inbox, she stood and opened the file cabinet to her right. Sitting on top, unfiled, was the folder she was looking for. Harbor Financial's Corporate Winter Camping Retreat. She opened it quickly and saw the signed registration form from the company, signed waivers from eight participants and the three-day camping schedule.

Thank God she'd found it.

Reed sounded his horn twice as he pulled up outside. She glanced up in time to see him jump out of the truck and head toward the door.

Her gaze landed on the addictions treatment center invoice and conflicting emotions swirled through her. Cassie might be able to keep the truth from Reed, but could she? It had taken all her strength that morning not to mention her own run-in with the man at the hospital. Her sudden change in mood and her hasty exit had confused him, but she couldn't be with him and keep the information to herself. She'd wanted to talk to Cass first... Now, she wasn't sure her friend would be her ally in telling Reed.

First they had to find her, and Reed had enough to

deal with right now. Hurrying to meet him at the door, she waved the folder. "I have it."

"Everything's there?"

She nodded. "Everything you need to know right now is in here," she said, locking the door and avoiding his gaze.

A THICK SNOW veil blinded them as they took the Ski-Doos through the trails toward the campsite zone listed in Cassie's file. Since the group wouldn't be officially missing for several more hours—their return time was scheduled for that evening—they weren't treating the mission as a search and rescue. Right now, it was deemed a call for assistance, therefore Wade was back at the station preparing to call the emergency contacts of the campers if he didn't get word that everyone was safe by six o'clock.

Wind blew her hair away from her face and tree branches whipped against her legs and arms as Erika held on to Reed on the back of the Ski-Doo. His breakneck speed through the trail was slightly terrifying, but she wished he'd go faster. Cassie's interrupted call to the state trooper hadn't given them much to work with, and they had no idea if anyone was seriously injured or if the group was snowed in and unable to make their way out without assistance. Erika's heart and mind were a mess. She'd only reconnected with her friend days before—she had to be okay.

Winter camping was a crazy idea to her and while she knew the unpredicted snow and avalanche warning wasn't Cassie's fault, she was irrationally annoyed with her friend.

Or maybe it had to do with the secret Cassie was keeping from Reed.

A secret they were *both* keeping.

Damn! Her life had gone from simple—work, eat, sleep, repeat—to conflicted, chaotic and confusing in a matter of days. Getting emotionally involved meant getting hurt. She had hardened herself against that possibility with her career, then she'd taken a break from her life and had opened herself up to all kinds of potential pain.

The roaring of the Ski-Doos racing through the trails drowned out the beating in her chest, but she was certain Reed could feel it pressed against his back. She held him tighter, hoping to reassure him that things would be okay. Or was it to reassure herself?

A moment later, they stopped the Ski-Doos at the site where Cassie's group had been camping. She got off the Ski-Doo and stood silently, scanning the area with the rest of the crew. Tent marks on the ground, partially covered by snow already... Footprints practically buried and an old campfire that had been put out hours ago. Several logs still sat around it, gathering their own light dusting of powder. The clearing was surrounded by trees and in the distance she could hear a water source. Nothing appeared to be out of order and there were no clues to any trouble the group may have run into.

"They were scheduled to leave here today at 10:00 a.m. and walk out through the south backwoods trail...along the mountain peaks," Reed said, reading the file. "But in this weather, Cassie would have checked the updated avalanche advisory system and seen it go from caution to danger."

"Not if the weather impacted her signal," Tank said.

The guy looked as white as the snow and, while they were all worried about their friend and her group, Erika suspected Tank was feeling the anxiety more than some of the others. The man obviously had strong feelings for her friend. Would this be the catalyst needed to make him finally act on those feelings once they found Cassie? Erika refused to believe there'd be any other outcome that day. She was staying positive, despite the dark clouds looming overhead and the heavy snowfall.

"Even if she couldn't get confirmation, I think she'd be aware of the danger of hiking south out along the mountain ridge as planned. I know Cass and I think she'd take the alternate route listed in the file," Reed said.

Tank nodded. "I hope so."

So did Erika. Big blankets of snow on the mountains looked treacherous, seemingly dangling from the peaks like marshmallows melting over a campfire. If they decided to give way, things would get so much worse—fast.

"The call came into the station at 11:56...almost two hours ago, so they might be as far as Canyon Ridge by now if they did take the mountain ridge trails," Tyler said.

Reed nodded as he stared at the snow-covered mountains to the south. "She must have known not to go that way. I'm sure they would have taken the north trails."

Erika thought his voice held a note of hopeful optimism, but it masked a layer of uncertainty. He was obviously struggling with his belief in his sister's abilities.

"But I think we need to cover both trails just in case," Reed said.

Tiffany nodded. "Okay, why don't I lead the support team members along the north?"

The least experienced members. They should definitely go the safer route—no question. The last thing they needed was more emergencies that day.

Reed nodded. "Yes. And Tyler, Tank, Cruz and I will go along the south."

"What about me?" Erika asked.

"You're with Tiffany's group," he said.

"No. I'm going with you guys."

"No, you're not. You're not an official crew member…"

"Stop. We are not doing this shit. Cassie is my best friend and I'm a doctor—if someone is hurt out there, I'm your best ally." Cocky, arrogant, she didn't care how she was coming across. She'd just gotten Reed and Cassie back in her life. The idea that they could be in trouble or injured and she wouldn't be there to help would drive her crazy.

Reed walked toward her, obviously pained with a similar dilemma. "Look, my sister means everything to me…and now you are…becoming someone I care deeply about. I'm not putting your life at risk."

"It's not your decision. If you say no, I'll follow you anyway." Hard-faced, she met his stubborn stare.

"If you get hurt…"

"Then I'll fix myself up. Let's go," she said with more bravado than she felt. The south mountain trails looked terrifying as shit. On a clear, sunny day she wasn't sure she'd feel confident hiking them, and on a day like today there'd be no chance in hell, but her friend needed help. The man she was falling in love with wasn't doing this without her.

"I want her with us," Tank said, joining them.

Her chest swelled with pride in the man's confidence in her.

"Me, too," said Tyler.

She stared at Reed.

"Fine." He reached for his backpack from the Ski-Doo and gave some final instructions to Tiffany's group as they headed toward the north trails. Then he turned to the rest of them. "We walk in. Noise and vibrations of the Ski-Doos will only make the avalanche conditions worse."

They all nodded, gathering their gear.

"Tyler, as we walk, please give Erika a crash course in her avalanche gear. There's a beacon, probe and shovel in her backpack."

"Will do," Tyler said.

Beacon, probe and shovel. She knew what a shovel was at least. Tyler had better be a quick teacher. Though she hoped she wouldn't have to use any of it.

"Don't worry. It's not brain surgery," Tyler said with a small smile. "If kids can learn this stuff quickly, you'll have no problem. Just stay close and I'll explain everything."

She nodded.

"Quietly, we move. No unnecessary talking. No noise. Silent steps," Reed said, checking his watch. "Mandatory breaks at every two hours."

Everyone nodded.

He glanced at her, and the silent worry in his eyes was stronger than she'd ever seen it before. This rescue had personal stakes.

She sent him her best reassuring nod, but the twisting in her gut grew stronger by the second. They hadn't had time to smooth over the abrupt, awkward way they'd left things that morning.

But there would be time to talk, to figure things out. This mission would be successful.

It had to be.

CHAPTER SEVENTEEN

FOUR HOURS LATER, they'd arrived at the end of the south trails, the road at the edge of the forest was coming into view and there had been no sign of Cassie or any of the campers along the way. Reed wasn't sure whether to feel relieved or even more nervous. Maybe they had taken the north trails out. Maybe they were back at the village by now. Safe. It beat thinking about the alternative—that they'd somehow gotten off trail and were stranded in avalanche territory now that the warning had reached critical. As they'd hiked, three snowslides had occurred on mountains in the distance and each one had brought a new sense of urgency.

He brushed the snow off his jacket and, reaching for his radio, called Tiffany. "Any news?" They hadn't heard from the other team in hours.

"No. We reached the trail's end ten minutes ago. No sign of them. No recent tracks to suggest they'd gone this way either…but the snow is falling so fast, it would be hard to see footprints…"

His stomach fell. They weren't safe. Despite Tiffany's attempt to make him feel better, his gut told them Cass wasn't waiting back at the station. Brother's intuition told him finding his sister wasn't going to be that easy.

"How would you like us to proceed?" she asked.

"Try the West Loop trail."

"That would have added hours to the trip… I don't think…"

"Just do it." The harshness in his voice wasn't intended. "Sorry, just…try it, okay." If they weren't on the north trails and they weren't on the south, where the hell were they?

Which way did you go, Cass?

He turned to his team and shook his head. "We need to double back and move in closer to the Chugach Mountain." He glanced at Erika. She was nodding her agreement with everyone else.

Why in the hell was she out here in this unpredictable storm?

The entire four-hour trek, his instincts had been on high alert. He had to find Cassie and her group, but he also had to protect his own team…including the woman he was falling in love with.

He followed behind the rest and she walked alongside Tyler, who continued to quietly brief her on procedure and actions in the event that the mountains did give way. For the first time, jealousy wasn't among his emotions. He knew how she felt about him and right now, they were all putting their lives at risk. They were all in this together. Tyler was the best instructor they had on avalanche safety.

As they moved farther south, toward the dangerous peaks, his radio sounded.

He held up a hand to halt the group.

"Wade, give me good news." Was it too much to hope that the group had made it back via another route?

"We got a tip from air patrol. A signal flare just went up forty feet from Canyon Ridge…"

A flare. Good to locate the group. Not so great in an

avalanche. His sister knew the risks of setting one off in these conditions so someone in her group must be hurt.

He quickly checked the camping file. Canyon Ridge was nowhere near the group's planned course. What the hell was his sister doing? She lived out here in these woods and she knew the dangers. There was no way this was a mistake. She couldn't have gotten turned around. Even in a snowstorm, his sister could navigate these backlands blindfolded.

"Okay, we are headed toward Canyon Ridge. We are going to have to start moving up the mountain, where the flare came from," he told the group, falling into step next to Erika. He'd brought along an extra search and rescue jacket for her this time, knowing it would be warmer if they were still out there by nightfall. In it, she looked like part of the team. And while his protective instincts told him he could never handle her being on these missions all the time…he felt more confident with her next to him. If one of Cassie's campers was injured, having her there would be an asset.

But his conflicted heart was something else he had to deal with. As soon as this was over and everyone was safe, they needed to talk.

THE FIRST SNOWSLIDE happened twenty minutes into the backwoods search.

Watching from fifty feet away, Reed held up a hand to halt the group as loose snow descended the mountain, a tidal wave getting wider as it traveled toward the base. "A sluff," he told the group.

Tyler had mentioned that those were some of the more common slides and they were rarely deadly. But from where Erika was standing, watching the snow pick up speed and size as it cascaded down the mountain, it didn't exactly look safe for anyone standing beneath it. A broken bone or being trapped beneath may not be deadly, but it wouldn't be much fun.

Reed checked the area for more loose snow and a few minutes later, they continued their slow-moving upward trek.

Had anyone ever told her that she'd be climbing a mountain in the middle of an avalanche warning, she'd have said they were insane.

Six hours in and her body felt the exhaustion of their efforts. The higher they climbed, the thinner the air and the worse the visibility. Snow was still falling in big, thick flakes, the wind tossing them around in swirling loops before they could land on the ground. Milder temperatures that week had made the snow damp and heavy but as it started to get dark and the temperature dropped below freezing, things were getting slippery.

"Wade is calling families now. It's officially time to call this a search," Reed said, his anxiety evident in his voice and stress etched on his handsome face.

As they slowly, cautiously moved higher, Erika could hear the deep rumbling of more sluffs in the distance, and her confidence waned. She wasn't trained to be out there. Tyler's crash course in avalanche safety had practically gone in one ear and out the other in her worried state.

Would I remember any of it if I needed to use it?

She clutched the straps of her backpack, hoping that at the very least, she didn't hinder the search. She didn't want to become a liability to the group. Everyone was exhausted and worried and the weather was really taking its toll. During the day had been difficult enough, but now as a heavy dusk settled over the trees and the temperature plummeted, their hopes of finding the group were waning. She'd heard Tyler mention something about setting up camp and resuming in the morning, but Reed was pushing on.

Tank was quiet, his fear written on his face.

Man, if Cass could see the guy now, it would erase all doubt about how he feels about her.

"I see red," Tank said, breaking his silence seconds later. "Over there, beyond that peak." He pointed to the left of them, several feet higher. "It could be a jacket."

Reed moved closer, climbing higher for a better view, and a second later he was waving them all forward. "I see the group. That was Cass," he said.

Tank's face, which had yet to show anything other than a deep fear, relaxed into a look of relief. Then, it quickly turned to one of determined focus as they hurried toward the group.

Erika did a quick count as brightly colored ski clothing came into view. Twelve. Cassie's file had listed eight corporate people and two guides, including her. They'd obviously picked up some hikers along the way.

Cassie must have heard them approach because she turned as they drew closer and she hurried over to them. "We have an injured hiker... Fell through a slab avalanche a hundred feet to this spot. My group saw the beacon as we were trekking out this morning," she said.

The worry and relief on her friend's face made a lump rise in Erika's throat. She was okay.

"So, you're okay? Your group is okay?" Reed asked, hugging her quickly.

She nodded. "We're fine. I hurt my foot on the trek

up here, but it's nothing serious. Probably just a sprain. But the injured man has broken bones and we can't get a litter in here without sending these mountains into a free fall," she said, casting a glance at the ominous snow peaks above them.

They needed to move fast and get the hell out of there.

"He's gone into shock and right now, we're all just trying to keep him from passing out."

"Where is he?" Erika asked. This was something she could help with. She pushed fear aside and focused on her medical training. This was the reason she was here.

Cassie led the way to the injured man, who was lying on several sleeping bags on the ground. His legs were clearly broken and one shoulder looked dislocated, his arm lying at a weird angle beside him. His head had several large gashes and blood covered his cheeks. He was covered as best as they could in bags and heated blankets, but moving him or trying to assess injuries was nearly impossible.

Fixing a broken clavicle on a conscious man was one thing. These injuries were hours old and the guy was in shock. Her professional oath wouldn't allow her to attempt anything here.

She pulled Reed aside. "This guy is barely hanging on. We have no idea the extent of his injuries. I'd like to help, but it's too dangerous to do anything out here." Even just removing the blankets from his body could cause further damage to him right now. He hadn't moved in hours, and his body wasn't self-heating.

"I agree. We have to get him airlifted out of here, but first we have to get him away from the high-danger avalanche zone. A chopper this close will certainly do more damage than good. We could all be snowed in."

More rumbling of shifting, falling snow in the distance confirmed his words. The sluffs may not be deadly, but they were dangerous enough and an injured person in shock would slow them down considerably. It was going to take several hours to get to a clearing. They all needed to mentally prepare for the trek ahead.

"Tank, I'm going to need your muscles, man," Reed said.

Tyler and Cruz had already started to assemble their best version of a litter out of blankets and sleeping bags. Everything was wet and heavy and the guy weighed at least two hundred pounds. This wasn't going to be an easy trek out.

Tank nodded. "Tell me what you need."

Within moments, Tank, Tyler, Reed and Asher—the injured hiker's friend—lifted him carefully in a hammock-style litter and the group began to make their way back to safer territory.

"These hikers were lucky you guys were in the area," Erika told Cassie. Her annoyance at her friend had dissipated the moment she saw her. She still had questions, but they could wait.

"Yeah, we saw the avalanche indicator this morning and decided to start our trek out earlier than planned, along the north trails where it was safer... We were making good time, but once we saw the beacon, the entire group decided that the best thing to do would be to check it out. I don't usually bring my camping clients out in this weather," she said, looking slightly distraught. "And I certainly don't try to turn them into search and rescue, but no one wanted to leave anyone out here."

Obviously Cassie was doubting her actions. "You

couldn't have predicted this freak snowstorm or this mild weather," Erika said, touching her friend's shoulder. "And you all did the right thing. Who knows how long these hikers could have been out here alone. There's no way Asher could have gotten his friend out by himself." She glanced at the man in the litter, now out cold. She hoped they weren't already too late. The extent of his injuries was bad and there could be more they didn't know about. He trembled beneath the heated blankets, and her practical, professional side suggested they were too late, but for the first time in her life, she refused to believe it. Yet.

A loud cracking sound blasted behind them and they turned in time to see the side of the mountain fracture just feet away...

The ground broke into large pieces and gave way beneath two of Cassie's campers, sending them sliding down the mountain between the cracks.

"Move!"

She wasn't sure who voiced the command, but they were all instantly running away from the cracking mountainside, down toward where the two campers had disappeared.

Erika could barely feel her legs beneath her as she ran alongside Cassie. She could barely breathe. Her pulse raced as she stumbled along the uneven, slippery trail, desperate to get away from the unpredictable terrain beneath their feet.

Silently praying they could find the two at the bottom.

After what felt like forever, they reached the base and relief ran through her when Reed located the two men immediately. Then her knees felt weak as she approached to assist. Both of the men had cuts on their heads and one man's wrist was clearly broken, the bone protruding from the skin in his arm, but her focus was on the other man on the ground...turning pale. His eyes were wide and his hand was around his neck.

He was struggling for air.

"He can't breathe," Cassie said, panic in her voice.

"Is he choking?" Reed asked.

"No." Erika had seen footage of a similar injury during her premed days. "Blunt force can fracture the cervical spine—C2 and C3..." Time was the enemy in this case. She dropped to the ground next to the man and tore off her gloves. "Can you speak?"

He shook his head, his eyes widened with fear. No air was getting into his lungs.

She carefully felt his spine along the base of his neck. She was 99 percent sure she was right.

He would die without a tracheotomy.

Oh God, she couldn't believe she had to do this.

She'd only ever performed the procedure in a sterile, safe, surgical environment. What if she was wrong? There were too many unsafe conditions...too many unknowns...

She did know this man couldn't breathe and at that moment, that was the only "known" she needed.

She forced a deep breath as he gripped her hands, silently begging for help. He had seconds.

Oh shit. "I need something sharp and a tube—a pen or a straw..." She kept her gaze locked on the man as she extended a hand to the group, waiting for someone to hand her what she needed.

Nothing. They all seemed to be in a trance.

"Hey! Wake up! All of you need to help. I'm going to perform a trache—something sharp and a tube now!"

Cassie instantly handed her a pocketknife.

Great. Reaching for her canteen of hot water, she sterilized it as best she could under the circumstances, then glanced at the group. If someone had a better idea, they could speak up any second now.

Nothing.

"I still need a tube… Cassie, sterilize your Shewee—fast."

Her friend quickly retrieved it and did as she was instructed, then handed it to Erika.

She swallowed hard, but one look at the guy's bluish lips told her she had no time.

Cutting a small gash into his lower neck below his Adam's apple, she quickly jammed the tube into the hole she'd created, as a stream of blood dripped down his neck.

The flow of air was instant and the man's body collapsed in relief.

Scurrying to her feet, Erika hurried away and threw up in the snow.

CHAPTER EIGHTEEN

"ARE YOU OKAY?" Reed asked for the tenth time as they arrived at Wild River Community Hospital. An hour ago, the group had made the call for the chopper, despite the avalanche risks. There were far too many injuries and too many lives at stake to postpone the pickup until they'd reached safer ground. Luckily, the mountains had cooperated and the group had been airlifted out without further disasters.

"Yes, I'm fine. I promise," Erika said. Color was slowly returning to her cheeks, but Reed still worried. The emergency tracheotomy had to be the most life-threatening situation he'd ever faced on a mission, and thank God Erika had been there. Her quick thinking had saved the man's life.

And damn, if he wasn't so very grateful for her.

Grateful and a million other things.

He grabbed her hand and held her back from the rest of the crew as they entered the hospital.

"What's wrong?"

"Nothing… I just need to do this," he said, pulling her into his arms and brushing her hair away from her face.

Her eyes widened. "We have an audience and I'm kinda covered in blood."

From the corner of his eye, he saw the crew members watching…saw his sister's surprised expression as she leaned on Tank to hobble inside, but he didn't care. All day, he'd felt tense and uneasy about how Erika had left that morning. He'd been desperately on edge throughout the search and now all he wanted, all he needed was her. To kiss her, to touch her…to show her that in such a short time, he'd fallen for her. "Let them watch," he said. Holding her face between his hands, he lowered his lips to hers.

She closed her eyes as their mouths connected and at least some of the tension of the day eased from his shoulders as she returned his kiss with passion and eagerness.

He'd missed kissing her. Missed the feel of her in his arms. And now that everyone was safe and alive, he just wanted to hold her close and savor the feelings coursing through him.

Right now, he didn't want to think about the what-ifs plaguing him or about the fact that their time together was quickly coming to an end. He just wanted to breathe easy knowing the hellish day was over.

"We should go inside," she said, pulling away a second later. "I want to check on Cass. I heard her cry out in pain as we ran down the mountainside and I'm pretty sure her foot is broken."

Everyone had received a few injuries today. His entire body ached, and this one would definitely go down as the most challenging rescue mission the group had faced. "Okay." Taking her face between his hands, he said, "And don't question yourself or your actions—not even for a second. You saved that guy's life."

She nodded, but her forehead wrinkled and she bit her lip.

Luckily, hours later, Dr. Smyth agreed with him.

"You'll have to teach me how you assessed the situation that quickly and effectively," he said, taking her hand.

She shook her head and gave an unsteady laugh. "I have no idea."

"She was incredible out there," Reed said. His admiration for her must be written all over his face, but he didn't care. He had no intentions of hiding his feelings for her from anyone.

"I just did what I had to," she said, looking embarrassed by the praise.

"They have him in recovery already and he's on anti-infection drugs for the incision. He'll have surgery tomorrow, but for now, he's doing fine. He was very lucky you were there," the older doctor said.

"Thank you, Dr. Smyth. That means a lot coming from you."

"What about the other hiker—the one who fell through the slab avalanche?" Reed asked.

"He's in surgery now to reset the bones in his legs and shoulder. It's going to be a tough road to recovery for him, but his friend is doing okay. They'll both be okay. Your sister took a risk helping them, but she saved their lives, for sure. You all did," he said, tapping Reed on the shoulder.

Then, turning his attention back to Erika, he hesitated before saying, "Tom's wife is here... She'd like to thank you, as well."

Reed expected her to hesitate or turn and run, but once again she surprised him. "A thank-you isn't necessary, but I can talk to her about what happened and why I did the tracheotomy."

Dr. Smyth smiled. "That would be great." He turned to Reed and nodded, seeming to give him credit for Erika's change of heart. It was unwarranted. Reed had nothing to do with it, but he'd seen the gradual change in her that week. "Can I borrow her for a few minutes?" he asked.

Reed nodded, squeezing her hand quickly before letting it go. "As long as I get her back."

AFTER A QUICK trip to the washroom to clean herself up, Erika followed Dr. Smyth down the hall toward Tom's room. She had no idea what to say. She was more nervous now than she had been on the mountain.

You'll just explain your actions. Simple. Straightforward. Easy.

Dr. Smyth gave her a quick hug at the door. "Stay as long as you want."

She took a deep breath as she entered.

Tom lay in the bed, hooked to the monitors and an IV dripping anti-infection drugs, a large bandage covering his throat. He wouldn't be able to talk until weeks after his surgery but he was okay. Next to him, a woman in a thick winter coat, with short blond hair, sat with her back to the door, but she turned hearing Erika enter.

"Hi, I'm Erika."

"Dr. Sheraton," Tom's wife said, rushing to hug her, new tears filling her eyes. She squeezed her so hard, it nearly knocked the wind from her lungs. "Thank you for saving his life."

She nodded, unable to speak. Her gaze landed on the strand of twinkling red-and-green lights in the hospital window and emotions strangled her. Losing a loved one any time of year was hard, but Christmas would have been heartbreaking.

The woman pulled back. "I don't know what I would have done if I'd lost him. We have kids. It's Christmas…" Her voice broke. "You are truly an angel," she said, wiping a tear from her cheek.

"I'm glad I was there," Erika said, approaching the bed. "This guy really didn't leave me a whole lot of choice in my actions." She should clarify her thought process for them, explain how she'd identified the problem so quickly…but right now, verbalizing how she assessed the need for the emergency tracheotomy was difficult. None of that seemed to matter right now. Just that he was alive. "I apologize if any infections…"

Tom silenced her by reaching for her hand and squeezing it. He smiled, only gratitude reflecting in his tired-looking eyes, and she held his hand tight. She didn't need to say anything. Didn't need to explain.

She'd done the right thing. Saving his life *and* being there now.

"OKAY, WHAT'S GOING on with you and my brother?" Turning in the front seat of Tank's truck, Cassie gave her a knowing look.

Erika's heart raced. She had no idea. Dating? Having sex? Friends? More than friends? And of course Reed wasn't there to add any clarification to her frazzled mind. He'd had to go back to the station to finish the paperwork and debrief the crew. She and Tank had stayed at the hospital with Cassie. Her foot was broken in three places, and the doctor didn't know how she'd been able to walk at all during the rescue.

Now Erika was sitting on the hot seat alone, fending

off questions from her friend. She should have gone with Reed.

"Me and Reed?" Guilt had to be plastered all over her face. Before the avalanche, they'd been questioning how Cassie would react to the news of them...together... now, Erika wasn't so sure her friend needed anything else that could potentially stress her out.

All of the corporate retreat people were doing okay, including Tom, and the company had signed waivers releasing Snow Trek Tours from injuries caused by acts of nature, therefore her friend wouldn't have to deal with any lawsuits, but Erika knew she still felt responsible for bringing them along on the rescue to help the hikers.

Adding this bombshell didn't feel right.

But her friend laughed. "No, you and my *other* brother. Yes, you and Reed!"

"Nothing?" Could she get away with that?

Cassie turned to Tank. "So, Reed's kissing everyone like that after rescues now?"

Tank shrugged. "As long as he keeps his lips off me..."

Cassie stared at her.

The pressure was too much. "Okay, fine... Something's going on. I'm not really sure what." That was the truth. She had no idea what was happening, except that her feelings for him were getting stronger each minute she spent with him. It was more than just sexual attraction...but she had no idea if it was love. She'd never been in love before. Was she supposed to feel this conflicted and slightly nauseous? Excited but definitely overwhelmed? Torn between what she wanted and what she saw happening realistically?

"There was a sexual energy between you both during the rescue—I could feel it the moment you all arrived."

"I think that was just nervous energy you were feeling." Letting her friend know that she'd gotten close to her brother was one thing. Admitting that they were having sex might be a little too much. She didn't have a brother, but if she did, she doubted that she'd want to hear about his sex life.

Which kinda sucked, because she wished she could tell her friend all about the mind-blowing experiences she'd had with Reed.

"Okay, maybe, but definitely afterward there was a vibe between you two, and that kiss outside the hospital—holy fucking shit."

Holy fucking shit was the perfect description.

But Erika was shaking her head no. Just kept shaking her head no.

"We all saw it," Cassie said.

"We were all very tired after the rescue…" Would her friend believe she was so exhausted and in pain that her imagination had exaggerated the kiss?

"Come on. Tank, you saw it, too, right?"

The guy glanced at Erika through the rearview mirror and she kept shaking her head no. Word about the night she and Reed had spent together at the station had obviously traveled through the group, but he just shrugged. "I didn't sense anything between them," he said.

Cassie shot her a look as if to say "No shit, he doesn't sense anything between us either," and sighed.

"I mean it was just a kiss. Reed's hooked up with tourists before," Tank said, winking at her in the rearview.

Too far, Tank.

She glared at him, hating that it was probably true. Was that all she was—another hookup? She didn't believe that.

Tank returned his attention to the road.

"Fine," Cassie said, "Keep lying to a woman who could have died yesterday." She turned back around in her seat as they pulled up in front of her condo.

Tank immediately jumped down from the truck and hurried around to the passenger side. Opening the door, he effortlessly scooped Cassie into his arms.

"I can wa…" Cassie started to protest. "Actually, never mind."

Erika grinned as her friend wrapped her arms around Tank's neck and he carried her up the stairs. A memory of her first night there, when Reed had carried her drunken ass up those stairs, flashed in her exhausted mind.

How were they going to keep spending time together unless they came clean to Cass? Told her everything?

And there was another conversation she needed to have with her friend, as well. She wasn't sure which one would be harder.

Tank stepped back to allow Cassie to unlock the door, and immediately Diva came hurrying forward. In the emergency, no one had remembered to check on the poor dog, and she whimpered with happy relief, dancing around Tank's legs.

"Sorry, Diva, we all forgot about you," Erika said. Bending, she lifted the puppy to Cassie.

"Hi, Diva! How's my girl?" her friend's excited, high-pitched voice had the dog going crazy in Erika's arms.

The puppy yelped happily, licking Cassie's face. "Did you miss me? Did you?"

The dog squirmed, excited to see her owner back safe and sound, her tail wagging so fast it whipped against Erika's arms.

Tank shot Erika a look. "Getting heavy," he mumbled.

She moved Diva away and allowed Tank to enter Cassie's condo, where he set her down on the couch.

"Thank you for…carrying me in," Cassie said. "It was unnecessary…but it was nice."

Tank looked uncomfortable as he shoved his hands in his pockets. "I'm just glad you're okay."

The two of them stared at each other with unconcealed affection.

"I'm going to take Diva for a walk," Erika said, grabbing the leash and hurrying outside. Talk about sexual tension thick enough to cut with a knife. It was too bad that her friend wasn't more preoccupied with a relationship of her own—then she'd feel a lot less guilty about her desire to spend the next seven days with Reed.

They could all hang out together… But then what happened at the end of the evening? Would Cassie be pissed if she spent the nights having sleepovers with her brother? Now that she'd broken her foot, she could probably use Erika's help a little more—walking Diva, helping her get up and down the stairs…

Securing Diva's leash, she zipped her coat higher as they headed right on Main Street.

Despite her exhaustion, the cool early morning air felt refreshing. She forced several deep breaths, replaying the events of the day before in her mind. Most of the rescue was a blur. She knew she'd done the right thing and she was glad she'd been there, but looking back on her actions, they surprised her. Not her emergency actions on the mountain as much as how she'd reacted at the hospital. For the first time, accepting thanks from a family member and checking on her patient hadn't made her feel uncomfortable. Giving them the reassurance that he was going to be okay had made her feel almost as good as saving his life had. The doctors had all congratulated her and thanked her for her quick thinking and clean work and she'd been there when they'd taken Tom in for spinal surgery that morning.

Dr. Smyth had said he was going to be okay. His recovery might take a while but he was alive and would be home with his family for Christmas.

She'd still requested a call from Dr. Smyth once Tom was out and in recovery. Leaving the hospital that morning had been tough. Getting close to a patient and his family was new to her. But she'd seen the value in it the night before. Her ability to comfort his wife had seemed to make all the difference for the woman.

Late morning cast a warm glow over the quiet village. The stores weren't open yet and the lights from the streetlamps flickered off one by one as she walked along the street. Diva stopped to pee once and seemed eager to return to Cassie's, tugging the leash back in that direction after only a few blocks.

"You missed her, huh?" she asked the dog.

Diva wagged her tail in response.

"Fine. We will go back…but if we interrupt something, it's your fault," she told the dog.

Great. Now even she was talking to the animal. A cute, adorable animal that she'd actually started to get used to. Liked, even.

Maybe she should get a dog. Something to keep her company. Someone to look forward to seeing after a long day...

She sighed, knowing she could never do it.

It wouldn't be fair to the dog.

She brushed away a feeling of unease as she reached the bakery. The smell of baked bread wafted through the air, making her stomach rumble. The Open sign lit up a second later and she contemplated going inside. Various breakfast pastries in the window made her mouth water. None of them had eaten in almost twenty-four hours and she could deliver breakfast muffins to the crew at the station, as well. She was desperate to see Reed. He'd been reluctant to leave her at the hospital that morning, too.

No dogs allowed.

"Sorry, Diva, you'll have to wait here. I'll just be a second." As she wrapped the dog's leash around a pole, her cell phone rang in her pocket.

The hospital.

Alaska General Hospital. Not the one she'd been expecting a call from.

"Dr. Sheraton speaking," she answered.

"What the hell were you thinking?"

She winced, her appetite vanishing. Obviously her father had heard about the emergency tracheotomy. She released a deep breath. "The man would have died."

"He could *sue* you."

"The patient and his wife both signed a release form

at the hospital, releasing me of any responsibility for any problems that might occur. They started an anti-infection IV the moment we arrived and the other doctors said the incision looked clean when Tom was rolled into surgery this morning."

"Tom?" His disapproval was evident.

Instant headache. Stress that had taken nearly ten days to dissolve was back in her shoulders and neck as she explained her actions to her father. "The fall through the snow crushed his C2 and C3. The man was suffocating. There was no time or any other choice. Besides, Dr. Smyth and his team are taking good care of him at Wild River Community. He's in surgery now."

"You spoke to Dr. Smyth?"

"Yes."

"And you stayed until the patient went into surgery?"

"Yes." Was all this a crime?

No, just out of character for her.

Diva tugged the leash as the cross light on the corner a block away turned to Walk.

The dog was desperate to get back to Cassie, and Erika was no longer tempted by the aroma coming from the bakery. Her father's tone had her stomach turning for a different reason. She unwrapped the leash from the pole and continued walking, listening to her father rant on and on about liability and risk...

She knew all of that. In the moment, she'd had to make the split-second decision about saving the man. She'd made her decision and it had saved his life. "Dad, it's a different environment up here. You know that. Decisions need to be made quickly." The space behind her eyes throbbed.

"Not by you. *You* are on vacation. What are you doing, running around the woods playing forest ranger, anyway?"

"It's mountain search and rescue," she said tightly. How easily her father dismissed something he knew absolutely nothing about. She had read recently that new medical students were actually being trained in these wilderness settings—it helped them improve their quick thinking and adaptability skills. Obviously her father hadn't read the updates...or cared.

"It's not your responsibility or your problem. You were supposed to be at a spa or shopping or anything else. Relaxing, getting your head back in the game."

Obviously, her head was in the game—the situation the night before only proved it—but arguing with him had never paid off. He'd always encouraged her to stand up for herself...just not against him or his authority.

Was he reprimanding her now as her father or her boss? "Yes, sir."

He didn't hang up and she sensed there was more, so she waited, oblivious to the cold wind whipping her hair against her face. Her anger and deep disappointment keeping her warm. A memory of Dr. Smyth's friendly, reassuring, impressed attitude the night before making her chest hurt. Why couldn't her father feel that way? Offer that kind of praise and understanding just once? No doubt Dr. Smyth had expected her father to react differently about this as well—she was certain he was the one who had reached out to tell him. She should have warned him that her father was different now.

"Dr. Smyth said they're looking for a new surgeon at

Wild River Community," he said a long moment later. She'd guessed right. Dr. Smyth had taken this opportunity to reconnect with her dad.

"I assumed they'd be replacing him on staff once he retires."

"Are you considering the position?" His voice was ice-cold, as though he thought he knew the answer and was disapproving already.

He obviously didn't know her at all. Her dedication and commitment to him and the hospital and their research should have told him the answer. "No. I'm not." The sinking in the pit of her stomach was nothing. She hadn't considered the opening at all. Alaska General Hospital was where she belonged. This sudden uneasiness had to be just the turmoil of the last thirty hours, lack of sleep and food and the realization that soon, she was returning to her life in Anchorage.

"Good."

Was it?

"Also, I've gotten your suspension lifted."

Suspension? "I thought this was a vacation."

"Same thing. You can come back tomorrow," he said.

What? The heaviness in her chest was for one reason only—Reed. The thought of leaving him earlier than planned made her throat constrict. "But I was planning to stay here for another week." She needed that time. Things were still a little awkward between her and Reed, and she desperately needed to talk to Cassie. She couldn't go home yet.

Diva stopped as they reached the other side of the street and instantly fell over...asleep.

"I need you here on Monday to go over preliminaries for the clinical trials," her father said.

Now he was including her.

"You'll be here?"

Was it really a question? "Yes. Of course."

A dial tone on his end indicated the end of the conversation.

Tucking her phone away, she picked up the dog and cradled her in her coat as she turned back toward Cassie's condo to pack her things and say her goodbyes.

REED SUPPRESSED A YAWN, struggling to keep his eyes open as he filed the last of the debriefing paperwork at the station. This one had taken forever. The search had been lengthy and complicated, with a lot of people involved and serious injuries. He'd needed hospital reports and statements from all the crew members. Cassie's other tour guide, Mike, had taken care of notifying family members of the corporate executives and filling out the required claims for Snow Trek Tours.

The words in front of him started to blur. He hadn't been getting much rest lately...even between rescue missions.

Though he was hardly complaining about the lack of sleep.

Reed checked his watch. After 10:00 a.m. His plan was to catch a quick nap, shower and then head to his sister's place. Tank had texted to say her foot was casted and she'd been released that morning.

Erika had surprised him by wanting to stay until Tom was in surgery. Her support for him and his wife felt like a breakthrough. Her time back in Wild River had certainly changed her. Or maybe it just brought out the real Erika. One she didn't feel she could be in her normal, fast-paced, stressful life.

"Hey, man, heading out soon?" Tyler asked, tapping him on the back.

"Yeah. Just finishing up." He felt like an old man as he got to his feet—every muscle in his body ached. Maybe Erika would be interested in reciprocal massages that evening. Though he wasn't sure running his hands all over her body would have the desired relaxing, therapeutic effect.

"Before you go, a few of us were wondering if you could sign off on this." Tyler placed a support member nomination form on the desk.

Picking it up, Reed scanned it.

The crew wanted to nominate Erika. He grinned. "This your idea?" he asked Tyler. "'Cause if you're still trying to get into her pants, you'd have to fight me for her."

Tyler raised his fists, then immediately dropped them. "I could take your old man ass any day, but that's not why I'm doing this. In fact, it was Wade's idea. I just filled out the paperwork—he had to hurry home to Kim." He gave a whipping leash motion and Reed laughed.

Funny how, a week ago, he'd been one of the guys giving Wade heck about his relationship and settled ways. Now, he understood the appeal. Tyler would someday, too.

"In that case, I'll sign this," he said, putting his signature at the bottom. "This is a great idea."

If only she really would consider becoming a support member. If only she was staying in Wild River.

He grabbed his coat and handed the nomination form to Tyler. "It's official." And while he knew she'd never accept the position on the team, she was here now and he couldn't wait any longer to see her.

CHAPTER NINETEEN

TANK'S TRUCK WAS gone when Erika arrived back at Cassie's. Her heart was as heavy as the sleeping dog in her aching arms, who conveniently awoke the moment she opened the condo door. She wiggled free when she saw Cassie.

"That was a quick walk," she said, her casted leg propped up on a stack of pillows on the couch. Tank had signed it already and the sight would have made her smile if she could summon any joy at all, but all she felt was sad and conflicted. She was leaving. Returning to Anchorage right now was the last thing she wanted to do.

"Someone missed you," she said, unclipping the leash and hanging it on the hook near the door.

"Well, it's good that you're back, Tank just ran out for breakfast. He should be back in a few minutes. I'm starving and I couldn't decide what I was hungry for, so I told him to get one of everything… What's wrong?" she asked as Erika entered the living room.

May as well get straight to it. "I'm going to head back to Anchorage a little early. Tomorrow."

Cassie frowned. "But I thought you were enjoying your time here. Was it the rescue? I totally understand if it shook you up a little…or a lot," her friend said, tying her blond hair into a messy bun at the top of her head.

Erika shook her head. "It wasn't the rescue. I was glad I could help. I just got a call from my...from the hospital. They need me back there." She wished it were true. Unfortunately, she believed that her father was dragging her back so she wouldn't get into any more "trouble" in Wild River.

"Oh. Well, I can understand that. They're probably realizing they can't survive another week without you." She studied her. "There's more. Spill it."

Erika paced the living room. "It's nothing. Just my dad. He found out about the emergency tracheotomy." She clenched and unclenched her hands at her sides.

"I take it he wasn't thrilled?"

"Ha!"

Cassie shot her a sympathetic look. "Erika, I know he's your father, but you've got to stop beating your-self up over needing his approval. You are a brilliant surgeon. Your patients are lucky to have you. Think about Tom and his wife—how grateful they were— and that was only one patient. You save thousands of lives every year. You can't keep fighting for your dad's acceptance. You don't need it, friend."

The stress of everything in the last twenty-four hours made her lips move before she could think. "You're one to talk."

"What does that mean?"

Shit. This was not the way she wanted to have this talk with her friend. In fact, now that she was leaving, she wasn't sure she should have it at all. She bit her lip. What would be the point in getting into this now? It really wasn't any of her business. It was between Cassie and Reed and their family. She'd been back in their lives for a week. Yet, she felt she owed it to Reed to call Cassie out on the huge secret she was keeping.

Still, she hesitated, searching for the right words.

"Erika, what did you mean just now?" Cassie sat straighter on the couch.

"Just that…" She took a deep breath. "Reed sent me into your office looking for the file for the corporate retreat…to get more information on your location." She paused. Staying unemotional and unattached was the way she'd avoided situations like this one. How had she gotten tangled up in the Reynolds family's dynamics?

"And?"

"And I saw a payment made to an addictions treatment center—for your dad," she said, hating the look of hurt on her friend's face, knowing she was the cause.

"Right. I'm not the most organized. I've been meaning to hire a new receptionist…to file things away and shit. Out of sight." Cassie forced a deep breath. "Did you mention it to Reed?"

"No."

Her shoulders relaxed. "Good."

Erika frowned. "Good?" Anger rose in her chest. She hadn't always been close to Reed, but she was now and Cassie's actions—keeping this from him—upset her. The friend she'd known would never hurt her brother, and this would definitely hurt him. "You know your brother is still looking for him, right?"

"Yes, I do. Erika, it's complicated."

"So complicated that he doesn't deserve to know his father isn't missing? That *you* know where he is." She fought the overwhelming sensation of guilt and hypocrisy. So did she and she hadn't said anything. But this was different. Cassie was family.

"I've only known for a few weeks," she said, staring at her lap. "I got a call from the addictions center a few days before you called to say you were coming here. And then, well, you've been here…and there hasn't been the right time to talk to Reed. I haven't even had the time to digest all of this myself. I thought he was dead."

"So it's my fault? My coming here?" Her friend's justifications sounded like excuses to her. If her mother was still alive and safe, and someone was keeping that news from her…

"No, it isn't at all your fault. I'm just saying that telling him will shatter him and I haven't gotten the guts to do that yet," she said, looking defeated. "I have tried, really, I have. But every time, I can't get the words out."

Erika understood that much at least. She sat next to her friend on the couch. A long silence fell between them. "Is your father's addiction the reason he went away?"

Cassie nodded. "I only spoke to him for a few minutes, but he seemed in bad shape. He's been struggling with alcohol issues for years. He and Mom met at the pub in Willow Lake…they fell in love when she was helping him through his first attempt at recovering… getting sober. He was okay for a long time. He stayed away from drinking and he was a great father. Then things started to change. As kids, we didn't fully understand, but we could feel the tension in the house. Dad would come home later from work and he and Mom would argue. Reed would excuse his behavior, saying he was working a lot and he was just tired or stressed. He always sided with Dad."

She took a deep breath. "Apparently, he fell off the wagon—bad—he spent his paycheck on a bender the weekend he disappeared and then he couldn't face coming home." She paused. "Then days turned into weeks, weeks into months, and he couldn't get back to us. He had no idea how to find his way. He preferred letting us all think he was lost, because in a way he was. Reed was wrecked when Dad left. He refused to believe that he'd ever just leave us."

Erika swallowed hard, her chest so tight she could barely breathe. Her own moment of truth. "I saw him a few years ago. He came in with…an injury." She'd spare her friend the details. "He'd been drinking on the job. Once he recognized me, he asked to be treated by another doctor."

Cassie looked pained.

"Sorry I didn't reach out to you then, to tell you. I wanted to. I almost did, but I didn't know how and we weren't…as close as we used to be. I wasn't sure if you already knew or if you'd even want to know."

Cassie nodded slowly. "I understand. I'm not upset—I get it." She paused. "And you haven't mentioned this to Reed?"

"No."

"Why not?"

Erika released a deep sigh. "Because I didn't want to hurt him."

Cassie nodded. "And you've only cared about him for five minutes." She paused. "I will tell him… I just need a little more time."

REED WIPED THE steam from the bathroom mirror and examined the extent of his injuries. Bruising along his left side and several deep-looking cuts along his chest and shoulder from their dash down the mountainside… they could probably use a stitch or two, but he'd been more concerned about the others. He'd been so busy, he hadn't even noticed any pain until the hot water had hit the open wounds.

Arriving home, he'd fallen onto his unmade bed, savoring the scent of Erika's vanilla body lotion on his sheets as he'd passed out. Three hours' sleep was barely enough, but he was eager to see her. He still couldn't believe what she'd done to save that man's life. He'd tried to think of what he would have done had she not been there, and nothing he came up with resulted in a man who would have survived.

Leaving her that morning hadn't been by choice.

Tank had still looked nauseous when he'd left him at the hospital. This rescue had been the only time Reed had seen the guy nearly break down with relief when the group had finally come into view—safe.

Tank's relief could have rivaled his own.

Man, he hoped his sister and his friend would smarten up and take a chance at being together. They both deserved happiness and the feelings they had for one another were obvious to everyone, including themselves.

His own feelings for Erika had shocked the hell out of him, but there was no denying they were strong. Would she be willing to try a long-distance thing when she went back to Anchorage?

Hearing his doorbell, he grabbed a towel, and a moment later opened the door to Erika. Such a sight for sore eyes. Why had he slept so long?

"Hi," she said, looking uneasy.

"Hi… I was just getting ready to come over to Cassie's. Everything okay?" he asked, stepping back and allowing her to enter.

Her gaze fell to his injuries and her eyes seemed to water.

"Hey, don't worry…these are nothing," he said, moving to wrap his arms around her. The cold of her jacket against his still damp skin made him shiver but he didn't care. He couldn't be this close to her without having her in his arms. "And now that you're here, maybe you can take care of me," he teased, lifting her chin to force her gaze to meet his.

She looked distraught and his chest tightened, remembering the awkward way she'd left his apartment the morning before. The kiss after the rescue had him thinking they were okay, but maybe not. "Hey, did I do something wrong?" Whatever it was, he'd make it right.

She shook her head. "No, definitely not."

But she had bad news, he could tell. "What's the matter?"

"I'm leaving," she said, sucking in a deep breath.

"Next week…right?"

"Tomorrow morning."

Too soon. "Why?" He stiffened slightly. Had things gone too far between them? Was she second-guessing how he felt about her? How she felt about him?

"My dad called. He needs me back at the hospital."

"The same dad that forced you to take vacation?" He'd never been close to Erika's parents, but he knew her father was demanding and critical and rarely gave his daughter credit. He'd always dictated her life, according to Cassie, and the fact that he had so much control over her still annoyed Reed.

She nodded. "He heard about the rescue. He wasn't happy that I'd taken such a huge risk."

"There was no other choice—Tom would have died. We all know that."

"He also heard about the job opening at Wild River Community once Dr. Smyth retires and I guess he's freaking out a little."

Reed's hope lifted slightly. "Were you considering that position?" Maybe mountain life had started to appeal to her, made her realize she could have a fulfilling career in a more laid-back lifestyle. She had grown up here, after all, maybe being back here reminded her how great it was.

But she shook her head. "No. My career…my life is in Anchorage."

That stung a little, but he had no right to hope that after their short time together, she'd consider such a drastic life change. "Of course."

She moved closer, resting her head against his sore body, but he didn't care—he held her tight. She was leaving the next morning. He thought he had another week of this. More time holding her, kissing her, making love to her… Convincing her to give them— together—a shot when she returned to Anchorage.

He kissed the top of her head. "How do you feel about going back so soon?"

"I don't want to leave you," she said.

He hugged her tighter. "Cassie's at home? Is she okay?"

She nodded, but he felt her tense at the mention of his sister. "Tank's with her."

He'd text the guy and make sure he stayed there for a while. He needed this time with Erika. A last few hours together before she left. There was so much he wanted to say…yet he had no idea how. It was too soon to claim he was in love with her, but there were no other words to describe the overwhelming sensations running through his body and heart when he was with her, when he saw her, when he thought of her.

She was it for him. He knew that. As crazy as it sounded, he'd fallen fast and hard for his sister's best friend. Now, he had to figure out how to show her. Find out if she was feeling even a fraction of what he was. Where they went from here, how they made this work, he wasn't sure, but if she wanted him, he was willing to try. More than eager to explore this connection between them.

He backed away slightly and kissed her forehead, her nose, her cheeks and finally her lips.

Taking her hands, he wrapped them around his neck, and placing his hands under her thighs, he lifted her, wrapping her legs around his waist as he carried her to his bedroom.

She continued to kiss him as he made his way blindly into the room and set her down on his unmade bed. Breaking their connection, he unzipped her jacket, removed it and tossed it aside.

Seemingly lost in a silent turmoil, she quietly removed her sweater and bra, then her jeans and underwear and, naked, she lay back against his pillow, waiting for him.

God, her leaving was going to suck the life out of him.

Dropping his towel, he lay on the bed next to her. Not touching, not kissing, just lying there staring at one another. Two people who'd connected on so many levels in such a short time...or perhaps the connection had started that night in the forest when he'd held her while she'd slept. A night when they'd been a source of unexpected comfort for one another.

He could see so many of his own conflicted thoughts in her eyes and he reached for her, pulling her closer. "You're sure you can't stay longer?" He kissed the top of her head as his hand slid the length of her side, caressing each delicate, soft curve, trying to commit each inch of her to memory.

"Unfortunately not," she said, and he could hear her desire to stay in her voice.

"Well, let's not waste any more of the time we do have," he said, gently guiding her onto her back and lying on top of her. He supported his weight on his arms as he separated her legs and placed himself between them.

He felt himself grow thick as his body touched hers.

"We should talk...about things," she said, biting her lip.

"We should definitely talk about things, but first I need to make love to you." He could show her how he was feeling so much better than he could tell her anyway. Lowering his head to hers, he slid his tongue along her bottom lip, tasting her, teasing her...

She gripped his head between her hands, letting her fingers tangle in his hair as she pulled him closer, connecting their mouths. She kissed him hungrily, with a desperate urgency of a lover knowing their time was coming to an end.

He slipped his tongue between her lips and explored every part of her mouth. His hips began to rock slowly, pushing his thighs into hers, his cock against her pelvis. He wanted her so bad. But not just right now...

Damn, she was right. They did need to talk. His own anxiety was rising with his desire. He had to know this wouldn't be the last time he was with her. Had to know she wanted more.

He reluctantly broke away and forced a breath to refocus his thoughts—not an easy task with her sexy, willing body beneath him.

"What's wrong?" she asked.

"I think we should talk first."

"Okay."

Rolling off her, he grabbed the bedsheets and pulled them over their bodies as he lay on his side next to her. Keeping her fantastic curves hidden might help him get through what he wanted to say without the urge to be inside her interrupting again.

He stared at her for a long, silent moment, hoping she'd speak first.

She didn't.

"Okay, so the thing is...this...whatever's happening between us, I don't want it to end when you go back home."

She looked happy...relieved. "Good."

"Good?"

She laughed. "Yes. Very good."

"Good, because I'm starting to fall...I mean, I'm having feelings for you that I haven't had in a long time...maybe even ever."

She nodded. "Good."

He laughed. She was right, communication was something she had to work on. But if all she could muster right now was "good," he'd take it.

"So I want to try to make this work. For real, you and me," he said, touching her cheek softly.

"G—"

He kissed her, unable to hear another "good." For now, knowing they were going to try a real relationship was enough. Pulling her on top of him, he let the blankets fall away and his breath caught as he stared at her beautiful, firm breasts. Her legs on either side of him, her folds pressed against his thick, hard cock. Her hands trailed down his chest and stomach and the look of need in her eyes had him feeling completely weak. He was powerless to the feelings he had for her, coming on so strong, so unexpected…

Reaching for a condom, he tore it open and slid it on before lowering her body down over the length of him. "Fuck, you feel so good. So warm, so tight…"

She swallowed hard as she lifted her hips up and down in a slow, torturously dangerous rhythm that had him practically panting for more. Watching her breasts rise and fall with her movements, her head tossed back in pleasure of her own and her dark hair cascading over her shoulder…he was mesmerized.

He lifted his hips to go deeper, needing to be closer to her, wanting this feeling of absolute pleasure to last.

She pushed down further and let out a small gasp as his cock plunged deep into her body. "Damn, you're so big and hard. I've never been with anyone who makes me feel so good," she said, rocking a little faster, a little more desperate against him.

"We're good together." And it surprised him that two people who were so incompatible on the surface could be so perfect together at the core. He felt he knew her, knew who she really was beneath the cool, professional exterior. She was letting him in, letting him see parts of her she hid from the rest of the world—a softer, caring, irresistible nature that he was drawn to. "I don't want to let you go," he said, reaching up to brush her long hair away from her face.

The look in her eyes told him she felt the same way and his heart pounded loudly in his chest.

Placing her hands against his shoulders, she rocked her hips faster, sliding up and down over him, until her breathing matched his and they were both searching for release. He gripped her ass, his fingers digging into the flesh, helping her motion, increasing her pace... until finally his body erupted in waves of pleasure, shooting throughout his core.

"Damn, Erika," he said, his eyes rolling back as he enjoyed the aftershocks of his orgasm.

He felt her clench tight around him, then her own vibrations rippled over his cock. Her body throbbing around him was almost too much but he pushed a final time, giving her the same rush of intensity he was feeling.

Spent, she fell against him and he held her close, pulling her into his arms as she rested her head against his chest.

They both lay there, lost in their own emotions, battling the one thought that he suspected was plaguing them both.

Could they really make this work?

CHAPTER TWENTY

WITH A HEAVY HEART, Erika climbed the stairs to Cassie's condo the next morning. She opened the unlocked door and immediately found herself wrapped in a big, warm hug.

"Oh my God. Look at you!" Arlene Reynolds stood back to take her in. "So beautiful," she said.

Erika blushed. Would Cassie's mother be as friendly if she knew how Erika had spent the evening before? Wrapped in her son's arms, making love to him over and over…both desperate to fuse their connection, make it as strong as possible so that it could survive what came next.

Had Cassie told her mother about them? She'd yet to talk to her friend since their uncomfortable chat the day before. All she'd wanted was to go to Reed—the one place she felt safe, the only place she could be herself.

Cassie hadn't asked any questions when she'd left the day before. She knew where Erika was going, but Erika needed to apologize to her friend before she left Wild River. She wanted her connection with Cass to be strong going forward so time or distance or arguments couldn't come between them.

But now that conversation might have to wait. "Hi, Mrs. Reynolds. Nice to see you."

"It's been far too long. I was so happy when Cass

told me you were coming to visit her. You two used to be inseparable." Erika closed the door and stepped over two heavy-looking suitcases still in the entryway. Reed had told her that his mother was coming to stay with Cass while her foot healed. Arlene had read about the details of the search and rescue in the Willow Lake backwoods newsletter. "It's such a shame you have to go back early. I would have loved to catch up with you," she said, looking genuinely disappointed.

Erika nodded, swallowing a lump forming in the back of her throat as she removed her coat. Arlene had been like a mother to her after hers died. The other woman had taken her shopping for her prom dress and taught her how to apply makeup. Seeing her now brought another wave of nostalgia that made leaving so much harder.

She had two hours before she had to catch her train and she felt guilty for having spent her last night there with Reed. She wasn't sure if Cassie would even want to talk to her.

"Cass, Erika's back!" Arlene called up to the bedroom.

Erika held her breath as Cassie made her way down the stairs, holding the rail with one hand and her crutch in the other. She bit her lip, but relief flowed through her when Cassie sent her an apprehensive smile as she hobbled her way toward them. "Do you see the size of those suitcases?" she asked, nodding toward her mother's things.

"Yes, your mom packs as light as I do," she said with a laugh, hugging her friend tight at the bottom of the stairs. "I'm sorry," she whispered.

"Me, too," Cass whispered back as she pulled away,

giving her a reassuring smile. "And you were right—
I will tell him."

Erika nodded slowly, no longer sure about the right
thing to do. Would the news about his father's whereabouts make Reed feel better or worse? For now, she
focused on the positive, the things she could control.
She and Cassie were okay. Their friendship had somehow survived ten years of almost no contact—one argument couldn't break the friendship ties they'd formed
in childhood. Emotions rose in her chest and not for
the first time, she regretted having to leave so soon.

What would happen if she told her father no? If she
took the rest of her vacation and went home a week
from now?

She'd be replaced on his research team.

"Seriously, Mom, how long are you planning to
stay?" Cassie asked, struggling to lift Diva off one of
the leopard-patterned suitcases.

"Until you're feeling better and the foot is completely healed," Arlene said.

Her friend's eyes widened.

Probably the same way they must have when Erika
had announced the unexpected length of *her* visit. She
grinned, remembering that awkward first night in the
bar. Reed had certainly warmed up to her quite a bit
since then.

Man, she'd been such an asshole. Thank God, her
friends had seen through her bullshit.

Her chest ached at the thought of what distance and
time might do to them all, but she pushed the negative
thoughts away.

Negative or realistic?

"That's not necessary—you don't have to stay that

long. I'm fine. I can totally get around here all by myself. You just watched me come down the stairs," Cassie was insisting.

Her mother waved a hand, rolling up the sleeves of her handmade holiday-themed sweater as though on a mission. "Nonsense. You nearly died. If Erika was staying, that would be different, but you need me," she said, already in the kitchen loading the dishwasher.

Erika smiled, feeling suddenly jealous of her friend. She missed her own mother so much... She hadn't had anyone take care of her or want to for a long time. A deep longing to stay, to be a part of this family and close-knit group of friends nearly choked her. But she'd only been visiting this way of life. She'd never had any intentions of staying.

She checked her watch. "My train leaves soon, so I have to finish packing..." Reed had dropped her off and said he had to run to the station for a few minutes, but he'd be back soon to drive her to the train station.

Cassie nodded, moving forward to hug her again. "Sure you can't stay? She will drive me insane."

"Be nice. You're lucky to have her," she said, kissing her friend's cheek.

"You're right. I am. I'll have to keep reminding myself of that." She laughed, following Erika over to her own open suitcase in the living room.

"Cass...where's the coffee?" her mother asked, opening every cupboard.

"She doesn't need coffee like the rest of us mere mortals," Erika teased, picking up a sweater from the back of the couch and folding it. It was the one she'd worn on the heli-skiing date and she could still smell Reed's cologne on it. She hoped the smell lasted—she'd need it once she was back in Anchorage. She was going to miss him so much.

"I'll be back in a few minutes," Arlene said, reaching for her coat.

"Where are you going?"

"To the grocery store to get coffee and other things I'm going to need to survive here."

"In that case, you'll also need to buy a coffee maker," Cass said.

"Oh, Cassie, you're not human," her mother said, leaving the condo.

"Or you could go home to your own coffee maker," her friend called after her as the door closed.

Erika laughed, zipping her suitcase.

"Remind me again how lucky I am," Cassie said, stretching out her casted leg.

"Very. You have a wonderful family." Her voice nearly broke and she ordered herself to pull it together. It was just Anchorage, not the moon. A short train ride away. She could visit anytime. They could visit her.

"Reed kinda grew on you, huh?"

"Not at all," she said, sitting on the couch next to her.

"Try bullshitting someone else," Cassie said, pointing to her wrist tattoo.

Erika fingered her own. From now on, she wouldn't be covering it up. "Okay, maybe a little bit. You're not upset that I spent the night with him, are you? It's not totally weird for you, is it?"

"I didn't get a chance to say it yesterday, but I'm thrilled for you both."

"That's such a relief to hear."

"You two are actually perfect for one another. You'll

certainly keep my brother on his toes." She studied her. "You are planning to keep this going, right?"

"We're going to try." She toyed with the hem of her sweater. "I'm not good at this, Cass. What if I mess it up?"

"Reed won't let you. I've seen the way he looks at you. You may have changed here in Wild River, but you've changed him, too."

Her pulse raced at what that meant. "So…what about you and Tank? Any progress there?" She needed to change the subject. Saying goodbye to her friend was tough and she knew saying goodbye to Reed in an hour would be nearly impossible. Keeping the conversation light was the only way to get through it. She was only returning to her life. Not dying.

So why did it feel like there was a hole forming inside of her?

"Nope. We take a step forward, then three steps back. Kaia's been asking about her mother a lot lately… As she's getting older, she has a million questions and it's tough on Tank. Every time he gets close, he pulls back like I've burned him. I'm trying to be patient but, damn, it can be infuriating that he doesn't see that I'm what they need."

Erika touched her friend's hand. "Hang in there. He can't resist you forever," she said with a smile.

"Right?" Cassie said with a hopeful expression.

"Definitely."

She checked her watch and stood. "Well, I should head downstairs. Reed will be here any minute." Her pulse raced at the thought of the painful goodbye awaiting her.

"Oh wait." Cassie struggled to push herself up, only sinking farther into the couch cushions. "Help."

Grabbing her hands, Erika pulled her to her feet. "See? This is why you need your mom."

"Okay, maybe." Cassie hopped on one foot to the kitchen. "I have something for you…" She opened the fridge and took out a white square box wrapped with a festive-looking red-and-green bow. She handed it to her. "To cure any chocolate cravings."

The Chocolate Shoppe logo made Erika's mouth instantly water. The smell of peppermint fudge revealed what was inside. Did her friend have anything to cure any Reed cravings she might have, as well? "Thank you. I can't promise I won't eat every last piece on the way home."

"Hey, I'm not one to judge. In fact, I may have opened it already and stolen a piece or three," she said with a sheepish expression.

Erika laughed. "I consider myself lucky to be getting any at all." She suddenly wished she had a parting gift for her friend, as well. Then, seeing Cassie's wrist tattoo, she rushed forward to hug her. "You really are the *Best* part of this friendship."

Cassie sniffed. "Don't make me cry. We're going to keep in touch this time."

"We will. I promise to try my best." Already she knew it wouldn't be good enough. Hearing Reed's truck pull up outside the condo, Erika nodded, pulling herself together. "He's here. I have to go."

She collected her suitcase and headed toward the door. "Relax. Stay off your feet as much as possible." She grabbed her red cashmere coat and put it on. "Doctor's orders," she said, earning a look from her best friend.

Sliding her feet into her heeled boots, she blew a kiss to Cass and left the house before tears could surface. She'd have even more emotions threatening her soon enough.

And it wasn't like she wouldn't see Cassie again soon…and they always had Facebook. Already, she was feeling the stress and anxiety that had subsided over the last ten days returning.

Reed was waiting at the truck. His gaze took in her formal coat and impractical boots and something in his expression told her she was already almost unrecognizable to him. The reality of it sucked the wind from her lungs. Reed had fallen for the person she'd been able to pretend to be while on vacation—carefree, relaxed, fun, adventurous…in real life, she was none of those things.

Hurrying up the stairs, he smiled as he took her suitcase. "Need me to carry you?"

"I think I can handle these—I'm sober today," she said, carefully descending the grate staircase.

At the bottom, he opened the passenger-side door for her. "I'm shocked Cassie let you go." He nodded toward his mom's car parked in front of Snow Trek Tours.

"She begged me to stay," she said.

He swallowed hard and simply nodded as he closed the door.

She forced a breath as she watched him cross in front of the truck. In tight-fitting jeans and a bomber-style winter jacket, a search and rescue logo baseball cap on, he looked like the last thing on the planet she wanted to walk away from. Maybe having him drive her to the train station was a mistake. Taking a cab would have been better.

Easier.

Leaving that morning after the intimate moments they'd shared in his bed would have been a better way to remember him...

Tears burned in her eyes. This wouldn't be as easy as they'd tried to make it sound the night before.

He climbed in behind the wheel and immediately reached for her hand, holding it tight as they drove along Main Street in silence.

Taking in the holiday decorations in the village—the storefront displays and the large center square Christmas tree they were lighting that evening—only depressed her further. Holidays here would be magical. Spending them with Reed would have been amazing.

Mariah Carey's "All I Want for Christmas is You" started to play on the radio and he quickly reached forward to shut it off.

Nope, there would be no listening to romantic, depressing Christmas carols for her that season either.

She stared through the window, her time in Wild River on replay in her mind. So short, yet it felt like a lifetime.

The train station platform came into view a lot quicker than she would have liked.

What was the worst thing that could happen if she stayed? If she told her father she was taking the extra time off as planned and she'd see him next week?

She'd piss him off and in a week, she'd only be feeling this way all over again.

No. Like a Band-Aid.

When Reed turned into the parking lot, she shook her head. "No, please don't stay. This is hard enough..."

Her voice broke slightly, so she just pointed to the drop-off zone.

"Your train isn't scheduled to leave for another twenty minutes. I'd like to wait with you." His voice was hoarse as he struggled to keep his own emotions in check.

"I'll never get on it if you do," she said, barely above a whisper.

He squeezed her hand and reluctantly did as she asked, pulling up in the drop-off zone where just the week before Cassie had picked her up. So much had happened in such a short time. When she'd arrived in Wild River, she hadn't even been sure she'd last a day, and now she wanted to stay. Just a little longer.

Putting the truck in Park and removing his seat belt, Reed turned to face her. "This is not goodbye."

She nodded, desperate to believe it was true.

"I have something for you," he said, releasing her hand to reach into the back seat of the truck.

"I hope it's not more fudge or I'll be unrecognizable the next time you see me." It was meant as a joke to lighten the heavy tension filling the cab of the truck, but all it did was make her heart ache wondering when that next time would be.

They'd compared schedules and made a ton of promises, but she knew herself…

He handed her a red-and-yellow S & R jacket, the Wild River Search and Rescue logo on the sleeves. Her name embroidered on the chest. *Dr. Erika.* She swallowed a lump that refused to go away. "But I'm not a member," she said.

"The crew decided to make you an honorary support member after the other night," he said, touching her cheek.

She fingered the patch. "Thank you. This means a lot." More than she would've expected it to. She'd never imagined that Wild River could feel like home again, but this week she'd felt like she belonged.

"*You* mean a lot. To all of us. To me."

Oh God, holding back tears was impossible. One slid down her cheek and she brushed it away. "This is crazy." Feelings couldn't grow this strong, so fast, could they? "In a good way." She could see his unease and uncertainty reflecting in his expression.

Man, she was going to miss getting lost in those eyes. Miss being wrapped in his arms...

Taking her hand, he kissed her palm and held her gaze longer than was safe, before glancing at the time on the dash.

Time she wished would stand still was ticking away far too quickly.

"You better go," he said, sounding as thrilled about it as she felt. Climbing out of the truck, he met her on her side with her suitcase. He set it down on the curb and reached for her.

She immediately walked into his open arms and hugged him tight. "I'll miss you," she whispered. Air couldn't quite make it into her lungs.

He smoothed her hair away from her face and kissed her forehead. "This is not goodbye," he said again.

Good. If he kept saying it, she might eventually believe it.

Standing on tiptoes, she placed her lips to his. The kiss was gentle at first, but quickly ignited as passion and anxiety and a desperation she'd never felt before took over. Her hands clung to his shoulders and he was a source of oxygen from which she was drawing life…

He held her tight to his chest and she could feel their hearts pounding in sync.

How did she walk away from this? This feeling of contentment and safety in his arms, the feeling of being loved and loving someone in return… She searched for strength in his kiss, but the longer she was engulfed in Reed, the more consumed she felt.

He broke away, fighting for breath, a long moment later and she knew it was time to go.

Now or never.

He held her tight as he said, "We will make this work. We will text and Skype…and I'm here anytime of day or night… And Christmas Eve. We are going to be together then—that's just two weeks away…"

Two weeks felt like forever. The night before in her half-asleep state, she'd said she'd *try* to make the trip back for Christmas Eve. She hadn't promised. The clinical trials were starting the week before Christmas…in her gut she knew getting back there for Christmas Eve was improbable, but she refused to lose hope that somehow they'd find a way.

She was unable to spend the rest of the season with him, but she was suddenly determined to find a way to be there, in his arms on Christmas morning. The only thing she wanted that year. It would take a Christmas miracle, but right now, when she was leaving the only man she'd ever fallen this hard, this fast for, Erika had to believe in miracles.

She nodded. "Right. Two weeks is nothing…"

He smiled. "I'll be seeing you, pretty girl…"

Okay, that was her cue to walk away. Instead, she dived back into his arms.

Damn, this was so hard.

"Two weeks. We can make this work. Believe in me, okay?" His words were meant to reassure, but all she heard was a pleading desperation not to hurt him.

And damn, she wished she could say for certain that she wouldn't.

Pulling away, she picked up the handle on her suitcase and plastered on her best fake smile. She blew him a final kiss as she headed toward the train. In a few minutes, once she was seated and the train pulled away from the station, tears would start to fall. In a few hours, once she was home, reality would make the last week feel like a dream.

CHAPTER TWENTY-ONE

REED SCANNED THE schedule on the station office wall the next morning, clutching his coffee cup like a lifeline. The day before, Erika had texted briefly to let him know that she'd arrived home safely, but she hadn't been able to call him until almost midnight, having gone straight to the hospital. Leaving her at the train station had been torture. A hollow, lonely feeling had stuck with him for the rest of the day.

When she finally did call, they'd talked for hours... and by 2:00 a.m., he still hadn't wanted to let her go. He'd been listening for the smallest indication that things were still okay between them. But as she told him all about the clinical trials starting the following week, all he'd heard were a million reasons why she wouldn't be able to get away again anytime soon.

Scanning the upcoming holiday season calendar, he couldn't find even one day where *he* could make a whirlwind road trip to Anchorage to see *her*. Three support members and one full member were going away for two weeks over the Christmas break, therefore all other hands were needed on deck with the tourist and ski season picking up.

He was leading another Hug-A-Tree session the following day and the last one for the year was scheduled for the following week. He couldn't hand those off to the other guys—it wouldn't be fair.

Marcus's support membership was being evaluated in a few days and he was hoping to become a full member. As a crew leader, Reed needed to be there for that. Having another full member would ease some of the pressure on him.

In addition, his mom expected to spend time with him and he was still needed at the bar—that month more than ever… The night before had seen double the usual number of patrons and it was only the beginning of December.

Things were only going to get busier.

He ran a hand through his hair and took a gulp of the steaming hot coffee, burning his throat. It was his third cup and the caffeine wasn't helping at all. If anything, it made him only more anxious and irritated.

What was it about women that drove men so completely crazy?

This had certainly never happened to him before. He'd dated tourists without developing feelings—some beautiful, amazing, interesting women. None had left him feeling this damn empty.

Erika wasn't just some tourist. She'd been a part of his past and suddenly someone he wanted in his future. Unlike his previous flings, this parting had been with a promise of more.

The cot in the corner of the station taunted him with flashbacks of their first night together. Her soft, silky body so ready for him… He hardened slightly at the thought. Damn, it was going to be a hell of a long three weeks. Everywhere he looked, he was reminded of her.

Sitting at the desk, he reached for his cell.

Thinking about you, he texted.

He knew not to expect an immediate reply, but five minutes later, he still got a twisting knot in his gut. She'd said her life was busy. He was going to have to have patience. But alone in the room all morning, waiting for an emergency call or a text from Erika had him seriously on edge. Tiffany and several other team members had invited him to help them decorate the Search and Rescue Christmas parade float, but he'd declined, and the sound of the Puppy Orchestra barking "Jingle Bells" drifting through the station walls was driving him insane.

There would be no escaping the sights and sounds of Christmas here in Wild River, and that sucked. Hard. Christmas was not a season for the lonely hearted.

When the door to the station opened an hour later and Tyler walked in, Reed had never been so grateful to see the guy. Anything to take his mind off Erika. "Hey, man."

"Hey."

"Heard your girl went back to Anchorage yesterday."

So much for taking his mind off it.

"Too bad. She would have made a great team member... I still can't believe she had the balls to do that tracheotomy right there on the mountainside."

Three days later and it was still all the crew was talking about. It had definitely spurred the conversation about having a trained medical professional on the crew. While they were all trained in CPR and first aid, that hiker would have died without Erika.

Tyler let out a low whistle. "You got yourself a good one, man."

Reed nodded, checking his phone. Nothing. He knew she was a good one. The best, even. The problem was, he already felt her slipping away.

It was after 2:00 a.m. when Erika finally locked her office door behind her and collapsed on her cot. Two surgeries and a four-hour meeting with her clinical trial team had her brain fried. She couldn't understand it. This was the same pace she'd been keeping before her vacation, so why did it feel nearly impossible to keep up now?

This was why a break was a bad idea.

She felt so out of the loop with the trials. Despite Darren withdrawing his request for a transfer, her father had moved him to Dr. Connolly and she'd been assigned a new intern while she was away. She couldn't remember the young female doctor's name if her life depended on it, and her coffee never tasted the same. She missed Darren.

The surgeries that day had gone well…but could have gone better. Over and over, she replayed each decision, torturing herself with the things she should have done differently. Both patients were in recovery—they'd be fine, but they hadn't gotten her best.

Though she was proud of herself for dealing with both sets of family members directly before and after the surgery. She'd met with them to discuss the procedure, answered their questions and even tried to give reassurances.

So, maybe the break wasn't such a bad thing. She was definitely approaching her role in a slightly different way. And hopefully in a few days, she'd be feeling like her old self. Get her routine back on schedule.

Hearing her phone buzz in her desk drawer, she retrieved it and, squinting in the dimly lit office, she read the text message from Reed.

Thinking about you.

Received 9:08.
That morning.
Shit.

A dozen times that day, she'd intended to go back to her office, where she'd forgotten her cell, to text him, but each time she'd gotten pulled in a different direction. Time seemed to move faster at the hospital. In contrast to the excruciatingly slow, thorough movements of a search and rescue, the pace here was lightning fast. An hour passed in what felt like seconds.

Reed had been on her mind constantly...

No, that wasn't entirely true. While he was there—in her mind and her heart—her job required focus and she'd successfully pushed all other thoughts away when she worked. Lives depended on that narrow focus.

Besides, thinking about him only made her miss him more. Lack of downtime was a good thing.

She sat back on the cot and texted him.

Sorry, it's been a crazy day... I miss you.

His reply was immediate, making her feel instantly guilty. She'd hoped his day had been as busy as hers and he hadn't been worried when she hadn't replied sooner.

Want to chat?

She did. She desperately did. But after an eighteen-hour shift, she could barely keep her eyes open. If she called Reed now, they'd be on the phone for hours, like the night before.

But she missed him. She longed to hear his voice. The night before, she'd talked nonstop about the clinical trials and after they'd hung up, she'd gotten the feeling that he'd been wanting something more from her. Needing something more.

Not only did she not know what that something was, she wasn't certain she could give it to him even if she did. A long-distance relationship was going to require a lot of communication, and while she'd grown a little during her time with him, this wasn't going to be easy on her. Being around him, touching him, kissing him was easier.

But right now, phone calls, texts and Skype were all they had.

Dialing his number, she blinked the tiredness from her eyes and cleared her dry throat. When was the last time she'd stopped for a glass of water? She was certain she hadn't eaten. Her new intern hadn't gotten the memo that she was fueled by espresso yet.

"Hi." His voice after the first ring sounded sleepy but happy, and she was glad she'd called.

She wanted to reassure him that things were fine... they were still fine. She also needed that reassurance—not from him, but from herself.

"Hi," she said, readjusting her pillow on the cot and settling in for the night. With less than five hours until she needed to be back there, there would be no going home. "Why aren't you sleeping?"

"Because my bedsheets still smell like you and I

can't close my eyes without seeing your beautiful, naked body lying beside me."

Despite her exhaustion, her body responded to the words. A dull aching in her heart mirrored the one in her pelvis. "I wish I was there," she said, closing her eyes.

"What would you do if you were?" he asked, his husky-sounding voice holding more than a note of desire.

Obviously he planned to steer the conversation away from talk of work that night. And that was completely okay with her. "I'd lie in your arms completely naked and kiss you, hard…savoring the taste of your mouth and lips…" She had no idea where the teasing, erotic words had come from, but they'd had an immediate relaxing, calming, yet arousing effect.

An unexpected and completely new experience for her.

If Reed was surprised by her response, she couldn't tell. "And then what?" he asked, the sound of his voice telling her he, too, felt this mix of longing and pleasure.

Closing her eyes, she summoned an image of his naked body—sculpted shoulders, muscular chest, abs and obliques that gave way to the sexiest V leading to his cock… She imagined running her hands over his body, feeling every inch of him—so hard, so sexy, so perfect.

She could feel herself getting wet and she wiggled her hips and clenched her thighs together as she answered, "Then I'd crawl lower on the bed, running my hands along your chest and stomach… Wrapping my hand around you, I'd stroke the length of your cock, slowly pumping up and down, watching you get thick and hard beneath my hand."

His breathing became heavier as he listened. "I'm touching myself just like that now. It feels incredible… Go on, what else would you do?"

Just the question had her imagination soaring. What she'd love to do to him right now. No longer tired, she unzipped her dress pants and slid a hand inside her underwear, touching herself. So wet. So ready for a man hundreds of miles away. "I'd lower my head to your cock and I'd lick you from the tip all the way to the base, swirling and circling around the shaft, as my hands continued to massage your balls." Her eyes closed tight, she imagined tasting him, wishing he were there. Her own chest rose and fell in a heavy, steady rhythm and her fingers massaged against her clit.

"Damn, Erika, I'd love to feel your mouth on me," he said in a heavy whisper. "I'm so hard right now."

Her entire body was on fire, need and desire flowing through her. Turning him on was turning her on more than she could ever have thought.

"Keep going…"

"I'd take you deep into my wet, warm mouth…all the way…in and out. Holding the base of your cock, I'd follow my lips with my hand, moving up and down…" Her own waves of desire demanded to be satisfied with each word.

"Fuck, I'm almost coming already. I wish I could grab your sexy ass and explore every inch of you while I watch you take me in your mouth."

Oh. My. God. So close to orgasm.

"I'd slide my fingers inside you and tease that sexy

little clit until you were begging for release... Are you touching yourself?"

She swallowed hard, her mouth watering at the thought of all the dirty, delicious things they could do if they were together. "Yes, and I'm so wet for you, Reed. Wet and ready..." She slid a finger inside her body and felt her muscles tighten around it. It was hardly Reed's big, solid, thick cock, but she'd take any relief in that moment.

"Think of me, sweetheart, sliding in and out of you...thrusting hard, deep inside your body..."

She pumped her fingers in and out, adding a second...then a third.

"I'd kiss you, teasing your lips with my tongue as my cock buries deeper inside..."

Oh my God. His words, her touching all had her on the brink. She quickened her pace as she heard his breathing grow heavier.

"I'm so close..." she panted, arching her back as the first wave of pleasure rippled through her and she nearly dropped the phone.

"Me, too. Come for me, Erika. I want to hear you come," he said, and she did.

Her head spun and her toes curled as her body convulsed in waves of pleasure. Sensations rippling through her body made her shiver as she pulled her hand out of her underwear, the intensity almost painful.

She heard him moan in his own release, and the aftershock of her orgasm stole her breath.

"That was sexy," Reed said a second later, sounding sleepy, but perfectly at peace.

She turned onto her side, clenching her thighs together as her body continued to tingle. "That was a first," she said, letting her eyes drift closed, a new exhaustion taking over.

"Not as perfect as the real thing, but until I can have you in my arms again, I can live with phone calls like these."

She could imagine the satisfied smile on his face. And for now, when all they had was each other's voice on the other end of the line, that's what she'd cling to... for as long as it lasted.

CHAPTER TWENTY-TWO

THE WEEK FLEW BY. Marcus's evaluation to become a full member had gone well. He'd been voted in by a unanimous decision, and Reed was relieved to have another permanent crew member to help at the station throughout the holidays. The Hug-A-Tree school programs were done for the year, but between one short rescue call, a search for a lost Labrador retriever and several ski patrol assists, it was Friday before Reed could see his mom.

Now, sitting across from her at Mountain Slope Café, he sipped his coffee, listening to her daily recap of life in Willow Lake. He hadn't lived in his small former hometown in a long time, but it sounded like not much had changed.

His mother's schedule was the same as always, though she had started a new Zumba class at the community hall on Thursdays. She'd been forced to change hairdressers because April, her longtime stylist, had moved to California. "The blond is too blond, isn't it?" she asked, removing her hat to reveal the ash-blond, shoulder-length bob.

It looked the same as always to him. "Maybe a little too blond," he said.

She swiped at him, put the hat back on and launched into the current drama between her neighbors. They were fighting over an old tree that sat on both their properties. They both wanted to decorate it for Christmas but couldn't come to an agreement on colored versus white lights.

Man, if only I had their problems.

Unlike Cass, he didn't mind his mom's nonstop chatter. She was entertaining and well, all he had to do was nod and smile.

Today, though, he fought the urge to tell her about Erika. It was really the only thing he wanted to talk about—when he did get a word in—but he wasn't sure what to say. Technically they'd been dating two weeks. He'd never told his mother about girls he'd dated before, but this was different. He was in love with Erika... though the lack of contact in the last few days was making him anxious.

Combine that with the ever-increasing awareness that Christmas was all around him—sights and sounds of couples in love and families excited to be spending the season together, all the things he'd barely noticed before—and he was feeling on edge. He wanted someone special to spend this season with...and every season.

He'd found the one. He just wasn't sure how it was going to work out. The late-night calls were all they had and eventually they wouldn't be enough. What did they do then? Did one of them move? Give up everything and relocate?

Would Erika even consider that? Would he?

Maybe he'd hold off on telling his mom anything just yet.

"How are things with you, sweetheart?" she asked just as the waiter set their food in front of them.

"Good." He folded a piece of bacon and popped it into his mouth. He barely tasted the salty, greasy meat. Food had lost its flavor lately. Nothing was like it was before Erika.

"How are things at the bar?" she asked between bites of her eggs Benedict.

He nodded as he swallowed. "Getting busier." The night before, they'd been at maximum capacity by ten—much busier than a normal Thursday night. He and Tank had been run off their feet. Thankfully, their seasonal staff was increasing that weekend. "We should put you to work while you're here," he said.

"Your sister needs me, even though she'll never admit it."

He cleared his throat. "So, how is Cassie?" He'd seen his sister only once since the avalanche rescue, but she'd texted him almost every hour of every day to tell him their mother was making her crazy.

His sister's texts were making *him* crazy.

Every time the cell chimed with a new one, he dived for it, hoping it was Erika. Unfortunately, her texts were less frequent. A lot less frequent...

But they still chatted at the end of each day.

Which was why he was exhausted. The late-night calls at the end of her long shifts were killing him, but it was worth it to hear her voice. Despite the stress of her job, she seemed so excited about the clinical trials starting the following week and so far he'd been successful in not asking whether they would prevent her from visiting on Christmas Eve. It was a new relationship and he didn't want to push her away by being needy or demanding. He wasn't that guy. He'd liked his independence just fine. The single, bachelor life had suited him great...until Erika.

Now, he was totally feeling capable of becoming a stage-one clinger.

"And she's grown an additional toe..." his mother was saying.

He blinked. "What?"

Arlene laughed. "Who's the girl?"

"What girl?"

"The one you're losing sleep over. You look like shit and you haven't been listening to me at all...and you keep checking that cell phone like baby Jesus is going to call, so out with it. Who is she?"

He'd never been able to keep things from his mother. Growing up, she'd had to play the nurturing role of mom and the kick-ass disciplinary role of father. He was still amazed at how she'd been successful at both. And still irritated that she'd had to.

"It's Erika."

Surprise registered on his mom's face, then she was nodding. "Makes sense."

"It does?"

"Yeah... You were always intrigued by her."

"I'm not sure I remember things that way." He'd always felt *intimidated* by Erika, but he'd refused to get close enough to her to be intrigued. Until that night in the woods, anyway, and he'd certainly gone out of his way to avoid her afterward.

But Arlene insisted. "You were. I mean, as she changed from a tall, skinny preteen to that amazing curvy body she has now, you certainly took notice."

He shifted in his seat at the mention of her body. A

body he'd kissed every inch of, touched every soft part of… A body he missed having next to him at night.

"But it was more than that," she continued. "She was different from the rest of you guys…she was quieter, more serious. She had a determined strength of character that appealed to you. She wasn't flighty and flirty like most of the girls Cassie hung out with."

He might have been interested in Erika from afar, but his interest came from trying to get her approval. She'd been so much better than the rest of them. His mother was right—she was smart and determined and she'd motivated his sister to do better. He'd respected her for that, even if they'd seemed too different to be friends.

That wasn't the case anymore. They were more alike than he could ever have imagined. And they fit together so well…at least they had when she was in Wild River.

"And of course, after that night in the woods…you'd already lost your heart."

He shook his head, refusing to admit to his mother that she was right. "No, back then, she was irritating and annoying and I struggled to understand her…"

His mother raised an eyebrow.

He sat back in his chair. His appetite vanishing the more they talked about the woman he was missing like crazy. She was right. His ambiguous teenage feelings for Erika had been the first step in developing this attraction and connection, and he was certainly hooked on her now.

"Well, you've certainly chosen well. True, I didn't get to spend a lot of time with her, but from what Cassie says, she's certainly able to match you in terms of drive and pigheadedness," she said with a smirk. "A surgeon, wow." She sipped her tea.

"Yeah…she's amazing. And busy," he said, checking his phone again.

Still no response to his good-morning text two hours before.

"Long-distance relationships aren't easy, but you'll figure it out if it's meant to be."

His mother was a firm believer in faith, but she'd always told them that anything worth having was worth fighting for.

He smiled as he reached across the table and squeezed her hand. "You're right. And this one is definitely worth the effort."

SHIT, SHE'D OVERSLEPT.

Late morning sunlight shining through the window was not a good sign. Panicked, Erika grabbed her cell phone.

9:58.

She'd missed her daily briefing with her dad. These late-night calls with Reed had to stop. They had to figure out a better system. She couldn't keep sleeping at her office either. Her back ached from that stupid cot and exhaustion was catching up to her.

How much longer could she keep this up?

Getting up, she straightened her skirt over her hips. She grabbed her lab coat from the hook behind the door and buttoned it, hoping no one noticed she was wearing yesterday's clothes. A trip to her condo sometime that day was necessary. She'd only spent a few hours at home in the week since she'd been back from Wild River.

Thank God messy buns were in style.

Grabbing a bottle of mouthwash from her desk drawer, she took a swig, gurgled it and spit it into the trash can beneath her desk.

She grabbed her patient files off her desk and stumbled over her discarded heels, losing the contents of the files all over the floor.

"Shit." She'd never felt this rushed, frazzled, unprepared and disorganized in her life. Luckily each piece of paper in the folders had a patient file number or her day would be getting complicated fast.

Gathering everything in a big pile, she shoved her feet back into her shoes and hurried down the hall to the boardroom.

"Erika, your intern clocked in an hour ago, she's been waiting in the staff lounge for you…" a nurse called after her as she walked past.

"She'll have to keep waiting." So much for trying harder with the new recruits. They should be taking the initiative anyway. When she'd interned, she certainly didn't sit around waiting for someone to tell her what to do.

Arriving at the boardroom on the first floor, she forced several calming breaths before opening the door. The room was full of doctors and the meeting had started without her. From the front of the room, her father didn't even glance her way as he pointed to a slide on his PowerPoint presentation.

She felt like a ten-year-old who'd failed a math test.

Every seat was full. She would have to stand there like a moron. Embarrassed and feeling judging eyes on her, she squared her shoulders.

"Psst," Darren whispered. "Sit here," he said, getting up from his chair at the table.

She quickly and quietly took his place with a grateful look and he handed her a double espresso and a note.

Sorry, I knocked on your office door for ten minutes.

She shook her head. Not his fault. Just her own. He wasn't even her intern anymore.

Then he discreetly took her disorganized files and set to putting them back together.

Tears burned the back of her exhausted eyes and the lump in her throat made it impossible to swallow the caffeine as she sent him another grateful look.

He winked at her as she turned her attention to the presentation at the front of the room. Her father was outlining the details of the trials and assigning different teams to different patients. She was so far behind. She may as well have been gone for months. Her father's gaze landed on her and the message was clear.

She needed to get it together.

Which meant no more long, late-night calls with Reed.

CHAPTER TWENTY-THREE

HE WAS GETTING the brush-off.

Days of barely any contact from Erika had Reed on edge. The brightly colored Christmas lights strung above the bar and the earsplitting sounds of Mariah Carey's "Christmas (Baby Please Come Home)" wasn't helping his mood.

Was this stupid CD on Repeat?

He'd heard this song a dozen times already that evening.

Grabbing a bottle of tequila from the shelf, it slipped from his hand and shattered on the floor.

Damn.

Going into the kitchen, he got a mop and broom and quickly cleaned up the mess.

"Still waiting on those tequila shots, Reed," Tank said, appearing at the bar with an empty wait tray. The man owned the place, but he couldn't make the simplest cocktail. Whenever he was forced to be behind the bar, everyone drank beer.

"If they'd like to come lick it off the floor, they can be my guest," Reed mumbled, tossing the shards of glass into the trash.

"That bottle's coming off your paycheck."

Tank's attempt at a joke earned him a middle finger. Opening a new bottle, Reed poured the six tequila shots and set them down on Tank's tray, spilling liquid over the sides.

"You good?" Tank asked.

"Peachy."

Tank walked away to deliver the shots to the obnoxious holiday party in the corner booth and Reed poured several pints of beer. Setting them in front of some tourists a little too abruptly, the liquid sloshed onto the bar.

"Hey, first day on the job?" the guy wearing an '80s style pro-ski club jacket asked.

The other guy snickered and Reed saw red. Picking up the glasses, he took them away. "Cut off," he muttered.

"Hey!" Ski-Pro called out. "What the fuck, man?"

Reed's jaw tightened. His emotions were on the surface and he felt ready to explode.

Tank intercepted, taking the glasses from him with an annoyed look. "Jesus, man," he muttered.

Reed had seen that expression far too many times that week already. Good thing his boss was also his buddy or he would have been fired by now. He just couldn't snap out of it. Unanswered texts, voice mail whenever he called and an overall vibe that Erika was avoiding him had him seriously on edge.

Grabbing a towel, he wiped down the bar, ignoring the sneers on the two men's faces.

Hope they don't plan on going into the backwoods while they're here.

Tank refilled the glasses to the top then delivered them back to the men. "On the house." Then, with a nod to Reed, he disappeared into the back office.

Shit.

Reed tossed the hand towel onto the bar and followed.

"Close the door," Tank said, collecting the darts from the board on his office wall and handing him the red ones.

"Not in the mood," Reed said, shoving his hands into his jeans pockets.

"But you'd rather take your shitty mood out on my paying customers?" Tank asked, still extending the darts.

Tank rarely called anyone out on anything. The guy had had enough.

Reed took the darts. "Sorry, man. I'm just..." He threw one arrow hard. It hit the edge and bounced off. "Just...argh," he said, throwing the second one...not even close to the bull's-eye, but throwing sharp, pointy things was helping a little.

"I've noticed. We all have." Tank threw his pair, both hitting the target. He shrugged. "Sexual frustration is something I understand," he said.

Reed retrieved all four, handing Tank the black ones, and threw his again. "It's been days, and just two text messages...short messages." Two brief "I'm sorry, work is crazy, we will talk soon" messages. Was this what she'd tried to tell him? Warn him about?

Two weeks ago, his heart had been aching at her leaving. Now it was breaking at the thought that with each day, she was moving farther and farther away and there was nothing he could do about it. He didn't know what to do with the pent-up nervous energy. He'd never felt this way before.

"She's a surgeon. Hospital emergency rooms are crazy, man. You know that. And Cass mentioned that her career is her life."

Yeah, and he'd thought he was okay with coming

second. Now, he wasn't sure if there was even a second spot on Erika's priority list. "I get that she's busy, but I think she just doesn't know how to balance work and life. She was so different when she was here."

"Everyone's different on vacation. She had no other choice but to relax. Is she coming back for Christmas?"

"She said she would try…"

"Hey, guys, when Reed's done sulking we have a full bar out here." Kelsey, their holiday hire, stuck her head in through the office door, her bright red hair falling into her eyes.

"Has anyone told you yet that you match the Christmas decorations?" Reed mumbled.

She gave him the finger. "And you've been playing the part of in-house Grinch perfectly."

That was true, but he couldn't shake his bad mood. Not having a girlfriend over the holidays used to be a blessing—he hadn't had to spend his tips on expensive presents—but now he was feeling the void with all the celebrating every night at the bar. His sister and friends used to be enough. Now there was only one person he longed to spend Christmas with.

"Seriously, guys, we can't keep up out here," Kelsey said, leaving the door open as she walked away.

"We're coming," Tank called after her. Turning to Reed, he said, "So, Christmas? Is she coming back or not?"

"We had planned on it, but honestly I'm not sure." Reed jammed the darts into the board.

Tank tapped his shoulder as they left the office. "I hate to be the one to say this, but I don't think this is going to end the way you want it to."

"Yeah." Tank was cynical about love and relationships, so Reed hesitated to take the words too much to heart. He couldn't give up on her yet. He'd told his mother that Erika was worth fighting for and he just needed to fight harder.

He'd talk to Cassie. She knew Erika the best and she was the most optimistic person he knew.

"Thanks for the chat, man," Reed said, returning to his post.

He just needed to block out the holiday music, the tacky decorations and the sickeningly-in-love couple in the booth across from him and do his job.

CLIMBING THE STAIRS to Cassie's condo hours later, he saw her lights still on, so he let himself in. "Hey, you still awake?" he asked, seeing her lying on the couch.

Their mom had left earlier that day and Diva was asleep in her food dish in the corner.

Cassie sat up and waved him in. "Yeah… Just going over Christmas bonuses."

Spread out on the coffee table in front of her were employee files and new Summer Adventure brochure proofs. It was December, but she was already thinking ahead to the next two seasons. His sister was one of the hardest working businesspeople he knew. Went to show, you didn't need a fancy MBA from an Ivy League school to be successful.

"Rough night?" she asked.

"It was busy, but no more than usual this time of year."

"You seem stressed and you don't usually visit at 2:00 a.m., so what's up?"

He sat on the couch. "Have you talked to Erika much since she left?"

Cassie closed her laptop, propping her sore foot onto the coffee table. True to his sister's nature, she'd had the cast removed early, opting for a smaller boot that she refused to wear. Trying to tell her otherwise was pointless.

"No... She texted once to ask if she'd left a pair of gloves here...and once more to see how my foot was healing, but I haven't heard from her in days."

Disappointment in his sister's voice matched how he was feeling.

"Right."

"Look, I pretty much missed what was happening between you two, but judging by your shitty mood and the dark circles under your eyes, I'd say you've got it bad."

He leaned back and rested his head against the couch cushions. "So bad." He wouldn't normally confess as much to his sister, but he needed her help. Unlike him, Cassie had been in love before. She'd experienced heartache. He just needed to know how to pull his head out of his ass and forget about Erika for a single moment.

"Well, Tank's about to fire you, so you better get your head on straight."

He blew out a long, slow breath. He'd been hoping for better advice than that. "Yeah, we talked."

"You threw darts, you mean." She rolled her eyes. "I swear that man thinks all of life's solutions are hidden in that freaking dartboard."

"Cass...can we focus on *my* fucked-up love life for a sec?"

"Fine. For a second," she said, swatting his leg.

"Okay, so what's going on? She's not available as much as you'd like?"

More like not available at all. "I'm not that clingy, Cass."

"Well, didn't she agree to come here for Christmas?" She pointed a finger at him. "To stay with *you*, I might add. I'm done with houseguests for at least a year."

There was hope in his sister's voice. Hope he'd almost given up on. "Yeah, but I'm not counting on it. She wasn't kidding when she said she works every day of the week and long hours. We've barely talked at all lately and I haven't asked her again about Christmas."

Cassie bit her lip. "Doesn't sound promising." She paused. "Why don't you go to her?"

"Christmas is our busiest time at the bar and three of the guys on the crew are away visiting family…" He shook his head. He'd already explored any angle he could to make that option work, but he'd dismissed it as a possibility.

"I don't mean just for Christmas." She took a breath. "Look, Snow Trek Tours is doing great now." She gestured to the files on the table in front of her. "I can easily repay you for the loan…"

"It wasn't a loan. I gave you that money. I'm glad things are going great for the business, but that's all because of you, Cass."

"Just hear me out. You could move to Anchorage and go back to school."

He scoffed. "I'm almost thirty."

"So? You always talked about being an EMT… With your training from the search and rescue, you'd probably be able to transfer in credits to a program and be finished faster…"

Excitement rose in her voice as she talked, but he continued to shake his head. The EMT dream had long ago left him. He loved his life on the mountain, felt fulfilled by his position on the search and rescue team. Anchorage was the last thing he wanted, even if it did have the one thing he wasn't sure he could continue to live without.

"Stop shaking your head and just consider it. As kids, it was all you talked about. Helping people is your thing. And Erika is in Anchorage. This long-distance thing is never going to work long-term," she said, gently.

So much for getting a more optimistic outlook from his sister. "No, I can't. A lifestyle change that drastic for someone I've only loved for a few weeks…"

His sister looked shocked.

"What?"

"You just said love."

No sense in denying it. He knew it was true. He loved Erika with all his heart. "Crazy as it sounds, I do love her."

"Well then you have to go after her. Even if that means sacrifices."

"I have responsibilities here. I don't hear you suggesting *she* move *here*. Give up everything she knows, everything she's worked hard for."

Why was it on him to take this leap of faith?

"She has a professional career saving lives. It's not as easy for her to find work here."

The Wild River Community Hospital had an opening, but Erika had said she hadn't even considered it.

"Reed, you could help people as an EMT in Anchorage, or go into nursing. You talked about that, too," Cassie continued.

"No."

His sister studied him. "Reed, be honest with yourself. Why is this life so hard to let go of?"

He stood and paced the living room. "It's what I do. It's all I've known." He had commitments and responsibilities here. Ones he couldn't easily walk away from.

Cassie was silent for a long moment, staring at her hands. When she looked up, she said, "You're chasing a ghost, Reed. Dad didn't go missing in the backwoods. He left us. No amount of searching is going to find him."

He needed air. The truth of his sister's words echoing in his mind was too much.

"How do you know?" Everyone had given up on finding his dad so easily. Not him. He wasn't sure he'd ever stop looking.

"Because I know where he is," she said.

He blinked, feeling the floor give way beneath him. His mouth went dry and his palms sweat. He dropped back down onto the edge of her couch and fought to steady his pulse. "How?"

"He contacted me a few weeks ago. He's at an addiction treatment center in Anchorage." She refused to look at him as she spoke.

Anger rose in his chest and he stood again. "Why the hell haven't you told me this? How long have you known?" What had she said? *A few weeks?*

What the fuck?

For the first time in his life, he wanted to punch something, break something. His fists clenched at his sides as he fought to control the shitty-ass roller coaster of emotions he was on.

Now of all moments, she chose to tell him. When his world was already rocked. What the hell did he do with this information?

Cassie struggled to stand and approached him. She reached for his arm but he yanked it away. "Tell me the truth, Cassie."

"I swear to you, Reed, I've only known for a few weeks." She looked pained and he forced himself to calm down. This couldn't have been easy on her to discover either. Not that he was letting her off the hook for not telling him sooner.

"He reached out to me as part of his recovery."

But he hadn't reached out to *Reed*. He couldn't decide which part of all this was worse.

"I'm paying for his treatment," she said, her eyes brimming with tears.

His sister never cried. Ever. The fact that his anger was bringing on this emotion made his chest hurt. He forced a deep breath and unclenched his fists. His father was alive, okay…and an alcoholic…still. He'd always hid it from the family, but as a teenager, Reed had seen everything his parents had tried to conceal.

He stared at the ceiling, his trembling hands resting on his hips. "Does Mom know?"

Cassie nodded. "We talked about it before she left. I asked her about him and she came clean. She said she'd always known that he was struggling with it, but it was easier to let us believe he'd gone missing."

Easier on who? He ran a hand through his hair. His mouth was sandpaper. An addiction, he could have dealt with. Maybe he could have helped somehow. Keeping this from them was wrong.

"She said she was always hoping he'd get his shit together and come back. Still hoping," Cassie said softly.

"She should have told us. *You* should have told *me*." That was the hardest thing to swallow. He and Cassie had always had each other's back. He couldn't help the feeling of betrayal.

"I know. I'm sorry. I just… He said *you'd* be disappointed in him the most. He asked for a chance to get better, then come back to you…a better man. Someone you could be proud of again."

Proud? Of a man who'd just walked out on them? Who'd chosen alcohol over his family? He could barely breathe as he stared at his sister, trying to see her side, trying to make sense of it. Any of it. "Why didn't you tell me? Did you think I couldn't handle it?"

"That's not it at all. I just didn't want to hurt you."

Too late. He nodded slowly. "I'm going to go."

"Reed, please," Cassie said, reaching for his hand.

"I can't do this right now, Cass."

Heading back outside, he took the stairs two at a time and walked down the quiet, deserted Main Street with no destination in mind, just away from the truth.

CHAPTER TWENTY-FOUR

TIME WAS FLYING BY in a blink and Erika's guilt kept rising. She started each day with the best intentions of reaching out to Reed to explain that things would slow down a little once the clinical trials started…and each day came and went with unanswered text messages from him as a million other things took priority.

Now it seemed impossible to reach out. To explain. Pushing thoughts of him aside was the only way she could successfully get through her busy days, but how could she tell him that?

His texts were becoming fewer each day and he hadn't tried to call the last few nights. Maybe he was slowly accepting that she was busy and he wasn't prepared to keep reaching out to dead air. While she wanted to beg him to not lose hope, that would be wrong.

She missed him, or at least she missed what they'd had in Wild River. She missed the connection with another person—a man who had made her feel more alive than she'd ever felt. She missed the freedom and the adventure and the excitement. She missed the woman she'd been in Wild River.

But that hadn't been the real her. *This* was her. This life was hers.

And she couldn't do this with Reed.

Her father was losing confidence in her as the head of the clinical trial team and several surgeries that week hadn't gone well.

It was either success in her career *or* love. Not both. Never both.

The sinking feeling in her stomach made the realization of what she had to do that much harder. She didn't want to end things with Reed. That's why she was avoiding him. Hoping somehow she'd come up with a way to make a relationship work.

"Dr. Sheraton to emergency." The call over the intercom was far too familiar this past week. With the weather getting colder—more snow and ice storms— and Christmas parties leading to more drinking and driving, she'd had six emergency operations that week.

One patient hadn't made it. Struck by a drunk driver on a crosswalk, the twenty-year-old college student had suffered internal injuries far too severe to save him. Devastation on the boy's mother's face when she'd delivered the news had broken her.

From now on, she was returning to her "no contact with the family" policy. What good did it really do? Hearing from Erika that her son wouldn't be there for the holidays had changed nothing for that poor woman. She'd still lost her son.

Slowly, her defensive walls were going back up. She needed them. She should never have taken them down.

She checked her watch as she rode the elevator to the first floor. Six thirty. Her evening was only beginning. A blizzard raging outside predicted a busy night for her.

When the elevator doors opened, she saw Reed standing in the emergency room.

Obviously *not* hurt.

And looking so unexpectedly amazing, dressed in a pair of faded jeans and a thick, thermal bomber jacket, his dark hair cut a little shorter but the scruff at his jawline was now almost a full beard. She stood frozen.

The elevator doors began to close again and he reached forward to stop them, entering the small space. "Hi."

His familiar cologne immediately filled the space and she held her breath. "Hi." She knew she'd mouthed the word, but no sound came out.

He took her hands in his and stepped closer. "Hi," he said again.

She looked down at their hands. His touch was real. His smell was real. He was really there. Not a hallucination from sleep deprivation.

"God, you look even more gorgeous than I remembered," he said. "And hot in this lab coat." He grinned, but the attempt to ease the awkward tension was lost on her.

She still didn't move. Him there in her space. Him in her reality was messing with her tired mind. "What are you doing here?" she finally said.

He gave a nervous laugh. "I missed you. I wanted to see you. *Needed* to see you, actually."

She nodded. Reed was here. In her elevator. Well, not *her* elevator, the hospital's elevator. Her hospital… Her mind was spinning. She'd been prepared to deal with a stab wound or a heart attack. Another car accident victim. Not Reed. Nope, definitely not Reed. She felt slightly dizzy. Her chest hurt and her palms were sweaty.

Shit. Maybe *she* was having a heart attack.

His expression looked anxious as he kissed her palms. "I've really missed you."

Yes, he'd said that already. She winced. Her palms were sweaty. She simply nodded again. He'd come all the way from Wild River to tell her he missed her?

"Can you say something please?" The elevator doors reopened. He hit the button to close it and then the one for the bottom floor.

"That's the maintenance floor," she said.

"I don't care." He pulled her closer. "Erika, I don't care where this elevator takes us. I just care about you. Seeing you, touching you...wishing you'd say something."

"Um...yeah, sorry, I just wasn't expecting you." Understatement. He'd barely contacted her at all these last few days and she thought... What had she thought? That he'd let her off easy? Let what they had just fade away without having to verbalize a breakup?

The cowardly way she'd been planning to.

His shoulders sagged and the smile slipped from his lips. "Well, I would have given you a heads-up, but you don't seem to be checking your messages frequently..."

His annoyance immediately snapped her out of a trance. "So, you thought a visit was better?" The edge in her voice was unfair and unintentional. She was excited to see him, her heart was filled by the sight of him, but what exactly was he expecting from her? Showing up unannounced when she was working wasn't the best way to get her attention.

Though it may have been the only way. It had worked.

The elevator stopped, the doors opened and closed and she hit the floor for emergency again.

He shoved his hands in his pockets and stared at the floor. "Sorry to just show up like this. Admittedly, it wasn't the smartest idea. But I didn't know what else to do. I guess I thought if I was standing here, you'd have to make time. Would want to make time for me."

She felt like shit. "I'm sorry, that came out wrong. I am happy to see you." Problem was, his theory had been right. Now that he was there, she did want to spend time with him, but she still had a job to do. She couldn't take the evening off and go back to her condo and make love to him and fall asleep in his arms. That was a fantasy. This was real life.

"Are you?" he asked.

"Of course... I've...uh, missed you, too." She reached out to touch his arms, but his hands stayed in the pockets of his jeans.

His sexy, faded jeans that hugged his thighs with the rip in the left knee. Damn, he looked good. Suddenly all of her ability to push away emotions and memories of him vanished and their week in Wild River came spiraling back like a bad '80s movie montage.

Unfortunately, her words had come seconds too late. His expression had changed to one of disappointment and she hated that she was the cause. He'd come all this way. For her.

She moved closer. "I really did. Let's talk in my office," she said, checking her watch.

He caught the motion.

"I'm obviously on the clock, so let's just get this out there," he said. "What I've come to say."

Her heart raced. There was zero air in this elevator. "Okay..."

"I'm in love with you, Erika."

The lump in her throat threatened to choke her. He loved her? After only a few weeks? Was that possible?

She'd been falling for him while she was in Wild River, but now that she was back in Anchorage she couldn't help but wonder if the mountains and the freedom and the excitement had tricked her into believing the feelings she was having for Reed were real. She cared about him more than any other man she'd ever been with, but love? Was she even capable of that?

But here he was saying the *L* word and damn, if he didn't sound sincere.

Which made her own hesitation even worse. If he was so sure, how could she not be? "It's so fast," she said. "We've only known each other a few weeks."

"I've known you my entire life," he said.

"You know what I mean."

His gaze burned into hers as he stepped closer and wrapped his arms around her. "I know. But since your sexy, annoying ass sat on my barstool, I can't stop these feelings that I'm having for the first time. Being with you was unlike anything I've ever felt. You challenge me in ways no one ever has. You make me want to work harder, strive to be better—for you. Before you showed up, I was completely happy with my bachelor life. Now, I want to leave it behind. I want something more. You've changed me, Erika."

It had been that way for her, too, and being in his arms now was creating a whirlwind of confusing, conflicting emotions she wasn't equipped to deal with.

She didn't do feelings. She knew odds and procedures. She knew how to make a heart keep beating, but not how to trust her own.

"I've been going crazy without you. Food has no

taste anymore. I can't sleep. Tank's on the verge of firing me and I don't blame him—I'm annoying myself. I'm trying to be patient and I'm trying to understand the lack of contact. I don't want to complicate your life…"

Too late.

He backed away abruptly. "That's what I am—just a complication?"

She'd said the words out loud? Or had he read the thought on her face? "No, of course not." Not *just* that, at least. "But actually yes. Not *just* a complication, but a complication for sure. I don't know how to be a top surgeon and a girlfriend, okay? I've never had to be both. And I'm sorry I'm sucking at it, but if I have to choose which one to be good at, I have to go with my career."

He looked as though she'd delivered a blow to the gut.

How could she ease the truth? Words had never been her friend and the only ones coming to mind now wouldn't make either of them feel better. She was quiet for a long minute, sending the elevator back to the maintenance room when it hit the emergency floor again.

She waited.

Say something, Reed. Anything.

She couldn't trust herself to say any more. But if he had any answers, any solutions on how to make this work, she'd be more than happy to hear them.

Nothing.

He stood there, silent, storm clouds passing across his blue eyes. It was torture to see him this way, but she had nothing to give him.

She sighed. "Reed, this is my life. My career matters to me."

"And I don't."

It wasn't a question. "That's not true," she said softly. She cared about him a lot, but he was asking for a commitment from her she couldn't make. Love? When did she have time to love someone fully? The way they deserved? The way he deserved?

He stared at his feet. Silent.

The tension around them was suffocating.

"So, that's it?"

The hurt in his voice was unbearable, but words refused to come. The right words, at least. "I don't know how to do this, Reed."

A glimmer of hope reflected in his eyes, like a tiny life preserver she wished she had the courage to grab.

"Can you trust me to help you figure it out?"

She wanted to, but, "What if I don't get there? Where you are?"

"Are you willing to try?"

It was a fair question, but he wouldn't be satisfied with her answer. "Not if it means sacrificing my career or not giving my patients my best."

He looked defeated as he nodded. "Then I guess I should go."

No! Her heart screamed at her to do the right thing. For once in her life to take a chance on something that didn't make sense. But years of ignoring her heart made it easy to silence it now. She nodded.

"And Christmas…?"

God, she wanted to give him the answer he was hoping for. But making another false promise would be too cruel.

"No."

"Okay." He hit the button for the elevator door and she resisted the overwhelming urge to reach for him, to touch him one more time, to kiss him one more time... She couldn't. That would be selfish. She had to let him go. And if those arms wrapped around her, those lips touched hers, she wouldn't have the strength.

"Bye, Erika," he said as he left the elevator. Turning back, he added, "You were wrong, you know."

No doubt she was wrong about a lot of things. "About what?"

"It doesn't hurt less when you're not expecting it." Then he headed toward the front door.

Her legs felt unsteady beneath her and she craved the safety and privacy of her office as tears threatened to fall, but the flashing lights of an incoming ambulance illuminated Reed's disappearing figure and the sound of sirens drowned out the breaking of her heart.

REED STARED THROUGH the frosted window of his truck at the Anchorage Addictions Treatment Center. What the hell was he doing here? Leaving the hospital, he'd been in a fog. When his surprise visit to Erika had crashed and burned he should have headed back to Wild River. Instead, he'd driven here.

Nothing good would come of this stop either.

Going to see Erika had been an impulsive move. A decision he'd made that morning. A desperate attempt to get things back on track. He hadn't expected her reaction. He'd foolishly thought that once she saw him, she'd remember how great they were together. How could he have been so wrong?

At least he'd known what he'd planned to say when he saw *her*.

What the hell was he going to say to his dad?

Years of anger, sadness and uncertainty were likely to all come pouring out. The man was at a rehab facility dealing with an addiction. This wasn't a good idea. Neither of them was in the right headspace for this.

An image of Erika's cool reception made him shiver. Would it be the same with his father? What would his dad say? He hadn't even wanted Reed to know where he was.

It was now or never. He had to grow a set and get out of the damn truck. He couldn't leave Anchorage without seeing him.

He climbed out of his truck and walked into the building. The waiting room was nicer than he'd expected. Beige walls and tan, comfortable-looking furniture. A fireplace and a small coffee and tea center set up beside it made the place look more like a hotel lobby than a clinic. Down the hall to his right, a set of doors led to an outside courtyard, and to the left was another hall, leading to intake rooms. Staff members went in and out, dressed in the same uniform of khaki pants and polo shirts with the Anchorage Addictions Treatment Center logo on them. Casual and comfortable.

His hands shook at his sides and he glanced outside.

"Can I help you?" a receptionist asked. The only thing giving away the purpose of the place was the fact that she was behind thick glass, speaking into a microphone. Her smile was warm and she had kind eyes—the perfect person to have behind the desk—but nothing could make him relax.

Too late to back out now. "Um, maybe. I'm here to see a...patient." Was that the right term?

"Okay. Are they in long-term care or have they just recently checked in?"

Cassie had said her dad reached out only a few weeks ago, but who knew how long he'd been here before that. "He's new, I think. Maybe a month."

"If he's recently checked into the thirty-day detox program, he won't be able to see visitors..." She turned her attention to her computer. "Name?"

"George Reynolds." He hadn't said his dad's name in so long, it stuck on his tongue. He folded his hands on the ledge as he waited for her to search the system.

"I see he checked in on November 22..." She continued to punch a few keys. "Are you family?"

"I'm his son."

"The only emergency contact I see on file is a Cassie Reynolds."

He swallowed hard. "That's my sister. Will I be allowed to see him?"

She studied the computer monitor and then shook her head. "It looks like he checked out yesterday."

Yesterday. He'd just missed him. "Did he complete the program? That wasn't thirty days."

"It doesn't look like it," she said, with a sympathetic smile. "A lot of people struggle to make it through the first time. It's very intense."

He nodded. His father had dropped out. What happened to wanting to come back to them a better man? Anger rose in his chest, replacing the empty hurt he'd walked away from Erika with.

So close to seeing the man after all this time and he was too late.

Not that he would have gotten the chance to see him anyway, according to the center's rules, but just knowing he was there, getting help, taking the necessary steps to get his life on track again would have been almost enough.

Obviously his father still couldn't put their family first.

He cleared his throat. "Did he leave an address or phone number?"

She shook her head. "We couldn't give it out even if he had," she said. "I'm sorry."

He hit the ledge with his fist, then backed away as her eyes widened. "Sorry... I'm sorry," he mumbled, hurrying out of the clinic and back into his truck. His heart pounded in his ears and his mind was a mess.

Coming to Anchorage had been a huge mistake. There was obviously nothing here for him.

CHAPTER TWENTY-FIVE

"FORTY-NINE... FIFTY," Tank said, taking the weight bar from Reed and setting it back in the holder. "Great job, man. Maybe one day you'll be lifting as much as me."

Reed was hardly in a joking mood. When his buddy had suggested the early morning workout session, he'd thought it might be just what he needed to blow off steam and ease some of the pent-up anxiety from the last few days. First, the argument with his sister, then the breakup with Erika—he was having the shittiest week of his life. He still hadn't been able to wrap his mind around the situation with his father, and despite Cassie's attempts to talk, he wasn't ready yet.

He was a mess.

Unfortunately, the workout was making him even more annoyed. Or rather his workout partner was.

As pissed as he was at Cassie, he was starting to get her frustration with Tank. He knew Tank's situation was complicated, being a single dad and all, but why was he keeping Cassie at bay, stringing her along and using her as a babysitter but never giving her what she needed. After his own experience with Erika, being in love and getting completely crushed, he understood how his sister must be feeling all the time.

It sucked, and it was time to call his friend out on it.

Tank leaned back on the bench and Reed handed him the weight.

He pumped out his reps fast and hard, but when he was finished, Reed didn't take the bar.

"Hey. Wake up," he said.

"I'm wide-awake," Reed said.

"Well, take the bar." Tank's crazy big biceps started to wobble under the two hundred pounds. "Reed, what the fuck, man?"

Reed took it and set it back. He didn't want to crush his friend, just get through to his big skull.

Sitting up, Tank shot him a look as he wiped his face with a towel. "You pissed at me now?"

He was pissed at everything and everyone lately. Keeping his mouth shut was what he wanted to do, but he couldn't. "Why do you think it's okay to string Cass along like this?"

His voice echoed off the concrete walls, and several people running on treadmills glanced their way.

"Cass and I are friends," Tank said. His tone clearly revealed that he thought this was none of Reed's business.

Maybe it wasn't. But right now he needed to try to make sense of this whole love bullshit. If people cared about one another, they should be together. No excuses, no running away.

He couldn't get Erika to see that and it was too late for his father to realize it, but maybe his friend and sister had a chance.

"You know she wants more than that," he said, quieter this time. Everyone knew everyone in Wild River and Cassie would kick his ass if she knew he was interfering.

"She knows I'm not able to give more. Reed, I've never mislead your sister." Tank guzzled some water from his bottle, then added more weight to the bench. "I've always been straightforward and honest with her."

"But you care about her?"

"Of course."

"So, don't you think she deserves to hear the truth— that you're just not into her that way? Let her move on?"

"It's not as simple as that." Tank removed the weights and put them back. "I'm done."

With the conversation, too, apparently. But Reed wasn't. "It's not fair to her."

"Life isn't exactly fair to any of us. Look, man, just because people can't commit the way you want them to, doesn't mean the feelings aren't there. And just because you're feeling something real for the first time and shit's not working out for you, don't take it out on the rest of us who have been struggling with the same complicated shit for a long time."

Reed swallowed hard. His buddy was right. His relationship with Cassie was none of his business. "I just don't want to see Cassie get hurt."

"Hurting her is the last thing I want to do. I'm dealing with things the only way I can."

The way Erika was dealing with things the only way she knew how. Why was life so messed up? Why couldn't things work out for someone, just once? He sighed. "Whatever you and Cassie are doing is none of my business. I shouldn't have called you out like that."

"You're protecting your sister, I get it. That's what families do—they look out for one another." Tank tapped his shoulder as he headed for the showers.

Families look out for one another.

An hour later, Reed arrived at Snow Trek Tours, a bell chiming above the door as he entered. Cassie sat at her desk, her head bent over a financial statement. Her blond hair was held back with reindeer antlers and the Christmas tree in the corner of the office was decorated with camping gear, skis and snowshoes. She looked up as he approached. "Hi, how can I... Oh hey."

"How are you?"

"I'd be better if my older brother would stop ignoring me," she said with a small smile.

"Yeah. I'm done being a dickhead." Ever since they were kids, they never let arguments last longer than a few days. They were too close to let disagreements—however big—get in the way of their friendship. He cleared his throat. "I, uh...went to see Dad when I was in Anchorage."

She took a deep breath. "And?"

He shook his head. "He wasn't there."

Her shoulders sagged. "Sorry, Reed. I know you were hoping..."

She didn't have to finish the sentence.

"So, anyway, I was wondering if you have plans tomorrow night." He shoved his hands in his pockets and rocked back and forth on his heels.

"Christmas Eve?"

"I hear there's a 'drown your holiday sorrows by getting shit-faced at The Drunk Tank' party if you're interested."

She laughed, relief appearing on her face at his attempt at putting the argument behind them. He still had no idea what to do about his newfound knowledge, but he'd get through one thing at a time. They'd get through it as a family.

"Brother, I've been attending that party for years. Am I to assume *you're* joining *me* this year?"

"I'll be there with bells on." If he was going to drown in holiday heartache this year, at least he'd be in good company.

It HAD TO be the quietest Christmas Eve on record for the hospital. Even the emergency room was quiet... except for the usual suspects—several older patients who claimed to be having heart attacks. Fortunately, it was only the stress of family visiting causing their mild, nonthreatening chest pains. Erika was certain that for some, they just wanted an excuse to leave the house for a while. The only patient she'd treated so far was an eight-year-old who'd stuck his tongue to a frozen pole on a dare and was being treated for frostbite.

Big, thick snowflakes fell outside her office window, creating the perfect Christmas Eve weather. She drew the blinds. Her office might be the only place completely void of any sights and sounds of the holiday. No artificial tree, no decorations, no snow from a can on her windows. A perfect refuge.

Sitting at her desk, she opened her inbox and was relieved to see several emails marked urgent from her father. They should help keep her mind off the place she longed to be. The person she longed to reach out to. She hadn't heard from Reed since the day in the elevator, but his disappointed expression had haunted her. Every time she closed her eyes, she saw him walking away.

Work. Focus on work.

She opened the first email from her father, but a new one arriving in her inbox caught her eye.

From Tom Marshal—the man she'd performed the tracheotomy on weeks before.

Subject line—Merry Christmas.

Ignore it and focus on work.

It *was* Christmas Eve. One holiday e-card wouldn't kill her. She opened it and an animated scene started on the screen. She watched, alternating between laughter and tears as the JibJab video reenacted the man's camping trip in the Wild River mountains.

The avalanche, the rescue… He'd even found her medical school graduation photo online and superimposed her into the video, arriving in a doctor's lab coat to save his life on the side of the mountain.

The video ended with him safe and sound in the hospital room, surrounded by his family. The photo of him they'd used was one of him hooked to machines after his surgery.

Obviously, the family appreciated his second chance at life and were dealing with the accident the best way they knew how—with humor.

Then the caption appeared on the screen.

I wouldn't be here this Christmas without you being there that day. Merry Christmas, Dr. Erika. You're our superhero. —The Marshal Family

The lump in her throat constricted her airways, and it was a relief to know the emergency room wasn't busy, in case these overwhelming feelings decided to kill her.

She'd received thank-you emails, cards and even flowers from families in the past, but something about this one felt different. It touched her.

She typed a reply to the family wishing them a Merry Christmas and then sat staring at time ticking away slowly on the bottom of her computer screen.

This night was dragging on.

Ignoring the other emails, she opened Facebook. It was a mistake, but she did it anyway.

Having fifty-six friends, it didn't take her long to scroll through the new posts. Stopping on Cassie's, she felt a wave of remorse so strong she struggled to breathe. She'd promised her friend things would be different this time... She'd promised Reed.

And if she could only find that work/life balance everyone talked about, maybe things would be different. She'd be able to keep that promise.

So far, she'd been unsuccessful. The next day, no matter how busy she was, she was taking time to call her friend to say Merry Christmas.

Maybe she should do her own JibJab video...

Lord knows, she had time.

Scrolling through her friend's recent posts, she scanned the photos of Cassie and Arlene decorating her artificial pink Christmas tree, Diva passed out on the homemade, quilted tree skirt with all four paws in the air. The red-and-green boots on the puppy's feet and matching sweater made Erika smile and tear up all over again.

Damn, she even missed the dog.

Next were pictures taken at the Christmas parade the week before. Cassie, Tank and Kaia looked like they belonged on a Christmas card. Their smiling, happy faces with the holiday backdrop made it impossible to know that the three of them were dealing with their own issues.

Or maybe they weren't anymore. Had at least one of them gotten their happy ending in time for Christmas? Just in case, Erika made a Christmas wish that her friend would get what she really wanted under her tree that year—a six-foot-two hunk of solid muscle who was also a single dad.

Pictures posted just an hour before made her heart skip… Christmas Eve at The Drunk Tank. Pictures of Cassie, Tank, Wade, Tyler, Tiffany and a redhead she was immediately envious of with her arm around Reed. The picture had her longing for a Christmas Eve that she hadn't had since her mother's death. One surrounded by family and friends… People she loved. A man she loved.

She stared at Reed's smiling face, committing the image to memory to replace his look of sadness and disappointment on the day they ended things. Watching him walk away had been hard…but the reality that things were over between them hadn't hit until now, when she was alone and the silence of her downtime only screamed how lonely she really was.

What she'd give to be there with them.

Damn, that trip to Wild River had been such a huge mistake. She'd been okay with her life until she'd experienced an alternative. She hadn't been able to miss what she hadn't known existed.

She hit Like on the photo and forced herself to shut down the app.

Checking her watch, she hesitated before calling downstairs to her father's office.

"Dr. Sheraton's office." His assistant, Kam, sounded as though she were counting the final seconds until she could go home to be with her family. It was almost eight o'clock. Her father should have let the woman go at noon… But he'd never put emphasis on the holidays. Not since her mother died. Neither of them did. There were no decorations in his home, no Christmas CDs in his car. He didn't send out greeting cards and his assistant bought her own gift. The holidays were just two days they had to get through—nothing special.

Unfortunately, they did mean something to her this year.

"Hi, Kam…is my dad still here?"

"Yes, he is. Can I place you through?"

She suddenly wasn't exactly sure why she was calling. "Um…no… I'll come by." She needed the elevator ride to figure out what to say.

Not that it had helped her before.

In fact, she wasn't eager to enter the space where Reed's scent seemed to linger, haunting her, so she took the stairs instead.

Five minutes later, she made up her mind that she would invite her father to go somewhere, anywhere, for Christmas Eve dinner. At this point, she'd settle for Chinese takeout. It may not be traditional…but they had no traditions anyway. She just wanted to be with family.

When her mother was alive, things had been so different. Every year they'd gone out the week before Christmas to cut down their own tree. They'd decorated in traditional holiday colors, the old handmade ornaments stirring warm and comforting memories… And they'd watch Christmas movies together every night, taking turns selecting the titles. Her mother always loved the overly sentimental made-for-TV ones and her dad used to tease her about it, then they'd catch him tearing up at the end, as well. Of course, he'd blame his watery eyes on the scented candles...

Could they ever get that family connection back?

Kam wasn't at her desk when Erika reached her father's office.

Good. Maybe her dad had finally sent the woman home to her family.

Knocking on his door once, she turned the knob and entered.

She came up short seeing several doctors on the clinical trial team sitting around her father's desk, studying the latest reports.

Had she missed a meeting memo? She didn't remember seeing one scheduled on her calendar. Damn, had she messed up again?

"Was there a meeting today?"

Her father met her gaze squarely. "We're going over the first week trial results."

Without her? "Did you buzz my office? I was in there."

"No, I didn't."

The other team members avoided her eyes.

What the hell was going on? "Can I talk to you? In the hallway?" she asked her dad.

He checked his watch. "We're in the middle of something here, Erika. It's Christmas Eve—these folks would like to get home soon. Can it wait?"

Was he kidding? Her spine stiffened. "We could talk in here if you'd like," she said tightly.

He stared at her.

She didn't dare flinch.

"I'll be right back," he told the group. The fact that

he didn't immediately admit it was an oversight and invite her to join the meeting spoke volumes.

"Why wasn't I invited to this?" she asked the minute they were in the hallway.

Kam reappeared at her desk and glanced their way with a sympathetic look. Erika's stomach twisted. She had been purposely excluded.

And why the hell hadn't her father let Kam go home to her kids yet? Christmas Eve might mean nothing to him, family might mean nothing to him, but it did to most people.

She forced her pulse steady as she waited for an explanation.

"You have a lot on your plate right now," her father said.

She gestured to the nearly empty waiting room down the hall. "Not really."

"Well, you wouldn't know by your lack of attention to detail lately."

Her mouth gaped and she slammed her lips shut. True, she'd been a little distracted when she'd first returned, but it hadn't taken her long to get back to her old self—her old workaholic self…

She wasn't sure that was a good thing, but it was certainly what her father wanted.

Yet, it obviously wasn't enough. "The vacation threw me off a little…but that's over now." She swallowed hard, an image of Reed burned into her mind.

The redhead in the picture was there, too. Who was she? A date? Had he moved on already? She felt sick.

"Really? Those reports are hardly accurate. You missed two of the candidates' first week results."

She clenched her teeth. "I didn't *miss* anything.

Those candidates are away for the holidays. You approved their request to leave Anchorage for a few days to see family, remember?" She wasn't the one who'd messed up and she'd be damned if she would let him make her feel inadequate.

He waved a hand. "Either way, the trials have started...the team is up to speed on things. I'm taking you off as lead to give you time to focus on your job."

He was what?

She shook her head more in disbelief than refusal. No matter what she said or did, his decision was final. "I can't believe you. For three years, I've been at your side researching this new drug, applying over and over to get it FDA approved, interviewing and researching the right candidates for this trial..."

"And you did great work."

Was that a compliment? She couldn't tell by the patronizing tone.

"I want to stay on." She deserved to be there when the drug was a success, when her father and the team were awarded the Lister Medal, which she knew in her heart would happen.

How could he not see that? How could he not want her to have that?

"I've asked Tim to step up and he's agreed." He touched her arm, but the gesture was more disciplinary in nature than affectionate. A silent reminder that they had an audience and not to make a scene. He'd been silencing her emotions that way for years. She stiffened and moved away.

No matter what she did, no matter how hard she worked, nothing would be good enough for him. She'd learned to accept that. But now, he was taking away something that belonged to her as much as anyone else in that room, maybe more so... Something deeply personal as well as professional. "I disagree with that decision. Tim lacks the experience I have." He couldn't argue with that.

"True. But he'll catch up quickly."

Logic was dissipating, emotion taking over for probably the first time ever regarding her career. "I don't understand."

"I sent you emails today looking for updates on subjects 65 and 34."

Subjects. No, *patients*. Real *people*. Mr. Keely and Mrs. Somers. Patients she'd actually gotten to know the last few days, and now she had a very personal interest in seeing them benefit from these trials. It wasn't just about the drug anymore. She fought the urge to correct him. "I was just replying to those emails, and as I mentioned, candidates were not available."

"I shouldn't have had to send the follow-up emails. A month ago, you'd have already sent the updates about those subjects without me asking for them."

She swallowed hard. That was probably true, but the hospital emergency department had been crazy that week and she'd thought he'd remember that he'd approved their exclusion...excuses. He'd only hear excuses. That's all they were. She'd set expectations with her past work ethic and in recent weeks, those standards had slipped a little.

She'd accepted it. But she couldn't expect her father to. "Yes, sir."

"I have to get back in there," he said, turning and disappearing into the room. "CC Tim on your replies."

Tim, her replacement. The man who would get the

glory for all her hard work. Worse, the man who would get to work with these patients and see the amazing results. Erika stood there for a long moment, contemplating the future of her career.

Unfortunately, all she could think about was the fact that despite everything, she'd rather be at The Drunk Tank than in that meeting right now.

ERIKA HAD LIKED Cassie's photo. The one from earlier in the evening of all of them together at The Drunk Tank Christmas Eve party.

What the hell did that mean?

No comment, no message…hell, she still hadn't Friend Requested him on Facebook yet.

Just a single Like.

But she'd been checking on them—that had to mean *something*, right? Was she wishing she was there with them? In that picture, next to him? For fifteen minutes now, he'd been driving himself crazy wondering.

Maybe he should call. She had to be awake… Damn, he desperately wanted to hear her voice.

Reed stared at her profile picture, her medical school graduation shot. So polished, so poised, so…not the woman he had known her to be. Sure, she was brilliant and successful, but whenever he thought of her, he thought about the quick-thinking, fast-acting, no-bullshit-taking woman who'd saved a man's life on the side of a mountain.

And he thought about the soft, affectionate, desirable woman he'd lost himself to. Unfortunately, he wasn't sure that woman wanted him anymore.

He sighed, tucking the phone away as he continued to clean up the bar after the Christmas Eve party. It was after midnight, so technically it was Christmas Day. Everyone else was gone. Tank had taken off early to put Kaia to bed and play the role of Santa. Cassie had gone to spend the night at their mother's house. Wade was with his wife and Tyler had found a lonely tourist to spend the holiday with...

Much to Kelsey's obvious dismay.

He'd always enjoyed their annual Christmas Eve party. They were a family. There was no one else he'd ever wanted to spend this night with, nowhere else he'd rather be. Until this evening, when his heart had been hundreds of miles away.

Surrounded by family and friends, it was easier to pretend, but at the end of the night, he was alone.

Was his sister right?

Was it wrong to expect Erika to make sacrifices to be with him when he wasn't prepared to make any of his own?

He lifted the barstools, setting them on top of the bar, then he ran the mop over the hardwood floor.

Claiming that Erika would be happier in Wild River with him was just arrogance and an unwillingness to accept the fact that she might not have fallen as hard and fast as he had.

Maybe she'd needed more time. He'd been unable to give her that.

He put the mop away and turned off the Christmas lights behind the bar. Shutting off the music, he locked up and headed home. He hadn't driven there that evening, knowing he'd be drinking along with everyone else, and now the streets were quiet, empty, haunted with memories of Erika everywhere he looked. Light from the streetlamps illuminated his path and a soft snow fell in big flakes, covering his tracks as he walked. The Christmas displays in the store windows held reminders of everything that was important in life. Themes of family, love, connections were all around him.

He loved it here. This was the life he knew. But how much would he have to give up if he wanted to hold on to it?

He stopped and took in the snow-covered mountains. He breathed in the fresh air and let it fill his lungs with new hope. There was very little he'd give all of this up for...but one feisty, sexy brunette who held his heart might just be it.

HER CONDO HAD never felt so lonely. Void of any holiday decorations was the way she usually preferred it, but she couldn't help but wish she'd at least put up a tree.

The sound of her neighbors' Christmas Day festivities coming from down the hall wasn't helping.

She wasn't scheduled to be at the hospital for another two hours. Normally, she'd go in early, but being taken off the clinical trials still stung. How could her father do this to her? She'd obviously given him more credit than he deserved, hoping some part of him still cared about family. About her. But it was all about the job.

And here she was turning out just like him. Almost thirty and the only future in sight was a mirrored image of this lonely holiday.

Sitting on her sofa, her coffee warming her hands, Erika stared at her cell phone.

She'd already called Cassie to say Merry Christmas, but the call had gone to voice mail. It was only just after nine. Her friend was probably still sleeping.

Resisting the urge to call Reed was killing her. She willed the phone to ring.

But he wouldn't call. Christmas or not, she'd hurt him.

Picking up the phone, she opened her photo gallery and scrolled through the pictures she'd taken of him shirtless in his bedroom.

Damn, he was hot. And more important, he was kind and caring and strong and everything she could ever hope to find in a man. She'd thrown it all away. Had losing him been worth it?

She stared at his gorgeous face.

She was an idiot. And there was only one thing that could begin to make her feel better.

Going to her fridge, she retrieved the box of peppermint fudge Cassie had given her and carried it back to the living room. She picked up her honorary search and rescue member jacket—the best and only gift she'd received that year—and put it on, desperate to find comfort in the thing that tied her to Reed...to another possible future?

Turning on her television, she flipped the stations until she found *It's a Wonderful Life*.

Perfect. The most depressing Christmas movie ever, her fudge and memories of the best week of her life.

Merry Christmas to me.

CHAPTER TWENTY-SIX

CALLS HAD COME IN steadily since Christmas Day and by December 31, Reed was running on fumes. Unexpected ice storms and rain had made the ski slopes and hiking more treacherous, but the holiday tourists, the ones who visited the resort once a year, were ignoring the warning signs and venturing out in unsafe conditions anyway.

"Just once it would be nice if these jerks thought about what their stupidity meant for the people who have to come save their asses..." Wade muttered as he and Reed climbed the side of Canyon Ridge, heading for the spot where a cell signal locator had predicted two missing hikers would be. The call had come in an hour ago and they hadn't covered much ground yet, the unpredictable terrain a concern.

Slow and steady. At least the avalanche warnings had been lifted.

Tyler, Tiffany and a new support member, Riley, were only a few feet behind with the litter and emergency supplies.

As he trod carefully on the icy, slippery terrain, Reed couldn't help but wonder if maybe he would be just as happy rescuing and helping people in a city setting—heart attack patients, work accidents. Making a difference a different way.

So far that week, they'd assisted three ski patrol calls and answered two search assist calls from the state troopers' office, and not one of the rescues had even thanked them. Not that he did this job for the praise, but getting yelled at by a man whose rescue had required outing his affair with his ski instructor was not exactly the motivation Reed needed to continue this job, especially when his heart was somewhere else.

Over the holidays, he'd spoken to his mother about his father. She'd been disappointed to hear that the man had checked out of rehab, but not surprised. She'd been more upset for Reed. Everyone had to stop worrying about him. He wasn't a child anymore. He could handle life's complications. If he was in Anchorage, maybe he could help. His father may not have been there for him, but Reed was strong enough to offer support if it meant getting back the man he'd once looked up to.

Though he knew it wasn't his father's being in Anchorage that was suddenly pulling him in that direction.

He squinted as bright red fabric caught his eye. "I think I see something over that ridge," he said, pointing several feet away to his right. At least the hikers had enough common sense to wear a bright color.

Unfortunately, they hadn't had enough sense to bring a compass, instead relying on their cell phone GPS systems to navigate. The station did a great job educating the kids about backwoods safety, but they needed a better training program for adults.

If only they could somehow make it mandatory.

Wade radioed the others as they drew closer to the ridge.

Careful of the false ground beneath them, Reed

peered over the side. "Hikers located," he said in his own radio. Two men sat on the side of the mountain on a ledge several feet below. If he had to guess, they'd been hiking up the side of the mountain, hoping to reach the trail at the top that the crew were standing on. They both still wore their climbing harnesses attached to the mountainside. They were secure, at least.

But the mountain terrain between the top and where the men had stopped was unclimbable. Snow was unpredictable—the frozen surface couldn't be trusted—and blowing snow in the area made for terrible visibility. He waved his arms and called out, "Hey! Steven! Craig!"

Both men turned to look up and waved when they saw him.

It was hard to be certain from that distance, but it didn't appear that either man was injured.

"How are we proceeding?" Wade asked, glancing toward the two men. He shook his head, his annoyance with these rescues at an all-time high. "They look like they're sitting around, shooting the shit," he said. "Fucking tourists."

It didn't help that it was Wade's wedding anniversary and he'd no doubt gotten an earful when he'd had to rush out on his wife. Reed placed a hand on his shoulder. "We will get back to rescuing locals soon enough, okay."

"Promise?" Wade mumbled. The others reached them and Reed walked them through the method by which they could get the two hikers to safety.

"Bringing them up here without jeopardizing our safety is dicey, so I suggest we take that side trail down to their location, then move south along the far path back toward the village," he said.

Tyler frowned. "Couldn't we just lower the litter here and bring them up one at a time? Seems faster."

Reed considered the idea but shook his head. He carefully stamped a boot toward the edge. A big chunk of snow broke off and fell. "The ground here is too unpredictable. Farther out, we have no idea what's false ground or not."

Tyler didn't look convinced. "That slope is steep, man. Climbing up to them isn't a great idea either."

Reed looked at the others. He could pull rank and insist they do it his way, but the two hikers weren't in immediate danger. Safety of the crew was number one priority right now and he wouldn't make a decision that could potentially put any of them at risk. "What do you guys think?"

Wade shrugged. "I'm with you. Someone would have to rappel down with the litter and I can't see more than a few feet away. I don't like that idea."

"Tiffany? Riley?"

The newer members seemed torn, but ultimately they sided with his idea.

Reed turned to Tyler. "You good with this?" Tyler's opinion was actually the most important. The guy would be next in line to become a lead crew member if Reed left. Which he'd been contemplating more and more each day. He hadn't told anyone yet, but he'd have to soon. Each day he appreciated his job less and less when it meant giving up on any potential relationship with Erika. And he wouldn't do this job if his heart wasn't fully in it.

Tyler released a breath. "It's your call, man."

Reed hesitated a fraction longer, but realizing Tyler probably had New Year's Eve plans that he was hoping to get to—that a pretty girl waiting on him might be clouding his judgment—Reed went with his initial gut determination. "Okay." Calling out over the ridge, he told the hikers to sit tight.

Wade peered over the edge. "Are they playing cards?"

Reed sent him a look.

"They could pack a deck of cards but not a compass?" Disbelief in the guy's voice made Reed laugh.

"I'll let you give them an earful as soon as we're back at the station, okay?" he told him.

"You better believe I will. You should have heard the one I got from Kim this morning…" Wade mumbled, wrapping his thick scarf across his face to block the wind. "I'll be in the doghouse for a week."

Reed envied him. What he wouldn't give for an opportunity to be in the doghouse with Erika. He had to make things right with her first.

As the crew moved along the side trail, the snow picked up and the covering of white, fluffy flakes over the glassy surface below made footing even more dangerous.

"Grab tree branches and really lock in your footing," he instructed, leading the way down the path.

Visibility sucked in these mountain ranges. This wouldn't have been his first choice of trails to hike in bad weather.

Keeping a close eye on his crew, Reed didn't see a large sinkhole in the path ahead of him until his foot fell through it.

His right leg dipped, dragging the rest of his body

down into the hole. He landed on his right side, slamming his shoulder against the hard, frozen ground. "Shit," he mumbled, regaining his footing. Throbbing in his shoulder was immediate. There'd be a deep bruise by morning. He was lucky it hadn't dislocated with that impact.

"Reed, you okay?" Wade asked, appearing at the edge of the hole.

The top of the hole was about two feet above him. His fingers barely grazed the top and the snow at the edge wouldn't support his weight. "Careful along the edge, we don't want it to give way."

Wade lay on his stomach and extended his arms over the edge. "Grab my hands."

"No disrespect, Wade, but I'm two hundred pounds with fifty pounds of gear." The slightly older man was maybe one fifty. He was strong, but Reed doubted he could hoist him out.

Luckily, Tyler appeared right beside him. "I'm sure Hercules here has everything under control, but I have a hot date tonight, so quit messing around and get out of there," he said.

Reed removed his gear and tossed it high to Tyler.

Then both men gripped a forearm and pulled him up. He winced at the pain in his shoulder and rotated it several times. "Thanks," he said, glancing down the rest of the trail. Were there any more surprises along the way?

"Rethinking this now, aren't you?" Tyler said.

"Yes," Reed said. "I don't trust that there aren't more of these." He rotated his shoulder again. The impact of the fall had him already feeling pain through his arm and chest. He didn't think anything was broken, but breathing was becoming slightly labored. "What do you think of taking the west trail down?" he asked, pointing to a different path, closer to the mountain's edge.

Tyler nodded. "It holds its own concerns, but I think it's better than these sinkholes."

Reed was lucky this one had only been eight feet deep. He'd seen others that were a thirty- or forty-foot fall. A tumble that far could break limbs, or worse. "Okay. We move slowly," he told the group.

"I wonder who's winning that poker game," Wade mumbled as they reached the new trail twenty minutes later.

Before Reed could respond, the ground disappeared beneath his feet and he was free-falling. His arms waved at his sides as he fought to find something to grab hold of, but there was nothing but air around him for a long three or four seconds.

His body hit the ground with a force that knocked the wind from his lungs and he was tumbling downward over sharp, jagged rocks and ice. Snowdrifts flew into his face, blinding him. He continued to pick up speed as his body crashed into boulders. He brought his arms up to protect his head but winced as it left his body exposed to the hard, crushing terrain as he continued down the mountainside.

The boulder that stopped him felt like getting hit by a freight train and he gasped for a breath, feeling pain everywhere. He struggled to keep consciousness as he blinked, lifting his head to scan his surroundings, but he saw nothing but white, blowing snow and the jagged boulders that had bruised his entire body. He slowly moved his arms and legs. Miraculously, nothing seemed broken in his limbs, but his stomach and chest were throbbing with pain.

A wave of nausea hit him as dizziness made him black out for a moment. He continued to fight off the darkness as he struggled to get air into his lungs, but breathing and staying conscious was nearly impossible. Each inhale was followed by a shooting pain in both sets of ribs and his eyelids refused to stay open.

Trying to remember his emergency training, he fought to focus his thoughts on survival, but only images of his family—Cassie and his mom, his dad…and Erika flashed in his mind.

Was he dying? Were these images his final thoughts?

No. He blinked and tried to swallow the saliva nearly choking him as the nausea grew stronger. A dizzy spell had him throwing up and his pulse thundered as he noticed blood on the ground next to him.

He couldn't assess the extent of his injuries and he had no idea where the blood was coming from, but it wasn't good. Pain gripped his chest and he moaned, clutching the front of his jacket. He was barely holding on.

He fumbled for his bag, unzipping it and reaching inside. He tried to twist his body, but the pain searing through him made him feel as though he were impaled. Luckily a glance at his midsection revealed that wasn't the case.

Blackness started closing in and he focused on survival. He needed his flare. He didn't know how far he'd fallen…and the way his mind was straying he knew he was badly hurt. Time wasn't his friend.

His eyes closed and he saw his mom and Cassie and

Erika—they seemed to be rotating around him in a circle, all talking at once, all wearing looks of concern...

His eyes snapped open again. He couldn't judge the length of the blackout. Could have been a few seconds or hours. His body felt ice-cold and the pain was subsiding.

Numbness. Shock was setting in.

His fingers crept along his side and, touching the flare gun, he pulled it out of the backpack. It was preloaded, but his shaky, weak hands struggled to release the safety.

His eyes refused to stay open and he could hear Erika's voice saying she didn't know how to make their relationship work.

He needed to stay alive to show her. Show her how much he loved her, how much he was willing to sacrifice for her.

He needed to survive.

Gripping the flare gun with both hands, he extended his arms toward the sky, ignoring the tearing sensation in his body, and pulled the trigger.

The loud bang was the last thing he heard as his eyes closed and his head fell back against the cold, hard ground and his body went limp.

Suddenly, his life was in the hands of his search and rescue crew.

ERIKA STARED AT the resignation letter in one hand and the offer of employment from Wild River Community Hospital in the other.

Her past. And her future.

If she could just summon the balls to actually go see her father and deliver the news.

Dr. Smyth had been surprised to hear from her the week before, but it hadn't taken the hospital long to put together an offer. They were eager to have her join their staff. And while it wasn't the salary she was making in Anchorage, there were other benefits that came with the job in Wild River.

Like Reed.

Since the holidays, things had gotten a whole lot clearer. Her feelings had started screaming louder than her common sense. She'd spent a lot of time thinking about her future, and he was the one constant she knew she wanted.

She missed Reed. She loved him. She was moving to Wild River to be with him.

At least, she hoped so.

What if he didn't want her now? What if she'd hurt him too much? Could he forgive her for letting him walk away?

She hadn't heard from him since that day in the elevator. She'd spent hours thinking about him and staring at Cassie's Facebook photos of him, trying to summon the nerve to send him a Friend Request, but it seemed lame. She wanted to be so much more than friends.

She could have called or texted him but she'd needed to get her head on straight, make her final decision and then move forward with it.

With him. If he'd still have her.

She'd thought about reaching out to Cassie to let her know of her decision, but she'd decided to wait. She was scheduled to start at the hospital in mid-January, which gave her only two weeks to get her condo on the market and find someplace to live near the hospital in Wild River. There were several places she was hoping to look at, but she needed to resolve things here before she made any more plans.

Her chest tightened and she pressed her palm to it.

Anxiety over the unknown was always worse than the reality.

She had to hand in her resignation and get it over with. Maybe her father wouldn't even care. They hadn't spoken since Christmas Eve when in one moment, he'd crushed her career hopes and her dreams of reestablishing the relationship they'd once had.

It broke her heart that they weren't close. More so now than ever before. Falling in love with Reed had opened her up to all kinds of emotions she'd successfully repressed for years.

And she'd fooled herself into thinking that if she worked hard enough, did what her father wanted, lived her life like he lived his, they could be close again.

She'd been wrong. She might have opened her heart, but her father's heart had been buried with her mother. She couldn't bring either one back.

Leaving her office, she made her way through the hallways of the hospital. The triage station had New Year's Eve decorations hanging above the desks and she knew the nurses had noisemakers, confetti and a bottle of champagne hidden in the kitchen for midnight. She'd never participated in the countdown with them before, but she just might this year.

Better late than never, she thought.

She'd do things right from the start at Wild River Community. Get to know the staff. Dr. Smyth would be there for the first few weeks to help her make the transition, and she was grateful the older man had offered to delay his retirement. His support continued to be something she could depend on.

Kam was away from her desk when Erika got to her father's office. She scanned the hallway. She'd been hoping to gauge her father's mood from his assistant… kill a few moments with idle chitchat.

Just get this over with.

Knocking on her father's office door, she waited.

She could hear him talking inside, and a quick peek through the open blinds revealed he was on the phone.

She refused to leave and come back…because she might not get the nerve again.

She sat on the bench outside his office, struggling not to feel like the nervous little girl she'd been whenever she'd had to tell her father something he wasn't going to like. She wasn't a kid anymore. She was strong and independent. A skilled surgeon who could make it on her own, out from under his wing that was suddenly feeling more like a shadow.

This was the right thing.

Whenever doubt crept in, she silenced it with thoughts of Reed.

Please let him still want to be with me.

Her father opened the door a minute later. "Come in."

She stood on shaky knees and followed him inside, shutting the door slowly behind her. She'd never had to quit a job before, but she suspected this had to be ten times worse. She straightened her pencil skirt and folded one leg over the other as she sat in the chair across from him. Possibly for the last time.

"Hand it over," he said as he sat.

Damn, was there anything he didn't know?

She slid the resignation letter across the desk.

He scanned it. "Do you want me to try to talk you out of it?"

Did he want to? She took a breath and shook her head. Her decision was made. Even if he did ask her to stay, she wouldn't. She needed to make a career, a life for herself. One she wanted.

With the man she wanted.

The next two weeks would be torture, working out her notice alongside her father and itching to get to Wild River to talk to Reed. She couldn't do it by phone or text. Apologizing to him, telling him how she felt, was something she needed to do face-to-face.

"No. I've made the decision and I'm accepting the position in Wild River."

He nodded.

She waited. There had to be more.

He was silent. He couldn't even give her a word. After all the years she'd put in.

"Do you need anything else from me?"

"No. I'll send this to the board. I trust you don't need a letter of recommendation, seeing as how you've secured a new position already."

Not a hint of emotion. No way of knowing if he cared that she was leaving or not. She was just another employee. She should be grateful that he was making this easy for her, but it stung a little, to be treated like a stranger.

"No, I don't." She stood. "Okay, so my last day…"

He held up a hand. "You don't have to work out a notice."

She straightened her spine and squared her shoulders. "Okay." She paused. "I assume Dr. Smyth told you?" She wasn't upset. The older man probably assumed this was a decision she'd discussed with her dad.

He nodded, not glancing up from the latest results from the clinical trials, which she knew from Darren were a great success so far. It still stung that she'd been cut from the project, but at least the patients were seeing results. "He called to gloat, I guess, for stealing my best surgeon."

Her jaw nearly hit the floor. His best surgeon? She recovered quickly but the hospital intercom sounded before she could verbalize any of the incoherent thoughts running through her mind.

"Dr. Sheraton to emergency. Stat. All available nurses and surgical staff to emergency. Stat."

Her heart raced. All hands on deck? She turned to leave and her father was on her heels.

Sprinting toward emergency, she approached the desk as the paramedics wheeled in a stretcher. The sound of the emergency helicopter on the landing pad outside made her pulse race.

They'd airlifted someone in. A highway accident?

Moving toward them, her knees buckled as she recognized the Wild River Search and Rescue logo on the red-and-yellow jacket...

Dark hair covered in blood...

Reed.

Her heartbeat echoed off the hospital walls. The floor beneath her felt unsteady. She forced a deep breath, trying everything to remain in doctor mode. That's what the man she loved depended on right now. "What happened?" she asked, taking the chart from the paramedic with a shaking hand.

Her father and Dr. Richardson were reading over her shoulder.

"Search and rescue volunteer…fell from the side of Canyon Ridge," the young paramedic said, wheeling the stretcher toward the hall.

"Injuries?" It was Dr. Richardson's question.

"Broken bones in both ankles and one wrist, a dislocated shoulder and fractured ribs on both sides… and suspected internal bleeding from damage to the spleen."

Her breath caught in her throat as she stared at Reed. Unresponsive.

"Wild River Community Hospital wanted him airlifted here," the young paramedic said. "Patient's name is…"

"Reed Reynolds." She could barely breathe as she touched the blanket above his chest. Internal bleeding, broken bones—his injuries were extensive. How long had he been unconscious out there on the mountainside? Her mind and heart were a mess. They needed to get him into surgery right away.

"Reed Reynolds," her father said. "Cassie's brother?"

And the man she'd been preparing to start a new life with, leaving everything she knew behind.

Now he was lying on a stretcher fighting for his life.

She nodded, unable to speak as they wheeled him down the hall to prep for surgery. At the doctors' station, she grabbed her surgical scrubs and headed toward the locker room. There was no time to waste.

At the doors, her father stopped her. "You resigned, remember."

Was he serious? Five seconds ago. "Dad, I have to help him…"

He studied her. "You can't perform surgery when you're this close to the patient. You know that."

She swallowed hard, watching through the glass as Reed was wheeled farther and farther away. Dr. Richardson was already in his scrubs at the sink, washing up.

Hospital protocol prevented her from operating on family and friends…and he was both. More than that. He had her heart.

He needed to pull through. He had to be okay.

"He needs me," she said.

"He needs a doctor with steady hands," her father replied, holding hers up in front of her face. "You're in no condition to perform surgery."

He was right, but this feeling of helplessness if she wasn't in that room might kill her. "I love him," she whispered.

Her father's arms around her broke the dam around her heart and tears streamed down her cheeks before she could try to stop them.

He smoothed her hair away from her face and held her to his chest. "Shh…it's okay."

She couldn't remember the last time he'd hugged her. Or offered any comfort. Even at her mother's funeral, he'd relied on others to offer her support.

How could he possibly know that right now was the most important moment he could be there for her? She clung to his lab coat as sobs escaped her. She couldn't lose Reed.

A second later, she took a deep breath and moved away. She couldn't waste time crying. "I can save him," she said. She held up her hands, willing them to be rock-solid. She could push emotion aside and focus on doing her job. This time more than ever, she needed to.

Her father nodded. "I know, but there's regulations for a reason." He took her hands and she couldn't deny their unsteadiness. The trembling was something she'd never experienced before and she couldn't honestly say she could pull it together enough to perform the operation successfully.

But leaving Reed's fate to another doctor made her nauseous. Dr. Richardson was a seasoned professional, but this was the man she loved. Being on the other side of this was eye-opening. Being the terrified one, watching helplessly while a loved one fought for life was the singular worst feeling ever.

"Will you do it?" she asked her father.

He hesitated. "Erika, I haven't performed a spleen operation in years... Dr. Richardson does them routinely." He glanced toward the operating room. "Once they begin, who knows what else they'll discover..."

She winced at the unsettling assessment but shook her head. He was right. Reed's injuries were severe and there could be more. Which was why her father needed to perform the surgery.

"You're the only person I trust to save the man I love." She took a deep breath. "Please, Dad. I need your help. I can't lose him." Again.

CHAPTER TWENTY-SEVEN

SIX EXCRUCIATING HOURS LATER, the door to the waiting room opened and her father reappeared.

Despite an urge to rush forward, Erika held back slightly to allow Cassie and Arlene to move in first, but she was right behind them.

The two women had arrived a few hours before and the three of them had sat together in the surgery waiting room, trying to keep their spirits up and thoughts positive. Arlene had recounted stories about Reed as a child and every now and then, they'd stop talking to hug, to cry, to pray.

Her father was the best surgeon in Alaska, Erika had repeated to the group. And Reed was a fighter, they'd all said. Anything to help ease the anxiety they all felt.

But as time had dragged on, the doctor in her was wondering what was taking so long and her mind went straight to worst possible scenarios. Her father must have been right when he'd said there may be other injuries.

Luckily, she knew by the look on his face that the surgery had gone well. Her shoulders sagged with relief as he removed his surgical mask and tucked it into the pocket of his scrubs. She rarely saw him dressed for surgery these days and it reminded her of when he'd come home after long shifts at Wild River Community Hospital.

Her father had been her superhero back then, just like he was now.

Stepping in to perform this surgery was something he'd never normally consider. But he'd done it for her.

"He's okay," he said, and the three women released sighs of relief.

"Thank God," Arlene said, hugging Cassie, new tears rimming her tired, stressed-looking eyes.

"Were there any other injuries?" Erika asked. Now that he'd confirmed Reed was okay, the doctor in her needed the details.

"No. He was lucky. The broken bones and the damaged spleen was the extent of them. He's covered in bruises—that tumble down the mountain was no joke."

Cassie shook her head. "Mountain life isn't for the weak."

"His skills as a rescuer no doubt saved his life. The quick thinking with the flare and the way he'd obviously protected his head was influential."

"Did you remove the spleen?" Erika asked.

"No. It wasn't necessary. The injury was a grade two. I was able to stop the internal bleeding and repair the damage without removing the organ."

"And his blood pressure and heart rate?" There was always a fear of heart attacks or stroke when the patient was in a situation like Reed's. She couldn't relax until she knew everything was okay.

"All fine."

Another sigh of relief.

Tank had spoken to Cassie and he'd filled her in on the details of the fall. Reed had been lucky that he'd been able to get his flare into the sky before losing consciousness. Otherwise, it could have taken hours for the crew members to locate him. As it was, they'd had to carry him out four miles on treacherous mountain terrain to safety.

The crew had pulled through for their leader and their friend when he'd needed them most. They were all lucky. Things could have been so much worse.

She shivered. She wouldn't think about that now. He was safe. Her father had saved him.

"He's stable right now, but risk of infection means we have him on heavy antibiotics and pain meds, so he is going to be out for a while." He checked his watch.

It was after 11:00 p.m. She'd been watching the minutes tick by for hours.

"Can we see him?" Arlene asked.

"Not yet. Give the antibiotics some time to kick in," he said. "We don't want to take any unnecessary risks. Once we move him into recovery, I'll get the attending nurse to come get you one at a time."

Her dad was bending the rules by including her. It was normally just family who were permitted to see a patient this soon after surgery.

She was grateful to him...for so much.

Arlene nodded, taking his hand. "Of course... Thank you, Alan."

Her father looked slightly uncomfortable at the familiarity, or maybe it was her grateful tone and touch. But he surprised Erika by covering Arlene's hand with his own. "You're welcome. I'm glad I was able to help."

Cassie moved in to hug him and her father flinched slightly but it wouldn't have been noticeable to anyone but Erika. He wrapped an awkward arm around Cassie and patted her on the back.

Erika was so proud of him. "Thank you, Dad," she mouthed when his gaze met hers above Cassie's head.

He simply nodded before turning to head back into surgery.

The three of them sat on the waiting room chairs they'd occupied for hours. Cassie spoke first. "Now if you'd been there, you could have performed this surgery right there on the mountain, saving us all a trip," she said through a new batch of tears.

Erika hugged her friend. "From now on, I will be…"

Cassie pulled back. "What do you mean?" she asked, wiping her tears on her sleeve. Judging by her red off-the-shoulder sweater and black leather pants, she'd abandoned New Year's Eve plans to be there for her brother.

"I've accepted the surgeon position in Wild River. I'm starting there in two weeks." Saying it out loud made it that much more real and made her even more confident it was what she wanted.

Her friend studied her. "You're doing this for Reed?"

Erika took a breath. "I'm doing it for me. And to be with Reed…if he's still willing to have me."

Cassie raised an eyebrow. "My brother has been the biggest downer since you broke his heart. His sulking has driven us all insane and Tank was getting ready to fire his ass. Believe me, he'll have you. Which means he's going to be extra pissed that this injury has taken him out."

Erika laughed, blushing as she glanced at Reed's mother.

"He's told me all about it, honey," Arlene said, smiling through her tears.

Reed had told his mother about her? About them? He was really that serious about her? Damn, he'd better recover quickly. She couldn't wait to tell him she loved him. Couldn't wait to be in his arms.

"Well, maybe not *all* about it," Arlene said with a wink.

Erika's laugh was mixed with her own unshed tears.

Cassie's cell phone chimed. "Tank, checking in. I better call him," she said, standing and heading toward the window for privacy.

Arlene moved to sit closer to Erika. "I'm so glad Reed found you." She glanced at Cassie. "Now if we could only get a certain someone else to smarten up."

"Agreed." Maybe living in Wild River, she'd be able to help give Tank the kick in the ass needed to commit to her friend.

Holding hands, Arlene and Erika sat, lost in their own thoughts as they continued to wait.

An hour later, Jill, a recovery room nurse, came to see them. "He's doing great," she said. "Heartbeat 130 and no sign of complications," she added with a nod at Erika.

"Thank you, Jill," she said.

"You can all see him now. Maybe two at a time?"

"You two go ahead," she told Cassie and Arlene. His mother and sister should get to see him first, and honestly…she needed a minute. How would she react, seeing Reed in recovery? It had to be better than seeing him wheeled into emergency in critical condition, but still…

"Okay, thank you, darling," Arlene said, gathering her coat and purse and following Jill to the recovery room.

"I'll just stay a minute, then tag you in," Cassie said.

"Take your time." If he woke up, would he even want to see her? He'd said he loved her, but she'd hurt him.

Standing, she paced the now empty room as the clock inched closer to midnight. In such a short time, her life had changed so much.

She had changed. Ten hours ago, she'd been confident in her decision and hopeful that Reed would accept her apology. Now, she was terrified. The guy had just had a life-threatening accident. He may see things differently when he woke. See her differently.

Would he forgive her?

She refused to give up. If it took her a lifetime of groveling, she'd find a way to prove to him that she loved him.

Hearing footsteps behind her, she turned in time to see a man turn on his heels and walk back down the hall toward the doors. She squinted. George? Not pausing to consider it, she hurried after him. "George…Mr. Reynolds?" she said as she caught up to him.

Dressed in a pair of stained jeans, work boots and a black thermal winter coat, he hesitated, looking toward the exit. His eyes were bloodshot and his complexion pale. He looked thin and nervous, running a hand through his long, disheveled hair when she reached him. "Hi…uh…I heard about Reed."

"How?" Had Cassie called her dad? Had Arlene? How much did Reed know about his father's whereabouts? He'd have a lot to deal with when he recovered. She would be there for him. For everything he needed.

"The Search and Rescue log online," George said.

"Whenever there's an emergency call, I, uh…like to keep an eye on the reports."

All these years, he'd been keeping an eye on Reed from afar.

He cleared his throat. "Erika, right? Um, excuse me, Dr. Sheraton now?"

"Erika," she said with a nod.

"Time flies… Last time I saw you…" He shoved his hands into too-baggy faded jeans and rocked back on his heels. "How is he? He going to be okay?"

"He's in recovery. A lot of broken bones and bruising. They—my dad—was able to repair the damage done to the spleen."

She saw him wince, followed by a look of relief. "Good…good. That's really good." He forced several deep breaths.

She tentatively reached out and touched his shoulder. "Cassie and Arlene are in with him. You can go in once they come out."

He shook his head quickly. "No. No. I, uh… He's okay, that's all I needed to know." He looked at the door, ready to flee.

Let him go or convince him to stay and see his son? Man, she was not good at this. "I'm sure he'd like to see you," she said. She really wasn't sure if that was true or not, but Reed had been searching for the man for years, so she chose to believe he would—on some level at least.

He lowered his head, staring at the floor. "Um… I don't think I can. Not today. Not yet."

She nodded. "Okay."

"You see, I'm afraid the memory of me is far better than any reality of who I am now."

Her chest constricted at the pain in the man's voice. All she knew was she'd take seeing her mother again over any memory any day, but her situation was different. And Reed had already been through a lot that day. She wouldn't force something she really knew nothing about. "I understand."

"I am trying to get better," he said, as though needing her to know. "And then I can come back to him. To all of them."

She hated that he seemed to be struggling to convince himself that would ever happen. She nodded. "Whenever that is, I'm sure Reed will welcome you home," she said as George headed toward the door, knowing enough about the man she loved to know it was true.

But would he welcome *her* back into his heart?

"Take care of them for me, okay?"

"I will," she said, waving to him as he left the hospital.

REED'S ENTIRE BODY ACHED, and it took a long minute to realize he was in a hospital room and not still on the side of Canyon Ridge, his body crushed between boulders. The tiled ceiling over his head and the dimmed lights were a welcome sight. While the IV in his arm and breathing tube in his nose weren't a great sign, he was overcome with relief that whatever injuries he'd suffered were being cared for. His team had found him and saved his life. Pain radiated through his core and his limbs felt slightly numb, heavy when he tried to move.

He turned his head, trying to focus, but his vision and mind were blurry. Just the slightest movement had waves of nausea washing over him and he forced several deep breaths.

Whatever drugs they had him on were making him hallucinate, because he was staring at Erika sitting at his bedside. She was the last image he'd seen on the mountain before his world had gone dark and in his distorted reality, he was seeing her now.

Man, he really had it bad.

He needed to get better, get out of there to see her for real. If this accident had taught him anything, it was that he needed to fight harder to prove to her that they should be together. If that meant moving to Anchorage, he would. If it meant reevaluating everything in his life, he would.

For her. Anything for her.

God, this drug-induced version of her was so freaking beautiful. Her dark green cashmere sweater hugged her beautiful curves, the slight V-neck giving him a teasing glance of the perfect breasts he longed to touch again. Her dark hair pulled into a low ponytail hanging over one shoulder and her mesmerizing eyes, full of concern...and love as they remained locked with his.

"Hi," she said, moving closer.

Damn, she even sounded real. He struggled to stay conscious and as his eyes flitted closed again, he reached out an arm toward the sound of her voice, not wanting it to go away, but he was too weak.

"Don't try to move...just rest," he heard her say, but the sound seemed far away. He wanted to bring it closer, make it real, but he didn't have the strength.

"I'll be here when you wake up..." she said, the sound fading into a deep echo as he fell back into a deep sleep.

What felt like only seconds later—but must have been hours based on the darkness of the room—his eyes opened again.

His vision was better and his mind was sharper. He felt less pain and there was only one thought on his mind—Erika. Turning his head slowly, he saw her still sitting there, asleep in the chair and covered by her lab coat. It hadn't been a dream...she was there.

Where was here? He'd assumed Wild River Community, but glancing around, he saw the Alaska General Hospital initials on the monitor above his head, still keeping track of his vitals. His breathing tube had been removed, but he still had the IV and he could feel the tightness of bandages wrapped around his midsection, his legs and one arm.

He'd had surgery. He vaguely remembered the nurse and the doctors wheeling him into recovery.

He must be in pretty bad shape, but all he felt right now was happiness that Erika was next to him. "Hey, pretty girl," he whispered.

Erika stirred, and her eyes opened. Seeing him awake, she tossed the coat aside and stood, straightening her sweater as she came toward him. "Hi again... How do you feel?" She placed a hand against his forehead and her touch was the only thing he focused on. No more pain. No more heartache. She was there.

He reached for her hand when she went to move it. He gripped it as tight as he could in his weakened state. "Not sure... I'm in Anchorage?"

She nodded. "You were airlifted here almost ten hours ago."

"What's wrong with me?"

"A broken wrist, two broken ankles, fractured ribs

on both sides and…you ruptured your spleen. My dad fixed it," she said. The look of concern on her face made him want to reassure her he was fine. Unfortunately, she still knew more about his condition than he did.

"Shit—that sucks." That would put him on his ass for a while. But the sight of her made it hard to think about the pain or his injury.

"You really gave us all a good scare," she said. "I was terrified we were going to lose you."

We. Not her. She'd been there how long? And what did that mean? "You've been here the whole time?" He struggled to bring her hand to his lips. He placed a soft kiss there when she nodded. He never wanted to let go of this hand. There was so much he wanted to say to her.

"Your mom and sister were here, too." She paused, then continued. "They're getting some rest in the hotel a few blocks away… I can call them if you want."

He shook his head. "I just want you." He did. So bad. He'd been devastated when she'd pushed him away, but he refused to walk away again without doing everything he could to show her he was more than willing to take her exactly as she was—limited time and all. He didn't want to interfere with her life or complicate it with guilt, he just wanted to be a part of it.

"That's good news, because I want you, too," she said, squeezing his hand gently and smoothing his hair away from his face.

He prayed this wasn't the meds playing tricks on him. That her touch was real, her words were real and the look of love in her eyes was real. He didn't want her to feel pressured or feel as though she had to be someone different for him. "I'm sorry I asked you for more than you could give...that wasn't fair."

"Shh... You were right to want more from me. I want to give you more." She paused. "I've made the decision to take the job in Wild River."

What? She was planning to move to Wild River? Since when—his injury the night before? He couldn't allow her to make a hasty decision like this that she might regret. Might eventually resent him for. "But you love your career here..."

"I love you more," she said. "And my mind is made up, so there's no point in trying to talk me out of it."

She loved him? He felt nothing but happiness as he grinned. "You love me? After only a few weeks?"

She slapped his arm ever so gently. "Apparently."

"I love you, too. So much, Erika. On the side of that mountain, I thought I was going to die and I needed to hold on long enough to see you," he said.

She kissed his lips gently. "You're here now. You're okay. We are okay."

He wanted to believe that, but asking her to sacrifice everything to be with him wasn't fair. Not when he'd already decided to give up everything for her. "I can't let you give up your life here...we can make the long-distance thing work...for now, until I can figure out something else." He'd apply to the university and pursue a career in EMT like he'd wanted to.

She was shaking her head no.

Forever stubborn. "I know we said that before and couldn't," he said, "but that's because I was being a selfish asshole..."

She put her finger over his lips. "Stop talking. There's nothing more to figure out. I'm moving to Wild

River. To be with you. And because it's what I want." She leaned forward and kissed his forehead, his nose, his cheeks and finally his lips again.

She smelled so good. He couldn't wait to be out of this hospital bed...and back in his own bed with his arms around her. He touched her face, drawing it toward his lips. Hers were soft, inviting, warm...everything he'd been missing, craving. The familiar taste of her vanilla lip gloss had all the memories of their time together spiraling back until he thought his heart would explode.

Her kiss was light, easy, as though she was afraid to hurt him. She pulled away slightly, but stayed close as she said, "And I'm applying for a real position on the search and rescue crew, so I can keep your ass safe."

He stared into the dark hazel eyes he could stare into forever. "I'll approve your membership on one condition," he said, kissing her with as much strength as he had, ignoring the pain, the exhaustion...none of that mattered. The woman he loved was in his arms, telling him he'd not only survived his accident, but he was going to leave that hospital with everything he'd always wanted.

"Which is?" she asked, kissing him again.

"You get a new ski suit."

She laughed. "Deal. Now get some rest so we can get out of here and start a life together."

He loved hearing her say that, and a heaviness lifted from his chest as his eyes drifted closed again. "You'll be here when I wake up?"

She kissed him softly. "I'll be here."

He believed she would be. He felt their connection in that moment more than ever before. "And you're not going to change your mind?" he asked, his words slurring slightly as the drugs coursing through his veins started to win the battle.

"About us—never. Get better so I can take you home," she said, and the implication of her words made his body feel like nothing would ever hurt again. Home. With her.

That's all he'd ever need.

EPILOGUE

Two Weeks Later

LARGE SNOWFLAKES FELL to the ground outside Alaska General Hospital. The festive decorations were gone and only the promise of a new year lingered on the cold air.

"I save your life, and you take my daughter away from me," Alan said, but Erika heard the teasing in her father's voice as he shook Reed's hand.

He'd been discharged hours before, her father signing off on his release. He still had a way to go in his recovery, but he was going to be okay.

"Thanks again for both," Reed said. They loaded his bag into the back of Erika's car and he climbed into the passenger seat.

In a few hours, Erika would be starting on a new chapter of her life. With the man she loved.

The last two weeks had been a whirlwind. She'd listed her condo for sale, packed her personal belongings and found a place to rent near Wild River Community Hospital—just until she could find a house she wanted to buy. She'd said her goodbyes to the staff at Alaska General Hospital…and her dad, and now she was ready to go.

More than ready.

There was nothing left to do here.

She hadn't second-guessed her decision once. Only excitement and happiness filled her heart as she turned to her father. "Bye, Dad. Thank you again for everything." She hesitated. "Don't be a stranger, okay. Skiing conditions in Wild River are great this time of year." The last two weeks they'd made some progress, but their relationship still had some growing to do and she hoped he'd make time for that.

She would. She refused to give up on him yet.

He pulled her in for a quick hug and she wrapped her arms around him, holding on a little longer than he was comfortable with. Feeling him tense, she reluctantly stepped away.

"This is for you," he said, handing her a manila envelope.

"What is it?" she asked. The last time he'd handed her a letter, the news hadn't been good. Or so she'd thought. Turned out, it had been the best thing to happen to her.

He was silent as she read the letter from the American Surgical Association recognizing her efforts in leading the clinical trials team.

Early results were showing amazing progress. Her father had asked her to rejoin the team, claiming she could even start her own trials in Wild River, but she'd declined. The drug testing was in good hands and she was moving on.

Until that moment, she'd pushed aside how much the trials and the success of the new drug meant to her. Now, the words swam on the page and a feeling of acceptance and pride overwhelmed her. She impulsively hugged her father again. "Thank you for this. It means a lot," she whispered. More than he could ever know.

"You deserve it." He cleared his throat, shoving his hands into his lab coat pockets. "Your mom would be proud and so am I."

A lump rose in her throat. It was the first time he'd mentioned her mother since she died. Maybe they would be okay. Baby steps.

"Dad, can I ask...? Why did you take me off the trials in the first place?" She hadn't had the courage to ask until now.

He hesitated, staring at his feet. "When you came back from Wild River, you were different and I saw a struggle in you I hadn't seen before. A desire to have something beyond all of this."

He'd been able to see that?

"I realized that maybe I'd been pushing you too hard and I was afraid that if I continued, you'd leave. I thought taking you off the trials would give you more time and freedom to explore the other things in life you suddenly seemed to want...a work/life balance, I guess."

"Oh, Dad..." He'd been trying to look out for her? He'd been trying to keep her happy and keep her there with him.

"I guess it backfired, huh?"

She moved in and hugged him again. "No. It didn't backfire. Not at all."

"I made some mistakes after your mom died..."

"Things changed. But that doesn't mean we can't change them again."

He kissed the top of her head and released her, then stepped forward and opened the driver's-side door for her. "Now, go before I call Wild River Community and tell them you're a terrible doctor."

She nodded and smiled, not trusting her voice, and climbed in next to Reed.

As she pulled the car away from the curb, she glanced once in the rearview mirror. Her dad stood on the curb watching and waving.

"What was that?" Reed asked, nodding toward the letter on her dash.

"Approval and hopefully a fresh start at being a family again," she said.

He smiled, taking her hand and squeezing it. "I love you."

Erika couldn't believe she was actually doing this—driving away from the career that had meant everything to her. But her vacation from her life had taught her how to live, and now her future was waiting for her just beyond those snow-covered mountains in the distance.

She released a contented sigh as her fingers entwined with his. "I love you more."

* * * * *

ACKNOWLEDGMENTS

A big thank you to my editor, Dana Grimaldi, for loving this book and helping me realize my dream of being published with HQN. I am grateful to Susan Swinwood and the entire team for welcoming me into the HQN family and for all the effort in editing, cover design and marketing support for this new series.

Thank you a million times to my agent, Jill Marsal, who continues to believe in me, even when I have my own doubts, and for always pushing me to be a better writer.

A huge thank you to SAR Alberta and The Rocky Mountain Adventure Medicine Team for their research help. All mistakes are mine alone.

And as always, I wouldn't be able to live this dream life writing uplifting love stories if it wasn't for the support of my family. My husband and son are my biggest supporters and cheerleaders and I'd be lost without them. You guys are my world.